Dear

Thanks etc. etc.

The Skeletal Bird

(I don't know how
to properly sign
books, which I
think is obvious)

Kathleen Sawisky

Kathleen Sawisky

The Code Series

Between Fire and Pines

The Skeletal Bird

The Skeletal Bird

The Code

Book 2

By Kathleen Sawisky

This is a work of fiction. Names, characters, businesses, places, events and incidents are either the products of the author's imagination or used in a fictitious manner. Any resemblance to actual persons, living or dead, or actual events is purely coincidental.

The Skeletal Bird: The Code, Book Two – First Edition, 2017

Copyright 2017 Kathleen Sawisky
All rights reserved, including the right to reproduce this book or portions thereof in any form whatsoever.

ISBN-13: 978-1548824693

ISBN-10: 1548824690

For Yago, my first fan

And for Yago's Grandma, who didn't make a big deal about all the swearing

Part I

Prologue

The woman tip-toed along the third-floor balcony. Placing her heel down would send sound reverberating throughout the whole structure and alert her enemies to her presence. She couldn't do that just yet. A single door along the left side of the hall remained unbarred, and she stepped through, a stranger behind her, keeping his distance.

The bedroom looked like it hadn't been occupied for years, which, according to the man, was exactly the case.

"There are things here for her, though," he said, voice grating from lack of sleep, violence, emotional exhaustion. "I made sure the bathroom was stocked."

"This is where she'll stay, then?"

"It is."

The woman rested her hand on the moth-eaten quilt that had been thrown over the bed, clouds of dust billowing from the small jostling. She leaned across the spread, pressing her head into the pillow, and exhaled. She imagined how microscopic pieces of herself would be left behind, and how the girl would touch it without thinking, and the two of them, in that instant, would be connected.

"We have to-"

"I know. Just give me a minute."

"They're bringing the boy back. We have to leave before he gets here."

The woman closed her eyes. "I'm not afraid of him."

"I believe you," the man replied quietly, "but I am."

Chapter 1

The robin had a broken wing. Or maybe it had been mauled. Kyle Powell wasn't a vet. The only thing he knew for certain was that the bird's landing on the old roof had been incredibly uncouth. Peering through the boards that had been hammered along the inner portion of the window frame, he watched it flutter around, awkwardly hopping on its one good foot as it tried to make sense of its predicament. The boy jammed his stubby thumb between two boards, careful to avoid any splinters, and wiggled it around. The bird's panicked beady eye swivelled in its head and, for a moment, Kyle imagined how the bird might see his thumb as a juicy worm and drive its beak into his soft flesh. But the bird was smarter than the boy, at least in that regard. It continued its frantic hopping, one useless wing hanging by its side, before finally collapsing in a heap on the black, tarred shingles.

Kyle could see its breast heave from the exertion. A crimson ribbon of feathers, washed-out in the moonlight. Birds were such delicate creatures, and their hearts were so small. His mother used to tell him that birds, rabbits, anything tiny and weak could be easily shocked, frightened to the point that its heart simply stopped beating. Scared to death. That was why it was important to always be kind to those that were smaller than you. They relied on your kindness for survival.

The Tall Man was not nice to people. Not at all. He treated Kyle just fine, came to visit him at least twice a day, always bringing food or a new game for his Nintendo DS. But in the evenings when the men and women below the house hauled dirt from their tunnel, Kyle could hear the Tall Man bark orders until his voice was hoarse and broken from the cold. He didn't like the Tall Man; didn't like the way the Tall Man looked at him with sad, green eyes, or the quiet lilt of his voice. And Kyle didn't like his room with the boarded windows where all he could do was watch the little bird with the broken wing struggle to find a way to reach the sky.

xXx

She didn't see the branch until it was whipping across her cheek, drawing a line of blood that dribbled down her face, smeared by the wind that broke over her as she darted between trees. It might have hurt if her skin wasn't frozen to the touch. That was the risk that came with forging through a snowed in Maine woodland in the dead of winter.

If I freeze to death, they're going to find me flipping them off.

She wouldn't have been out for so long if she wasn't back tracking, creating layers of footprints over footprints to try to throw off her pursuers. Every extra second counted. Her guardian had held back, told her to run, and she obeyed because, frankly, any argument with Jim Wilkinson usually ended with hurt feelings and the girl didn't have time to deal with that sort of emotional baggage. She ran because he told her to, because after three long months on the run, the hawks had descended and begun to rake their talons over vulnerable flesh.

Her eyes had adjusted to the encompassing darkness of the forest around the same time she stopped being able to feel her toes. When they had first arrived at this haven, a secluded campsite populated with quaint log cabins that were, mercifully, abandoned in the winter, Jim made her memorize the surrounding land. That first night after they rolled in on fumes and received their keys from the wary caretaker, he sent her out into the woods and told her to come back when she could walk the whole thing blind.

It didn't take long.

Over the last three months, Jim's training had integrated with her desire for survival. She began to listen to her body, its demands and protests. It was a distraction from the lost souls, lingering on the mortal coil long after they had punched out. Someone had once told her that the dead had a habit of sticking around where they weren't wanted. At the time, the girl had thought it a horrible prospect, to be haunted by those who had left her behind. As the months wore on she began to wonder where her ghosts were at and what was keeping them so silent.

If her calculations were right, and the girl was confident they were, she was only a few yards west of the main road that led into the sleepy little hamlet. Follow that a quarter mile east and she would be in the town centre. Populations meant crowds, witnesses, people who could gum up investigations by going to the police, or worse, the press, with what they had seen on the night so-and-so was snatched from the street. No, these enemies wouldn't pursue her into the town; it was too much of a risk. Even if she and her guardian were relative newcomers, the locals would rally around them. It was unlikely they would allow anyone to be pulled into an anonymous van and *disappeared*, as Jim had described it.

When the girl had arrived with her guardian two weeks earlier, looking for a place to stay, the small townpopulation greeted them with polite informality and kept their opinions to themselves. In private, questions were asked. These weren't the usual travellers. When in town, the girl never showed any signs of trauma. If anything, she seemed abnormally well-engaged for a teenager. She chatted, asked questions, said *please* and *thank you*. When asked her name, she said Laura Palmer and then laughed, saying her parents had a sick sense of humor. The man she was traveling with was her uncle, and they were headed out west to see a sick family member.

They never questioned why Laura Palmer's uncle seemed to always be in a foul mood, or why the girl always had her arms covered, even at night when they sat in the roasting diner and picked away at their meals. She could be openly sweating and still refuse to remove her sweater. Once, she rolled the sleeves up to her elbows, and then later heard a waitress claiming that she saw a hint of a scar. She was right, of course; the flesh was still pink and raw, and Laura Palmer wasn't comfortable showing it off just yet.

On the other hand, Natalia Artison would have loved to show off her scar. To her, it was a badge of honor, a sign of her survival. It proclaimed *Here I am. I live.* A flagrant *fuck you* to the people who had pursued her and her guardian to Maine. She survived where others did not. If she stopped to ponder that for too long, she would find herself slipping into some inconsolable miasma. So, she smiled and carried on and pretended she was Laura Palmer, much to Jim's aggravation, because *he* was the one who told her she could pick her own name. No one was ever the wiser.

Two weeks was longer than either of them would have liked to stay at the campsite, except that the snow had fallen and their rental car had busted and a series of events had conspired to keep Natalia and Jim as close to the lake as possible. Townsfolk seemed to accept this, as these weren't the first world-weary travellers to extend their stay in the quaint hamlet. For their part, Natalia and Jim hunkered down, tried to integrate themselves into the society without rocking the boat or drawing attention to themselves.

They had been on the run since the end of September. They changed their names frequently: hair colour, too. Natalia had become accustomed to wearing contacts and her wardrobe now consisted of several items that would have appalled her mother, had she still been alive. But that was the Old Natalia. New Natalia was in survival mode, and New Natalia understood that taking on a different name meant taking on a different persona, and something as simple as the shoes on her feet could make or break that identity.

In the privacy of the cabin, she tried to remain Natalia Artison. She wore an old leather jacket, men's sized, too big for her and ragged. She wore jeans with rips and patches and tee shirts with video game emblems and what she called *stupid looking hipster bird*s, designed by NYU art grads who thought themselves altogether too clever for their own good. She kept her messy hair in a ponytail, because when it brushed against the brand at the nape of her neck it still stung horribly. In town, she would cover it up with scarves or a turtleneck, because Laura Palmer was a fashionable girl. Laura Palmer lived her whole life innocent and protected. Laura Palmer hadn't been at the Siege of Alcatraz. Laura Palmer hadn't been declared dead and mourned by what was left of her friends and family. Laura Palmer wasn't branded with the mark of a devil.

Only Natalia Artison was. Only Natalia Artison was a living, breathing threat to men and monsters alike.

There were shouts coming from behind her now. Friend or foe? It didn't matter. Jim had given her explicit instructions, and one of his many rules was that she never deviate from those first instructions, no matter what. He could be coerced into trying to get her back, he could be under the influence, drugged, anything. And, as he put it so mildly, just because he was looking after her didn't mean he didn't value his own life, too. If he had to fake his way through it, pretend to call her back, he would.

Natalia knew she was getting close to the creek that carved the woods in half and divided the resort. It was a couple of yards wide, nothing to worry about, but the water ran fast and deep, and if she went under she would be a human popsicle in no time. Her foot hit the ice and she felt it shudder and crinkle like layers of tissue paper.

Don't think about it. She planted her second foot in front of the first and kept moving, because moving meant life. It only took a single moment of hesitation to become a victim, and she refused. She *absolutely refused* to be what they wanted her to be.

The snowy ground crunched beneath her feet and she was free of the river. Nothing to fret about.

Natalia kept running. She could see the edge of the dirt road that connected the resort with the highway. Her shoes were soaked through and her jacket was heavy on her torso. It would be a short walk to the town, unless those pursuing her thought to try their luck with the main road.

She broke through the tree line and clambered up the side of the ditch, nearly falling on her ass when she hit the icy asphalt. A few hundred yards away the road turned a corner and joined the main artery of the town. One lonely street lamp marked the change from dirt to pavement. Natalia felt her breath catch in her throat as she caught sight of a humanoid shape flitting in the beam of light, as if caught in an exhilarating dance. She blinked once, and the figure was gone.

There were those who had departed from their physical form, but left incorporeal pieces of themselves lingering, and when the wind caught Natalia just right she could swear that their voices echoed around her, offering advice, and consolation in the hard, cold days of her new world.

Then there was the one who had never really lived on the same plane as the rest of the world. A consumer of spiders and grubs, he picked dirt from his teeth and sharpened his nails on gnarled old bones. A Hollow Man, who whispered *hush* in her dreams and drew her increasingly away from her old life. He embodied all that was surreal in her world. His presence, effervescent and inescapable. Sometimes he felt so close that she might be able to touch him or draw him to her reality where he would be crushed under the spirit of everyman.

But at her core Natalia wasn't sure she wanted to share a world with the Hollow Man, and so when she felt him near, Natalia found it best to simply continue on with her day to day activities and pretend he was not there.

It was close to midnight by the time she reached the local dive bar, the Salty Dog. When they had first arrived in town, Jim had scoped it out as a potential meeting place in case things went to hell. When it became clear that they would be stuck in northern Maine, Jim tasked Natalia with making friends with the bartender/owner, a short-tempered brute with hulking muscles, who went by the name Bear and, according to locals, had never been called anything else. He hadn't been pleased to see a young girl come traipsing through the door, but Natalia, or more correctly, Laura, had eventually won him over. She never caused any trouble, never tried to order booze. She would just sit quietly and drink a soda with a white and green striped straw, to avoid ruining her lipstick she said, while her uncle read the newspaper or made phone calls.

Bear was the sort of person who was an ally, even if he didn't realize it.

The Salty Dog was quiet. Only a few locals huddled over the bar, red noses dipping in and out of piss-poor beer like bobbing bird contraptions. Natalia stepped up to the counter, using the mirror behind Bear to case the rest of the bar's occupants in their faded crimson leather booths. She knew every face and name, had spoken to each of them at least once. No one, she figured, had been hiding or biding their time, waiting to pounce.

"You're out late, kid." Bear was cleaning a glass with a dirty rag. A perpetual cycle of dirt and rot.

"Has my uncle been by?"

Bear's nose twitched. A tell. "Huh, haven't seen him. You wanna give him a call?"

"No, thanks. Do you mind if I wait? Maybe warm up a bit first?"

"I'll bring you tea."

"Got coffee?"

"I'll put a fresh pot on."

Natalia shook her head. "I don't need anything special. Just something to keep me awake for a while longer."

Bear tipped is head to one side in acknowledgement and silently slid a paper napkin across the counter, then pointed to his cheek.

Natalia had nearly forgotten about the cut to her face, but with feeling quickly returning, she knew the blood would be flowing free. She accepted the napkin, pressed it to her cheek. "We had a fight. I ran. It was stupid. Those woods are *totally* not safe at night. Biffed it right into the side of a tree." She played up the lingo, the teenage verbiage. It made her more of a character; an entity separate from herself.

Bear nodded, saying nothing further, and Natalia slunk across the bar to one of the booths, where she was dwarfed by the leather seats and the poor lighting. She buried her fingers in the pockets of the coat and drew out an old watch. She had found it in the cabin, hidden under a sofa cushion, and claimed it as her own.

What time had they attacked the cabin? One of many questions that would need addressing. Natalia could hear Jim in her head, listing off reasons why they had been found.

We were too careless, we were sitting in one spot for too long, we felt too safe.

They came as darkness had sequestered the cabin from the rest of the resort. Jim had been reading in the living room and Natalia had been doing homework, or what passed for homework when on the run. They came through the sliding glass doors, smashing their way in like a herd of buffalo, rolling over the cabin with gunfire and violence. Jim pushed Natalia towards the door and told her to run.

She complied. Out of fear, and now, shame.

It had been at least an hour. Jim had never explicitly told her how long she ought to wait for him, but she guessed when the Salty Dog closed in two hours Bear would become less accommodating.

As if summoned, he appeared at the table, setting a freshly brewed cup of coffee beside her elbow and a basket of fries from the kitchen.

A man after my own heart.

"All right, Laura? You're looking a little battered."

Natalia forced a grin and snagged a fry from the basket. "Just cold. I'm still not used to it."

"Any word on when your new rental will arrive?" Natalia could tell that Bear was waiting for an invitation to sit down. Maybe he wanted to speak about the state of her home life. Natalia would have even indulged him if that were the case, except there was no time for pleasantries. Not tonight, when the living and the dead were both on the hunt.

"We're hoping just a couple more days. A family friend is passing through town and he said he'd give us a ride if it didn't turn up. You know how those rental agencies are."

Bear nodded sagely. He probably had no idea what she meant. Truth be told, neither did Natalia. But these were the things that were said, small talk to keep people and their questions at bay.

"Good. That's good. We'll miss you around here."

"Won't miss my uncle, though." Natalia smirked in spite of herself. She and Jim were polar-opposites. He was a brooding, angry sort of man. She was...well, Natalia wasn't sure what sort of person she was. There had been no time to mourn the dead that had been buried after the Siege of Alcatraz, and no time to scavenge the old pieces of herself from what had been torn apart. Maybe that was what had made learning how to fire a gun so easy. She filled the void of who she was with things that she never should have known. There was still sarcasm, oh yes, and a quick tendency to anger, but everything else was a collection of thoughts and experiences and skills that the Old Natalia would have never obtained.

Bear grinned at her and shook his head. "No, can't say that we will." Realizing he wouldn't be getting an offer to sit and talk, he turned and sauntered back to the bar.

Natalia sat in silence, eating her fries and drinking her coffee, always with one eye on the door of the bar and another on the patrons.

An hour passed. Only crumbs of fries remained in the basket and hope was dwindling. Natalia was about to give up when the door opened. She shifted, reached through the pocket of the jacket where a rip let her grasp the pistol that had been tucked into the lining. If she was going to die tonight, she was going to go down fighting.

Jim stumbled through the door of the bar, grabbing at tables and chairs for support as he tripped about like a drunken fool. In one hand, he held a half-empty bottle of something horrendous that he had purchased during a trip to the main street a few days ago. It had been full when Natalia saw it last. Behind him, as equally plastered by the looks of it, was an old ally.

Natalia wasn't fond of Max Havstead. Certainly, he had taken a bullet for her, more than once, and nearly lost his leg in the chaos prior to the Siege. But secrets had a habit of revealing themselves over time, as the layers of lies protecting them disintegrated in people's memories. Max had given her up to the Special Operations Initiative, the Agency that had employed her parents and, by all accounts, pulled all the strings in her life without her realizing it. It was Max who had told them about the nesting doll and the secret she carried. He had unwittingly been the one to put the target on her back. Natalia was not pleased to see him and, had they not been in a precarious situation to begin with, she would have aimed the gun at him.

Both men were stumbling, laughing, making merry, as drunkards often did. Jim was wearing a dark jacket; his undershirt looked like it had been splashed with liquor. As they passed by the bar, Jim slid his bottle over with dramatic flair, stepped back, and motioned for Bear to take it. When the lumbering owner didn't move, Jim leaned in again snatched it back up before spinning, spotting Natalia, and offering her a dramatic wave.

This is how Child Protective Services gets called.

Bear and the rest of the bar patrons shook their heads, casting Natalia pitying looks.

If only they knew the half of it.

Max dragged Jim over to the booth where they slid on the opposite bench, and Max reached for the cold coffee.

"What the *hell* are you doing here?" Natalia leaned over the table, swiped her mug back, and levelled her best annoyed teenager glare at him.

"Not now." Jim grunted, pulling one hand from inside his jacket, where he had been supporting his abdomen. His fingertips came away red and wet.

"*Shit!*" She clasped a hand to her mouth and leaned in closer. "How bad is it?"

"I've been stabbed worse, if that's what you're asking." There was a wet sort of raspy sound to his words. However he was wounded, whether it was a bullet or a knife, it had probably punctured his lung.

"Were you followed?" Max asked, once again going for the coffee.

Natalia slapped the top of his hand with her spoon. "No, no one. Were *you?*"

"Jesus, don't-" Max halted midsentence and mid-eye roll. "I have a car back at the resort."

"You *walked* here, with him like *that?*" Natalia gestured wildly at Jim, then, realizing she was starting to raise her voice and needed to stop drawing any more unwanted attention their way, said, "You can't go back for it. We don't have time."

"We took care of the ones at the cabin," Max told her softly, "but you're right, the minute they don't check in-"

"Who *are* they?" What she meant to ask was *who do they work for?* Terrorist or government; either way they were probably screwed.

"Later," Max said. "We need to get out of here."

Natalia glanced around the bar, settling her eyes on one of the well-known drunkards of the area. Big Al? Something cliché like that. She could see Bear eyeing her up in her peripheral vision, as if he knew what was going through her head. She slipped out of the booth and grabbed her empty coffee cup. "Just give me five minutes. I'll get us a truck."

"Better hurry." Jim leaned back in the booth, forcing a loud laugh, as if to maintain their farce. "I seem to be leaking."

At the bar, Natalia set her cup on the counter next to Big Al, and inched closer to his left side. He was sitting with his jacket draped over the stool and under his ass. There was no way his keys were in the breast pocket, unless he was trying to unlock his crack. They had to be in one of the waist pockets of his jacket. All she had to do was get them out and get away without anyone noticing.

"Your uncle seems like he's had a bit too much this evening," Bear said.

"Old school friends just bring it out in him, I guess," Natalia replied casually. "How much do I owe you for the coffee and fries?"

"On the house." Bear was on to her. His voice had taken on a steely tone, and his gaze had hardened considerably, given the familiarity of only an hour earlier.

"At least let me pay for Al." Natalia already had her hand in her coat pocket, fishing for the dollar bills she always kept in case of emergencies. She let some coins clatter to the floor and muttered something about being clumsy as she knelt to pick them up. Her shoulder brushed against Al's jacket; the keys in his pocket offered a slight resistance.

So far so good.

Reaching for the scattered coins, she let one hand drift up towards the pocket and felt the key ring loop around her finger. Just as she pulled back, she heard Bear above her.

"Find all of them?" He was looking at her from over top of the bar.

Natalia quickly feigned brushing her hair back behind one ear, letting the keys slide from her fingers and down the sleeve of the jacket, where the layers of leather muffled any jingling.

"Here." She laid a handful of dollars and coins on the bar. It was about three times the amount that Big Al's Coors Light would have cost, but she figured Bear might turn a blind eye if she offered a substantial tip. "Thanks for the food, Bear."

"You going to get your uncle home?"

"Sure thing. Safe and sound."

Chapter 2

It didn't take long to find Big Al's truck in the parking lot. It was a newer model, some flashy Ford that could deal with the substantial snowfall and, presumably, a post-apocalyptic wasteland. They managed to wrangle Jim into the front seat, and Natalia crawled into the back while Max started the truck. They sped off into the night, leaving the dreamy hamlet behind. The moment they crossed the town line, Natalia leaned between the front seats and swatted Jim's hand away from the inside of his jacket. The left side of his shirt was splattered with red, map-like stains. He groaned as she shoved her hand roughly against the wound.

"Don't complain. It's for your own good." She shot a wicked stare at Max. "What the hell is going on?"

Max looked calmer now, as if whatever fight he had intervened in had put him back in his place. Natalia imagined that since his leg had been wrecked by Cain Ferigon he probably hadn't seen much field work. Another reason to question why he, of all people, had shown up at their door.

"Caulder's been trying to track you and Jim since you left San Francisco."

"We knew that he would. That's why we *went* on the run," Natalia said. Jim had given her extensive history on as many of their enemies as he could. Harrison Caulder fell in the number two slot. Director of East Coast branch of the Special Operations Initiative. Widowed five years. One sister, one nephew. Lonely and, Natalia had quickly learned, a massive tool, although Jim had reminded her that she shouldn't insult hammers and wrenches in such a way.

"He was always a few steps behind, until he got tipped off about a pair who showed up in Maine. Sent a scout to check it out. They almost didn't believe it was you two until they saw you alone in town one day and you did something, I don't know, Amy-ish."

I'm doing things like my mother? God help me.

Max continued. "Caulder sent a team of cleaners out to finish the job, but Meghan got word of it and sent me ahead to bring you home."

"Home? Oh boy," Natalia drawled. "I've always wanted to step in front of a loaded cannon."

Max smirked. "The Twelfth has been collecting evidence, but it's too inconsequential to make any difference. We can wave proof in front of a tribunal, and he can defend it as a by-product of the trade. We've only got him if he oversteps, and he won't do that unless you're right there in front of him."

"So, we're *bait?*" Natalia gawked.

"For lack of a better term, yeah."

"Oh, oh yeah," Natalia said loudly. "That sounds *great.*"

"Nothing bad is going to happen. Jim is too well-trained."

"I am *quite literally* trying to keep his intestines inside him at this *very moment.*"

Max glanced sideways, as if to confirm Natalia was exaggerating. Satisfied, he turned his attention back to the road. "Don't use *literally* like that when you don't mean it."

"Holy shit." Natalia gawped at him. "We *can't go back there.*"

Jim coughed and growled. "Don't knock it, kid. We've been on the run too long. There are a lot of risks when we're constantly changing up like that. It's time to end this."

"You don't have the strength to end this right now." Natalia reminded him. "You barely have the strength to take a piss!"

"Then I suppose I won't have to worry about him trying to kill me then, will I?"

That was just like Jim, that macabre humor. He understood his own mortality, and he never hesitated to make fun of it. Natalia did not appreciate his seemingly lackluster outlook on his life. Death had been too prevalent recently, and she wasn't keen on losing anyone else to an axe, metaphorical or otherwise.

"You're such an asshole," she muttered. "Fine. We go back to New York. Then what?"

"No idea," Max admitted with a shrug of his shoulders. "I was just told to bring you back."

"Meghan sure knows how to pick my favourite people in the whole damn world."

Max's dark skin looked like it might have blanched slightly. "Listen, about the whole doll thing. I didn't know it would end up with Caulder. I had no idea it would turn into...this."

"You can apologize to Jim when this is over. He's the one bleeding to death right now."

"Drama queen." Jim coughed, wet and wispy.

Max nodded. "I know. I just thought I ought to say...well, no one's been impressed with me since they found out, so..." Max let the sentence hang, as if it somehow summed up whatever point it was that he was trying to make.

"Plus, your knee." Natalia's voice softened. To be honest, she didn't really care that Max had been the one to reveal her secret to the Agency. It was something she should have done herself. Those choices felt like they had been made a lifetime ago; she had taken on a hundred names and personalities since then. Natalia found the prospect of trying to hold on to her resentment far too exhausting.

"Let's just forgive and forget, yeah?"

He looked remarkably happy with that. "Oh yeah, that would be fantastic. If you don't mind telling everyone else you don't hate me, that would be great too."

"Don't push your luck." But she smiled, hoping to illustrate that she wasn't serious.

"Still bleeding here," Jim croaked. "Hospital would be nice."

Max shook his head. "No hospitals."

"He could *die*." But Natalia could tell by Max's expression that Meghan Sirano had probably made it perfectly clear that as long as Natalia got back to New York alive, other casualties were not a problem. That was how the game was played. People were prioritized; the ones who had the most value usually knew the most or had the greatest monetary amount attached to them. After that, people became expendable. New agents could always be trained; new bodies could always be risked.

Natalia was not considered expendable. She knew too much.

A little bit of knowledge can be a dangerous thing. Natalia couldn't recall where she had first heard that phrase. It was altogether too relevant to her now. A little bit of knowledge was all it had taken for her to be severed from her old life and thrown, damaged, into the world of the Special Operations Initiative. One string of numbers, so inconsequential to look at, had acted as executioner and spilled the blood of her family all around her.

The simplicity of it sometimes left her feeling queasy. How such an innocuous thing could wield such power was beyond her. As they had explained, she was protecting more than just a random string of numbers. Those numbers led to people, and those people all had families, and those families did not deserve to die because of someone else's mistakes. That was why Natalia held her tongue, why she chose not to break despite the fact that Jim was bleeding profusely into her hand and she had been shot at only hours before.

Hundreds of people, trusting her to hold her tongue. Even then, there were some who had not been so lucky. Her parents, for one, and her sister, Beth. All three, victims of the Code in their own way.

If only they knew. It never did Natalia much good to dwell on those sorts of things, so she focused her attention on ensuring Jim's internal organs remained safely encapsulated in his body.

They drove for hours, cutting across state lines until, entering New York proper, Max decided they could afford to stop for a few minutes and put new bandages over Jim's wounds. He was looking worse for wear. The sickly bubbling noise was in every breath he took. Natalia wondered if then he would die too, not from old age but from being caught in the crossfire, from putting himself between her and disaster. There had been too many deaths; sinners and innocents alike. The only thing they had in common was the unnecessary nature of their deaths, all connecting back to her.

Max told her to sleep, that she was muttering to herself. True, she had been awake for a solid two days. Jim only let her sleep five hours at the most each night, and she was usually up by five-thirty each morning to start the daily routine that Jim had forced onto her. An hour of basic evasive techniques, then a quick collaboration over new identities, and they were out the door.

So, she slept. And she dreamt of the dead.

When Natalia woke, she felt like she was on the brink of a psychotic episode. Her vision was blurred from sleep, and, try as she might, she couldn't blink away the gauzy veil. Hands gripped her and she felt herself lifted free, the cold air on her skin. The smells, medicinal and metallic, made her eyes water from the overpowering stench of *nothing*.

There will always be people to help you.

Voices she recognized. Friends.

The Twelfth.

They were speaking in short whispers that matched their methodical movements. The actions of people who had worked together enough to interpret the slightest shifts in body language. Light blossomed against Natalia's eyes, and she felt sticky vinyl press against her face.

"Natalia, stay still, ok?" Max. Oh lord, what were they doing? She tried to shift, but found that she was encased, unable to move beyond a few inches left or right before brushing against cold vinyl.

"Max, we need to go *now,*" someone shouted in the background. "Zip it up!"

"I'm sorry, this is the only thing we could think of. Just stay still. It'll be over soon." Max tugged up a zipper, blocking the light from her eyes.

She was awake now, confused. Then again, there were a few things to consider. She was still armed, and heavily at that. If Max were about to toss her under the metaphorical bus, he would have taken the knife that was clearly strapped to her thigh. No, better to assume that something had gone wrong on their surprise road trip, and Max had been forced to change his plan.

The bag smelled old, musty: like chalky bones and sour meat.

Don't think about corpses or human juices. Think about puppies and kittens.

She couldn't be certain, but it felt like the van was speeding. The trip up to that point had been hurried, but never drifted into the realm of illegal. Something had happened, and Natalia prayed it was nothing to do with Jim.

Jim! Oh shit, where is he?

He couldn't look after himself, or so Natalia told herself. It helped her, to justify her intrusion in his life, as if it was necessary to ensure he continued to eat and change his clothes and not wander aimlessly off a cliff while scowling at village children. He was particularly good at scowling.

The imagery made her smile, and Natalia decided, whatever was happening, or about to happen, she would remain calm, aim straight, and not hesitate when it came time to pull the trigger. With Jim out of commission, she couldn't afford to let a second be wasted by fear. She had faltered in the past, and the regrets were palpable, a bitter taste on her tongue.

The vehicle lurched and Natalia felt her cloth coffin slide across the bubbled surface of the floor. She hoped that whoever was driving knew they would have to move fast. It wouldn't take long for anyone to glance inside the van and realize that this wasn't an average transport of a body.

The van stopped, and Natalia could hear voices outside. She imagined the back doors being flung open, someone gripping the bag and dragging her out, throwing her into the snow, and then planting a bullet in her skull. Or maybe they would just fire randomly into the bag, and leave her gasping for air as her blood pooled over the cold, steely floor.

They began moving again, and Natalia exhaled sharply through her clenched jaw. A slope, she felt her heels crush against the doors of the van. A sharp turn, and a hollow, echoing sound, as if they were driving into a parking garage.

The driver cut the engine and feet clomped all around. The doors opened, and hands gripped the bag and dragged it backwards.

"Don't move." It was Max. Natalia could make out his shadow above her. She was hoisted through the air and settled on some sort of cart. The wheels squeaked and rumbled across pavement, bumps that rang through Natalia's skull and made her eyes water.

Suddenly there was light overhead, filtering through the black mesh. Even in the bag, Natalia could tell it was white, medicinal light. The sort found in hospitals and morgues and labs. She was shifted again, her bag hauled from the cart and settled on a soft surface.

The zipper was pulled down and light flooded in. Natalia bolted upright, covering her eyes with a free hand while balancing herself on what she realized was a medical examination table. Max stood before her, looking amused by Natalia's discombobulation. Next to him was George Bedlam, who she hadn't seen since she and her old guardian had been forced to escape a hospital back in September. Her head swivelled, as if on a dowel, stiff and mechanical.

"Jim?" she croaked.

"We split up," Max explained as he eased forward, hands raised, prepared to calm her should she lose what little grip she still had on her sanity. "He's already up in surgery in the medical ward."

"And where am I?"

Max gestured behind her and Natalia turned. Small, metallic cubbies lined the wall behind her. Just wide enough to fit a human body.

"A morgue?"

"*The* morgue," a voice said behind them.

Meghan Sirano, Supervisor of the East Coast Division of the SOI, came marching through the doorway with the look of a general heading over the top for the final push. Natalia had met her a few times, none of which had left the girl with a deep sense of trust in the woman. She was cold, with sharp features and a matching pantsuit that looked like it had been trimmed to perfection by an X-ACTO knife. She had never seemed particularly approachable, unlike Aurora Lansford, the communications supervisor, who came trailing in behind.

Meghan snapped a clipboard from Aurora's hands and thrust it towards Natalia, along with a pen that she presented as if it were a lit cylinder of dynamite. "Sign here." She pointed to a sheet of paper.

"What am I signing?"

"No time, Natalia. I need you to trust me."

"It's ok, Nut." Bedlam was at her side. A slight comfort. "I've got your back."

Natalia signed the paper, then watched as Aurora leaned forward and flipped through the stack to another page, pointing to a second, then third line. Jane Hancock all the way down; blue pen that smeared across the paper from the shaking of her hand. Meghan placed her own signature next to Natalia's and shoved the clipboard back to Aurora.

"Fast as you can, Aurora."

Aurora was a step ahead, already tossing a tablet onto the nearest instrument tray, snapping photos of the documents, fingers flying across the screen as she input information from the form. Natalia watched, vaguely aware of the intensity. Meghan glanced nervously at her watch and to the door of the morgue, as if expecting a troll to barge through at any moment.

George Bedlam had just located a blanket to throw over Natalia's shoulders when the brushed silver doors flew open and a man Natalia could only assume to be the Massive Tool himself, Director Harrison Caulder, marched through, flanked by two non-descript security sector personnel who looked prepared to draw blood. The director's hand jutted forward, one accusatory sausage finger nearly driven straight through Natalia's chest.

"Natalia Artison, you're under arrest."

She jolted back, not at the accusation, but at the audacity with which he launched himself towards her. Had George Bedlam not been standing on the other side of the morgue table she might have toppled right onto the floor.

"For *what?*" She tried to sound as indignant as possible, but it was proving difficult given the level of exhaustion she was facing.

"It's fine." Meghan laid a hand on Natalia's shoulder and offered her most insincere smile to Caulder. "I'm afraid the director is a bit behind on the times. He hasn't been made aware of your new rank in the Agency as *trainee.*" Meghan's smile was wolfish, and Natalia was forced to do her very best to not break character at this strange revelation.

Serves me right for not reading the fine print.

Caulder's face had turned a vibrant shade of red, matching the exhaustive patriotic tie that was knotted securely at his neck. He turned to the agent on his left and barked, "Go check this!" At his command, the agent scuttled from the morgue and Caulder turned back towards Meghan. "You think this will protect her?"

"I think," Meghan began slowly, "any action against an agent or *trainee* within the SOI has to be investigated by Internal Affairs, and they don't take kindly to anyone trying to take the law into their own hands."

"You're playing a dangerous game," Caulder warned, before shifting his gaze to Natalia. "You and *Agent* Artison both."

"What game is that?" Natalia asked innocently. "Monopoly?"

Caulder spluttered something, but Natalia wasn't done yet. "Clue?" she asked. "Is it Guess Who?" She looked back towards Bedlam, smiled brightly. "I bet it's Guess Who. Does your character have a really punchable face?"

Caulder looked as if he might spit acid, but instead elbowed the two security agents out of the way and stormed from the morgue.

"That right there is why people keep trying to shoot you," Bedlam said serenely. "I see it now. It all makes sense."

Natalia grinned cheekily and turned her attention to Meghan Sirano, who was staring at the swinging doors, looking bewildered, as if she hadn't expected him to give up quite so easily.

"What, uh, what happened there?" Natalia asked. "Did I agree to donate a kidney, too?"

Meghan smiled and shook her head. "I'm sorry. It was the only thing I could think of. We knew the cleaners were catching up with you and Jim, and we just couldn't afford to have you out in the open anymore." Aurora cleared her throat and Meghan gave her a wicked stare. "Cain Ferigon was spotted heading west out of Houlton four days ago."

"Shit." That had been close to them. Too close. Natalia closed her eyes and envisioned a grand wind sweeping over her squirming stomach, settling it. Visualizations and meditation; one of Jim's handy tips for survival. "So, now what?"

"It's like I said to Caulder," Meghan explained. "If he wants to get you now, he runs the risk of bringing Internal Affairs into it, which means Caulder is going to have questions that he'll have to answer. It doesn't stop him, but it'll throw a wrench or two into his plan."

"And Cain?"

"The whole of the east coast is on alert," Bedlam said softly. "He won't get within ten miles of New York without someone alerting the right authorities."

Natalia could now see the delicate pink scars that littered Bedlam's face. His prominent widow's peak was ragged from old wounds that had stalled the hair growth. His nose had been broken since she had seen him last, though his wireframe glasses did a decent enough job at hiding it. He looked worn, and Natalia pushed through her memories, trying to recall if he had always been like that or if perhaps his own experiences with Cain in September had somehow pre-emptively aged him.

Bedlam must have sensed she was giving his appearance a thoughtful onceover. He rested a hand on her shoulder. "Everyone has their eyes peeled for him. I *promise*."

Nodding once, Natalia turned back to Meghan. "Jim's been teaching me how to fight."

"Oh, he has, has he?"

"I asked him," Natalia interjected quickly. "I wanted to be able to defend myself. Now that I'm a-"

"A trainee."

"Right. Now that I'm a trainee, I'd like to learn more. The real stuff." Until that point, Jim's training had involved what he described as *Street Fighter Lite*. It was the sort of training one pursued when one was certain they were going to be mugged behind a sleazy bar, not when they were facing a terrorist. He had let her shoot a gun, but only after ensuring she knew each component of it forwards and backwards, and understood how everything functioned. Even then her aim was atrocious and made him cringe.

Natalia wasn't keen on the idea of killing again, and she knew Jim wasn't looking for an opportunity to put a weapon back into her hands. No, what he taught her was survival. Escapism, language, attitude. The sort of things that offered a person a sense of confidence, so they might walk down the street without fearing for their life. She could pick locks, knew where to stab, and understood what to look for when she suspected she was being followed. Trade craft, he called it.

Learning the skills and, perhaps more importantly, the nerve to kill another human was an entirely different matter, and that struck Natalia as odd. She had already killed, more than once, in fact. Those were ghosts she was quite content to avoid revisiting, if possible. But now, as a trainee, she would have to face them and survive as the champion, the conqueror.

"Well," Meghan said slowly, "Jim has good instincts for these sorts of these things. When he's feeling more up to it, we can have him start giving you some proper lessons. And we can arrange for you to join the other trainees." Her eyes narrowed, and she added, "If you're absolutely sure. This was really just meant as a distraction for Caulder if nothing else-"

"Of course, I'm sure." Natalia hid her mouth with a hand and yawned. Exhaustion was settling over her like a heavy blanket.

"Can we continue this later?" Bedlam asked. "She needs sleep."

Meghan tipped her head to the side, still analyzing the girl sitting in front of her on the autopsy table. Finally, she conceded with a nod. "Take her upstairs. Get one of the docs to do a cursory exam and then find her a bed." Meghan stepped back, Aurora in her shadow. "Welcome to the SOI, Agent Artison."

"Flip," Natalia said, pushing herself off the autopsy table and letting Bedlam take her by the elbow. "She really doesn't seem keen on it, huh?"

Bedlam directed her through a small door off the morgue and down a narrow hallway that was lit by the same horrendous blue lights as the rest of the basement. "To be fair, none of us were when she brought it up." They reached a small elevator at the end of the hall and Bedlam jabbed the button with his thumb. "But then word came through about Cain, and she made a good case about you having at least the minimal skills needed to protect yourself."

On the elevator, Natalia leaned against the brushed silver and closed her eyes. The gentle lurch of the ascent sent her head spinning, and she gripped the handrails in a half-assed attempt to keep herself upright. "And it pisses off Caulder," she said, sleepily.

"That's an added bonus," Bedlam agreed. They stepped off the elevator into an inexplicably bright artery that smelled heavily of iodine and lemon Pledge. So clean, it burned the back of Natalia's throat, and might have made her eyes water if they weren't already closed from the exhaustion. She let Bedlam push her in whatever direction was required. Doors and hallways passed by, already long gone by the time she could comprehend how they fit as individual components into the structure of the building as a whole.

Bedlam helped her onto a soft hospital bed, although she couldn't remember entering a room where such a bed existed. With some fumbling Natalia managed to squirm her way under the covers and turned on her side so she could see Bedlam. He was talking, but the words were thick and slow, like maple syrup poured on fresh snow. Natalia exhaled sharply, closed her eyes, and let the visage of Bedlam bleed into darkness

Chapter 3

When Natalia woke up next, she had lost all concept of time.

Stretching her legs under the blankets, her joints give satisfying pops, like boney firecrackers. After a quick check to ensure her limbs were still attached, she rolled from the hospital bed and tested the ground under her feet.

The floor isn't lava, dummy.

The world of the Agency was inherently dangerous; that had been made explicitly clear by Jim over the course of their three months on the run. It wasn't just the high mortality rate. The SOI attracted a sort of person who lived and breathed chaos, who thrived in the heat of battle, like scavengers who feasted on the misery of others. Natalia was a stranger in a strange land, trying to navigate the world without a compass. Signing those papers the day before – had it really only been a day? – had given her a direction, a place to go. But every step towards that goal oozed unfamiliarity, and Natalia wasn't certain she was equipped to handle it.

Beyond the privacy partition was a large, open ward. Dozens of pale blue curtains were drawn closed. A man in an austere white lab coat glanced up from a clipboard, nodded in her general direction, and pointed with the end of his pen to the sectioned-off bed at the furthest end of the ward. Natalia followed his unvoiced directions and gently pushed back the curtain. There, sleeping remarkably peacefully for a man who had been stabbed less than twenty-four hours earlier, was Jim.

Natalia exhaled sharply through a clenched jaw and shook her limbs loose, finally feeling the nerves of the last few days depart her. If he had died...Natalia didn't want to think about that.

No more ghosts, she thought grimly, settling in the chair beside his bed. *And no more dead, either. I've had enough.*

Someone had left a magazine on the bedside table, a poor man's coaster for the water jug and cup. Beneath the glass, the distorted face of a reality show star ballooned and the headline indicated he thought he had the capacity to run a country. She began to flip through the pages aimlessly.

Within the hour, she could hear the ward bustling with activity, doctors and nurses trotting about and delivering orders. Natalia was thoroughly engrossed in the ludicrous articles in the magazine when the curtain around Jim's bed was dragged unceremoniously open by a woman who was, for once, completely unfamiliar to Natalia.

"Huh," the woman said blandly. "So, it's true."

"Pardon me?" Natalia folded the magazine shut and sat up in the chair, her body protesting the unexpected motion.

"The spawn of the Artisons." The woman laughed quietly, as if it were some private joke, and tossed her hair. "Someone mentioned you had joined our ranks."

Am I talking to a cliché? On closer inspection, Natalia could see that the woman's face was hard and scarred from years of fieldwork. Penny-sized milky scars dotted her face and arms. "Sure have," Natalia said. "Who are you?"

The woman smirked, but didn't offer her hand in greeting. "How many more are going to have to die for you?"

"Oh, wow," Natalia said, "we're just going straight to that, huh? The art of conversation really is lost."

The woman had an unnatural, almost comic-like look; eyes too brown and too big for her face. Natalia's dad would have called her a Disney princess.

"Your parents were a cancer to the Agency," the woman sneered.

"What's that supposed to mean?"

"Spare me the naivety," the woman spat back. "You ought to know the truth. If you don't it's only because they're pr-"

"Enough." If Jim had been awake the whole time, Natalia hadn't noticed. Despite looking wan, he spoke with conviction. Jim feasted on the disaffected nature of others; if this kept up, he would be on his feet and dancing in a matter of hours.

"You of all people should-" the woman began.

"I said *enough*, Leah. Learn when to let shit go."

"Fine." The woman tossed her hair again and turned around. "We're all really looking forward to dying for her."

"Get off the cross," Jim snapped back, "we could use the wood."

Natalia snorted and clamped her hand over her mouth, theorizing that hysterical laughter might not help either of them, and it certainly wouldn't endear her to the agent who was now stalking off, snarling wicked comments to the doctor as she passed.

"Um." Natalia turned to Jim, then pointed towards the door. "I don't think she knows what cancer is?" Jim smirked but said nothing, so Natalia asked, "What the hell was that all about?"

Jim, clearly still sleepy from coming out of his dozing state, tried to shrug unsuccessfully, wincing from the pain. "People around here, the ones that are good at their jobs, they don't make friends. Can't afford them. Your parents were very good at their job." It sounded wise, but the words were slurred. He grimaced, shifted in the bed, annoyed.

"How is that my fault?"

"It's not." He collapsed backwards with a huff. "Just ignore them. Task Force Three is full of assholes, and Leah Beaumont is the worst of them. She's got half the story, and only knows a quarter of the words."

xXx

Boredom settled in soon enough. Jim's recovery involved more sleeping than Natalia was comfortable with, and left her lonely and isolated in the medical ward. More than once over the following days Rebecca Pulson, George Bedlam, and even Max came to visit her, to urge her to come out with them for lunch, but Natalia refused. Leaving Jim's side, even with him stabilized and out of danger, seemed like testing fate. If she was by his side at least she could be certain he couldn't go anywhere without first asking her permission.

Sometime during the third night, Natalia felt the sensation of a hand resting on her head. A familiar scrunching of her hair, fingertips patting her skull. Cologne, like Christmas spices. The smell of a man who enjoyed a good celebration, in whatever form it might take.

"Troy!" She bounded out of the chair and into the arms of her godfather, Amy's best friend. She hadn't seen him in over a year; he had been living overseas, a perpetual bachelor pursing a young French woman who, as Amy had described it, was as flighty as a mocking bird and about as graceful as an ostrich. Apparently it hadn't worked out.

Troy Winters embraced her, a tremendous squeeze that lifted her off her feet. "How are you?"

There was someone from her old life, a real, living person who crossed the threshold of one reality and entered the next. She could hardly believe it. "What the hell are you doing here?"

"Erm, yeah, the thing is..." Troy trailed off, and Natalia didn't need an answer.

"The Agency." She sighed and rolled back a shoulder, stiff from sleeping curled into the wooden armrest of the chair. "You too, huh?"

"Your parents and I - we never wanted to tell you or Beth." His face shadowed at the mention of Beth.

Natalia didn't have the energy to deal with more sadness, and she could see Jim staring at her out of the corner of her eye, wary, waiting to see if she would succumb to her emotions. "It's ok. I was a kid. I would have never been able to keep the secret."

"You're still a kid," said Troy.

"That is up for debate," she replied smugly.

Troy seemed pleased by this response and turned to Jim. "Looking a little worse for wear, Wilkinson."

"Nothing a little bloodshed won't solve." Jim grunted, trying to right himself on the hospital bed. Natalia was quick to his side, offering what support she could. When Jim was more or less settled, Natalia turned back and found Troy looking at her, frowning.

"What?"

"Your parents didn't want this for you."

"They also wanted me to take to the piano, but it never stuck."

Troy's mouth twitched, maybe a half a smile, and Natalia reckoned she had soothed the savage beast, at least for a day or two. He had always been protective of her, and of Beth. It stemmed from his loyalty to Amy Artison, unshakeable even as their friendship waned and frayed over the years. There was no doubt in Natalia's mind that Troy would have a select thing or two to say about her playing chicken with a terrorist.

Jim must have sensed a pause in the conversation, as he interjected, "There's a team meeting later today, Natalia. I think Rebecca was going to give you the dime tour and let you wander around for a bit."

"By myself?" She raised one eyebrow at her guardian. "That seems a little risky, don't you think?"

Troy and Jim shared an uneasy look and Natalia immediately regretted mentioning it. Jim glowered in a way that only he could manage, and said, "Leah Beaumont was up here two days ago to take a gander, like she was part of some sort of freak show."

Troy sighed. "The Third always was Caulder's pet, but I wouldn't worry about it. Meghan's made sure there are eyes on you as long as you're around here."

"How delightfully big brother," she drawled.

"Yeah, yeah. Government spying is bad and all that shit." Jim nodded towards the door of the hospital ward. "Do yourself a favor and go find Rebecca. You're ok, kid, but you smell like three days worth of stress."

"A true gentleman." But Natalia grinned. "Glad you're not dead, Jim. Try to keep it that way, yeah?"

"Only because you asked so nicely."

The two men watched as Natalia hobbled off in search of Rebecca; a taciturn silence fell between them. Jim had never hated Troy, nor particularly liked him. Troy had been part of Amy's group of friends, and Jim had always existed on the periphery of that sphere. He and Troy worked well together, but they were from different worlds. The fact that they were colliding now, when Natalia was between them, only served to reinforce their indifference for one another.

"So," Troy said.

"Let's just get this out of the way. You want the kid?"

"Excuse me?"

Jim wasn't one to be drawn in by anyone feigning ignorance, let alone Troy Winters. "That's why you're back. You were Amy's best friend. It makes sense that you would want to look after her kid. So, you want to take her or not?"

"Tired of her already?"

"I didn't say that. I made a promise; one way or the other I'll be watching her back. But if you're going to throw a fit about it, I'm not going to fight you. She'd probably be more comfortable living with someone she knows."

"Someone who isn't you?"

"Someone who is part of her old life, before all this shit went down. Before Steven."

Troy hummed a moment. "Don't get me wrong. I'd love to take her. I think having her stay with someone like *you* is probably just as damaging as handing her over to Cain."

"Ouch." But Jim didn't try to sound offended. Troy wasn't wrong; he just had the tact of a two-by-four up the side of a head.

"But," Troy continued, "I don't know what she wants. I only know what *Amy* would have wanted for her, and I think we both know that isn't you."

Jim was hardly in a position to disagree, although he liked to imagine if things had been different, if he hadn't ended up the walking disaster he was, perhaps Amy would have approved of him looking after her child. Perhaps she would have even encouraged it.

"Natalia's a smart kid, and it's not my place to step in. She's headstrong, like her mother. We'll let her make her own decisions. If you change your mind, if she gets too much to handle then sure, yeah, I'll take her. For now, it'd probably be best to leave her where she is."

Jim was surprised to find himself relieved to hear that. He kept his face stony, not wanting to reveal his satisfaction lest Troy try to use it against him later. It was something he had begun to realize about himself since Natalia came under his care; Jim had an active interest in the day-to-day operation of the world around him. Knowing that his choices could impact her made him more cautious about his choices, and opened his mind up to other possibilities. Accounting for a second person changed the entire equation, and Jim wasn't entirely opposed to that.

Chapter 4

Natalia met Rebecca outside the hospital ward and found herself pulled along by the sleeve of her jacket towards the chrome elevators. She remembered the woman from the time before Alcatraz. Rebecca had been there, a good friend to Steven and, by association, someone Natalia was certain she could trust implicitly.

"Task Force Twelve gets the fifth, sixth, and seventh floors," Rebecca explained as the elevator stopped and they stepped into the hallway. "Locker rooms and day rooms on five. Office space for senior agents on six. The main office space, we call it the Hive, that's on seven. Task Force Three has their floors above us. Everything after that is shared space; armoury, weaponry, training facilities, stuff like that."

They pushed through a set of double doors at the end of the hall and entered a locker room.

"This'll be yours-" Rebecca trailed off as they neared a row of lockers painted a dull shade of iron. They had been personalized; some were dotted with stickers and magnets. Others had photographs stuck into the vents, or pressed against the metal with the help of gummy tack and tape. One such locker was covered in a mishmash of new and old; photos and clippings that were layered on thick, like a disorganized memory box. Natalia had to squint to make out the individual faces. Steven, Jim, Rebecca, Troy, her parents. And there, in a handful of photos, her and Beth, some of them together, some of them apart. Natalia approached the locker and tugged an image from the collage.

It was her family. Amy, Marcus, Beth, and Natalia. Some silly family portrait they had taken during a vacation years ago. But no, it only *felt* like years ago. It had just been last spring. The memories were so close that Natalia thought she might be able to reach out and caress them with her fingertips if only they would manifest themselves in the physical world.

"Oh yeah." Rebecca looked sheepish. "Those belonged to your folks. You can take some if you want. If you need them, or something. They were supposed to clean them off before you got here, but..."

Natalia did need the photos. Everything she owned before this began had been engulfed in liquid fire. What was left were memories, and even those had been tarnished by Cain. Maybe with a picture or two she would be able to rebuild them in a way they would be untouchable, even to a monster like Cain.

"It's fine." Natalia would take a few pictures later. The family ones. Start her own collage on her own locker. "You said mine's over there?"

"Oh sure," Rebecca said, nervously ducking her head to hide the rising colour on her cheeks. "Come on."

A few doors down they stopped in front of a locker that sported her name and title on a magnetic tag that hung lopsidedly on the door. It was full of clothes, shoes, makeup – all in her own size, own choices, as if someone had taken a snapshot of her life before the Siege of Alcatraz and tried to replicate it.

"Some of the clothes belonged to your mom. She had quite a wardrobe stashed away and we thought maybe you'd like to keep them."

Natalia gripped the edge of a blue sweater. It was soft, alpaca. Beth had been furious when Amy wore it to work one day and didn't bring it back, claiming she had spilled tomato soup on it and the whole thing had been ruined. Her mother had done that a lot, fashioned little lies that she used to shift her life from one palm to the other, like a magician with a coin. It seemed effortless to Natalia. She never would have known if it hadn't all gone to shit. Leaning in, she inhaled the scent of the sweater and smiled. Her mom's scent. Jasmine, neroli. Sometimes Natalia would catch a whiff of it as she walked down the street, and fight the urge to react. Laura Palmer wouldn't react. Laura Palmer connected no memories with that scent. Laura Palmer didn't give a shit about Chanel No. 5 the same way Natalia Artison did.

She pulled back from the fabric, cleared her throat pointedly. "So, now what?"

"You can shower over there." Rebecca pointed towards the back of the locker room. "There are towels. I left some shampoo in your locker. When you're ready I'll finish showing you around if that works for you."

Natalia nodded and pulled the blue sweater from the hanger. It would do just fine.

After she had soaped the grime of the last three days from her skin, washed her hair of the blood and dirt that had settled at her roots, and done a cursory catalogue of her scars, Natalia emerged from the locker room feeling refreshed and moderately more human. Her skin burned from the hot water blasting against the brand at the nape of her neck. It was healing well, or so she thought, twisting about and trying to observe it in the foggy mirror. The symbol, a simple infinity sign within a circle, was a thread that tied Natalia between worlds. Try as she did to resent the scarring of her body, Natalia was beginning to find a small measure of comfort in it, as if it kept her connected to what she had lost.

Rebecca was waiting patiently for her in the hallway. When Natalia emerged, she gave a satisfied nod. "So, there *is* a kid under all that grime." She laughed at her own hilarity and motioned down the hall. "Come on, I'll give you a quick tour."

She dutifully followed Rebecca up one floor to an open, industrial-looking space, all tiered walkways, shiny silver rails, and glass cubicles where agents worked earnestly away on this and that.

"This is the Hive," Rebecca said, dodging an occupied chair that rolled across their path. "The Twelfth and the Third have their own independent tech and comm agents as support. This is where our people work, along with all the junior agents and trainees." She pointed down a hallway that branched off from the room. "We're having a meeting down there. You can come if you want, but I don't think you'll hear anything that you haven't already been told."

Code for 'we don't want you to hear what we're going to discuss'. It didn't bother Natalia much; she was still coming to terms with the sudden expansion of her personal existence into the Agency. Somehow, sitting in a boardroom, pretending to understand what was being discussed, did not interest her. "What'll I do in the meantime?"

Rebecca shrugged and patted her on the shoulder. "Whatever you want. Explore, read, go piss off the Third. There's a cafeteria on the second floor if you're hungry, and Jim is still in the medical ward if you want to go visit him. No one will stop you now."

I wouldn't be so sure about that. Natalia watched Rebecca turn down the hallway and disappear into the conference room.

Suddenly, the noise and bustle of the Hive crashed over Natalia, igniting all her senses and splitting her in a hundred different directions as she tried to understand it. People shouting at each other from across the elevated floors, tossing about lingo and acronyms so their conversations barely constituted a grammatically complete sentence. Small groups of agents were huddled around screens built into the walls, watching as the projections changed rapidly from faces to maps to row after row of intel.

Natalia felt sick, bombarded by what was happening around her. Colours, noises, sounds. Beads of sweat clung to her hairline, and her heart thrummed in her chest. No discernable rhythm, just a panicked *patta-patta-patta*, urging her to give into that fight or flight instinct.

Flight it is. She grappled at the doorframe and propelled herself down the nearest corridor, towards the elevator, trying to not trip on her feet as the world swayed around her. She thumbed the button for the elevator, and stumbled clumsily onto the lift. It was only as the doors slid closed that she realized she had been holding her breath.

The locker room seemed as safe a place as any to collect her thoughts and take a few minutes to pull herself back from the edge of a breakdown. It hadn't been the first time she felt crushing anxiety when surrounded by so much action. Since the Siege of Alcatraz, she had developed a few eccentricities, least of all a dislike of too much hustle and bustle. She had battled claustrophobia for a while, until Jim pushed her into the closet of a motel room and told her to *deal with it*. There was no simple fix for the anxiety that reared its head when she was in the middle of too much action. Jim would give her a hard time about it if he knew how she had made an awkward escape from the Hive. His solution would probably be to send her to a mosh pit.

After a few minutes of solitude, and what passed for meditating in her world, Natalia found the lockers that had belonged to her parents and began to shift through the layers of pictures that had collected over the years. Happy faces, frozen in their bliss, with no concept of how their lives would be so violently cut short. Natalia ran her fingers across eyes, noses, and mouths, trying to identify something in their visages that might indicate they were carrying the heavy burden of the Agency. Nothing. Picture perfect. Always *on*.

She ran her fingers over her mother's face and frowned.

Who the hell were you when you weren't my mom?

A door opened and closed and voices broke through the heavy silence: cheerful laughter, sarcasm, and joking. Teenagers.

Natalia placed the photo beside her on the bench and glanced up as a young woman no older than her walked in, accompanied by two men the same age. They all stopped in their tracks when they saw her.

"Hey!" The girl drew out the vowel awkwardly as she sidled up beside Natalia. "Anna Monroe, trainee. I hear you're one of us, now."

Natalia shook Anna's hand as the taller of the two young men raised his fists in the air and chanted, *"One of us! One of us!"*

"I'm-"

"Natalia Artison." Anna smiled widely, showing off an endearing gap in between her front teeth. "You're all the others can talk about. Well, you and your parents."

The boy who had been chanting cleared his throat pointedly and Anna blushed. "Not, like, their deaths or anything. That's not what I meant. Can we start this conversation over?"

Natalia grinned. "Suits me just fine."

"What are you doing here? We thought you'd be at the meeting."

"I figured I'd snoop around for a little while." Natalia waved one of the pictures from the locker. "A trip down memory lane seemed called for."

Anna's face drooped and she hopped over the bench to sit next to Natalia. "Yeah, I guess you don't have any pictures, huh?" Anna kicked out her feet and began to play with a strand of her corn-coloured hair. "I'm the same way. Parents died in a car bombing back home. The Agency looks for things like that, yeah? Sorry excuses, little whelps like you and me. When I left I couldn't bring much with me. Just the memories, eh?"

Natalia could already tell she'd enjoy Anna's incessant need to fill silence with talk, if that was indeed what she was doing. Natalia leaned backwards and made eye contact with two boys who had been holding back. The first, whose ability to chant rivalled even the most enthusiastic sports fan, looked like he was suppressing a laugh. The other, with an austere face and dark wind-swept hair, looked as if he had been asked to swallow a lemon, and then the rest of the citrus orchard.

"Oh, rude." Anna tapped her forehead dramatically and pointed to the first. "Ben Richardson and-" she halted at the sight of the other boy. Natalia had seen pissed-off people before, and been the cause of them more often than she liked, but the venomous look he was currently sporting was particularly impressive. Before she could make some offhand comment about it, he spun around and marched from the locker room.

Anna sighed, aggrieved, and waved her hand dismissively. "Martyn Garland. He's..." She looked to Ben, as if seeking some sort of assistance in explaining what had just happened.

"You shouldn't mind him," Ben said, settling on the other side of Natalia. "His mom was part of the security sector. Way I understand it, she died the same time you and your sister were taken back in September."

There wasn't much Natalia remembered from that time. In the early days after her mother's death and the fire that had devoured their lives, she and Beth had been caught up in their collective misery, and paid little attention to the agents who had been assigned to watch over them. The simplest actions, from making meals to folding laundry, had seemingly taken place like magic. Natalia was no fool, though; she knew those agents had been responsible for keeping her and Beth within the realm of the sane.

Until they were slaughtered with ruthless efficiency by Cain's people.

"Oh, god," Natalia said numbly.

"He doesn't think it was your fault or anything!" Anna interjected. "It's just, you know. It's hard getting over it. He's looking for someone to blame, same as everyone else around here. That's why the Third has a stick up their collective asses. Martyn's still just mourning her. He'll come around eventually."

"Oh." Natalia exhaled in a low whistle. "I don't know about that. Seems like people generally don't care for the Artison name around here."

"Probably because it's spelled in a stupid way," Ben suggested, and winced as Anna punched him on the shoulder.

"That's more like it." Anna smiled, turned back to Natalia and patted her shoulder sympathetically. "Don't worry about it. You've got your own shite to work through."

As grateful as she was for Anna's generous claim that she had enough to worry about, Natalia felt distracted by Martyn's pain. It was a mutual sadness, one that should be shared with another person, but he was still angry. Had she ever been angry about it? Maybe about Steven's death, and Beth's too, but there was an incessant feeling of exhaustion that claimed her whenever she thought about the total loss of her family. Sadness was strenuous enough; what room did she have for anger?

Plenty, she thought, *under the right circumstances.*

Chapter 5

When Natalia and Jim stumbled through the front door of his house, they were greeted enthusiastically by Jim's German Shepherd mix. The dog had been staying with a friend in San Francisco, and then accompanied them for several weeks after they fled the city. A close call with one of Caulder's lackeys just north of Montello left Jim uncomfortable with the idea of hoisting his dog around with them. Cooper was flown home, first class, and stayed with Rebecca until that very day.

He greeted Natalia with a wet kiss to her cheek and then solemnly lowered his belly to the ground in front of Jim as a show of obedience. Jim, who had told Natalia he wasn't entirely certain how he had trained Cooper, rolled his eyes and tossed his bag to the floor.

"Two bedrooms downstairs." He pointed to a hallway directly to her right. She had nearly missed it amongst all the dark wood and weak light from the ancient wall sconces. "Another two upstairs, and mine. Pick whichever you want. I'm going to bed." Without another word, Jim dragged himself down the hallway, up the stairs, and disappeared around the corner.

Natalia stood in the foyer, Cooper by her feet, and stared around in bewilderment.

"Ok," she said, then exhaled slowly. "This isn't the weirdest place you've ever been."

No, that award was cinched by Alcatraz.

Deciding it might be nice to have a bit of space from Jim, and inherently drawn towards rooms on the ground floor where she wouldn't have to worry about plummeting to her death, Natalia picked up her backpack and trudged down the hall. It took her a few minutes of blindly running her hands along the wall and walking into corners before she finally located a light switch. With one flick, the sconces flared to life.

She found the two bedrooms, as advertised, and paused between them. *Whichever one you pick, you have to stick with it. This is going to be* your *room.* In another life, another time, the decision would have been made by her parents. They would have told her where to sleep, what colours she could paint the walls, what bedding she would be allowed to have. Now, with freedom someone her age could only dream of, Natalia couldn't even decide which bedroom to step into first.

It's not that important, she told herself, stepping into the bedroom on her right. *It's just a room.*

Someone had made the bed long ago. When she fluffed the sheets, a soft cloud of dust rose and tickled her nose. Cooper sneezed and tried to bury his face under his paws.

A bed is a bed. Kicking off her shoes, Natalia crawled under the covers, patted the bed as an invitation for Cooper to join her, and closed her eyes. She could feel sleep settling into her skull like poured cement as Cooper's nose pressed into the palm of her hand.

In the middle of the motel room, Natalia hears the door open, and the creaking floorboards. She is still in that pleasant place between awake and dreams, but her heart begins to jackhammer in her chest all the same. Instinct rising, giving way to action. In one smooth movement, she rolls of the bed and drops to the floor as a blade is plunged into her pillow. They would have to pay to replace that.

She looks up over the edge of the bed and scowls at Jim, who steps back, looking unimpressed.

"Really?" she asks. "Really?"

"You have to be prepared."

"I have to have one night of complete sleep. You aren't Mitzi McNinja; you don't have to plunge a dagger into my pillow every night to keep me on my toes."

"Who the hell is Mitzi McNinja?" Jim looks appalled, like he can't believe the word 'McNinja' just left his mouth.

"It's...never mind. Please, can't I just have one *uninterrupted night of sleep?"*

Jim looks almost hurt by the request, as if these little night-time stabbing adventures were somehow about more than just keeping his ward prepared. But the look passes and the austere guardian returns and clears his throat. "The minute you let your guard down, they will find a way in."

Natalia heaves an intense sigh and drags herself back into bed, where she settles her head on the shredded pillow, sending a wave of feathers billowing up. "Wake me up in an hour."

That was how they worked. An irregular harmony that they were both unaccustomed to. Every night, beginning the day they left San Francisco. Jim was right; it kept her on her feet, alert. She was learning how to hone her body, to listen to its needs and wants. She wasn't strong by any physical measure, but she no longer felt weak. Now, staying in what would be her home for the foreseeable future, Natalia felt prepared.

That night, Jim did not wake her up.

She pulled herself out of bed before the sun had breached the horizon. Cooper rolled over the covers and snuffled his face beneath the pillow. He gave a sigh of what Natalia could only assume was contentment and she smiled.

"Glad at least one of us can enjoy it."

Pattering around in her sock feet, Natalia tried to take in the small details of the home. The smell of old cigarettes clinging to walls, the dryness of the air. There was a strange disconnect between the aesthetics of the house and the rest of the world. Old hardwood, old wall sconces; everything seemed antique. But the air, the presence of the house, was modern and bleak. She had circled around to the main artery that branched out from the foyer and stalled. The frosted glass doors of the living room glowed warmly, inviting her in.

She imagined that Jim would be less hospitable.

She pushed a door aside – it creaked on the rails that guided it. Jim was awake, papers spread out before him on the coffee table. All around him, a mishmash of the old and new. An upright piano that looked like it had been pulled from the Warsaw Ghetto; leather couches with pristine throw pillows.

"Thought I'd let you rest." He didn't glance up, apparently not concerned about the change in schedule.

Natalia perched on the settee across from him and pulled her legs up to her chest. "What are you doing?"

"Looking over some files." He turned over a piece of paper hastily, as if he only just remembered who he was talking to. It was too late. Natalia saw the corner of the image. Everything about the day Amy Artison had died was burned into Natalia's mind. She could smell the coppery blood, nearly taste it on the air. She heard the books and glass crunching beneath her feet. She felt the anxiety of what was waiting around the corner. It never really left her.

But Natalia couldn't picture her mother's corpse. It was a strange, blurred memory that Natalia couldn't sharpen no matter how much she tried to recall the moment. Even now, catching a glimpse of the blackened skeleton that had once been her mother, Natalia could not call the memory out of the darkness that obscured it.

"I shouldn't have them out," Jim said matter-of-factly. Remorselessly.

"Steven had them too." Natalia leaned forward, made a motion to grab the folder. Jim gently slapped her hand away and she recoiled, more out of shock than anything. "Really?"

"Orders," he grunted, beginning to collect the papers. "Besides. You're not ready for them."

"What makes you so sure?" She didn't expect a response, and in classic Jim form, did not receive one. With a sigh, she kicked out a foot and said, "Can I ask you a question?"

Jim arched an eyebrow at her, his face otherwise emotionless. Natalia had come to understand that about him long ago. He showed nothing, gave nothing away, and offered his enemies no opportunity to manipulate him into action outside of his control.

"Is it going to be a dumb question?"

Blunt as a children's spoon.

"I was just wondering about Martyn Garland."

"Oh," Jim almost looked defeated, as if the topic was somehow infinitely less interesting than he had hoped. He had been prepared for a fight, and now that one wasn't coming he was disappointed. "What about him?"

"Anna said his mom was there when Beth and I were taken, at the old safe house."

Jim nodded, but said, "I'm still not hearing a question."

Natalia rolled her eyes. "Ok, so *was* his mom there?"

Jim smirked, apparently proud of his ability to aggravate a teenager into proper grammar and sentence structure. Natalia would have argued that it was hardly an achievement given that six months ago she was an earnest academic who took pride in her ability to string a sentence together, at least when compared to her peers. Living with him had damaged her desire to impress anyone with her rhetoric.

Jim Wilkinson didn't give a flying fuck, and as such, neither did Natalia.

He was searching through a folder marked *PERSONNEL.* It was stamped with the date of the fire that had gutted Natalia's old life. Once he found the right paper, he pulled it free and passed it over the table. "Vivian Garland. She was a nice woman. Hard, though. Made more so when her son joined, I think."

Looking at the picture of her, Natalia could see the resemblance between Vivian Garland and her son. The same dark features; warm, brown eyes like tilled earth. Natalia knew that face. The last time she had seen the woman, she was strung up from a balcony, skin grey and flesh bloated, blood drip dropping from her toes and dotting the safe house floor like a Jackson Pollock.

"You know better than most," Jim said after a few moments, "when someone you love gets caught in the crossfire, you don't just bounce back from it."

But Natalia didn't know that. She imagined it was a worldly truth. Pain and heartache wrenches on the soul and leaves damaging bruises on the spirit, on the *self*. Those damages leave ephemeral pain that resonates in the trenches of the person, so even when the pain seems as if it is gone, bones and body continued to reverberate from it. But Natalia didn't feel such pain or the reverb of a plucked string echoing throughout her body. It was as if the sound of death was dampened in her ears and in her soul.

Natalia didn't feel the damage she knew must be there, and it frightened her. What was she, if not capable of reacting to such sadness in her life?

She wanted to explain this to Jim, in the hope that he might understand her predicament and provide some sort of guidance to how she might once again *feel*. Yes, that was it. She wanted to feel. The pain, the horror, the exhaustion, and sadness; all of it, all at once, so she might commiserate with others who had lost something of value.

She must have been silent for some time, because Jim leaned forward and dropped a file he was holding onto the table with a resounding *smack!* Natalia jolted at the noise, and glared at him. "I was thinking."

"I know," he replied stiffly. "Time for thinking is done. Now you move on. That's how survival works in this business, kid."

"Thanks, tips." Still, Natalia couldn't shake the feeling of having lost something of herself in all of the violence. It frightened her to think that what she had lost was not her innocence, or her naivety, but her memories, and all the small day-to-day traits that had made her Natalia. What was her survival worth if she lost her hold on those integral, seemingly innocuous pieces of herself?

"Natalia-"

"I'm going back to bed," she said at once, pushing herself off the chair. They didn't need to talk anymore. There was nothing left to say. Nothing Jim would understand, at least. That was how Natalia understood the world around her. Her pain was a solitary struggle, and Jim could never share in it. Nor, Natalia thought, would he be willing to.

xXx

Rebecca was in the kitchen the next morning, sipping coffee and chatting gaily with Jim. There was an envelope on the island with Natalia's name on it.

"Look who's up!" Rebecca grinned and pushed the envelope towards Natalia with her elbow. "Got something for you. Couple things actually, but we put them all into the same envelope. Save the trees."

Jim was rolling his eyes behind her, and Natalia had to bite her tongue to keep from laughing.

"What is it?" she asked, reaching for the envelope.

"Open it. It's not happy stuff. Not really, but it'll be good for you at least."

The first paper was a statement of both her parents' life insurance policies. Natalia's immediate reaction was to glance up towards Jim, who simply shook his head and dipped his nose back into his coffee cup.

Right. They're dead. Dead is dead.

The combined numbers were impressive. Evidence of her parents thinking ahead.

"They had private, plus the Agency policy," Rebecca explained. "With that, you should be set for the rest of your life, school included. We were calculating just how much the Agency policy would get you. You could get over thirty bachelor's degrees with it alone. Not that you'd need to."

Mom and Dad were looking out for us...for me. It was bittersweet. The money would have been split between her and Beth, but there was no Beth now. So, Natalia had a ridiculous amount of money to her name and no one to share it with. Rebecca handed her a pen and Natalia signed on the dotted lines.

"There's another one too, but, uh, it caught us off-guard."

Natalia scanned the paper but couldn't make heads or tails of it. She leaned across the counter, grabbed Jim's coffee cup from his hand and took a sip. It stung her eyes. Not just coffee. She raised an eyebrow at him and he shrugged.

"Who's Andrew Wagner?" she asked, returning the hair of the dog from whence it came.

Rebecca glanced over at Jim. He shrugged again. A man of few words.

"When you and Beth were taken to that warehouse, where your dad... Well, we tracked down the old owner. He was in a palliative care unit, cancer. Didn't have any family, and he...I don't know. He seemed *sad* to hear what you were going through." Rebecca left it at that.

"This is a *lot*." Natalia waved the paper in front of Rebecca and Jim. "What do I do with it?"

"Donate it, save it, invest it. Whatever you want. It's yours now. That's just what was set aside. There'll be more after the estate sale, too." Rebecca cocked an eyebrow and frowned. "I, uh, sort of figured you really didn't care about rooting through his belongings and finding stuff to keep."

"No." Natalia drew the vowel out long and thing. "Should I? Should....*someone?*"

A thought tickled some irrational portion of Natalia's mind. She imagined, if only for a moment, lounging on a chaise, dripping in diamonds, commanding the attention of some butler with a British accent and sassy personality. Daydreams were quickly squashed by the reality of the matter. Not all the money in the world could protect her from what was coming, of that she was certain.

Natalia caught Jim giving Rebecca a strange look and knew at once that they were communicating on a level that she was not, nor would ever be party to.

Rebecca turned quickly. "I'll get the documents to the lawyer, and the funds will get transferred over to your account. Then...well, what do you guys have planned for today?"

"Shopping," Natalia replied, "and I was thinking that maybe I'd see where I'm buried."

It was a concept that had baffled Natalia from the moment she and Jim were free of San Francisco and travelling under assumed names. She had been declared legally dead after the Siege of Alcatraz. Her friends mourned her, a headstone was placed next to her parents' grave, and that was that. The only people who knew the truth were part of the Agency. It struck Natalia as sad, to think that her parent's world, and in turn, her own, was so small that life moved on relatively seamlessly without any member of the Artison clan there. Granted, she had never had a lot of friends, and those she went to school with were never *best* friends. She knew it was a cavernous blank spot in her childhood, and yet she had never been lonely.

"That's always fun." Rebecca was altogether too enthusiastic about the idea. "I had to die once. Only for a month. It pissed my dad off even though the Agency told him I was ok. Said he hated having to open up all the sympathy cards."

"What do I do if I see someone I know just walking around? What if they see *me?*"

"Usually they're too shocked to say anything. They chalk it up to memories," Jim smirked, "and if they try to talk to you, you throw on an accent and pretend you don't know them."

"That's cruel."

"That's necessity. We don't pretend to die for shits and giggles. When it happens, it happens because something has gone very, very wrong."

"Like Alcatraz."

"Like Caulder." Jim pushed the papers towards Rebecca in a not-so-subtle gesture that it might be time for her to go.

"I need to get back, anyways." Perpetually unoffended, despite Jim's attitude, Rebecca collected the documents, carefully placed them back in the envelope, and gave Natalia a wave as she turned to leave the kitchen.

"I know it's hard," Jim said after the front door slammed shut. "Once Cain and Caulder are dealt with things can go back to normal."

"Oh yeah," Natalia said. "*Normal.*"

"Go get ready," Jim said before taking a swig from the coffee cup. "Max'll be here soon."

After showering and dressing in the last of her clean clothes, mercifully free of holes, save for one small tear in the right knee of her jeans, Natalia pulled on the old leather jacket and slunk out into the hallway. Jim was already there, boots on, annoyed expression to match. Next to him stood Max, who appeared moderately more pleased to be there.

"I'm your cover for today," he explained. "Good thing too. Rumor has it Caulder's been on a rampage since you got back. Wouldn't be surprised if he tried to run you off the road."

"You've got some James Bond car with rockets on it to stop him, right?"

Max laughed and turned towards the front door. Natalia had nearly missed his mangled right ear. Another thing she had forgotten, or at least pushed to the background of her traumatic memories. Despite all he had done to contribute to her current woes, Natalia could hardly deny how much Max had risked, and lost, in the process.

They piled into the car, with Jim notably quiet for the most part. A few minutes on the road, the cell phone that she had been given by Aurora trilled in her pocket. Natalia fished it out and found a message from Jim.

We're going to be babysat all day. Don't get into trouble.

She was in the process of texting back when the phone trilled again.

Turn off the damn ringer.

They reached the cemetery by late afternoon. Jim's mood had darkened considerably, starting around the time they entered the mall, before dropping rapidly with each teenager they passed. It was a relief when Natalia realized she had everything she needed and they could head to the cemetery.

The sky was a burst of pink and red, the colours of the Asiatic lilies that her mother would grow reliably every year, and the air was cold with the promise of new snow that would soon cover the city. Natalia was buried next to her parents. There were wilted flowers near her headstone. It was sweet that someone had cared enough to put them there. She replaced them with two daisies pulled out of one of the bouquets she was carrying. One went on Amy's grave, the other on Marcus'.

"Weird," she said lamely.

"What is?"

Natalia knew from Jim's tone that he wasn't particularly keen on hearing what she thought was weird, but a part of her found it amusing to force him into conversation when he didn't want it. "Who decided where they got buried?"

"It was in their wills, I guess."

"Weird."

Jim sighed, aggravated. "For fucks sake, what is *weird?*"

"Mom always told me she thought it was a waste of space to get buried. She wanted to be cremated."

Jim cocked his head at Natalia and shrugged. "So, she changed her mind. People do that all the time."

Natalia wasn't convinced. It didn't seem like something a person just *changed their mind* about. Those sorts of fundamental beliefs kept people grounded in reality. Her mother had never seemed changeable. She believed what she believed and there was never any arguing with her. That wasn't a conversation to have with Jim, though. He wouldn't be interested.

"Do you want to talk about it?"

Natalia was sure she heard Jim retch a tiny bit as he spoke, and wasted no time in changing the subject. "Where is he? He's buried here too, right?"

Jim nodded and pointed to a small slope north of them. "Just up there, I think."

They found Steven Delarno's grave without much difficulty. There were plenty of footprints and flowers enough to suggest the local florist would not be left wanting any time soon. The inscription in the marble was crisp and fresh. *Husband, Father, Friend.* Simple enough. Natalia felt her cheeks flush. Her generic Gerber daisies wrapped in yellow cellophane were going to be lost among the roses and lilies, and yet only her small offering felt appropriate. The hoity-toity didn't seem to suit Steven.

"He's had some visitors," Jim observed, drawing one foot through the muddy snow. It was true. Steven's grave looked practically new, as if you could peel back the dead grass and find his corpse smiling up at you. All teeth and bones and withered flesh.

"A popular guy." Natalia stood for a moment, then placed the flowers at the foot of the grave. Out of the way, separate from the rest of the world that Steven had occupied. It wasn't that his impact on her had been the greatest, it was just that his had been the last, and she didn't feel as if she belonged to the club.

"I miss him," she said.

"Me too."

Natalia knew Jim wasn't pulling a fast one. Despite his constant mood since taking her in, Natalia had begun to learn how the tone of his voice revealed more than his expression or posture ever could. They didn't talk about the loss of her first guardian, and Jim's best friend. Talking about it made it real, rage and grief alike, and neither Jim nor Natalia were prepared to face life without Steven Delarno.

Not yet.

"It isn't what I thought it would be like," she said at last.

"What isn't?"

Natalia looked up at him, half expecting Jim to be staring off into the distance, biding his time. "Life," she said finally. "And death."

Jim didn't speak for a moment, then leaned down, adjusted some of the older flowers on the grave so Natalia's small bouquet stood out among the other offerings. When he stood up again he said, "Usually isn't."

A moment of silence longer and Natalia turned. "Let's go."

Chapter 6

If Natalia and Jim thought they'd be given leave to exist without someone watching their every move, they were sorely mistaken. Someone from Task Force Twelve was stuck to them at every conceivable moment. Two days after visiting Steven's grave, Natalia happened to be in the living room and glanced out the window to see Bedlam and Rebecca sitting in a car, eating crullers and watching the house.

"How long have they been out there?" she asked, as Jim strolled in from the kitchen.

"Since the dawn of time, I reckon."

Jim, at least, seemed to be healing from his wounds. He was walking more confidently and didn't groan every time he leaned over to tie his shoe. Still, whenever Natalia did catch him wincing or clutching at his side, she felt her heart speed up.

She had left something of herself on Alcatraz, taken more with her. A fear, deeply embedded, that another might lose their life because of her inaction. She had lost one guardian, and even if Jim wasn't as forthcoming as Steven, she didn't want him to die. If anything, the thought of him dying nauseated her to the point where she couldn't think straight.

"When can we start training?"

"What's your hurry?" Jim glanced at her over the rim of his coffee cup, a smirk curling the edge of his lips. Always half a smile, as if he kept the other half to himself. "Somewhere to be?"

She snatched the cup off the table. In the last few days, she had realized Jim had a bad habit of leaving his dishes around. He must have gotten to them eventually because they always disappeared, but coffee cups were an exception. She didn't want them laying about where the aroma of rye whiskey and black coffee could momentarily distract a co-worker or, worse, give someone a reason to remove her from Jim's care.

You can't get rid of me that easily. She moved towards the kitchen and kept talking. "I want to be *capable*. I want to be a fearsome warrior! Take no prisoners; bend no knees."

By that point, she was in the kitchen, and the silence from the living room caused Natalia to reason that she had once again crossed the line of civility with Jim and he was no longer willing to entertain her. She was surprised when she turned and found Jim leaning against the doorjamb. "Being capable is more than just being physically fit. You know plenty already. You *are* capable. You're just not..." Jim looked around, clearly struggling for words. "You're just not there yet. It comes in time. With experience."

Cooper was at her feet, wagging his tail and looking intensely concerned. Natalia crouched down, smoothed his ears, and gave him a kiss on the head. He leaned forward and began to lick her arm.

"Experience, like training?"

Jim glowered. "Worldly. Hardships."

Natalia laughed.

"You'll know it when it happens," Jim said shortly. "I'm still aching, and I'm not opening up a wound just to appease you. Go take up knitting or stamp collecting if you're bored."

Natalia bit back the smart reply that was on the tip of her tongue. Capable as she might be, she knew there was no winning an argument with her guardian. Any amount of pushback caused him to drive in his heels more firmly, and then she'd never learn to dodge a blade or scale the side of a building. With a defeated sigh, Natalia whistled for Cooper and slumped out of the kitchen with the dog at her heels.

Jim watched, mildly amused that his fearsome dog was absolute putty in the presence of Natalia. It wasn't entirely surprising; some pets just had an instinct about the needs of those around them, especially those who were heavy with hurt. Cooper would be a good friend to her, protective, and perhaps give her some of the basic companionship that Jim knew he was unable to provide in his own interactions with her.

Without realizing it, he had been clutching at his wounded side throughout the conversation. It was a spiky sort of pain, but one that Jim recognized as part of the healing process. He wanted to get back on his feet, to start Natalia on the hands-on training. Sure, she knew how to fire a gun; not well, but she could keep one clean and had the basic idea of aiming. She knew the rules, and when to follow them. More importantly, she understood when to break them like her life depended on it. Often it would. The one thing she had taken to was escapism. Jim reckoned it came with her knack for climbing trees that Amy had told him about years ago. Natalia had fallen only once, and miraculously not broken anything. Amy had tried to put an end to her excursions after that, but there had been no stopping Natalia.

She might never be a good fighter, Jim thought as he moved around the kitchen island, running his hands over the granite countertops and refamiliarizing himself with his home. *But she'll keep her enemies on their toes.*

He opened a cupboard above the sink and pushed aside a box of old minute rice to retrieve a bottle of something foul and brown. Natalia knew of his drinking habits, but it seemed prudent to at least maintain the air of secrecy. Neither of them said anything. Jim didn't let it impact his work, and Natalia didn't try to lecture him on how all the booze and cigarettes would send him to an early grave.

Oh yeah, you're a good role model. Jim downed a sharp swig of scotch straight from the bottle and began to paw through the contacts in his phone until he found Tess' number. If they were both going to be stuck at home, it would be nice to have some company.

xXx

Theresa Everett always made herself at home. It was a mentality bequeathed to her by her Haitian grandmother who had, as Tess put it on more than one occasion, gall enough to invite herself to the Devil's den and make herself a cup of tea. Tess embraced it, if only because she rarely had time to dither around pretending to respect some unspoken social norm. She puttered around Jim's kitchen, pouring herself a drink from the hidden bottle of scotch. Jim watched her, amused.

"You want some truffles while you're at it?"

"Cheeky." She ran her finger around the inner rim of the glass, rotating it gently on the marble surface. They could hear Anna Monroe chatting gaily in the background, apparently determined to integrate herself into Natalia's life like a fishhook.

"How're things going with Anna?"

"Oh, fantastic," Tess said brightly. "No one's tried to kill her yet, so she's doing quite well for herself."

"Not much practical experience then?" Jim grinned. Tess flipped him the bird as she moved into the living room and plopped down on the nearest couch.

"She's a natural," Tess continued. "Bright, witty. She's got the right personality for this."

"Yeah?" Jim said. "Well, Natalia's really sarcastic."

"Natalia is dealing with some *intense* shit," Tess said, swirling her glass as she looked around the living room. "Can't blame her for finding her own way to deal with it." Tess narrowed her gaze at him and pushed an errant curl from her face. "You and I know that better than most, wouldn't you say?"

"That's different."

"Different but the same," Tess agreed. "Does she know yet?"

"About?" Jim wasn't particularly keen on having this conversation, but since returning home, he had known it was inevitable. There were only so many people left he could talk to about the *incident*, and Tess, in all her non-judgemental kick-assery, was more than willing to discuss it.

"Jesus, Jim. You know exactly what. What did Cain *show her* in *bloody Alcatraz?*"

Jim heaved a sigh and leaned back on the couch, allowing himself a moment to slump and be, as his mother would have called it, a *schlub*. "The trees. Crime scene photos of the whole family. And pictures of Steven's kid, dead on the table."

"Shit." Tess followed suit in leaning back into the couch, balancing her glass on her chest. "See, this is exactly why none of us should have kids. Too much room for manipulation."

Jim raised one eyebrow at Tess and she winced, hiding her face behind her own glass she said, "No offense."

He snorted a non-committal response, one he knew Tess could interpret as forgiveness for the slight.

"What did Steven say? How'd he explain it to her?"

Jim shrugged half-heartedly. "He didn't. Not really. Neither did I. We just... Shit." He shifted forward, depositing the glass roughly on the table and placing his head in his hands. Tess was one of the few people he felt comfortable enough showing his full spectrum of emotions around. Anger *and* sadness; the two pivotal parts of Jim Wilkinson.

"We didn't. Neither of us. It was... Well, it moved too fast, you know? And I just didn't."

"You didn't want to, you mean." Tess looked unimpressed. "For fucks sake, Jim. She is a part of it, whether she knows it or not." She yanked back the sleeve of her shirt and presented her forearm. Her own tattoo, long since mangled in a desperate attempt to erase her connection to their shared past. What had she done? Jim remembered some story about her getting drunk one night in Beijing and taking sandpaper to the infinity symbol after a close encounter with one of Cain's cronies. He gave an involuntary shudder at the thought and reached towards his own mark, burnt and distorted. Infinity, twisted and curled from where fire had licked at it.

"We don't get a pass on this," Tess said shortly. "We don't get to forget what we've done, Jim. We made Natalia part of this. She needs to know what Steven died for."

"Nothing," Jim spat back, though his heart wasn't in the bitter statement. "He died for nothing."

Tess leaned forward, more earnest now, and hissed, "He died for *her*. Don't you ever, *ever* forget that."

She leaned back, satisfied that she had sufficiently chastised Jim. "So, moving on. How are you feeling?"

"Right now? A little annoyed, if I'm honest."

Tess smirked. "I meant physically. But sure, annoyed works too."

Jim prodded his side with a finger and grimaced. "It's nasty. Been a while since I've gotten a gash like that. We were lucky Max got there when he did."

Tess ground her teeth a bit. Overhead Jim could hear the skittering of the girls as they perused his small library and, he was surprised, laughed about this and that. The sound didn't carry throughout the house very well, but Natalia's laugh was unmistakable. It was the same as Amy's.

"The Third are getting pretty goddamned bold," Tess said, after a moment of listening to the laughter. "Meghan's sent multiple complaints to the Council, but our overlords won't hear a word of it. They're as spooked as Caulder that Natalia's a ticking time bomb, and they figure turning a blind eye to this will absolve them of any responsibility."

Jim could understand that. They didn't know her. They hadn't been there or seen her during the most horrific moments of the Siege of Alcatraz. They didn't realize how fear had turned into blind determination and forced Natalia to dig her heels in so reluctantly. She might very well be willing to watch the world burn if it meant preventing Cain from getting what he wanted. Jim couldn't help but admire her, just a little bit.

"Maybe we need to put her in front of them. Let them see for themselves that she won't talk."

"I don't think it'll help," Tess admitted. "They've made up their minds. Or Caulder was persuasive enough to convince them it was for the best. We're on our own with this."

"Seems funky," Jim said. "I don't know much about what went on in those early days, but Rebecca said Caulder's mind was made up about the whole thing pretty quickly. He never even gave her a chance."

"Does that really surprise you?" Tess asked. "He isn't exactly known for his composed, rational thought process."

"Yeah, but to open with both barrels like that?" Jim shook his head. The liquor was giving him that pleasant buzz; the sort where he knew his reactionary skills were peaked. It wasn't enough. He needed to dull the pain. Darkness was settling over the city and soon it would be time for bed, which meant another sleepless night accompanied by memories of burning orchards. "It just seems like he's gone way off the deep end."

"He's been director of our branch for how many years? Now a kid shows up with the capacity to dismantle it if she falls into the wrong hands? He's protecting his interests." Jim balked and Tess held up her hands in defense. "I'm not saying he's right. I just understand *why* he might see no alternative. Not for ourselves alone, and all that jazz." Tess stood up and stretched, walked towards the windows, and pushed a curtain aside with her pinky. "She has you, anyways, and the whole of the Twelfth. It's not like she's going to be hung out to dry."

"We can only do so much," Jim reminded her, sharply. "Cain, Caulder. They have resources that we don't. When shit goes down you *know* it'll go down hard."

"Jim."

"Tess."

She glanced back over her shoulder, already pulling her hair into a ponytail and reaching for the gun at her hip. "They're here."

Jim was on his feet before the words had left her mouth. It came with the experience, and a history of fuck ups that had taught Jim and Tess to understand each other's motions and movements. Hair being pulled back meant things were about to get serious.

He pushed back the curtain and saw the shadows from across the street already forming like an oily mass about to descend upon them, pushing their way into eyes and ears, noses and mouths, to choke those who stood in the way of their prey.

Natalia.

The front door flew off its hinges with a bang.

Natalia was surprised to find herself connecting with another person. More than that, someone her own age. Certainly, she and Anna were woven from different thread, but that didn't seem to impede their ability to talk about the usual teenage things. They perused the small library Jim had built in a secondary bedroom upstairs, taking turns asking questions and getting to know each other as they looked through the books. Anna was, Natalia learned, the offspring of two Irish physicists who immigrated to the US eight years after their daughter was born. They passed away within a year of each other, mother from cancer, father from self-pity, as Anna put it, leaving behind a pre-teen daughter who was thrown into the foster system and eventually plucked out by a well-meaning Tess Everett.

"There was this afterschool program my foster parents sent me to. Whole thing was just an excuse to get me out of the house. We thought maybe Tess was a creeper at first. After a few months, child services picked me up and told me I was moving in to a new house, just like that. Can you imagine?" Anna laughed gaily and flipped through a textbook. "When I saw Tess, I thought for sure I was going to be some sort of child victim. Emaciated, locked in a basement. Turns out she'd been scouting for new recruits after a group of trainees went sour and she liked the way I punched another kid on the court." Anna shook her head and muttered, "Fucking Derek."

"Seems sort of predatory to me," Natalia said shortly, not meaning to be judgemental. She backtracked quickly. "I mean, you were a foster kid, part of the system. Isn't that preying on the weak?"

"Oh sure, if I'd been left with no other choice. But she introduced me to Caulder and Meghan, explained what the SOI did, and said if I wasn't interested they'd hook me up with a good family who wouldn't toss me out on the street the next time I got into a fist fight." Anna beamed. "I've been Tess' ward for just over five years now, and they make you do this biannual psych test with the resident shrink. Makes sure you know your options, that you're healthy, smart, not being manipulated. One year I saw her accompany a kid right out of the Agency because he just cracked under the pressure: admitted he didn't like it and wanted a normal life."

Natalia wasn't convinced, but tried to remind herself that her own experience was hardly the norm, and she wasn't in a position to cast judgement on anyone. Anna seemed happy, well-adjusted and, perhaps more importantly to Natalia, she seemed like someone who could be a friend. Natalia hopped off a ladder that was leaning against one of the shelves, tugged her jacket, *Steven's* jacket, around her waist, and flashed Anna a smile that was returned in kind.

"It'll be good if-" Natalia didn't have a chance to finish the thought. A vicious boom exploded from down the stairs. All at once it was chaos.

Tess was screaming from the ground floor. "*Anna!* Take her and run!"

Natalia didn't have a chance to react. Anna's hand was around her wrist and drawing her out into the hallway. Gunshots now, silenced. They should have known, they should have known.

"Come on!"

They skittered into the main hallway that ran the length of the second floor, and Natalia felt the fear hitch in her throat. It was dark, with row of small wall sconces lining either side of the hall to provide a meager glow. Just enough for Natalia to see the shadows of the black-clad men and women approaching from both sides of the hallway, blocking off their escape.

"Jim!" Natalia raised her voice, turned in a circle, and prayed she'd hear him respond. Nothing. Just grunts. Gunfire. "Jim, we've got company up here! Did you invite them in? *You're not supposed to invite them in!*"

"I don't think they're vampires," Anna said shakily, placing her back against Natalia's in a show of solidarity. She could feel Anna's fingers against the palm of her hand, one finger pressed in like a trigger, and then three fast taps.

Three. There are three on her side. Natalia narrowed her gaze, made a quick count, and repeated the process. Another two facing her directly. Five experienced agents against the two of them was hardly a fair fight.

"Come with us," one shadow ordered, and Natalia felt like she was being pranked. A faceless, nameless enemy, summoning her to the dark side. She laughed, and a ripple passed over the shadows, as if they knew what such a simple, defiant act would mean. "Fight, then."

"Get their masks off so we can ID them," Anna whispered.

Natalia watched as the talkative assailant reached for a monstrous knife strapped to their thigh. It glinted in the pale light, and Natalia saw the motion, the tightening of the knuckles over the hilt. The shadow bolted forward. Crossing the path of a hallway, a blurred mass leapt from the darkness; Cooper latched his jaws on the knife-wielding arm and dragged the man to the ground, where he began to tear and rip at the arm until it released the blade.

Seeing the opportunity, perhaps the only one they might get, Natalia slid for the knife. Using the blood-slicked flooring, she let the momentum carry her past Cooper and bowled into the legs of the second assailant. She slashed wildly and felt a spray of hot blood splash over her face like holy water. A cry, and the woman she slashed kicked out, catching Natalia in the chest and throwing her against the wall. She pulled herself sideways, towards Cooper, who had leapt upon the first man and buried his muzzle in the delicate tendons of his neck. Vicious, without mercy.

The hardwood by her ankle splintered and Natalia's head snapped towards her feet. The woman was crawling towards her, using a knife of her own to propel her across the bloodied floor. Natalia kicked with her heel, sending the blade spiraling backwards. Behind her, Anna was overwhelmed; too many attackers, too fast. Natalia had to help her.

Jim greeted the first assailant with the butt of an axe he had brought inside after chopping kindling. The nose splintered and the assailant screamed, dropping his gun, hands flying to his face. Without pause, Jim dragged the black hood from his face, making the split-second recognition he needed that yes, this was someone from the Third. Yes, this was an attack on his home and a direct violation of a closely held Agency rule. Jim dragged the man's hair backwards and punched the blunt head of the axe into his gut, driving the man to his knees where Jim could give him one last hit to the side of the head to render him unconscious and, perhaps, a bit permanently damaged. Nothing that would stop them from being held accountable, though.

He could hear Natalia screaming at him, and knew that in the few seconds the door had been blown off the hinges they had gotten in through the back door and swarmed the house. Tess seemed less concerned about leaving any survivors. Anna's cries could be heard from above, and both Tess and Jim understood that any engagement in battle meant that the Third didn't plan on leaving anyone alive.

Call it tit for tat then.

Jim brought the blade of the axe across the chest of the closest goon, dropping the figure wordlessly and transitioning to the next, battering his way towards the nearest staircase so he might make his way to Natalia and pluck her from the carnage, away from all of it.

Just as he had promised.

Despite all his years of engaging in violence, both actively and reactively, Jim always found the structure and weakness of the human body fascinating. People were remarkably capable of heavy acts of violence against each other, but it only took a swish of an axe to cleave them from the waking world. Another body here, another soul there. Jim figured out long ago that if there were a Hell he'd surely be going there, and no amount of repentance could change that.

He was closer to the front door now, to the stairwell that hid in the shadows and would take him to the second floor. Tess cried wildly behind him, and he turned to see her tackle another assailant by the waist. She brought her knife down into their hooded face. Once, twice. Yet they kept streaming in, like a hydra split in two, four, eight. Relentless in their pursuit. Jim saw Anna down the hall. She had gotten her hands on a gun and with a single, self-assured pull of the trigger, taken down a figure that had raised its own hand against Tess.

Jim heard Natalia's cry, and raced for the stairs.

At a holler from Tess below, Anna looked wan. Natalia screamed at her to go.

No more. Please don't let any of them die.

The Third she could take or leave. Fuck them. But Jim? Tess? No. Not them.

She spun as Anna disappeared from her peripheral vision, and found a single figure still standing. She had long discarded her mask, and Natalia was unsurprised to find it was the same woman who had accused the Artisons of being a cancer in the agency. What had Jim called her? Leah. Something like that. Unimportant, invisible. She smiled at Natalia, turned her head to one side, and cracked her neck, her large eyes bulging in the dim glow of the wall sconces.

"Go on," she said, nodding towards the knife that lay at Natalia's feet. "Pick it up."

Natalia complied, not because she thought she stood a chance against a senior agent who had, for whatever reason, decided she wanted the girl dead, but because following her rules might buy Natalia a second or two to come up with a plan.

"You should have just come with us," Leah said. She was walking with a limp now, and Natalia realized that in the confusion she was the same assailant who Natalia had gouged with the blade when the battle began. It was a weakness; maybe one she could exploit if only she knew how.

"You could have saved them," Leah said, voice crackling. A crash came from the floor below.

"They sound like they're doing pretty ok on their own," Natalia replied. She could feel the heat of the wall sconce on the top of her head. She was covered in blood but none of it her own save for a few splinters in her hands that were acting as spigots.

Leah limped across the bloodied hardwood and swatted the knife from Natalia's hand. The blade skittered across the hardwood, well out of reach. It was a show of dominance. Natalia wanted some cheeky reply to fly from her mouth and impale the older woman through the heart, but her own fear betrayed her.

The audacity to attack, when day was bridging the night, in a home of a colleague. It was supposed to be safe. *They* were supposed to be safe here. If not here, then where?

Leah's fingers, wiry and claw-like, found Natalia's neck and slammed her against the wall, lifting Natalia until her toes dangled above the hardwood. Her breath smelled like blood as she leaned in towards Natalia and whispered, "It's nothing personal, kid."

A blade slid into Natalia's side, like a hot knife through butter. She screamed and saw stars burst in front of her eyes, blinding her to the hateful face of Leah Beaumont. It was as if the jaw of an ungodly beast had clamped around her hip and wrenched its head backwards, tearing her flesh and twisting her bones as it tried to gut her. Then, from the left, Natalia heard Jim yell. She craned her neck to look at him. Every nerve in her body burnt at the movement. She saw her guardian at the top of the stairs, blood dripping from his forehead and from the axe that he clutched in his white fingers. Leah stepped back, pulling the blade smoothly from Natalia's side, letting the girl slump to the floor where hot, tacky blood began to spill out from between her fingers.

Natalia blinked and the axe was spinning through the air. She blinked again, exhaling slowly, allowing time to slow with her, and the axe jutted from the curve between Leah's breasts. Leah looked down, astounded, and tipped forward, face first onto the floor.

Jim froze, and he hated himself for it. He froze at the sound of metal splitting flesh and at the sound of the blade sliding into Natalia's side, between her ribs. He froze as Leah pulled the blade free and let Natalia drop to the ground, spilling the blood of a child. When he finally acted, he did so without thinking. His axe arced through the air and nestled itself into Leah's chest, felling her where she stood. The floor was sticky, and as he ran to Natalia he thought he could feel the hands of the dead reaching up from the mess, trying to hold him back.

Natalia was crying, clutching her side with such intensity that Jim thought she might inadvertently injure herself further. Her head turned towards him, and her eyes widened. She reached out, throwing her bloodied hand towards Jim, crying his name, though for the life of him he could not hear her voice. He turned, sliding in the blood and grime, and threw himself to one side as a figure behind him tried to drive a blade into his back.

Jim tackled the figure, and together they crashed backwards into the stairs, tumbling down half a flight to the middle landing with a thunderous *crack!* A boot struck Jim in the middle of his chest and sent him flying to the ground floor, where the only saving grace was the pile of bodies at the foot of the stairs. The figure came at him, pouncing from above, when a single gunshot rang out. The figure tumbled from the air like a shot bird.

The gun hung loosely from Tess' hand, and Anna was sporting a nasty gash on her forehead, but they both stood. They both lived.

Jim threw himself upwards, stumbling up the stairs to the hallway where Natalia had fallen.

Where he had left her.

Empty. Empty save for the dead bodies piled atop each other like autumn woodpiles, and the smear of fresh, red blood from a body dragged along the hardwood, then lifted, taken down a flight of stairs, and out into the night.

Chapter 7

Sticky and cold. Summer days in a childhood that was far removed from her memory, relegated to nostalgia and regret. Spilling red Kool-Aid down the front of her shirt, fearing the repercussions from her parents for the stains would never come out, no matter how much they bleached it. Natalia tried to roll, felt her side open like a gaping mouth, crimson spittle dripping from the torn flesh. She was going to die.

Voices far, but near. Echoing in a metallic chamber. "We're *fucked!*"

Ha! Natalia groaned, and felt someone cuff the side of her head viciously. It didn't do much: a distraction from the pain of the stab. *Mercy, mercy.*

"Did he set us up? Did Caulder-?"

Ah, that explains it.

"She's bleeding out. We're going to have to ditch the car. How many did we lose in there?"

Don't fall asleep. You need to stay awake for what happens next.

Then, as if she were carrying a conversation with herself, Natalia thought, *What happens next?*

A baptism, a voice replied.

"Let's just drop her. Let's drop her somewhere and get out of town."

"Caulder's going to be pissed."

"Who the fuck cares what he thinks."

Words entered her mind in fragments, blurred by the sensory overload. In the dim light of the car, she could see the shaking, shadowed figure of a captor, leaning over her, fruit punch dripping from his lips while spiders festered at his jaw line, devouring the syrup to grow, grow, grow.

"We're far enough. Let's get this over with."

The passing street lamps surged and grew black limbs that curved around the car and grasped at the glass, screeching like claws across ice. The heady, sweet smell of death filled her nose; flesh already rotting away. Was that her? Was she already dead?

A door opened and the world outside spun as fingers grabbed her arms and dragged her from the car. Snow and ice filled her, her belly scraping along the ground as she squirmed against the hand that collared her. They tossed her forward lazily, and she inhaled a mouth full of ice particles. Voices spoke behind her; the pulling back of a hammer in an ancient pistol. She wanted to roll around, to turn on her back to face the one who was going to cast her out of the land of the living, stare him in the eyes as he pulled the trigger. Such drastic moves weren't in her future; the cut was deep and pulsating and the hot blood was melting the snow below her. Natalia let her eyes settle on the horizon, buildings rising from the inky black water that stretched out before her. And the sun, just setting beyond it all, reflecting off glass and setting the sky afire.

Behind her, a gunshot.

The man standing over her moved violently to one side. Natalia felt a spray of crystalline ice strike her face from where a bullet narrowly missed her cheek. The bank of ice she was lying on shifted, crackled from the disturbance. The shelf broke, taking Natalia and her would-be executioner down a short, steep slope towards the black water. They hit the surface, and the air jutted from her lungs; water muted her senses and the body of the man pinned her beneath the current. She reached up, stretching until her fingers broke through into the air, but she was weak, so weak from the blood loss, like a newborn kitten, runt of the litter, and without the strength to fight for her share of a meal.

Darkness spiderwebbed around her eyes, flooded through her senses, dulling her to everything but her heartbeat thrumming in her chest, announcing that she lived.

xXx

Jim wasted no time. Tess and Anna were driving back to the Agency together; Jim would take his own car; once he dealt with one particularly gritty detail, he planned on being back on the road to find Natalia. Tess called ahead, to alert Meghan and the rest of the team about what had transpired. Meghan immediately began trying to call Jim, but he was in no mood to be berated or, worse, hauled in from the field for questioning. There was no time for bureaucracy.

After clearing security, Jim took the elevator straight to the administrative floor. Caulder's receptionist tried to stop him, but one withering look set her in her place. Jim barged through the door, and Caulder leapt to his feet.

That was when Jim punched him. It was satisfying to see the way his flesh curled around Jim's knuckles and whiplashed backwards, throwing the director off his feet.

"Have you *lost your mind?*" Caulder gripped his mashed potato nose, blood already streaming through his fingers and splattering across his desk, soiling his paperwork and picture frames.

"Where is she?" No time for pleasantries. No time to address who threw the first stone, or who punched whom first. Jim advanced again, curling his fingers in preparation for another strike. "Where the *hell* is she?!"

"You're on immediate suspension!"

With a growl, Jim slapped a desk lamp from its perch and sent the whole thing shattering at Caulder's feet. He jumped backwards, still clutching his nose with one hand and motioned frantically to someone behind Jim.

He felt the electric jolt of the Taser before he turned. It was a foolish mistake on Jim's part, and one he could have easily avoided if he had kept his head. After all, he was supposed to be helping Natalia. Saving her. He couldn't do that with thousands of watts of electricity racing through his body. His jaw locked and he fell to the ground, the maroon carpet scraping his bruised cheek. All at once he was and was not being dragged by the security forces through the hallway of the administrative level. He was and was not conscious and aware of the voices above him, laughing and berating him for his failure.

He was and was not a breaker of promises.

When Jim came to, his tongue was covered in metallic-tasting film, and he was lying face-down on the cold cement of the parkade. A security agent tapped his ribs with a boot and said, "Get up. Get out. Don't come back."

He managed to struggle his way to his car and clamber into the driver's seat. Despite the singed smell of hair and flesh, Natalia's citrusy perfume clung to the inside of the car and wormed its way into Jim's mind. Not as vibrant as a strike from a Taser, but equally as painful.

With hands on the steering wheel, Jim inhaled sharply through his teeth and held his breath until his lungs burned and his eyes watered. Reaching for a crumpled pack of smokes that he kept in the center console for emergencies he saw his hands shaking, covered in dried blood, and wondered how much of it was hers. He flicked his wrist, forcing away the jitters from his fingers, banishing them like a bad omen.

Inevitable. It was inevitable, he told himself. A bump in the road. An unfortunate attack on his home. But he would get her back because this wasn't Cain they were dealing with. This was the Third, and they played by the same rules that Jim had been taught.

The difference, Jim thought as pulled the cigarette from between his teeth and watched the glowing embers eat away at the paper and tobacco. *The difference is that I want her to live.*

From across the parkade Jim could see a figure emerge from the elevator and brush by the two security agents who were still standing there, waiting for him depart. The figure must have chastised them, because they turned and left the parkade, shoulders slumped. Jim stubbed out his cigarette in the ashtray and stepped out of the car. Troy looked infuriated, as Jim had expected, but the anger had to be short-lived. Minutes, if not seconds; anything more would be eating into the time they needed to trace Natalia.

"What the *hell happened?*"

Jim braced, half expecting Troy to lash out, to shame him for his failures, but even as they met below the prying eyes of the Agency, Jim could see that Natalia's godfather had already been briefed on what had happened. He knew exactly what had gone down; he just didn't *like* it.

"The Third came for her. We held them back but they got through. I don't know how many got away, but it was a goddamned massacre in there."

"Meghan's furious. Said to tell you to stay the hell away from here. Aurora updated me. They pulled out one still alive. Courtney Glover; gunshot wound. They're bringing her back here, but she'll be under heavy guard."

"How many dead at the house?"

"Eleven."

"Jesus." Jim ran a hand through his hair. Did he remember that many? No, it was too much of a blur. He needed sleep, time to think, pull it all together.

"Six more already down in interrogation, and another eight are AWOL."

"That's the whole of the Third?"

"Every last one of them," Troy said.

"And Caulder?"

"Total denial," Troy said. "Calling it a mass revolt. He won't be held accountable, not like this."

"And we'll never get him to admit otherwise." Jim slammed a clenched fist against the closest cement pillar. "Fuck! Every minute he holds his tongue is a minute we lose sight of her." He turned to Troy and narrowed his gaze. "I need you to get me in to talk to Glover."

Troy nodded. "I can do that."

xXx

The next morning Tess was waiting for them both. She would accompany Jim to the subbasement while Troy found one or two creative ways to hold up the security forces that would have to respond the moment Jim's face was spotted on camera.

They split up at the parkade, with Troy taking one elevator up towards the security floor, and Jim following Tess down towards the sub-basement. Cameras lining the hallway blinked off, one after another, a momentary malfunction thanks to Aurora's handiwork. It would buy them enough time to enter the interrogation centre, where men and women who specialized in the more intricate aspects of the human psyche could utilize their own form of malice to get the answers they needed.

It was where people disappeared.

The cameras never stopped tracking people in the hallway, and at the far end, a sensor measured body temperature in the enclosed space, to monitor how many people came and went. They couldn't override those sensors without more time, which meant the minute they were in the room the wheels would begin spinning.

Time was rarely on their side in this profession, now even less so.

At the end of the hallway, they were greeted by George Bedlam. He looked tired, although Jim couldn't tell if it was from sleepless nights with a new infant at home or the general stress of the job. He was willing to put his money on both.

"I gave her the sodium thiopental ten minutes ago or so. She should be waking up soon." Bedlam glanced down at his watch, and Jim saw his hand shaking with the motion. "You'll have five minutes at most, so use it well."

At knocking from the other side of the door, Bedlam twitched. Jim hadn't seen his so twitchy in quite some time. It was no secret to the Agency that since his experience in Vancouver, Bedlam had been willingly holding himself back from field assignments. Something about fatherhood and, so the rumors went, the experiences at Cain's hand. He shook the tremors free, reached for the door handle and glanced back at Jim.

"Ready?"

Jim nodded.

"No more than five minutes, Jim." Bedlam pushed the door open. "Go."

The temperature in the room fluctuated easily; one more technique to break the person tied to the chair. Now it was freezing, and Max, who had been stationed on the other side, was wearing his jacket and two pairs of gloves. In the center of the room, both wrists handcuffed to the rails of a medical gurney, sat a wan, shivering Courtney Glover. She was a young thing, maybe only a few years into adulthood. Having supped on the poison of Harrison Caulder, she now found herself unwittingly part of his plan. In that way, Jim pitied her. He understood how enigmatic leaders like Caulder worked, how easily they drew the weak to them with honeyed words and promises of grandeur.

It made little difference now. She had shed blood for his cause. That made her as much a part of this as anyone.

Max held back, only nodding as Jim passed him.

Under the light of the single, bare bulb, Jim saw the fresh gauze that had been applied along Courtney's right shoulder where she had taken a bullet. She would live. Her head lolled from one side to the other, her eyes flicking back and forth, as if she was trying to watch every car on a speeding train. Her gaze fell on Jim, but he could tell her mind was a world away. Too far to make her useful.

"Glover," Jim said, leaning forward. "You know me?"

"Agent Wilkinson." Her mouth spread into a smile and Jim saw a front tooth had been broken and her face was speckled, not with freckles, but miniscule cuts. "You want something?" She was slurring her words, a by-product of the compound Bedlam had administered. Jim knew better than to ask how Bedlam had gotten his hands on it.

"Where were they taking her?"

Courtney rolled her head to one side, giggling like a child, and said, "Oh, no. Nope."

"Glover, tell me. Where were they taking Natalia?"

"To the river. Drop her like a fish back into the deep." Glover giggled again, opened her mouth wide, and ran the tip of her tongue over her broken tooth. Her tongue split with the motion, and blood ran down her chin.

"*Which* river?"

"Gowanus, the canal. Nice and quiet." Courtney laughed again, her jagged tooth glistening from the light overhead. "She can sink like a stone."

"Where along Gowanus? Come on, Agent Glover, that's a big area to cover."

Courtney swallowed the laugh, suddenly sombre. "An empty lot by Union. No witnesses."

"Which side?"

Courtney shook her head, and sent a spray of tears flying in all directions. "No. I didn't want – I didn't want to. I'm sorry. I really am."

"Courtney." Jim lowered his voice, hoping a kinder, gentler approach might somehow reach the most innocent part of her mind that was untroubled by the drugs. "She's just a child."

As she shook her head, Courtney whispered, "Me too, me too. Got some dolls, you know. Collected them-"

"Courtney."

"East," she sobbed. "The east side."

Jim glanced over his shoulder towards Max who was already heading back towards the door to share the news. Courtney's behaviour suggested she was past the point of no return and fading fast, and, quite frankly, Jim had gotten all he needed from her, so he turned to leave.

She spoke again, this time more earnestly. "He told us to."

Jim paused, turned, and faced the young woman. "Who did?"

Courtney grinned through the snot and tears. "We were so scared, you know? Everyone was scared. The director said it was for the best. Now we don't have to be scared anymore." She furrowed her brow. "But I still feel scared. And sad now, too."

Childlike, the height of innocence, and yet there she lay, bloodstained. The hands of a killer. But weren't they all in the end? And Harrison Caulder had made Courtney one of them, as he had all the rest.

Jim turned once more and left the crying woman behind him.

He wasn't surprised to see Meghan and Caulder marching down the hallway, this time with three security agents in tow.

"This probably isn't going to go well," Tess said, hand drifting towards her belt, where a pistol was snapped in her holster.

"Let's *not* start a fight we can't finish, eh?" Bedlam growled beside her. Even then, Bedlam planted himself in front of Jim, as if knowing that a battle was inevitable and they should be prepared.

"Agent Wilkinson, you have been *suspended*," Caulder snarled as they approached. "What the *hell* are you doing in a restricted area?"

"How do you like that?" Jim asked lamely. "I come here and get Natalia's location through some measured interrogation and that's the thanks I get."

At his words Meghan's anger broke, if only for a split second, before returning in full force. "Where is she?"

"They took her to Gowanus Canal, east side of Union street, to an empty lot where they can dump her body." Jim narrowed his gaze at Caulder and added, "Under *his* orders."

"Bullshit," Caulder snapped back. "You're just looking for a reason to start a fight."

"You're scared. They're *scared*." Jim angled between Bedlam and Tess and jabbed a finger at Caulder's chest. "We're *all* fucking scared, and you played on that. You manipulated them, made them your lackeys. She's a goddamned *kid*, and instead of protecting her you sent the Third after her like a fucking *fox and hound*."

"Jim." Meghan didn't raise her voice. Level and consistent. That was how she worked when new information entered the scene. She knew how to shut down her voice, to make herself seem impartial. It gave her the chance to sneak in under the radar and land a killing blow where one wasn't expected.

"Get a team, go check it out," she said.

"Meghan, this agent is *suspended*!" Caulder protested.

"His only concern is Natalia's welfare. We might as well utilize that earnestness while we can." She looked back at the agents and gave them a curt nod. "Get out there."

It was a free pass they could hardly say no to, especially given the likelihood that Jim might decide to try to take down the director again before security planted a barrage of bullets in his back. Besides, they had places to be.

Meghan heard Caulder dismiss the security agents behind them after Jim and his band of renegade envoy had departed. A dangerous move on their part, but she could hardly blame them. Her own fury was brimming, so close to the surface of her skull that she thought the top of her head might pop open to release the pressure.

No, contain yourself.

"He's finished at this Agency," Caulder said, turning for the elevator. "Wilkinson is *finished*, do you understand me? You can't save him this time." He touched his nose, as if to reaffirm that it had indeed been broken the day before.

"Sir-"

"The gall of him, to attack me and then to interrogate Glover, *unsupervised no less*!" They stepped onto the elevator and Meghan decided to let him have his little rant. It would give her more time to plot a course, and a better chance to corner him. "What the hell were the others thinking? They'll be lucky if they have careers in the *security sector* after I'm finished with them. I tell you, Meghan, I can't believe..."

Meghan didn't much care what precisely Caulder couldn't believe. She was in a sort of shock of her own. She knew as well as the next person that any form of torture or interrogation was never one hundred percent correct. Whatever they had done to Glover, she hadn't even bothered asking, as a doctor was on his way down and would file a full medical report soon enough, had revealed enough to Jim that he felt secure in his position. Secure enough to confront Caulder and place the blame squarely on his shoulders.

As much as he was a pain in the ass, Jim rarely acted out without reason. His choices were measured. The anger she had seen in him over Natalia's kidnapping was no more out of place than the anger he presented after his run-in with Cain or the resulting failures. Meghan trusted Jim's instinct as much as she trusted his word. That was why she had let him take Natalia away from San Francisco. As much as she had believed in Steven, there was no doubt in her mind that Jim Wilkinson had the self-determination and the tendency towards violence needed to protect the girl.

If only they had acted sooner.

No point in worrying about what's been. Meghan smiled slightly, because if that were true, life would be much simpler for all of them.

She had followed Caulder to his office, his ravings ringing through the hallways of the Agency, until she closed the door forcefully behind them and spun to face him.

"*Did you?*" she demanded.

"Did I *what*, Meghan?"

"Did you order the Third to go after her?"

"I didn't order-"

"Casually suggest, then, whatever, I don't care. The point is, did you make the call?"

"How dare you speak to me like that."

Meghan stepped forward and planted her palms on his desk, leaning across the glass top in the hope that it would give her an air of intimidation. In her peripheral vision, she could see splatters of black blood that had been missed during the cleanup the day before. "Now is not the time for your sententious rhetoric, *sir*. Did you order Natalia's execution, yes or no?"

"I-" Caulder faltered. He turned abruptly, and Meghan thought for a moment she saw his shoulders heave with...a sob? No. That was too human for someone the likes of him. It was only as he turned around again that she saw he had been reaching for a photograph on the small table behind his desk. Wordlessly he handed it over. The framed image depicted a young boy, maybe no more than ten, in a school uniform. He was wiry, with thin, blonde hair that was a little too shaggy for his small face.

"He hates getting his hair cut," Caulder said, as if reading Meghan's expression. "It drives my sister batty. It'll be longer now, I imagine."

"Sir?"

"My nephew, Kyle." Caulder settled behind his desk, unlocked a drawer, and pulled out a nondescript manila folder that he passed to Meghan. "He's been gone since late September. Missing. We thought maybe he had run away, he had a fight with Lisa before he left for school that day, but..." He sighed again, motioned for Meghan to open the folder. Inside there were phone transcripts, dating all the way back to the first of October, not long after the Siege of Alcatraz. A hasty glance confirmed what Meghan dreaded.

"Cain?" she asked, looking up.

"He let me talk to Kyle, albeit briefly. His demands were clear. He'd give me Kyle back in exchange for-"

"For Natalia." Meghan finished. "And you wouldn't do it."

"I know what sending her back to Cain means, Meghan. I know as well as you, and even Agent Wilkinson. I'm sure I'm many things in your eyes, but I'm not condemning every agent in ouch branch, *and* their families, just to save Natalia Artison. If-" he ground his teeth, snatched the folder back out of Meghan's hands, and settled behind the desk. "*If* she's dead, Cain has nothing to work towards, no reason to keep Kyle."

"How do you know Cain won't just kill him?"

"He wouldn't," Caulder said. "Even then...I'd trust him." At this Meghan laughed cruelly and Caulder scowled. "I *have to trust him*. At his core, I think Cain has a set of morals, the same as the rest of us. I've got no choice but to believe that he'll keep Kyle alive."

"You think killing her will give you the upper hand?" Meghan asked. "You're playing a dangerous game with him."

"I'll play dice with the bones of the dead if it means protecting my family, same as anyone here." Caulder took the photo back, pressed his fingers to the glass and for the briefest moment, Meghan saw the façade of a man, built out of the Agency's beliefs and ethics, break down and leave him raw and wanting.

"You'll be held accountable, one way or the other," Meghan said at last.

"I know," Caulder said finally, looking up to her. "Just promise me you'll bring him home."

xXx

The drive to Gowanus Canal left Jim antsy. They were losing light fast, and that would make their search of the area that much more difficult. Not that he expected to find much. The Third had too much of a head start on them. It would be a scramble to catch up.

If there was anything to catch up to.

The thought of finding Natalia dead hadn't occurred to Jim until Bedlam mentioned it grimly during the drive. There were plenty of *what ifs* and worst case scenarios that he kept talking through until Jim finally had to politely, but firmly, tell him that he wasn't helping. They would find what they would find, and that was just the way it was.

He didn't earnestly believe that, however. Natalia was a fighter, even if she didn't know it yet. The sort of person who had a will to survive bred into her, like some precise genetic mutation that only presented itself when the going got tough. She would have preferred something snazzy like healing powers or the ability to laser off someone's eyebrow at five paces. At least, that was what Jim imagined she might tell him. So, despite what he said to Bedlam, Jim wasn't afraid that they would find Natalia's corpse mangled, dismembered, executed. She was a survivor out of spite, if nothing else.

They arrived at eastern bank of the canal, just off Union Street as Courtney had said. There was an empty lot that slopped away from the road, nearly hidden beneath a thick line of black trees that had been planted to try to hide the polluted canal from the eyes of the everyday person. A break in the trees, nearly invisible unless one was looking at it from the right angle, showed a small dirt road that had been cut into the earth, and fresh tracks that had disrupted the snow.

The convoy cars pulled off the paved road, driving until they were through the trees. A single sedan sat abandoned on top of a knoll that sloped dramatically towards the edge of the canal.

"I'll run the plates," Bedlam volunteered. Jim could hardly blame him for wanting to stay in the car. The air was bitter, and a cold breeze was rushing in from the canal, bringing with it the stench of pollution. That, and Jim reckoned if there was anything to find, Bedlam might not want to see it.

The first indication that something had gone wrong for the executioners of the Third was the back passenger side door that was ajar. Jim and Tess leaned down and clicked on their Maglites.

It looked like the set of a horror movie. Blood splattered the inside of the car; soupy puddles of it on the floor, congealed from the cold. And a single agent who Jim recognized from the Third. Warren Foster. Not a pleasant guy: not the sort to be crossed, from what Jim remembered about him. The back of his head looked like someone had put their fist through a cherry pie. Peering back towards the road, Jim knew the treeline could provide enough cover for someone who was waiting. The rest of the car was peppered with buckshot that had gone wide.

"Not what I was expecting to find," Tess said, stepping back from the car and drawing the beam of her Maglite along the ground where a trail of blood extended across the snow in wide, pink swathes, before disappearing into the canal below.

"I get the feeling Warren didn't expect it either." Jim followed the blood trail across the ground, down the steep slope to where Max was hunched over another body. This one was face down in the snow, with a single bullet in the back of the head.

"Two shooters then," Jim said.

"You think?" Max asked.

"Unless they managed to drop the shotgun they used to take down Warren Foster and line up a shot with a rifle before anyone had a chance to react."

Max didn't look discouraged by the thought. He had a lead stomach when it came to these sorts of things. Running a hand over his right ear, scarred from the mangling it had taken months earlier, he sighed. "Blood keeps going from here, down the slope."

Jim turned and saw Troy kneeling at the edge of the canal. There was a break in the icy ground, a mini avalanche that ended in the polluted canal. The chill in the air bit deeper into Jim's face. He exhaled slowly, imagined Natalia's body tumbling towards the water with the wave of snow and ice, disappearing beneath the brine.

Troy glanced up, saw Jim watching, and lifted his hand out of the water, bringing with it a dripping black lump. As Jim came closer, he saw it was Steven's jacket – Natalia's now. Her cloak of infinite protection. She wore it everywhere, and had it on the night before.

A third body was half submerged in the canal, one booted foot thrust up through the water like a beacon in the night.

Troy glanced back at Jim, shook his head, and pointed towards the shifting ice floes.

"Nothing?" Jim asked, though he already knew the answer.

The wind was picking up, and the air was frigid. Anyone who went into the canal and then came out would need to be warmed up or risk hypothermia. If they came out at all. The cold in his face descended into Jim's bones, but he wasn't certain if it was a by-product of the wind or subtle guilt.

"We've got bullet casings up here!" Tess called from the treeline.

Jim stared into the darkness; the canal was inky in the approaching darkness. It swallowed the reflections of the city lights from the other side, devouring his sense of hope. The water took everything for itself and offered nothing in recompense, not even the bones of the dead. Jim crouched next to Troy, pointedly ignoring the half-face of the man who had been pulled from the water.

"We'll drag the canal," Troy said without looking at Jim. He too was staring into the abyss of the polluted water. "If she's there, we'll find her."

"She won't be," Jim said frankly. Even now, the words came naturally. Natalia couldn't die when there was so much left to do. Cain wouldn't let her die, and Cain, Jim was convinced, had eyes on her always. "Someone else was here. Had to be, to kill these men, to get to her."

"Cain."

"Maybe." *Yes. Always Cain.*

"Jesus Christ, Jim." Troy shook his head and turned his face towards Jim. "Why the hell are the Third acting like this?"

Jim tipped his head to once side, felt the stretch in his tendons and sighed. "Fuck if I know, but they're relentless. Or they were."

"You think this little adventure might be enough to convince them otherwise?"

"Tess and I quartered their forces. The ones that made it out alive are on the run; the rest are locked up. Whether we like it or not, we've got one less enemy to deal with now."

"Might be too little too late."

"Might be," Jim agreed, standing up. His bones creaked from the cold. "I need to get some sleep. Call when you hear about the bullet casings, yeah?"

Chapter 8

The pain in her side was dulled. Nothing more than a cold splash against her skin. Then again, maybe this was death. Maybe in death the pain of the waking world was nothing more than the delicate touch of a blade, only there to remind the dead of what it had been like to live.

She rolled and hit a cement floor. The pain came flaring back, shocking her senses like a sparked match. Bright, alert, confused. Natalia could hear her own ragged breathing echoing around her, and the lights, far above her head, were cold and white. She scampered away from the bed she had fallen from, nothing more than a small cot with a tangle of blankets. There was a door at the far end of the building, a warehouse.

Focus, dammit!

Natalia threw herself forward, launching to her feet and towards the door. She jerked unceremoniously backwards as a chain around her wrist pulled taut. Realizing she was pinned, with only a few feet of range, Natalia hauled herself around to the head of the bed, crouched low, and closed her eyes.

Breathe. You need to focus.

She inhaled deeply, from her belly, and felt the air settle heavily on top of the fear that was bubbling up through her stomach. She imagined the breath as warm, fresh, and heavy, like a hand-sewn quilt, capable of crushing her fear under layer after layer of coloured squares.

One, two, three...

Now think. Where are you?

Not Alcatraz. Please, don't take me back to Alcatraz.

Natalia left a piece of herself on the island that night. Among the fallen soldiers and the dead that Cain had sacrificed without a second thought, as the siege wore on and the dead began to mount, Natalia left a piece of herself behind to rot. And when Jim had at last drawn her away from Steven, she had felt herself severed from the last of her innocence. The lingering spirit of a child who had lain beside her guardian and chosen to die.

Then there was fear, so real. It was cruel, because the island never disappeared. It still existed, with a half-functioning prison on the Rock. And somewhere amongst the cells and the cement was a girl waiting for parole.

Fuck Alcatraz and all her memories of it. *I'd rather die,* she decided.

At the far end of the warehouse, the door opened, and Natalia shrank further into the corner. She wasn't entirely certain why, or what it might accomplish. She was trapped, no two ways about it. But cowering, even for a moment, felt natural.

"Natalia?"

There it was. A familiar voice. Not one she was keen on, if she were honest. The last time she had heard it was on the island and...

Awful things happened on the island. Awful, dreadful things that had crushed her between two types of evil and left her struggling to repair damage to a person she didn't even know had existed at the time. It was like building a puzzle without an idea of what the picture was meant to look like.

Natalia turned stiffly so she could peek above the cot, her chains rattling. There was no element of surprise, but she felt vaguely more secure pretending that she was hidden. It gave her those desperate extra seconds she needed to find where she had buried her courage and dig it out.

Pete. Peter Cobbs. One of Jim's allies behind bars, at least for a short time, until Cain had intervened. Pete had not taken the betrayal lightly, and it had nearly resulted in Jim's death.

Instead, someone else paid the price. A notch on the belt, that's what Jim had called it during one of their late night drives, moving from one state to another. A notch on the belt, and nothing else. Jim didn't want to talk about the death of Preacher, and Natalia decided it was best to respect that.

But now, staring at Pete approaching her, Natalia hoped she wasn't about to join Preacher in the great beyond.

"What the hell are you doing behind there?" Pete demanded, fists planted on his hips, somehow still sounding good-natured despite it all. "Chrissake, get up, kid. You're *hurt*. Get back in bed."

"Pete, I-" Natalia wasn't sure where she was going, or what she planned on saying. He was one of the last people she had ever expected to see again, let alone in a state that could be considered, well, personable. Gripping the edge of the cot, Natalia pulled herself into a standing position. She couldn't straighten out completely; her left side felt bunched together. Suddenly aware of the pain ebbing through her body, she looked down and pressed her hand against the already bloodstained shirt. It came back red and sticky.

"Aw shit," Pete said. He stepped forward placed a hand on her shoulder and gently drew her back towards the cot. "Sit down. I'll get Hank back in to check your stitches. Guy's a retired doctor," he added, seeing Natalia's confusion.

"Just, just stop Pete. Stop for a second." Natalia reached out with her manacled wrist and grabbed Pete's hand. "Where *am* I? What happened? I have *questions*, Pete."

"Sure you do," he said with a non-committal shrug. "Of course." He slung himself down on the cot; it creaked and buckled under his weight. Was he always so monstrous? Somehow prison made everyone seem smaller than they really were.

They sat in dead silence for a moment as Natalia tried to wrap her head around the absurdity of the situation. Pete, oddly patient, said nothing but stared at her in wonderment.

Finally, Natalia raised her shackled wrist and gave it a shake. "Can you take this off?"

"Ah, ha. No. No, I'm not going to do that, kid. Last time you woke up in a strange place you stabbed someone."

"That's fair, I guess." She shifted uncomfortably on the bed, then pulled one of the many blankets out of the pile and wrapped it around her shoulders. She struggled a bit, what with her one wrist firmly chained to a pipe on the wall. Pete helped her adjust the blanket then returned to his inert position. She nodded slyly at him and asked, "How's, uh...how's prison treating you?"

"Early parole," he said lamely, and Natalia knew better than to question him. It was one of the things she and Jim had doggedly pursued during their off hours while on the run. Who had made it off Alcatraz alive; who had been found, massacred, by Cain's people; and who had disappeared without a trace.

Pete fell into the latter category and that was, as Jim had put it at the time, a very bad sign. It meant, as far as Natalia could tell, that she needed to approach the next topic carefully. Pete was not the ally he had been in Alcatraz, whether either of them wanted to admit it or not.

"Where am I, Pete?" she asked at last, trying on a meek voice, hoping that it might subtly remind him of her youth and give her a bit of an edge.

Pete raised an eyebrow, and Natalia knew he wasn't buying it. "One of the Reapers' warehouses," he said slowly. "We keep extra rides here, supplies, shit like that. Figured it would make a good staging ground for, uh..."

Natalia narrowed her gaze at the mountainous man and began to work through his statement in her head. That was another one of Jim's little bits of training. You accomplished much more by staying silent and analyzing your opponent's language. People were very precise for a reason, and Pete was no exception.

"Oh, shit."

"Now, kid, just calm now."

Natalia began to pull at the chain on the wall, determined to either pull the metal free or her arm from the socket, whichever came first. "Fuck, fuck, *fuck*," she grunted.

"Just stop, stop, ok! You're going to hurt yourself."

"I should be so lucky to injure myself before Cain shows up!" *Cut an artery, split a vein, drain me dry. Whatever it takes to keep me away from him.*

Pete's hand was on her wrist now, gently, but pointedly preventing her from dragging her arm back any further. With one skillful movement, he purposefully pushed Natalia down on the shoulder. "Stop, ok? Just let me explain."

Despite how they had left things at Alcatraz, with Pete's determination to kill Jim and hesitant alliance with Cain, Natalia found herself unwittingly prepared to listen to whatever yarn he had to spin. She had trusted him in Alcatraz, for the most part, and was willing to extend that same trust again.

"We're just using the warehouse as a place to get some supplies shipped to; then Cain-"

"Nope!" Natalia declared, as she pulled earnestly at the chain.

Trust was a short-lived sort of thing.

"Just, *stop*. I know you're scared, but if you give him the Code then-"

"Oh, you are too damn old to be that naïve, Pete." Natalia dropped the length of chain and scooted to the other end of the cot. "He's a killer, he's a *bad* person. Why the hell would you work for him?"

"A man has his monsters," Pete replied quietly. "Cain's giving me a chance to deal with mine."

"You mean Jim? He's not a *bad* person, Pete." *Cold, calculating, indifferent a solid ninety percent of the time, but not bad.* "You don't have to do this."

"I'm already a sinner, kid. What does harm does a little more pride or greed do in the long run?"

"Jim saved my life on the Rock, Pete. And, and so many times afterwards. It isn't right."

"No, I get that. You got loyalties and I admire that. Thing is, Cain wants you back, and he's going to be just as ruthless as he was before." Pete sighed, stood up, and looked down at her. "We're getting three more shipments tonight. Cain's representative is coming around midnight tomorrow to check it all out. After that, they start shipping it to wherever the hell it is that he wants it. You've got some time to think about it, but I wouldn't waste it."

"And if I say no?"

Pete shrugged one shoulder unhappily. "Then I guess you're going back to Cain."

Hours passed and the compound began to buzz and turn with activity. Every so often one of Cain's mercenaries would troop through the other side of the warehouse and pay her no heed. Pete reappeared only once to offer her some food, a microwaved TV dinner. She accepted it, only because it was still carefully packaged and she couldn't find any sign of tampering. He sat and smoked beside her in silence while she picked away at the Hungry Man Meal.

"How you feeling?"

Natalia didn't respond. There was no point. The man beside her was not the same loyal beast who had protected her in Alcatraz. He was a different figure, a victim of his own anger. She would offer him as much of her spirit as she did Cain.

"Come on, kid. You could at least talk to me; jokes or some shit like that."

She continued to pick away at the peas and carrots in her microwaveable tray.

Pete pulled out his crinkled pack of cigarettes, popped one up with his thumb, and offered it to her.

"I don't smoke, Pete."

"Maybe you should." He pulled a Bic lighter from his pocket, tucked it into the half empty package, and handed it to her. "You never know."

"Sure, if Cain doesn't kill me the lung cancer will."

"I ain't going to let Cain kill you."

Her head snapped towards him, eyes narrowed. "You'll never be able to stop him. You're too angry with the rest of the world."

Pete had opened his mouth to shoot off a reply when the warehouse doors opened and a man with an impressive growth of facial hair strode forward. "Last shipment is here."

"Got the keys?" Pete nodded towards Natalia's handcuffed wrist, and man's eyes went large. Pete shrugged his broad shoulders. "She won't get far, hurtin' like she is. Might as well let her stretch her legs."

He looked unconvinced, and a moment of silence passed before he relented with a sigh and leaned in to uncuff her wrist. Up close Natalia could see he was wearing a leather vest, faded, and covered with embroidered patches. Another biker, perhaps?

Natalia rubbed the red skin where the cold cuff had bit in to her flesh and smirked. "My dad was really into ZZ Top too, you know."

He took a step back, confused, and Pete let out a bark of laughter. "Shit, Lonny, she's right. You got the beard an' everything."

If you're going to die here, you might as well piss off a few people while you can. Natalia pushed her meal aside and, somewhat unwillingly, allowed Pete to help her to her feet. Her knees buckled and he caught her by the shoulders, picking her up like a rag doll.

"Ok?"

"Just sore from sitting." She shook off his bear-like paws and muttered a thanks. Eyeing the ZZ Top impersonator warily, she glanced over his leather vest, studded with patches and shiny emblems. "Mickey Mouse?" She pointed at a golden pin that sat just below his heart.

Lonny grinned sheepishly and pulled his vest forward, as if to put the pin on display. "Took my grandkids to Orlando. They bought it for me."

"Sweet," Natalia said with a genuine smile, and she meant it. It was easy to forget that everyone had a family, everyone had a story. Some of them even involved normal things like family vacations and going to the movies.

"All right." Pete flapped a meaty hand towards Lonny, who smiled and winked at Natalia before turning around. At his gentle nudge, Natalia realized she was meant to follow, Pete at her side.

It was an impressive compound, with stacks of orange, green, red, and black shipping containers as far as she could see, guarded by a long line of predatory-looking Harleys that stood before the precious cargo. Dinnerplate-sized lamps illuminated the immediate area, but Natalia could see that the further the shipping containers went, the bleaker the world became. She could make out the slim outline of a barge pulling away from the dock, having delivered whatever it was they had been waiting for. Large barrels lined the side of the warehouse, all marked *Gas* and *Oil* and fitted with spouts for the convenience of refilling and tending to the bikes. A handful of mercs were pulling the door of the nearest shipping container open and shifting a lamp to illuminate its contents. Pete took Natalia by the arm, directing her towards the container.

It was filled to the brim with guns. A few LMGs that she recognized from Jim's flashcard training. Crates marked with munitions symbols. There were Kevlar vests, helmets, visors. Everything a person might need if they were planning on arming a small rebellion.

Why is he showing me this?

Natalia knew better than to ask. She placed the cigarette pack in her back pocket and began to roll the lighter between her hands in an effort to keep her fingers functional as the cold began to nip at her. The man with the ZZ Top beard turned, offered a thumbs up, and Pete moved on to the next container. Inside, a man was bent over an open wooden crate, flicking a flashlight over the contents. The smell hit Natalia and turned her stomach; sickly sweet molecules that clung to everything inside the crate.

Before they had been dragged back to New York, Jim had been obsessively forcing her to read books on everything from ancient weaponry to modern bomb making. When they were on the road, she would use the data on her phone to read Wikipedia articles, finding herself curious enough to devour the information even without being ordered to. She had gotten bored of reading about the Hell's Angels in Canada and somehow stumbled on the article for plastic explosives. C4, Semtex. When they stopped to get the oil changed at an automotive shop, Natalia hung close to the car, taking in the foreign scent of the fumes, and tried to wrap her mind around how something so integral to their daily life could be utilized to create such a destructive compound.

Pete cleared his throat and the man tipped his head slowly towards the front of the container. With his flashlight swinging up towards the ceiling, his face was partially illuminated, and Natalia felt her stomach surge. The whole of the left side, ear, chin, nose, and cheek, was a mess of bubbled scar tissue, old and white, like an iridescent paint that had been blobbed onto his skin. One eyelid drooped lazily, no longer useful, as scarred as the rest of his face.

"Meloy," Pete said, utterly emotionless.

"Got a spill from one crate." His voice sounded like a rock tumbler fighting a chunk of concrete. Too much smoking cheap cigarettes and drinking even cheaper booze. "I'll get someone to clean it up. Cain accounted for that when we ordered it. We've still got enough."

"Good." Pete turned around and began to direct Natalia towards the side of the warehouse.

Oh, a lovely stroll in the dead of winter. She rubbed her hands along her bare arms and exhaled sharply. "How many of those containers belong to Cain?"

"Enough for you and your *friend* to be worried." Pete didn't look at her, instead staring straight ahead as they wandered around the outside of the warehouse.

He's letting me see the whole compound. He's letting me.

"What's in them?"

"Weapons, different kinds. Guns, explosives, shit like that."

"Did he tell you why he needed them?"

"Nope, and I didn't think to ask. None of my business."

They turned the corner and Natalia caught sight of another warehouse. "All those people out there...are they his?"

Pete pointedly ignored her question. "Tomorrow night one of Cain's people'll come, make sure everything's as it's supposed to be and give it the all clear. Then we'll move it."

"Where to?"

Pete laughed. "Even if I knew, think I'd tell you?"

"I can hope. Why the secrecy? Cain doesn't trust you?"

"Probably only a handful of people he *does* trust, and no, I wouldn't count myself among them."

"What's going to happen after you take the containers to Oz, or Narnia, or wherever the hell they're going?"

"Then you'll go with his representative."

"And if *my* people don't arrive in time?" Natalia demanded. "What then? You just let me go back to Cain?"

"I don't know, kid. Haven't thought that far ahead. Depends."

"Depends on what? Your sense of morality?" Her feet were cold, her toes frozen. One foot went wide under her and the toe of her shoe clipped the side of a barrel that rang with a *clung*.

Pete was quick on the uptake, grabbing Natalia by the shoulder to steady her. He laughed and Natalia felt her cheeks flush from the embarrassment. "Shit, kid. I ain't got a sense of morality. Not one lick of it."

"In Alcatraz-"

"Alcatraz was a life or death matter. Alcatraz was before I knew about Cain, about your guardian. Things change. Things are always changing. You ought to know that."

"Nothing about that time gives you even the slightest sense of obligation towards me?" Natalia stopped in her tracks; the cold was hitting her hard and fast, and left her feeling dazed. Not a good sign for an escape. "Nothing about that time matters to you?"

Pete shook his head and opened the door to the warehouse, having come full circle during their short talk. "It's about survival, kid. Always has been. Ask anyone, hell, ask your guardian. He'll tell you the same thing. Ain't no room for morality or obligation in a world like this."

xXx

The canal was dragged, but as Jim predicted, there was no sign of Natalia. Rusted tin cans, yes, and an old mattress that had been hollowed out by the aquatic life, but no body of a young woman stabbed in the liver. It was a positive sign, but a frustrating one. Natalia was in the hands of someone unaffiliated with the Agency, and the trail had dissolved in the polluted waters of Gowanus.

It was mid-afternoon the next day when Aurora called to give him the news on the bullet casings that Tess had found at the treeline.

"Fingerprints on them belong to an old friend of yours."

"Shit, do I want to know?"

"Hard to say. Your buddy from Alcatraz."

"Pete?" He didn't have many people he'd have referred to as *buddies* in Alcatraz.

"The one and only. One of sixteen inmates to disappear after the Siege. We did some cursory searches on him. His ex and kids were in Raleigh, but she moved out here in late September with their youngest. Security figured she wasn't a threat, so we haven't been keeping eyes on her."

"Have there been any sightings of him in the city?"

"Not a one. His gang's been pretty quiet from what we've been able to tell, not that they're ever at the front of our radar. We've got no reason to think he's reconnected with them."

"What's Meghan got to say?"

"She ordered us to put together everything we have on the local chapter. At the very least, we can send people in to scope it out to see if there's any sign of Pete. It's not much of an update, but I figured you'd want to know."

"Absolutely. Thanks, Aurora."

Jim put his cell phone down and glanced across the worn table at the woman staring at him. All auburn hair and sad green eyes, she looked at him hopefully. If there was one word to describe Angel Holloway, it would be *hopeful*. When they were teens, caught in lust, she was hopeful for them. When their relationship crumbled away, ever hopeful. Now, older and wiser, and still carrying hope like an inextinguishable flame that refused to be buffeted by even the most violent of storms. Jim envied her for that hope.

"Nothing new," he said. "Not really, at least."

"Shit." She pressed her thumb to her lips and furrowed her brow. "Are you ok?"

Jim shrugged and looked down at the deep gouges where prongs of forks had been driven into the table. Smooth blemishes in the hardwood from the bottom of spoons pressed into the surface. He knew most of the dings and scratches in the furniture and along the walls. Most, not all. The price for living in the shadows.

Angel puttered around; washing coffee mugs, opening and closing cupboards aimlessly, as if she might find Natalia tucked inside one of them, her limbs contorted over her head so she might fit next to the box of Lucky Charms.

"Jayson will be home soon," she said, "if you want to stay for a nightcap." When Jim didn't respond, she turned and said his name.

"Sorry," he said. "I was thinking. Do you still have that gun safe?"

"That bad, huh?" Angel crossed her arms and leaned against the doorjamb. "Sure do, in the basement. Still a couple of your unregistered ones in there, thanks so much. I took them to be cleaned when you were away, so they should be working fine."

"Ammo?"

"Bedsides table. Seriously, Jim. Is it that bad?"

"It might be." He pushed back on the desk chair and stood up. "Lead the way."

xXx

To the credit of Pete and the mercenaries that Cain had at his disposal, they treated Natalia with more respect than she expected. They fed her regularly, let her go to the bathroom whenever she needed, and frequently took her handcuff off, under strict supervision, to ensure that she was comfortable. Their resident doctor came back twice to check her over, although Natalia was less and less convinced that he held an actual medical degree.

Doctorate of Philosophy with a minor in the squishy parts of the human body. Her stitches were holding and she didn't have a fever. Still, he gave her another shot of antibiotics, what she *hoped* were antibiotics, and made her promise that she would tell one of her guards if she started feeling the least bit off colour.

Just as Jim had explained, everyone had a set of rules they wanted to adhere to. Some people concerned themselves with children or equality or law and order, but no individual necessarily had to believe in all of them at once. She was still a child to these men and women, and worthy of being looked after. That didn't mean they couldn't also work for the same man that had tortured her; he wasn't there, hawkishly draped over their shoulders and guiding their actions. They could make their own decisions.

Natalia, although she wouldn't admit it, was grateful for the care she had received, even if they were just prepping her like a calf being sent to the slaughter.

That changed the next night, when Cain's representative arrived to look over the order and ensure everything was as it should be. Pete had been increasingly on guard, and had gone out of his way to avoid Natalia's eyes. The few words he exchanged with her were terse and, at times, seemingly apologetic. She was left alone after that, made to pass the hours by herself, with only the sounds of movement from the outside to entertain her. The skies outside were blanketed with heavy, dark clouds when she finally heard the front gate of the compound squeal open. A convoy of hefty vehicles, trucks probably. Mercenaries outside speaking, exchanging well wishes, and then boots crunching over old ice and snow.

The door to the warehouse opened and Natalia gave a cry of alarm.

There were few people in the world she feared as much as Cain. Few people who incited such a sense of vulnerability within her. And she hated vulnerability, because that was what had gotten Steven killed and put her and Jim on Caulder's shit list. Vulnerability eventually led to death. Before that, though, stood one man.

Duncan.

She didn't know much about him. Not his last name, not what sort of family he might have. Jim had only told her the barest details; he was a rapist, and a child killer. In Alcatraz, he had booked a permanent stay in segregation, yet still commanded a small army of inmates who didn't mind that he knew the location of at least six dead children and kept it to himself. Duncan had set his sights on Natalia and, were it not for the intervention of Jim, Pete, and Preacher, he might have succeeded. He joined Cain's crew, and had made it quite clear that he had a certain physical interest in her. One he was willing to wait to cash in.

Now he stood before her, markedly proud of himself.

"Fuck," was all Natalia could say.

"Not yet." He laughed and turned around, leaving the warehouse just as nonchalantly as he had arrived.

Natalia looked up at Pete, found him unwilling to catch her glance. "You can't be serious. You can't let him take me."

"Kid-"

"Pete, please! Just, just kill me, ok? If that's how this is going to play out then just kill me because I *cannot* go with him. Please. Please, Pete."

"I have to go show him the stock," Pete mumbled, shame clouding his voice.

"Pete! Don't do this! *Please!*"

Her cries echoed through the empty warehouse, and Natalia glanced frantically around. She was trapped, that much was clear, and she had wasted precious time hoping that help would come when, even if Jim and the Agency were on her trail, they would most likely be too late.

Berate yourself later. Right now you need to think.

There was no way to uncuff herself from the old piping that stretched up the wall. Near the top of the warehouse wall was a window, cracked open to let in a brisk winter wind and siphon out the smell of oil and gas. She drew the cuff up and stood on the cot. The pipe was old and rusted, thick enough that she could wrap her hands around it. Whether or not it would support her weight was another issue entirely. Bracing her foot against the first joint, Natalia began her ascent.

She was nine feet or so above her cot when the pipe intersected a metal joist and she could no longer drag herself up. Gripping the part of the pipe that levelled off, Natalia pushed on the window with her free hand until it opened another few inches and the voices from outside could flow in freely.

"We've accounted for everything." That was Pete. He was monotone, and Natalia could hardly blame him. "It's all here, minus one oil drum that spilled in transit."

"I'm going to have to check for myself." That was Duncan.

"Fair enough."

"I'm surprised," Duncan drawled. "You're risking a lot letting Cain use this place without sharing the spoils with your buddies."

Pete's voice was rigid as he replied, "I'm aware. I'd like to get cleared outta here as soon as possible."

There was a clanging of metal, and the sound of rummaging. Duncan, checking the goods, confirming their mutual partner wasn't getting played. "Cain wants the shipment on the road by midnight. You ride with it and the ones Cain's hired. I'll stay here with the kid and a skeleton crew."

If Pete had anything to say about this arrangement, Natalia wasn't interested in hearing it. She couldn't count on him, so his response was irrelevant. Doing her best to avoid a misstep that would lead to her plummeting to the ground where she would surely break her back, Natalia shimmied back down the pipe and onto the cot. She had to think fast. There would be no way to escape while Cain's mercenaries were still present. Too many, all heavily armed. She would have to wait until they were on the road. That would be fine, except it left her alone with Duncan and she was certain he wouldn't waste any time.

She ran her fingers over the pipe, along the screws and the drywall.

There is always a way out. Jim's teachings, doggedly pursuing every thought she had. Natalia figured the screws were just about the right size. She could see where the pipe was fused together. If she could get enough leverage... Natalia tugged her small switchblade from her pants. A gift bestowed on her by Max during his drug-induced frenzy some months earlier. It had taken a life, and more than once Natalia had wanted to get rid of it, but Jim always coached her against it. She pressed the tip of the blade into the screw. It fit, if only just. With a bit of force the screw began to turn away from the drywall.

Twenty minutes later, she had four of the eight screws removed and discarded in the crack between cot and wall. She could hear voices approaching the warehouse and brushed the drywall dust from her jeans. If they noticed anything out of the ordinary, she would be back to square one.

Pete strode in, alone, and Natalia's stomach turned. His posture was slumped, shoulders caved in towards his chest and head bowed so he might avoid eye contact. But Natalia wasn't satisfied by that. He had been instrumental in plucking her out of the hell that had been Alcatraz, and now he was leaving her to the very wolves he had beaten back.

"We're leaving now. Gotta take the shit to Cain."

Natalia had considered begging once more, trying one final time to elicit and emotional response from the convict in the hope that he might change his mind and help her or, worst case scenario, cast a killing blow to save her from Cain. But no, damaging one of Cain's toys was a quick way to a shallow grave, and Pete was in survival mode. But then again, so was she.

Natalia knew however she played her cards now, it was a *Hail Mary* and nothing more. "Your gang, the Reapers, they don't know you're using this place, do they?"

Pete's eyes widened and he looked around, stalling on the open window above the bed. He frowned at her and shook his head in disbelief. "No, no they don't."

"That's risky, isn't it? They'll be mad."

"As hell."

"Well, then," Natalia said, settling with her back against the wall, casually hiding her makeshift renovation project. "That makes two of us."

If Pete had anything left to say, he kept it to himself. Shame and guilt, pulsing together beneath his skin left him wan, sickly looking. He opened his mouth to speak and then closed it again. There were no words; nothing he could say to justify his choices. Pete turned to leave the warehouse and didn't bother to look back.

The metal cargo containers creaked as they were pulled across the open compound and into the barren streets. Natalia listened until silence settled over the complex. A few voices murmuring here and there, people laughing and the smell of cigarette smoke drifting in through the open window.

Natalia pulled out the blade and began to work away at the last of the screws. She was out of time. Cain, Duncan, it made no difference. Death was death; it was faceless, nameless to her.

Another screw dropped free and she moved on to the next.

xXx

Jim was already on the road when Aurora called him with the news.

"The Road Reapers have a compound on Staten Island, just off Edgewater Street. CCTV picked up movement; some eighteen wheelers carrying big-ass loads, and a couple beater sedans riding on their tails. We confirmed last year that it's supposed to be their winter storage place, just a place to store the extra rides. No reason for anyone to be there."

Jim knew about the compound. He knew about all of them. Before entering Alcatraz on his ill-fated mission he had read and reread the dossiers compiled on the more *popular* inmates. He knew more about Pete's life with the Road Reapers than he did about himself. The compound was far from the local chapter's clubhouse. It gave them an air of deniability if things went south.

Jim glanced in the rear-view mirror; Steven's leather jacket was sitting there. Angel, bless her, had dried it and insisted Jim take it with him.

"She'll be cold, and she needs something comforting."

She was a smart woman; never ceased to amaze him.

"Jim?" Aurora had been waiting for him to speak.

"Yeah, I'll meet the team there."

"Meghan wanted me to emphasize that if you get there before them, not that either of us expect that," the sarcasm was palatable "you are not to proceed without reinforcements."

"Copy that."

"I mean it, Jim."

"I know. I know. I'll be good." *For now.*

xXx

Natalia's fingers were stiff from the cold. She should have closed the window, but being able to hear what was going on outside was proving invaluable, and she was willing to battle the cold for a few minutes longer if it meant knowing how close Duncan was to the warehouse.

Two screws left. The knife slipped from her fingers for a third time and Natalia swore. She could hear talking outside. Voices, growing louder until one moved away, leaving the familiar humming of a man Natalia wanted to stab in the throat. Natalia placed the switchblade into her back pocket and gave three solid tugs on the pipe. The door opened and Duncan strode through.

"Miss me?"

"Like a bullet in the head." Natalia shifted her weight on the cot, careful of her wound. She would need as much leverage as possible. She gave another tug on the handcuff and felt flakes of drywall scatter around her wrist.

"I've been thinking a lot about you lately."

"Gag me with a spoon." He was less than five feet from her. She felt the pipe shift; the drywall cracked. It might as well have been a cymbal clashing next to her head.

"You look better in this light. Pretty. It was hard to tell at Alcatraz, but now I see it."

Wait for it. One last gentle pull and she felt the pipe pull from the drywall. She kept her arm braced, making it look like she was supporting herself out of exhaustion.

"The rest of them, they wouldn't mind seeing you dead at the end of all this. I think I'll try to keep you alive for a while." One more step, and he was in swinging distance. "Get to know you a little more intima-"

Natalia had never taken to softball, but she imagined Marcus Artison would have been proud of the swing she took at Duncan's skull. He hit the ground hard, and Natalia levelled a second hit into his side. She might have continued bringing the pipe down on him until he was paste, but there was too much risk of the convict rallying and taking her down. Natalia tossed the pipe aside and bolted for the door.

Chapter 9

Natalia hadn't thought far beyond escaping the warehouse. She reasoned the fresh air would bring with it a dozen other options that she could pick from, a buffet of escape possibilities. But the moment she hit the open plaza, her mind ground to a halt. Jim would have been sixteen steps ahead, having already decided which booze he would knock back when he was home safe and sound. Natalia, on the other hand, was having trouble remembering how to walk thanks to the pain that had flared around the incision on her torso.

She followed the outer wall of the warehouse, hugging the shadows until she saw the front gate. It was guarded. Six men. Probably the handful that Duncan had mentioned leaving behind. Looking back, Natalia could see that there were still at least thirty some-odd storage containers near the dock. Some of them open, their contents exposed to the elements. Others stacked whimsically on top of each other, without rhyme or reason to the order.

They probably suck at Tetris, too.

Duncan was bellowing from inside the warehouse, raising the alarm. Natalia scampered across the exposed square and towards the maze of crates. The snow had been pressed into submission by the trucks, leaving an icy rink underfoot.

At least you aren't leaving a trail.

She crouched in the shadows and watched as the warehouse door was thrown open violently. Duncan stumbled out, bleeding profusely from a head wound.

Good riddance. I hope he forgets how to do math.

He retched, spat up a bit of vomit, obviously not able to handle his pain, and Natalia smiled. Duncan leaned on the barrels of oil and gas for support, and clawed his way to the sentries at the gate.

The idea began as a small spark, flickering around her with the cold winter air. Then as she watched Duncan disappear around the corner of the warehouse, it burst into a flame, and Natalia reached towards her back pocket. Cigarette and lighter still firmly in place. What was it Jim had told her?

Nothing is better cover than chaos.

She waited until the few remaining sentries had followed Duncan and were out of sight. Time was limited, but that was ok. She snagged a wrench that had been casually discarded in the snow and slipped back towards the front of the warehouse. After a panicked few seconds of maneuvering, the spigot popped off the gas barrel. Natalia went down the line, snapping spigots and plugs from the vats until the iced over yard was drenched in sweet, noxious fumes. When the closest barrel was light enough for her to drag, she pulled it through the warehouse doors. With a bit of encouragement, the barrel tipped on to its side and rolled towards the back of the warehouse, where three dozen bikes stood at attention. Shined to perfection, all chrome and pristine leather.

This should piss them off.

The floor was sticky with the pooling gasoline, and the fumes were beginning to make her dizzy. Natalia skipped back outside, a strange giddiness forming in the pit of her stomach. She could hear the sentries yelling, warning that hiding would do her no good. She took a second barrel of gas and repeated the process. The snow muffled the sound of her rolling it across the plaza towards the first of the cargo crates. One door still hung open, revealing heavy artillery.

With a well-timed kick, Natalia forced the barrel into the container, its contents covering the floor and seeping into the various unmarked crates. It was like a surprise bag. Who knew what would come of it? All Natalia was certain of was that it would provide a significant *distraction*.

Taking a jerry can full to the brim with gas, Natalia began splashing it around the rest of the shipping containers, feeling remarkably giddy from what she guessed was a combination of blood loss and fumes. There, crouched in the darkness, with lighter in hand, she waited.

Duncan and the sentries rounded the corner, having made a full circuit of the compound, and stared in shock at the mess of oil and gas covering the ground.

Look at me.

"Come on, you sonuvabitch," she hissed. "Look."

Duncan's head snapped up, and Natalia smiled. She was kneeling by the end of her trail now, lighter in hand. He yelled for the sentries to fall back. The flame struck the gas.

Natalia was bowled over by the force of the explosion that came at her from every direction. She stumbled back, blinded by the white-hot light that swallowed the warehouse and its contents in a cloud of flames. If Duncan and his cronies had been caught in the blast, she couldn't tell. It was a distraction, pure and simple, and one, she hoped, that would send a message to her allies.

I'm alive.

Duncan would have to circle around the warehouse to circumvent the fire before he could reach her. It bought Natalia the precious few seconds she desperately needed.

Her fingers were frozen, locked up from her extended adventure in the cold. She had to keep moving. Anything less than a sprint and she would risk letting the cold invade her body. The frigid air was already slowing her down, mentally and physically. Turning towards the nearest cargo box, Natalia gripped the padlock and pulled herself upwards. It was a scramble; her body didn't cooperate well when faced with the slippery metal. Two false starts, then Natalia managed a wild scramble on top of the container. It gave her a better view of the chaos she had created. The sky was flooded by orange flames, like a Halloween decoupage. A beacon in the night. She kept low, creeping along the top of the connecting containers. All that was left was to stay one step ahead of Duncan and the other mercenaries, find a way off the compound, and get to safety.

Easier said than done.

xXx

Jim saw the explosion as he was crossing the bridge into Staten Island. He wanted to be upset, knowing full well who had caused it, but truth be told he was impressed. The fire could be seen from blocks away. Whatever Natalia had done, she hadn't held back. Already on the phone to Aurora, he relayed that there was an unexpected disruption in the general vicinity of the compound.

"CCTV has three bikes leaving the area about forty-five minutes ago, along with three cargo containers hooked up to trailers. Coverage of the Reapers' clubhouse out in Bay Ridge shows a shit ton of action. Looks like they're scrambling, hitting the road," Aurora reported.

Jim wasn't a fan of gangs, and hated one-percenters even more because they acted primarily on their emotions. Nothing would make them more irrational than a fire taking out their property. As hilarious as he found it, Natalia's action risked putting them on a shit list, and Jim wasn't certain either of them could afford to make more enemies.

With the team less than a half hour behind him, Jim hit the gas and braced himself for the scent of smoke. Thick, blackened tendrils that would envelop everything in their path if given half a chance. And among all that chaos and destruction, God willing, was Natalia.

xXx

Natalia reached the fence that stretched around the compound, hoping that her elevated position on top of the shipping container might give her an advantage when scaling it. Now, in the light of the blaze, she could see thick spirals of barbed wire topping it, and knew she was shit out of luck. As much as she wanted out of the compound, she wasn't interested in gutting herself in the process, strung up on the barbs while she bled out like some demonic scarecrow.

Turning back, she made a wild leap across the gap separating two stacks of cargo containers. Her aim was off, and the sheet ice on top of the crate caught her foot. She hit the side of the container with a bang and felt her body surge backwards as gravity took hold. Pain electrified her brain as she scrambled forwards. When she was safely atop of the container, she doubled over, hands groping at her side where she had been stitched up. Her fingers felt hot, and when she looked, they were shiny and red.

Shit.

Boots stomped through the darkness, crunching snow and debris that had scattered from the explosion. They were coming at her from multiple directions, probably hoping to corner her. With only one potential direction still unexplored, Natalia turned east, towards the docks. Given her options, death by hypothermia didn't seem *that* bad.

She eased herself over the edge of the container and felt her feet lose traction on the metal underneath her worn soles. As she slammed chin-first onto the last shipping container, the switchblade popped from her pocket, skidded across metal, and over the edge of the container, out of sight. Natalia scrambled to regain her traction and angled herself over the container, where she hung freely, two feet above the ground, before dropping into the snow.

Natalia's fingers were curling around the hilt of the small blade as Duncan threw himself out from between two shipping crates and tackled her around the waist. Together, they skidded across snow and ice, onto the ancient dock extended over the black water.

Natalia drove her hand upwards, hoping to spear him in the neck with her small but versatile knife. Duncan slammed her arm back down and delivered one sharp punch to her face, and Natalia felt her cheek tear from his knuckles. She rolled sharply, narrowly avoiding another strike, and brought her elbow down on a small bundle of nerves near his shoulder and neck. Duncan howled in pain and jolted backwards from the shock.

Her side was bleeding heavily again; she could feel it, warm and slick on her belly as she crawled across the fractured wood, towards the water. She'd never beat him like this, so running was her only choice. Head for the water. Escape and evade.

Duncan launched himself on her again, and the boards splintered around their bodies, sending man and child crashing into the grotty water. Natalia kicked out, landing a hit in the middle of his chest, and twisted about to propel herself back to the surface. She broke through with a gasp, one hand on the fractured remains of the dock, and had one foot out of the deep when Duncan's hand shot upwards, gripped her submerged leg around the thigh, and dragged her backwards.

They were tangled together amongst old netting and wooden pallets that had been left to pollute the river; two animals lunging at each other, hoping for the chance to make the killing strike before the other found an opening.

His hands were around her neck, a vile and personal attack on her body that told of all the pent-up rage consuming him in the months between his failure to rape her in Alcatraz and now.

Natalia's hand was caught in the netting, her head pounding from the lack of air. She wrestled with the plant life under the water, and in a split second her right hand pulled free from mess of rope and she plunged the knife directly into Duncan's chest. Once, twice. Over and over again, like a piranha diving in and out, picking bits of flesh from its victim. The water around them turned brown, as the current mixed the life of Duncan with the polluted bay.

Natalia kept stabbing until flecks of white bone began to chip from his sternum and her lungs begged for air. She stabbed until he began to sink, caught beneath the old Dust Devils and flat tires and redundant VCRs that had been tossed carelessly away. Duncan would join them; the undesirable, the broken things that no one wanted to touch.

She lost her grip on the switchblade as it struck muscle, and a clanging in her head sounded a frightful warning. Out of time.

Natalia began to kick towards the surface, but her feet were caught in knots of old fishing line, and the handcuff on her wrist was looped around a length of twisted metal. Try as she might, Natalia could not break free. Every kick tangled her more completely among the lengths of criss-crossing wire and thread. The glow of the fire above was dimming, and polluted water was streaming down her throat, into her burning lungs.

And then. And then.

She was on the edge of the dock, coughing up blood and water, vision blurred and marring the face of the figure already creeping back into the shadows. Hollow.

There was a gun beside her, dry and functional, which was more than she could say for herself. Her lungs burned from the water she had inhaled. Frost was already gleaming on her hair and skin. She was bleeding, cold, and now very bruised.

Natalia ran a hand across her side; it came back sticky and red. A slow leak, and one she wouldn't have to worry about yet, if she could get out and get help for herself. A few loyal stitches were holding strong. She didn't want to test her luck any longer. With one painful push, Natalia was back on her feet and limping across what remained of the dock.

She didn't look back. She didn't want to see the face of a dead man screaming up at her.

At a first crossroad made by the shipping containers that had avoided the brunt of the explosion, Natalia crouched to check the gun. The mag was half full, plus one in the chamber. It wasn't much, but she might be able to pop off a shot or two at any merc who tried to corner her. She rubbed her hands against the metal of the gun. She had awful aim, and it would be made worse by the cold.

Keep moving. Keep moving. Rest too long and you'll freeze to death.

She inhaled sharply and listened. Feet crunching snow. How far? She couldn't tell. Her hearing was muddied by water and a pounding headache. Which direction? Behind her. Someone yelling about the docks. They would be on her in no time at all.

You have to move.

As she stood up, her knees creaked, protesting their miserable treatment. She slipped between two shipping containers and glanced towards the sky to try to orient herself. It was a blanket of orange, with embers floating above her head like gentle drifts of stardust. She would head right, then, towards the fence and hope that the sentries hadn't returned to their post. If she couldn't sneak over, then she would just see herself out like a proper lady.

It was a struggle to move, back and forth, between cargo containers that were beginning to look like hulking monsters that had been pulled from the ocean and laid out to die. She could hear the voices of the mercs rising around her, floating out of the shadows, but the cold and violence was taking its toll on her mental state. Try as she might Natalia couldn't orientate herself towards the entrance of the compound.

Not good.

That sealed it. Natalia picked up her pace, ignoring the prints she left in the snow in favor of the speed she needed to escape the maze of cargo containers. She made a sharp turn from between two of them and found herself back in the light produced by the lamps that had not been damaged in the explosion.

The cold, thick barrel of a gun shoved rudely into her back. Natalia choked back a gasp, more of annoyance than anything, and slowly raised her hands. A voice from behind growled something unintelligible, but before Natalia could reply she felt the gun jolt away. A horrendous gurgling noise, and fresh blood sprayed on the snow at her feet.

Natalia turned and saw Jim remove his arm from around the mercenary's throat, knife rammed deeply into the curve between neck and shoulder.

"Jesus, Jim." Natalia stepped forward, awkwardly reaching out for him, an instinctive motion that stalled when she remembered that Jim wasn't the touchy-feely sort. She stopped short of embracing him and feigned brushing her hair behind her ear.

"Ok?" His voice shook. From the cold? Certainly not because he had been worried about her.

Natalia didn't give it a second thought, choosing instead to press one hand against her bloodied side. "They stitched me," she croaked, "but it isn't holding."

Jim's eyes widened slightly; the most shocked he was capable of showing, as far as Natalia was aware. Then it occurred to her that while they were standing around, shooting the breeze, the wolves were descending.

"Duncan was here! A-and Pete! He's bringing Cain. We have to go before he comes back. He wants to kill you, and he didn't tell the Reapers he was here, and-"

"All right, all right. Here, take this." Jim shrugged off his jacket and tossed it at her. "We need to get you somewhere warm."

If there was one thing Natalia had learned in her four months of training, it was that there was never time to ask questions when in the middle of an active warzone. She hobbled along, only keeping pace with Jim because anything less would earn his ire. At the front of the compound Natalia gaped at the car that had been driven straight through the gate; Jim said nothing, instead pointing at the car and telling her to get in. Natalia scrambled into the passenger's seat, and a moment later Jim threw the car in reverse. Sparks and paint flew around them, and Natalia could hear shouting inside the compound.

"They're coming," she whispered.

"Just hang on," Jim said, wrenching on the steering wheel, pulling them free from the last of the debris.

The heater was cranked at full blast, directed to her toes and face, but Natalia shook like an electrified mouse. She explained frantically, in broken sentences, what had happened since she had been taken from the house. When she reached the point where Duncan entered the story, Jim's knuckles turned white around the steering wheel, and Natalia saw his jaw flex as he ground his teeth.

Whatever he's thinking, it can wait.

She finished by telling him that Duncan was dead, lost to the sea. It seemed pertinent to avoid mentioning how it had come about. Jim already thought she was capable of great violence after she killed her Beth's murderer back in Alcatraz. In so many ways, Natalia could not consolidate those actions, and the actions against Duncan, with who she was in the here and now.

Jim was on the phone with the Agency, relaying the situation to Aurora. If Natalia had wanted to discuss her fears about becoming a serial killer, it would have to wait.

Jim pulled the hard to the left and Natalia's skull bounced off the passenger window. She glowered at him, a pointed comment about his motor skills on the sharp edge of her tongue. But Jim was frowning. No, he looked *frantic*.

"You're sure?" he asked. "Absolutely sure?" Aurora responded with something that was equally unpleasant. Natalia scanned the darkness, trying to orient herself. They weren't headed off Staten Island anymore, but deeper into its bowels.

"Ok then," Jim said, exhaling sharply through his teeth. "Track us, and get the others to our location as soon as possible."

The call ended and Jim tossed the cell towards Natalia.

"What is it? What's happening?"

"Agency's been tracking the Reapers from their clubhouse. They reached the compound and-" He glanced askance at her and frowned. "You had to blow up their shit, huh?"

Natalia pulled a dramatic face and shrugged. "I was bored?"

"Yeah, well, your boredom has just put us in their crosshairs. Cain is bad enough, you do *not* want to fuck around with one-percenters, Natalia."

"Well, shit." Natalia felt cold clutch at her stomach. She had heard stories about the vengeance of outlaw gangs. It was brutal stuff. The sort of violence that put them in league with Cain, perhaps even above him. Being followed wouldn't be such a miserable thing if it weren't for the dead of night. The roads were empty, and the damage to the sedan was distinctive. The gang could cover plenty of ground and corner them in some back alley.

"How long until reinforcements get to us?"

"Too long." Jim tugged on the steering wheel again, sending the car spinning in another direction. Natalia braced herself this time, and narrowly avoided cracking her head on the window once more. As they moved deeper into the forgotten neighbourhoods of Staten Island, Natalia was certain she could hear the thrum of Harley motors descending upon them like a thousand bees forced from their hive.

They had crossed an invisible barrier dividing the borough from its industrial roots and the new age post-modern developments. Most lots had been abandoned to builders who had wanted to gentrify the hell out of the neighborhood but lost their financing in the crash. Edifices boarded up, half falling over on themselves, as if exhausted by the process of trying to continue standing upright. Half-built novelty pie shops and boutiques that catered to dogs imported from small European nations. It was made all the more sombre in the stillness that accompanied the night.

Bright headlights came from Natalia's side, giving her a moment to say, "Oh, shi-" before a truck that had carted away one of the shipping containers slammed into the side of the car and sent them spinning into the corner of the nearest building.

Natalia felt like her head had lifted from her shoulders in that moment, and she was being pulled from her body and made to watch what was happening through a sheet of mesh. Jim, yelling something as he slashed at the airbag. The front of the car was in two pieces, split cleanly down the center by the building. Somewhere behind them, a horn was blaring.

Jim was looking at her now, speaking, but the sound of crunching metal was echoing through her ears. Jim's hand was on her shoulder now, drawing her back from the daze, yelling at her. "*Kid?*"

Mental check. Fingers and toe responding. Head attached to neck. Her side was bleeding, but that was beginning to feel more like a consistent irritation than a life-threatening impediment. "I'm ok!"

"Then get down!"

Her neck ached as she craned her head backwards, trying to make sense of where they were in relation to the truck that had plowed into them. The back windshield was shattered, and through it she saw Pete's furious face, spiderwebbed in the broken glass; a hundred thousand angry eyes, all resting upon Jim. She saw a hundred thousand sawed-off barrels point towards the car, and saw a hundred thousand fingers squeeze the trigger.

The window shattered, and the air over their heads split as the pieces of buckshot struck the car and decimated what was left of the windshield in front of them. Natalia shrieked and felt Jim push her sideways to the door. She fumbled for the handle as another round peppered the left side of the car. The door was crushed from the impact with the building, but with a strong push from her shoulder, the twisted metal cracked from its hinges and hit the ground.

"Jim!"

"Get to cover!"

Natalia rolled, hit the pavement hard, and felt debris from the crash slash through the jacket and into her back. Superficial cuts at best, and not something she could focus on. But the pain from the stab wound, the punches she had taken from Duncan, and the car wreck, left her feeling as if two sets of metallic hands were driving into the top of her skull in an attempt to rend her brain in two. She could hear Jim struggling through the debris on his side of the crash as Pete loaded another round of buckshot and called his name, summoning him to fight.

Staying as low to the pavement as she could, Natalia scrabbled towards the back of the car. She could feel the reverberations on the ground now; a dozen bikes, racing towards the sound of the crash. Bad enough Pete was there, prepared to drive his fist through Jim's throat; throw in the Road Reapers and they were about to enter the rapids of shit creek. Natalia glanced under the car, and saw Pete's heavy boots hit the ground and begin to stomp across the pavement.

"Jim, watch-"

"*Run!*"

He won't hurt me. He's not after me. Natalia clambered to her feet just in time to see Jim dodge Pete's first wild haymaker. If either of them heard the approaching bikes, they didn't care. This was about settling whatever issues they had been clinging to since the Siege. Natalia crawled over the back end of the car as Jim narrowly missed blocking one of Pete's punches. The hit threw him off his feet, giving Pete an opportunity to pummel Jim's face into wet, sucking paste.

She raced towards them, commanding them to stop, only to jump backwards as Pete threw out a hand to stop her from interfering. But she had to, because Jim's life was in danger and she couldn't fathom burying someone else.

Do something!

In the glint of the cold, winter light Natalia saw a wine bottle, carelessly discarded, miraculously whole. She snatched it up by the neck and knocked the end against the corner of a dumpster before leaping forward and driving the jagged emerald glass into the soft spot between Pete's shoulder blades. He howled and swung around with a clenched fist, landing a hard, angry blow on Natalia's side where she had been so carefully stitched back together. The hit sent her reeling sideways; she slid to the ground and watched the world blur and contort. The pain was palpable, like hot metal on her tongue. She blinked, saw Pete staring in horror; the self-realization of one's worst choices, and the consequences of them laid bare.

Pete was a broken man, and they both knew it.

Natalia blinked again and saw Jim's bloodied fingers sweep the ground for something.

Blink. A thick piece of rebar in his fingers.

Blink. Pete's temple, bloodied and cracked open like an egg.

Blink. Pete fell, eyes still on Natalia, until unconsciousness descended on him and he was out cold.

Jim was struggling to his feet as Natalia pulled her hand away from her side. Her fingers were glossy, like a candy apple at a carnival. She tipped over and felt Jim's arms brace her.

He was speaking now, but his voice seemed far away, through a tin tunnel that narrowed at the end. She was on her feet and walking, but leaning heavily on Jim, allowing herself to be guided away from the wreck, from the unconscious ex-inmate.

"Where-" She wanted to ask where they were going, but as her mouth opened she felt nausea swell up her throat. She vomited pain and acid and the little food she had yet to digest, and still Jim pushed her on, forward. The world tipped out of sync; buildings distorted and rose high above her head, much further than they should have, and the pavement slanted away from beneath her feet then came rushing up towards her face. But she didn't feel herself hit the ground, because the pain was psychological, and what was there for her to feel when her brain could no longer function?

Chapter 10

When she was younger, Natalia used to equate driving through snow at night with going through space in warp drive. Snow and stars, whipping by her at a trillion light years per second; their place in the cosmic universe unknown. She would never be able to return to any of those exact moments and observe them in detail, because by the time she recognized them, they were already a lifetime behind her. Now, lying in the back seat of a hotwired car, Natalia watched the snow from the other side. She saw the flakes as lonely, distant constellations, hanging in the nothingness of night, continuing to exist as she was carried beyond them. She wanted to stop and see each one, to pluck them out of the air and hold them in her hands as they dissolved, and she wanted to imagine what little, insignificant world they might represent.

Jim's voice was hazy and distant in the front seat of the car. He was giving her instructions, telling her what to do next. Whatever. She'd earned a chance to rest, but every time she closed her eyes he would holler something rude at her.

Uncalled for.

She wanted to ask where they were going, but every time she tried to speak she felt as if a piece of her left with her breath. The car lurched to a stop, an abrupt end to warp drive. Natalia rolled from the seat and struck the floor of the car, spreading blood among the empty bags of Doritos and discarded coffee cups. Jim pulled her out, and Natalia tried to find her feet in the snow. It might have been comical if it weren't for the pain and ever-increasing sensation of light-headedness that accompanied her up the sidewalk.

They reached a covered porch, and Jim hammered his fist on a green door with crisp, white trim.

"Quaint," was all Natalia managed to mumble, before the door opened to reveal a woman with a mess of auburn hair and large green eyes, heavy from sleep.

"Jim, wha-" On realizing that Jim was not alone, her features became alert and she stepped aside, making room for Jim to help Natalia into the foyer.

"How bad?" The woman took Natalia's other side without hesitation.

"Bad enough. Can you deal with it?"

They reached the bathroom at the end of the hallway and the woman stepped back, letting Natalia's weight fall onto Jim. She was starting to feel woozy. The woman was speaking but her voice was hollow, far away from Natalia.

"I can try. Get her lying down, on the floor."

Natalia felt her body touch the tiled bathroom floor, but couldn't recall how she could have possibly gotten there. Someone had placed a rolled-up towel under her head.

Kind of them.

The woman had tied back her hair and had replaced her pajamas with seafoam green scrubs. Jim was sitting on the edge of the bathtub; his hands were on Natalia's head, gently patting down her hair.

Sort of nice. Like a family.

"Natalia?" The woman leaned over her, shone a flashlight into her eyes. "Sweetie, we're going to roll you onto your side, ok?"

"Okee dokee," Natalia said with a wheeze. "Sorry 'bout the blood."

"Just keep talking, kid." Jim knelt at her other side, helped the woman peel off the blood-soaked jacket and roll up the hem of her shirt.

"I just cleaned this, you know." The woman laughed anxiously and tossed it into the tub. "Honestly, Jim. She's picking up your bad habits."

"Jim?" Natalia bunched her fist and drew it close to her belly, hoping to dispel the pain that had settled itself deeply into every conceivable part of her body.

"I'm here, kid. Not going anywhere."

"Sorry." She had wanted to say more, but even the single word slurred through her lips. "I was stupid."

"Just hold still, ok? Angel's going to patch you up."

"We really need to take her in to the hospital."

"We can't, not with things the way they are."

"Fine, fine."

"Jim?" Natalia felt his cool hand on her forehead again and exhaled in relief. "I'm gonna just sleep for a couple minutes, 'kay?"

"No way, kid. You need to stay here, ok? Keep talking. Tell me about how much ass you kicked back there."

Natalia smiled.

At the mention of ass-kicking, Jim caught Angel glowering in his direction, and he shrugged helplessly and mouthed "*what?*" as if he didn't realize she didn't approve of him encouraging Natalia to kick anything, let alone someone's deserving ass.

It wasn't long after that that Natalia finally lost consciousness, and Angel sighed deeply in relief.

"This'll be easier if she's out of it. Too much pain."

"How does it look, really?"

Angel discarded a bloodied piece of gauze and gently adjusted the clamp hanging out of Natalia's side. "It'd be easier to tell if we were in a *hospital.*"

"That's not-"

"I know, I know. There's a fresh roll of gauze under the sink. I need you to keep it clear. Jesus, I can't see a thing."

"She lost a lot of blood," Jim said, pulling out the sealed, sterile roll of white medical gauze and peeling it open. The bathroom tiles were crusted red.

"Of course she lost a lot of blood. That's what happens when you have a lacerated liver. We'll keep fluids going into her, and I can probably sneak a bag home from the hospital. Do you know her type?"

"B positive," Jim replied.

Angel smiled to herself and ran the back of her hand over her face, pushing a strand of hair aside. "We'll just hook a tap up to you, then." Jim opened his mouth to protest and Angel rolled her eyes. "I'm kidding Mr. Sensitive. Move that clamp to my right. Hold it there." She reached for a syringe in a black medical bag under the sink, and ordered Jim to fill it with a bag marked *Saline.*

Jim did what he was told. It wasn't so much that Natalia was at risk, but that Angel had the capacity to level him with a single withering look, and he knew better than to test her when she was in *Doctor Mode*.

A few minutes later, she announced that she had found the injury, and began to suture it up. "I'll hit up work for some supplies once we know she's out of the woods. Where the hell did you find her, anyways?"

Jim explained what had happened, from when he had seen Angel the night before to the explosion at the compound and their run-in with Pete. It seemed best to not mention the fact that the Road Reapers were probably on the warpath to find whoever had destroyed their compound. From there he let Angel stitch in silence, watching as she carefully worked around the delicate flesh of an already-scarred young woman. Her dedication to perfection was reassuring, as was her steady hand. Before moving on to lacing the flesh back together, Angel counted her discarded gauze once, then twice, just to be sure. When all her instruments were accounted for, she began to close up Natalia's side.

"You know," Angel said, "when I told you I wanted to meet her, I didn't expect it would happen like this."

"That makes two of us."

"You're right, she does look a fair bit like Amy."

"Thank goodness for that."

Angel snorted, shook her head, and continued stitching in silence. When her handiwork was done, she pulled out her stethoscope and grabbed a watch from the countertop. Jim watched, completely stationary, until Angel removed the stethoscope and leaned back, satisfied.

"Her BP isn't bad, all things considered," Angel said as she stood up. "Get that cuff off her arm. There are washcloths under the sink. Try to clean her up while I go make the spare bed. And scream if anything changes."

Jim located a washcloth and ran it in warm water before gently working away at the grime that covered his ward. Dried blood crusted her arms, dappling her skin in the few pockmarks he recognized from some half-assed explanation about childhood chicken pox. She was bruised; that was a greater concern. There had been no time to get the whole story from Natalia, but the beating was evident on her face thanks to a new array of bruises splotching her cheeks and nose. Her brief mention of Duncan had made Jim sick. He would ask Angel to talk to her about it, whatever had happened.

Pete's actions would undoubtedly linger on her, too. Another figure whose transformation she had witnessed during the most frantic moments of the storm, destroying any lingering hope she might have held about the biker. She was learning the hard way that trust was fickle at the best of times.

There was a handcuff attached to her wrist. It looked as if it had been moved around, worn until her skin was raw and bloody. There was a bolt cutter in the basement. They could deal with it later. Everything could be dealt with later.

She was pale from the blood loss; her old scars shone like swaths of lustrous paint on her skin. Knife wounds, scrapes that had been just deep enough to leave her marked. Some of them would fade. Scars had a habit of doing that when they were left alone and their memories weren't given time to fester. It was the scars that left nothing visible that were a concern; the ones that marked a person's soul, and left their minds diseased from the pain. If Natalia showed any sign of *those* types of scars, Jim had never noticed, nor had he ever bothered to ask. He didn't want to know. He had his own shit to contend with.

"Ok, got her cleaned up?" Angel was at the door. She had changed from her scrubs and was holding a syringe in one hand. "Antibiotics. Let's head any fever off at the pass."

Jim nodded and stood back as Angel pressed the needle tip beneath Natalia's skin. He winced instinctively, and Angel glanced back over her shoulder, one brow arched in unvoiced amusement. "It's not the needle," he protested.

"Oh, *I know*." Angel drew the syringe back and wiped a cotton ball over the small pearl of blood that dappled her skin. "You bring her, ok? Be careful of her stitches."

Jim gathered Natalia in his arms and was surprised to find she weighed so little. She still hadn't recovered much of her weight loss from Alcatraz, although her training had led to the development of some muscle mass. Jim followed Angel down the hall towards the guest room and laid Natalia on the bed.

"Now scoot out of here. I put a pair of my old pajamas through the dryer. She needs out of these wet clothes."

Jim was already halfway out of the room by the time Angel had finished talking. It didn't take her long to put Natalia into the woolly clothes. She had helped nurses do it enough times at the hospital, and Jay, when he was younger.

"Ok, you can come back in."

Angel turned on the bedside lamp, which cast a warm, golden glow that touched Natalia's pale cheeks and made her look remarkably peaceful, given the circumstances. The shadows of bruises that layered her bare skin were more than enough to break the illusion.

"I'll check on her every hour. If she's not improving by this evening then we'll have to take her to the hospital." Jim opened his mouth to protest, but Angel put up her hand. "We can use an assumed name, whatever you need to do. The fact that I had enough supplies to deal with her immediate problems is a miracle in itself. Now you, sir, need to get to bed."

"I should-"

"You won't do her any good being asleep on your feet. You've been awake for nearly twenty-four hours. *Go to bed.*"

Jim cast one more look towards his sleeping ward and then leaned down to kiss Angel on the top of the head. "Thanks."

"Yeah, I want *my* guns back, too."

xXx

Jim awoke with Angel's arm around his waist, and, for a moment, he felt blissfully at peace. Then reality came barreling back and he remembered where he was and why he was there, and just how close they had been to utter devastation the night before.

He carefully shifted off Angel's arm and turned to glance at the bedside table. It was nearly eleven in the morning. He had been asleep for a solid seven hours, and while it wouldn't be enough to bring him back to fighting capacity, it was better than nothing.

"I checked on her an hour ago," Angel murmured from beside him. "She hasn't gone anywhere."

"Sleep for now. I can take it from here."

Angel rolled over. "Make me coffee."

"Can do." He leaned down and kissed her hair, inhaling the scent of flowery shampoo and iodine. Perpetually clean.

Tracking down his emergency clothes in Angel's closet, Jim dressed and felt the ache in his ribs from his beating at Pete's hands. He navigated the crime scene that was the bathroom, as neither of them had the strength to clean it up in the early hours of the morning, and took a hot shower. When he had done a quick self-assessment to determine what damage he had suffered the night before – two cracked ribs and more bruises than he liked to admit – Jim left the bathroom and made his way to the kitchen.

Jayson's bedroom door was cracked open, but his bed was empty. The calendar had him down to work a morning shift at the shop. He'd be home in an hour, maybe two. Hopefully by then Jim would have the place cleaned up.

He made two cups of coffee; he left one next to Angel's side of the bed while the other accompanied him to the guest room.

Natalia had shifted in the night, a good sign. She was still asleep, with her left arm extended above her head, twisted like a serpent. Her hair had pushed away from the back of her neck, and the pink scar of Cain's brand radiated like it was on fire. He could forgive many things; Caulder's cruelty, Steven's death, all the lies, but the brand was different. Marking her in such a way felt distinctly personal to Jim. It indicated a level of desire and control that Cain was attempting to exert over her. Looking at Natalia now, having survived all that was thrown at her, Jim thought it was almost comical how badly Cain was failing.

"Well, kid." He settled on the chair beside her and took a swig of his coffee. "What are we going to do with you, huh?"

He rested a palm flat on her head and winced. A fever. Her forehead was dappled with sweat. Jim took a damp cloth that had been discarded next to the bed and laid it on her forehead.

"Your mom would kill me if she could see you now." Jim leaned back in the chair and sighed. "Steven too, he'd be mad as hell."

Jim knew he ought to call in to the Agency, to tell Meghan where they had ended up. He had been able to call last night, after hotwiring the car and pulling Natalia into the back seat, but knowing that the Reapers were only minutes behind him had kept the conversation short. He had Natalia; they were safe, and going off the grid. That was all any of them needed to know for now. They couldn't stay hidden under Angel's roof forever, especially now that the Twelfth was the only field-rated team stationed at the New York Branch.

Caulder would have no choice but to stop his relentless hunt for Natalia's head and leave them to their work.

Jim sat by Natalia's side, running various scenarios through his head while he tossed his phone from hand to hand, trying to decide whether or not it was worth giving up their location for a few slim pieces of information that might help pull the chaos of the last two days together. More importantly, the mistakes. The missteps. There were so many, and each one helped bring Jim and Natalia here, to a lacerated liver and a fever that wouldn't quit.

He was pissed at her. She had made at least two dumb decisions that he was privy to; she hadn't run when told to at the house, and she had intervened with Pete. Simple choices, easy for someone like Natalia, who was usually contrary for the sake of being contrary. Having the shit kicked out of her would do nothing to send the message home. Lighting up the compound, too; it would make enemies of the wrong people. All things to talk about later, when she was awake.

Jim heard action out in the kitchen and, figuring he was no good to his ward just sitting there, left the guest room to find Angel puttering around, pulling brunch materials from the fridge. The side door opened, and a young man, only four years older than Natalia, was trooping through, knocking snow off his boots and tossing a knitted beanie onto a peg by the door.

"Just in time," Angel said cheerfully, glancing up at her son. "We're about to do brunch. Or...linner?" She glanced at the stovetop clock and nodded, satisfied. "Linner."

"We?" The young man glanced towards the doorway where Jim was leaning and grinned. "Hey, Dad. I thought you weren't coming until this evening."

If he died right then and there, his son, Jayson, would be the only proof that Jim Wilkinson had ever existed. He was the product of a young, foolhardy relationship between Jim and Angela Holloway, born not long after they both graduated from high school. It was probably doomed from the start. They were too young, too naïve. The selfishness of youth easily dismantles even the best intentions. Still, Jim and Angel did their best, and made the adult decision to stop trying to be a couple and simply be parents after a year of living together. They both came from broken homes, and approached the amicable separation with the intensity of hyenas. Every holiday was spent together, expect when Jim was working, and they held Sunday dinners religiously.

Even though his relationship with Angel hadn't worked out, Jim still regarded her as one of his best friends, and on more than one occasion had threatened to dismember a potential suitor, much to her vexation and Jay's amusement.

"Yeah, well. I ran into some...*issues* at work last night, and..." Jim waved a hand around the kitchen, as if it illustrated his point. As far as his son knew, Jim worked in military intelligence collection for the government. It was the sort of description that seemed just complex enough to avoid further investigating. Angel only knew a sliver more; that sometimes this intelligence collecting involved guns and weeks spent away, overseas, out of contact. It was the most Jim could offer either of them without feeling as if was putting them in harm's way.

"Is that why the bathroom looked like a warzone this morning?" Jay asked innocently. Angel glanced at Jim, and Jay added, "And why there's some random chick in the guest room?"

"She's, uh, the kid of some old coworkers." Jim explained, reaching for the coffee pot to refill his mug. "They died and-" He glanced towards Angel, hoping for an out.

"Oh, I told him *all* about your adventures," Angel replied over her shoulder as she began to chop vegetables for a salad. "You nearly gave *me* a heart attack when the news started reporting about Alcatraz, thanks so much."

"Is that her?" Jay asked, eyes wide. "The news said she died there."

"Yeah. It's...complicated." Jim ran a hand through his hair and forced a smile. He had no qualms with his son knowing he had been at Alcatraz; he just hoped Jay was wise enough to keep it to himself. "She doesn't have a lot of fans out there."

"You'd never guess, judging by the state of the bathroom." Angel handed the knife off to her son. "I better go clean it up. Finish off the salad, Jay."

"Yes, ma'am!"

"Jim, you can help me. This is mostly your fault anyways." Angel was joking, but the words still cut deep. He wasn't the sort to cling to guilt; he found it a waste of mental space. But anything Angel said was an exception. She told it like it was, and any criticism, however lighthearted, was cocooned in an element of truth.

Angel was shoving the ruined bathmat into a garbage bag and tossing around Lysol wipes like they were going out of style. How one small girl contained so much blood was beyond Jim.

"What happens next?" Angel asked, working away on the stained grout.

"When she's awake, I'll call the Agency, get someone to come over to debrief her and update us on what's happening. We'll get out of your hair soon enough."

"Oh, Jim. I don't mean it like that. I've got no problem with either of you being here; I just need a timeline, what with the holidays coming up."

"Shit." Jim glanced down at his watch and was surprised to find the date much later than he remembered. Christmas was in ten days. "I didn't even realize-"

"I'm sure you didn't!" Angel laughed and shook her head. "You've been a little busy. Any chance you'll be able to come for Christmas dinner?"

"I, uh, sure, but Natalia-"

"-is obviously welcome," Angel finished. "It'll be her first Christmas without her family, right?"

Jim nodded.

"Well, she can stay as long as she needs. It'll be nice to have an extra couple of x chromosomes to even the playing field." Angel laughed again. "I hope she keeps you on your toes. You could use someone like that."

"That's why I've got you and Jay."

"Someone more *permanent*," Angel replied, tossing a bloodied wipe at him. "I don't get to be there for your big fuck ups, no matter how much I'd like to be, if only to harass you about it later. Someone has to remind you to *feel* things once in a while."

"I feel plenty."

"Nice things, then." Angel turned her back to him and began to scrub the bathtub.

Chapter 11

Jim admittedly hadn't thought much about the holidays. He never did. If it weren't for Angel and Jay insisting on his presence, he probably would have been content to let the time pass unmarked by any formal celebration. To him, December never meant anything pleasant. Snowdrifts covered the dead and dying, unhappy presents to be revealed at the spring melt, when bones jutted from the earth and reminded those who had survived the winter that the cycle of life and death ultimately left no survivors.

He ate with Jay and Angel, then asked his son to go pick up Cooper. Angel had an afternoon shift at the hospital. It would give Jim time to think, plot.

"Her temperature is going down." Angel stepped back from Natalia and wrapped a stethoscope around her neck. "And her lungs sound clear. I'd say she's out of the worst of it. We'll give her another dose of antibiotics when I'm home tonight, just to be safe."

Jim thanked Angel for her care and settled back in his place next to Natalia's bed. It wasn't the first time he had watched over her as she recovered from an injury, much the same way she had looked over him on their return to New York.

Angel's reminder that this would be Natalia's first Christmas without her family was not lost on Jim. She hadn't said a thing about it, perhaps having forgotten herself. But, Jim figured, it was more likely she just didn't *want* to think about it.

I should get her a present. Shit.

Jim couldn't remember if the holiday had ever been a big deal to Amy or Marcus. They were away more often than most operatives, and Jim was certain they had missed their fair share of important occasions. Christmas mornings and school recitals. What sort of childhood disappointments did Natalia keep to herself? More than that, what the fuck did a nearly sixteen year old girl want for a present? Makeup? A pony? Shit. It seemed like he would need Angel's expertise for yet another thing.

Look at the mess you've gotten yourself into now. Jim rubbed the sleep from his eyes. It was only late afternoon, but his entire schedule had become a jumbled mess thanks to the last few days. *Maybe you should take Troy up on his offer.*

But just thinking it made Jim feel wrong. He had no love for Amy Artison, or Marcus, for that matter. They had made his life miserable on multiple fronts. If it hadn't been for Steven, Jim would have never even considered looking after their kid, let alone training her to follow in her parent's footsteps. But Steven, big softy that he was, had taken to the girl, and she to him. Looking after Natalia seemed like the least he could do to repay his friend.

Jim wasn't willing to admit that the girl had endeared herself to him, but as he watched over her and realized how familiar her form had become, how each new imperfection stood out on her flesh, he figured he was too far in to make it out unscathed. Little bruises, new cuts, they built upon each other, slowly stripping away what was left of the old Natalia, leaving a new, hardened figure in their place. The metamorphosis of Natalia was nearing completion. He had been a constant throughout the process and it wouldn't be fair to divest himself from her simply because he was more comfortable in his curmudgeonly ways.

Natalia shifted, rolling so her back was to Jim. The light from the hallway spread across the nape of her neck, illuminating the pink brand that Cain had seared onto her flesh back in Alcatraz. Jim rolled up his left sleeve and pressed two fingers to his own mutilated tattoo. His efforts to distort it in the prison had worked at the time, but now, flesh recovered and ink in place, the image of the infinity symbol was clear once again, if not a little distorted. Natalia had been so perceptive that even marring his own flesh twice over hadn't prevented her from recognizing the connection the symbol made between her, Steven, and Jim.

It all linked them back to Cain.

Jim leaned back in the chair and closed his eyes. Maybe this time it would be different. Maybe December wouldn't take away everything he cared for, and his dreams wouldn't be haunted by women and children swinging from trees. And maybe, just maybe, Natalia wouldn't ask about Christmas.

He was fairly certain he'd need some kind of permit to get her a pony.

xXx

Natalia woke with a start. She had been dreaming. Some nightmare she hadn't been able to shake herself out of, where she was being crushed as the Alcatraz chapel collapsed over her head. Steven was nowhere to be found in it. Just her, alone, as hunks of rubble clattered down around her. She kept ducking, hoping she might be spared a killing blow to the temple. But the earth swelled under her feet, and she was tossed to the chapel floor just as the last support beam snapped free and dropped.

Natalia bolted, grabbed violently for her own neck, and felt a heavy hand press against her shoulder.

"It's fine. You're safe. *You're safe, kid.*"

Even now, Jim's clear and concise annoyance was more than enough to calm her. A man perpetually put off by everything she did and said; the consistency was reassuring, if nothing else.

Her side ached, and as her vision cleared, she reached down with one hand to gently probe her wound. It was bandaged carefully, with thick rolls of gauze stretching across her midsection, wrapping around her like a brace. A chair creaked beside her and she craned her head to one side. Jim was staring at her, arms crossed defensively.

I'm about to get a lecture.

Natalia opened her mouth to speak first, but Jim held up a hand to silence her and exhaled slowly through gritted teeth. "No. No excuses. You wanted to learn how to fight, how to kill, and now you know. Now you're a part of this life. That means you follow the rules. When I say run, you *run*. When someone else tells you to run, you fucking run. You follow the rules because they are what keep you alive."

"You – I couldn't just let you *die*." Her voice cracked, and she felt her own annoyance rise. She had only just woken up. Was now *really* the best time to have this conversation? "Pete would have killed you."

"That isn't your problem."

"Uh, I think it sort of is." She wanted to be angry, to give him hell for berating her less than three minutes after she woke up. She wanted to tell him that he couldn't pretend they weren't important to each other in some grand, cosmic scheme. She wanted to tell Jim he was acting like an *ass*. "I'm not going to let someone else die for me."

Jim was already stomping out of the bedroom; if he heard, he gave no sign of caring about her opinion.

Natalia bit the inside of her cheek to still the sensation of failure rolling through her stomach like a hurricane. She felt ashamed, foolish. Not just because it had nearly cost her what little life she had left, but because Jim was pissed off at her and she *knew* he was right. She hadn't followed his rules, and it had brought her perilously close to the edge of disaster.

It was a struggle to roll over without putting any pressure on her side. The slightest twitch in the wrong direction set an agonizing current through her body, causing her to spasm upright in the bed. The blood drained from her face and she swallowed her nausea.

"Whoa, no." A woman standing at the door of the bedroom brushed by Jim, flashing him a dagger-like stare as she knelt next to Natalia. Jim appeared apathetic. "You ok?"

Natalia nodded quickly and gulped for air.

"Going to throw up?"

Natalia nodded again and the woman barked at Jim to bring the garbage can from the bathroom. A moment later it was at her feet, and Natalia retched. There wasn't much to leave her save for several days worth of undiluted stomach acid. When she was done heaving, Natalia felt marginally better and sheepishly accepted a damp cloth from the woman.

"Sorry," Natalia said, wiping her face.

"I've seen a lot worse in my time. Think you're up to standing?"

With some manoeuvring, and considerable assistance from the stranger, Natalia navigated the small hallway, through a door, and into a quaint kitchen painted robin's egg blue, with a sloped ceiling. It looked like something from a calendar that featured British cottages and textiles with floral prints.

Natalia settled on a tall stool at the island in the middle of the room, and the woman began to fuss around her. In the natural winter light streaming in from the windows, Natalia had a better look at the woman. She was Jim's age, but where he had frown lines, her face was creased with laughter. She looked serious in her own way, but even as she pulled an expansive medical kit from a cupboard, Natalia could tell this woman was the sort of healer that patients were drawn towards.

From behind them, Jim announced that he was going out for a smoke and disappeared to the front of the house.

"One or both of us is in trouble," the woman said with a knowing smile. "What did *you* do?"

Natalia shrugged half-heartedly as the woman, without a word, lifted the hem of her shirt and began to unwrap the bandage. "Didn't let him get turned into putty."

"Shame," the woman said with a cheeky grin. "He could use some softening up." The last of the bandage fell away and the woman grabbed a pair of individually wrapped latex gloves from the medical kit. After they were in place, she began to poke around the incision.

"You've avoided infection, thank goodness. I'll give you one last round of antibiotics before we're done, just to be sure. Let me just put a smaller bandage on..." The woman kept working and Natalia glanced around the kitchen. The house they were in had to be old. The ceilings were slung low and the walls were proper bubbled plaster. All the windows were double-paned glass and looked like they could withstand a hurricane.

"Now." The woman straightened up and pulled out a stethoscope from a drawer. "Let's just make sure your lungs are clear."

Natalia followed her instructions. Deep breath in, hold it, release slowly. Rinse and repeat over and over until the woman stepped back, draped the stethoscope around her neck and nodding approvingly. "Your lungs are clear too. Amazing. I was sure you were going to end up with pneumonia, but your fever has been going down. I'd say you're in the clear, Natalia."

"But, um, who-"

"Oh god, I'm so rude. Sorry!" The woman offered Natalia her hand. "Angela Holloway, call me Angel. I'm a doctor," she added hastily. "I don't get some wild kick out of poking and prodding people."

"Oh, uh." Natalia smiled and nodded. "I remember you from last night."

"Two nights ago, missy. You've been asleep a while. Jim's told me all about you. Oh, before I forget..." She leaned over the opposite end of the counter and plucked Steven's jacket from the opposing stool. "That's the second time I've had to clean it in as many days. See if you can't keep it dry this time, ok?"

"Thank you." With some difficulty, Natalia managed to pull the coat over her pajamas, which she just realized she was wearing. "So, um, I don't mean to be rude but-"

"Where are you, why are you here, and how does any of this relate to Mr. Crabby outside getting lung cancer?" Angel moved towards the stove, plucked an old-fashioned teakettle from a burner, and began to fill it from the tap.

"Something like that."

"I'm an old friend of Jim's. This is my home, to be more exact, my kitchen." She lifted the kettle, and gave it a little shake, and grinned. "This is my kettle. That is my fridge. That Spiderman mug is my son's, although he'll deny it if you ask him."

Natalia smiled. She liked Angel.

Before the conversation could continue, the side door into the kitchen banged open and a young man, only a few years older than Natalia, struggled through the door, dragging a fresh-cut fir tree behind him.

"Oh good," Angel said wryly, "I was just saying I needed to clean up the entire house again."

"You're the one who always wants a real one." He pulled off his gloves, spied Natalia, and gave her a nod. He looked familiar, Angel's eyes certainly, but there was something else she couldn't place. "Hey, there. I'm Jay. I, uh..." He glanced at Angel. "Where's Dad?"

"Your father is on the porch, cutting another couple months off his life. Just keep the tree outside for now. Can you watch the kettle; it's for tea. I have to go talk to him."

Natalia's head was spinning. She had received a handful of information that had blown her entire world wide open. Jim had a son, a family. People he had never mentioned before. People who were probably capable of dealing with him for extended periods, and, indeed, might even subject themselves to him for joy. There were no pictures in his house, no indication that anyone cared about him or that he cared about anyone in return.

Natalia was lost in her thoughts when Cooper came bounding through the kitchen door, covered in snow, and wiggled down in front of Natalia's stool. She eased herself to the floor and knelt to greet him. He was happy to see her.

At least someone is.

He whined, nudged at her side gently with his nose, as if to ask, "What the hell have you been doing?"

"I'm ok, buddy." She had lost sight of him in the battle at the house. He seemed to have survived unscathed.

"He likes you," Jay said.

"You sound surprised." Natalia ruffled Cooper's head and stood up to face Jay.

"It is my dad's dog, so..." He drew out the last vowel and Natalia grinned.

"That's a good point." She shifted from one foot to the other and said, a little more slowly, "I had no idea about...well, any of this. Jim never mentioned having a family." Even as the words came out of her mouth, Natalia realized how it sounded. She blushed slightly, lowered her eyes, and tried to stammer an explanation before Jay jumped in.

"Oh, I know. Believe me. I get it. My dad is a private, *private* sort of guy. I think he likes to keep his personal life and his work life separate. Which would make you an anomaly."

"Not the worst thing I've been called," Natalia said. It was difficult to comprehend. She assumed that Jim had brought her here because there was no other option. Perhaps that was why he was so upset with her, over the clashing of two worlds that he had spent so much time trying to keep divided.

Not my fault, Natalia decided as she watched Jay from the corner of her eye. She could see the similarities between father and son. A half-smirk on Jay's lips, the same as Jim. The only difference being that Jay seemed to genuinely be in a pleasant mood, and Jim wore his own smile as a protective barrier against the rest of the world. Natalia had found herself adopting it too, but she wore hers as neither a projection of joy or a shield. It seemed to her to show a sort of slyness she wanted to evoke to those around her.

Be wary of me. I'm not what you think.

Kathleen Sawisky

Chapter 12

Jim knew he was being too harsh with Natalia. He was annoyed, because Steven had given his life to protect her, but Jim wasn't keen on doing the same, and by standing her ground, she had risked her neck. The harshness was a necessity. It was the only thing he could think of to reinforce the wall between them. It was for the best, to protect both of them from their social malfunctions and their emotional failures.

Out on the front porch, Jim lit up a smoke and inhaled deeply, until the caustic fumes were deep inside his lungs, nibbling away at the edges of his plural membrane. Another step closer to death. He wasn't smoking as much these days, mostly out of necessity. The health of agents was constantly under scrutiny, and he didn't need anyone telling him his lung capacity wasn't up to snuff. Still, every so often he needed that instant cool-down. There was something cathartic about the process of lighting up a cigarette and watching it burn into nothing.

He didn't want to go back inside. Inside meant talking to Natalia and explaining why he never told her about Angel or Jay or any of it. Inside meant seeing the guilt written on her face and having to apologize for what he said or, worse, not said. A *thank you* might have been in order, but that would only encourage her to disobey again, and they couldn't afford that.

The front door opened and Angel stepped through. She had pulled a shawl over her shoulders, but it was hardly useful in blocking out the chill of the December air. She would have to go in soon, and she would drag him along with her.

"Got another?" she asked.

"You don't smoke."

"No," she agreed. "Maybe I want to see what all the fuss is about."

"It's not worth it." But Jim pulled the pack from his jacket pocket all the same. Before he could react, Angel had snatched it out of his hand and thrown it as far as she could towards the street. Half a second later, it was run over by a truck.

"That seemed...unnecessary."

"You promised me you'd stop," Angel noted sourly.

"I also promised I wouldn't get shot again, and that's happened a couple times."

"I don't want to hear about it. I don't want *our son* hearing about it. And I also don't want Natalia hearing about it, but I suppose she doesn't have much choice in the matter."

"What's eating you, Angel?"

"Do you always treat her like that?"

"Like what?" Jim knew where this was going, but figured he was better off playing ignorant for a few moments longer.

"Like she's a burden on you. Shit, when you brought her here you looked like a panicked-"

"Like a *what*, Angel?"

She finished quietly, "Like a panicked father. I know she's only your ward, but she's also *Amy's daughter*, and the fact that you're looking after her has got to mean something to you. Saying those *awful* things, Jim, it's not good for her. It's not *healthy*."

Jim sighed and rubbed his tired eyed. "Angel..."

But she was on a roll, because try as she might, Angela Holloway could never stop being a mother or a doctor – both something Natalia was in desperate need of. Angel leaned on the banister of the porch, exhaling small orbs of hot breath. "You said she saw someone from Alcatraz?"

Jim nodded. "Two of them."

"Are you going to talk to her about it?"

Jim cocked his head and frowned. "What the hell would I say?"

"You could ask her how she's feeling after seeing people from a *goddamn prison* that she was trapped in. It's a fairly inspiring conversation piece."

She was right about that.

"There's a lot of...*history* there. I don't know if I'm the best one to talk to her about it."

"Like it or not, you're the *only* person for that conversation. Come on, Jim." She clapped him on the shoulder and offered a bright smile that hit him in right in the stomach, a reminder that not all was lost. There was still some beauty in the world. "Let's go make sure our son isn't burning down the kitchen."

xXx

Natalia had followed Jay into the dining room with a hot cup of tea clutched between her palms. They sat and chatted about this and that; remarkably innocuous details of their lives that might have otherwise gone unobserved if not for a precise question asked at the right time. She learned he was in his first year of trade school, studying to be a mechanic. She learned that Angel had gotten pregnant in her last year of high school, and while it didn't work out between her and Jim, he had remained a devoted father, or at least the best he be could while saving the world. She also learned that Jay only knew a small fraction of what Jim got up to.

Within a half hour Angel had joined them, whispering to Natalia as she passed that Jim's tempered had cooled somewhat and he had gone to call the Agency to relay what had happened over the last forty-eight hours. Natalia was surprised to hear that he had been keeping them under the radar for so long. If he hadn't contacted anyone to tell them that she was alive, it was probably because he genuinely didn't trust those in power or their intentions. She could hardly blame him.

Angel began to casually interrogate Natalia about her life. Even with her basic training, Natalia could see Angel making mental notes about favourite pastimes and subjects in school. It was becoming increasingly clear to Natalia and, she suspected, to Jay, that her residence in the small house might be extended through the holiday season. Angel, it seemed, planned on integrating Natalia fully into their lives before the end of the week.

Eventually Jim reappeared in the dining room. Whatever conversation had taken place had not ended the way he was hoping. Angel was quick to her feet, clearing away empty mugs of tea and a plate of jelly cookies that no one had touched. With a pointed look from his mother, Jay grabbed his own mug, and together they left the dining room.

"We've been told to stay put," Jim announced, settling at the head of the table and unconsciously pushing his phone between his hands. "According to Meghan, Caulder's been recalled to Washington to answer to the higher ups. That's one less thing to worry about. *But,*" he added swiftly, "the Road Reapers are raising hell about their compound going up in smoke, and they're looking for answers."

"Oh," Natalia said.

"Yeah, so what have we learned from this?"

"I... shouldn't set things on fire?"

"Unless you own them, right."

Natalia let a smile break across her face. If Jim was cracking witticisms, it meant his wrath had been eased and they could return to their normally scheduled programming.

"The three trucks that you saw leaving the compound headed north, south, and west. CCTV couldn't track them, but we know one of them doubled back. Aurora's people are seeing if they can track plates to find out where they're heading. That just leaves-"

"Cain," Natalia finished.

Jim nodded. "He hasn't been spotted in the city yet. That's good. We've got to figure he's close by though. Orders from Meghan are clear. We stay off the street until cooler heads prevail. The minute you're in fighting condition, I'm supposed to teach you, and I quote, 'how to not die.'"

"Oh yes," Natalia drawled. "Let's teach me that."

Jim nodded brusquely and pushed the chair back. Natalia wondered if he might say something, perhaps berate her further for not listening to him when push came to shove. Instead, Jim stood up, turned around, and walked away, leaving Natalia alone in a home she knew nothing about, surrounded by people who had been strangers mere hours earlier.

"Yup," Natalia said, leaning down and rubbing Cooper's ears, "this seems about right."

Part II

Chapter 13

The bird died a few days after landing on the ledge of the roof, finally succumbing to its wounds, dehydration, and hunger. Kyle was glad its suffering was over. Hours earlier a murder of crows had descended towards the house, flitting along the branches of the old burnt trees, and, perhaps hearing the weakened cries of the small creature on the roof, flocked to it and began to peck at its belly.

The boy slammed his fists against the wooden boards, hoping to draw the attention of the crows away from the bird that was, credit given where credit was due, fighting valiantly against its attackers. Three or four of the crows zipped away from the bird and began to shove their beaks between the boards, pecking fruitlessly at the boy as he stumbled backwards, into the arms of the Tall Man. Hearing the cries of the poor creature on the other side, the boy couldn't help himself. He turned and buried his head in the Tall Man's jacket and began to cry. He wailed that he wanted to go home, and the Tall Man stroked his hair and begged him to be silent.

Kyle finally worried himself into a deep sleep, and did not see the Tall Man approach the boarded window, hissing through his teeth, forcing the crows to scatter and leave the half-demolished corpse of the bird lying listlessly on the roof. He would have to do something about it, or else move the boy, but even as he considered his options, the sky opened up and the snow began to fall in thick, relentless drifts, covering what was left of the crow's meal.

xXx

Days in Angel Holloway's house passed slowly. It wasn't from lack of activity. There was Christmas baking to be done, and decorations to set up. Lengths of tinsel that Cooper would snag in his jaw and fling about the house as if to proclaim that he was helping. Angel involved Natalia in all of it, and wouldn't hear any protesting. In the evenings, they would play board games, or watch old holiday classics. *The Muppet Christmas Carol,* Gonzo reciting Dickens, and Rizzo bemoaning the loss of jelly beans. Natalia had watched it last year by herself, the rest of the family having chosen to eschew that particular tradition. Her parents were busy and Beth had been trying to woo someone over text using only emoticons and abbreviations. Small, invisible rifts that were marking the breakdown of their family unit. By the time anyone bothered to join her, Ebenezer Scrooge was already throwing himself at the base of his tombstone, bemoaning his fate.

Angel made popcorn and hot cocoa. Natalia was certain she had entered an alternate reality.

Jim kept to himself, opting to spend his evenings sitting on the front porch to smoke or, during the cold snap, in the living room with his attention on the street. He was a more effective guard dog than Cooper, and Natalia reckoned he wouldn't have a problem with sinking his teeth into the neck of anyone who came near his family.

He had barely said two sentences to her since offering her a brief overview of their situation. That suited Natalia fine.

Three days before Christmas, Natalia took Cooper into the backyard to give him a bit of exercise. Jim was back there, smoking on the back step.

"You're the worst," Natalia declared, sitting down next to him. "Angel will kill you."

"She can try," Jim shrugged. "It's not every day."

"It shouldn't be *any day.*"

"All right, all right," he grunted and flicked the cigarette onto the step, smothering it under his boot heel. "Better?"

Natalia didn't say anything, choosing instead to ruffle Cooper's head as he brought over a neon tennis ball that he had dug up from the snow.

"What's on your mind?" Jim asked.

Natalia inhaled sharply, steadying herself to tell Jim how much his words had hurt her. But she faltered, because the last thing she wanted was a battle that she knew was already lost. She lied. "It's just weird, seeing you in this totally different environment. I'm used to it being all murder and guns. Big explosions." She spread her fingers wide and moved her hands apart. "Boom."

He picked up a stick and tossed it across the yard. Cooper looked at him, unimpressed by the feeble effort on Jim's part. "It's not usually like this. I'm just not eager to be caught with my pants down."

"You think there's a big risk out there?"

"Big enough," Jim said. "The Reapers aren't the sort to just give up, disappear. You ruined a warehouse and a few of their bikes."

"I'm beginning to think I should apologize for that."

Jim stared at her, expectantly, then said, "You're not going to-"

Natalia joined in and mimicked his words. "I'm not going to apologize for that."

He smirked and nodded. "Can't ask you to. Either way, I think we need to be on our guard."

"You don't want to be here, right?" Natalia asked. She looked over her shoulder; Angel was in the kitchen, holding out a dishtowel to Jay, as if to blatantly suggest the necessity of him picking it up and doing something useful. "You're worried about them."

Jim tipped his head, as if examining her for a hidden microphone. "Sure," he said evenly. "Who wouldn't be? They've gone this long without being impacted by the job. I'd like to keep it that way."

"Decent of you," Natalia said. "I can think of a few people who should have taken a page out of your book."

Jim frowned and Natalia winced. They didn't talk about her parents. They didn't talk about Steven. They didn't talk about anything of substance unless it had to do with the many ways she could kill a man with a small kitchen implement. Bludgeoning wasn't considered a *real* choice, either. Too easy, he had said.

"You need to talk about it?"

"Nope." It wasn't just that she didn't want to talk about it. It was the fact that Jim approached every conversation with the enthusiasm of a politician kissing his hundredth baby for the day. He always seemed resigned to the fact that it had to happen, but he wasn't keen on the journey he would have to take to get there. Natalia wasn't ready to discuss her feelings with the analytical approach of a robot.

"Jim, can I ask you something?"

He grunted a response that she took as *yes*. Without a cigarette between his teeth, Jim didn't seem to know what to do with himself.

"What happened with Cain? I know you don't want to talk about it, neither did Steven. I want to know why he's so damn *angry*."

"Aw shit, kid." Jim ran a hand through his scraggily hair and rubbed his face. He was getting a solid layer of scruff, and it gave him a dejected, hobo-like air. "We, no, *I*. *I* fucked up. I was team lead and I didn't see the signs when I should have. He snapped, and became the monster." Jim looked at her with a steady gaze. "He became *your* monster."

"That doesn't answer my question."

"I know," Jim said matter-of-factly, "but it'll have to do for now."

"Those pictures, the ones I saw in Alcatraz. Jim, they were *horrible*."

"I know, I was there."

"Do you dream of them?" She didn't have to clarify what she meant. Did he still dream of bodies swaying in apple trees, seconds before they went up in flames? Did he still smell the charcoal flesh and the roasted apples? Yes. Everything he did or said, or experienced was bound in those memories. For ten years, they had been inescapable, and in another ten years... Well, Jim figured he wouldn't have to deal with them for another decade. Not if he had any say in it.

He didn't speak immediately, choosing instead to let the lacuna between question and answer suggest what he was certainly Natalia already knew. "Every night," he said at last. "Every single goddamned night."

"I dream of Steven, and Beth." Natalia drew a toe through the snow, leaving an icy crevasse. "Never anything real. But I see them." And how true it was. If Jim knew how to respond, he chose to say nothing. Natalia looked up towards him, eyes wide. "I miss them."

"I know." He placed a hand on her shoulder and Natalia shuddered. Jim retracted sharply, moved his cigarette from one hand to the other, before finally saying, "I need to know. I should have asked sooner but, well, shit." He turned his head, spat. "What went down with Duncan – did he hurt you? Did he-"

"Angel already asked." Natalia didn't want Jim to finish the sentence any more than he did. "No, he got the drop on me, tried to beat me senseless. But he didn't...*do* anything."

Natalia saw the slight heave in Jim's shoulders, as if a weight had been lifted. "You need to talk about it?"

"No, not right now." Natalia stood up, prodded her side with a finger, and winced. "Maybe some other time."

Tipping his head to one side, Jim conceded the point. "Don't tell Angel I was smoking."

"Sure, but you owe me."

"What do you want?"

She glanced back, looked towards the kitchen window where Jay and Angel were talking. "Nothing anyone can give me."

Chapter 14

Natalia heard the low rumble in her dreams before she recognized it in the waking world. An earthquake, rocking her memories of Steven's sleeping frame. The earth splitting open and spiders spilling out of the cleft that would devour them all.

She woke with a start to the sound of engines revving and threw off her bed cover, instincts kicking into high gear. Natalia rarely slept with pajamas on anymore; always pants, shirt, clothes that required little addition to make it look as if she were an ordinary girl in the middle of the day. Socks already on her feet, she reached for Steven's jacket and shoved her feet into the new sneakers that Jay had brought her. Rainbow shoelaces. He thought she could use something bright in her life.

Natalia flung open her bedroom door and made a beeline for the living room. Jim was already there, dressed, leaning against the front window, staring into the night.

"Jim-"

"I hear them." He looked back at Natalia and, for the first time, she saw that she had mistaken his coarseness for something else; defense, to avoid his fear. There was nowhere to hide it now, no way to placate the surging emotions. He was afraid. His two worlds had unexpectedly collided and created a spark that had just been buffeted into a flame.

"Go wake up Jay. I'll keep watch," Natalia said, reaching inside the jacket, pulling out her SIG Sauer, and double-checking the magazine. It was full, clean, like new. Jim had spent the previous evening quizzing her on the parts of the gun and showing her how to take it apart and clean it. In true Jim fashion, he made her put it back together again, timing her until she had it down to mere seconds. As with everything he taught her, it seemed as if that knowledge was coming in handy much sooner than either of them had anticipated it might.

Jim canvassed the street, searching for the ostensible threat that was preparing to launch itself out of the gloom and claw its way into his life.

"*Go,*" Natalia hissed, pushing him lightly on the shoulder.

Jim strode back into the belly of the house, whistling for Cooper as he went. He was hollering instructions, ordering his son out of bed, opening the back door so Cooper could run free. Whatever was coming, it was no place for a pet. Angel was working a night shift at the hospital, thank goodness. One less person to worry about. Natalia inhaled sharply, pressed herself against the glass, and watched the road. Two days until Christmas. They had done remarkably well, given the circumstances. Natalia had almost begun to feel *normal.* But it was inevitable they would return to their ways: Jim, the inveterate curmudgeon, and Natalia, the walking warhead.

She could hear Jay complaining loudly as Jim pulled him forcefully into the foyer and began tossing jacket and shoes at his son.

"Where're we going?" Jay asked, rubbing sleep from his eyes.

"Out. Now. Go get your mom from the hospital." Jim pressed a folded letter into Jay's hands. Instructions. Maybe even an explanation. Outside wind picked up a drift of snow, clearing away the drifts long enough for Natalia to catch sight of a man sitting in a parked car across the street.

An angry, withered face stared back. Eaten by fire on one side, a twisted mess of weeping wounds and black stitches.

Jay was saying goodbye to her, but she ignored him. She knew that face.

"Natalia, we need to go. We've got to try and take them off Jay's trail."

The back door slammed, and a thought jostled Natalia's memory, tipping off a shelf where she had laid it to rest, spilling out.

Like oil. Like spilled oil.

"Shit!" She bolted backwards towards the door and flung it open as Jay disappeared behind the backyard fence where his truck was parked in the alley. "Jay!" she screamed, because they were already discovered. There was no time for subtlety. "Jay! Stop!"

Natalia threw open the back gate as Jay's key slipped into the lock. He paused, seeing her approaching, and stepped back from the truck. An instant later she plowed into him, driving the young man into a snow bank. Engines revved down the alley, headlights flaring like lighthouse beacons, trying to draw them out of the shadows. Jay struggled in Natalia's grip, but she pressed her hand over his mouth.

"Shut up!" she hissed. The bikes drove closer, and Natalia wedged herself deeper into the snow bank, taking Jay with her.

Muttered voices, ragged from years of smoking the most caustic cigarettes they could find. She wondered where Monster Mask had gone. What had Pete called him? Meloy. Remember that. Remember, because someone, somewhere, wants to know that. Even as the bikes drew closer, kicking up snow and clods of frozen earth, Natalia tried to process it all. Pete hadn't told the Reapers about using the compound, but Meloy had been there. Was he playing both sides of the field? Trying to take advantage of Cain and the Reapers alike? It would be stupid of him.

Engines rumbled and voices conferred, and Natalia wondered what they were thinking. Would they storm the house? Destroy the years of work Angel had put into creating something secure and beautiful for her son? Would they move on, assuming their prey had already escaped?

Gunfire shattered the silence. Glass breaking, metal and tires punctured. And then fire. A ball of it flaring into the sky. Even hidden in the snow bank Natalia could feel the heat against the top of her head as Jay's truck exploded, shrapnel cutting through the night, smashing windows of nearby garages and homes. As quickly as they swarmed, the bikes continued down the alley, back into the night, leaving behind only the smouldering remains of Jay's truck flickering like an overly enthusiastic bonfire. Through the flames, Natalia could see Jim, still in the backyard, tucked into the shadows, watching in horror. She lifted one hand, a meager thumbs-up, and pulled Jay out of the snow

They stumbled across the alley and met Jim next to the flaming wreckage of the truck. In a different light, with a different perspective, it might have seemed pleasant, could have almost passed for *festive*. Sirens were already beginning to wail in the distance.

"What...the fuck." Jay stared at what was previously his truck, dismayed.

"We need to get to Angel," Jim said, looking at Natalia. He didn't say it, but she could read his expression clear enough.

"Mom took the car, so," Jay gestured feebly at the remains of his truck.

"Kid?"

Natalia glanced behind her shoulder to the carport of a neighbour, three houses down. "Right," she said. "I'm on it."

"Are you going to," Jay turned to his father "is she going to hotwire a car? Why didn't you ever teach me to hotwire a car?"

"Because I wanted my child to grow up *not* a criminal." Jim caught him by the collar and pushed him past the wreck. "Go to the cellar, *outside* entrance. I've got a black duffle bag stashed down there. Go get it."

"Dad-"

"*Now*, Jay."

Cooper whined at his feet. Leaning down, he brought his face close to the beast and let the dog nuzzle him worriedly in the neck.

"Go on, boy. Go for a walk."

Cooper turned nervously in a circle, whined. From down the alley Jim could hear an engine start.

"Coop, *go!*" He kicked a skiff of snow at the dog. It was a shock, more than enough to send Cooper loping to the open gate at the back of the alley and disappear into the darkness. He would go to one of the neighbour's houses, or be picked up by animal control. Either way he would be safe.

A car pulled rudely out of the parking spot and reversed down the alley. Jim had been teaching Natalia to drive out of necessity, for a moment just like this. She had complained that he had no patience with her, so Angel had volunteered to take her out to practice, assuming they could have the necessary legal papers forged. They never had a chance to start.

Natalia put the car into park and climbed across into the passenger seat as Jay reappeared with the bag hoisted over his shoulder. Jim pushed him into the back seat, tossed the bag in after him, and slid into the driver's seat.

Jim saw Natalia glance at Jay in the rear view and then catch his own eyes. "I saw someone out there on the street," she said, more to Jim than to Jay. "I thought..." She didn't need to finish her sentence. Whatever she thought was accurate. Vehicles didn't just go up in flames like Jay's truck had unless they were encouraged to.

"Jay, call your mom. We're going to pick her up. Natalia, eyes open. You get a weird feeling, you let me know."

The teens complied, Jay fumbling with his cell phone and Natalia reverting to the partially honed sense of danger that Jim had been coaching her on. He knew he had trained her well, and it was strongly credited to instincts she probably didn't realize she possessed. At the end of the day, she was born and bred for this job, and, on some intrinsic level, she probably understood that. That small, insignificant fact scared Jim more than anything. He imagined the dreams Amy and Marcus had for their daughter. How they hoped she would succeed, go to university, be a scholar. She would have researched something important, world-altering.

Yes, Natalia might have changed the world if she had never been taught how to shoot a gun.

And what aspirations did Jim have for Jayson? Easy. He had prayed that his son would never be privy to this life, and yet here they were, fleeing through the darkness, two days before Christmas, in a car that had been hotwired by an almost sixteen-year-old girl. Jim would need other dreams for his son now, but later, when this was over.

"Dad-" Jim glanced towards the rear view. Jay's eyes were large as dinner plates. "She's not picking up."

"You know where she was tonight?"

"Working emerge, I think."

Jim adjusted his mental compass and made a left turn at the next intersection. Natalia was still on high alert, gun placed carefully in her lap, one hand on the grip while her other furiously texted. There was no need to ask any questions or direct her to act. Their time on the road had been as much about survival as it had been teaching her to throw a punch, something she still wasn't very good at.

Focus on the road. Focus.

Meghan would handle the important things on the Agency's end. The right people would be notified, the right resources would be allocated. The only task Jim and Natalia would be assigned at this stage was survival.

Jay almost... Jesus, if Natalia hadn't-

No safe houses. It was too much of a risk. They would have to move at least three vehicles before they settled on one they could trust. The Agency could start looking into the movements of the Reapers. By then Jay and Angel would be long gone. Jim had already decided on that. There was too much risk to them. No, Jim had to meet the gang head on, and he would bring Natalia to sweeten the deal.

Steady there, you. Starting to sound like the person you left in Alcatraz.

The problem, as Jim saw it, was this: There was no way to know if the Reapers were acting of their own volition, stalking and pursuing Natalia and Jim because she had gotten a little overenthusiastic with some gasoline and a lighter, or if they were acting under the orders of a higher power; someone like Cain. Jim doubted the latter. Pete had always talked about the Reapers appreciating their independence. They never associated themselves with other one-percenters unless it was necessary, and those relationships were short lived.

That meant that Jim and Natalia had to fight a war on two fronts: The Reapers and Cain. Now, with the bikers on his heels, already poisoning the water that his family sipped from, Jim's priorities had been altered. Cain could wait; he was a patient man, after all. The Reapers? They shredded their way through darkness, leaving chaos in their wake. They wanted a fight, and Jim would find a way to bring it to them.

Chapter 15

"You bitch!" Alfred Jennings was frothing at the mouth, lurching about on the gurney, spouting racial epithets that Angel hadn't considered might be used against her half Welsh, quarter Scottish, quarter German ancestry. She wanted to be offended, just because she was sure *someone* ought to be, but she couldn't bring herself to care much for the ravings of a drunk who was gagging for another fix.

"Mr. Jennings, the reason you are tied down is because we caught you drinking our hand sanitizer. When we took that away, you started to suck on alcohol swabs, which, by the way, we will be charging you for. Your best bet at this point would be to cut your losses and give your liver a breather."

She turned away before Jennings had a chance to spout another round of verbal abuse at her. The nurse behind her paled.

"He's harmless. Brainless, but harmless." Angel patted the nurse on the shoulder. "Keep an eye on him. Security is right outside the door if you need them. We'll check his levels in another hour. Don't let him out of the restraints."

"Sure thing, Angie."

Outside, the emergency room was buzzing. Pre-Christmas misery had set in and the drunks were out in droves, trying to forget ex-wives and lost lovers who wouldn't return phone calls at this time of year, or at any other, for that matter. Angel couldn't wait to go home.

As she filled in the update on Jennings, her mind kept drifting back towards what was waiting for her. A son, loyal and kind, and an ex-lover who gave her every ounce of support she could ask for. And her very own Little Orphan Annie.

She had known Amy Artison from way back when, Marcus, too, and while they had always seemed a little too high and mighty to her, Angel couldn't help but feel for the loss Natalia was suffering. She wasn't dealing with it, that much was clear. Jim, too, wasn't dealing with it well. Angel had never worried about the place Amy Artison had in Jim's heart. They were always doomed to fail.

Jim and Angel, on the other hand? They were destined to succeed as friends and parents, nothing more. She could sleep beside him or smack him up the side of the head for his ignorance and not worry about offending his delicate male sensibilities. Natalia's presence changed that. Was it upsetting the balance? No. But it added an element that Angel wasn't sure about. She was already fond of the girl; perhaps overly so. It wasn't her place to be a mother to Natalia, though. Not without knowing how Jim felt about the whole situation first.

Angel shook her head and pushed the thought from her mind. Natalia wasn't her child to raise.

There was a commotion down the hall, but she ignored it. Security was always tight around Christmas. All the sad souls came out of the woodwork to hoist their misery and complaints upon everyone else. Just another-

Gunshot.

Angel dropped fast, head snapping in the direction of the noise. Men, burly, bearded, wearing stained leather jackets and grim expressions. Brandishing guns and pointing at...her? Angel scrambled to the other side of the counter just as another gunshot rang through the hallways, striking a nearby orderly in the arm.

What the fuck, what the fuck-

Then another gunshot, this time closer. A call and response, like an old camp song. Angel looked up to the opposite end of the hall and saw Natalia standing there, all five-foot-five of her, small and intimidating, holding a gun. She was stretching her hand out towards Angel, beckoning her forward.

"We have to go!"

"Natalia, what-" Angel reached out and was dragged around the corner, wrist in vice-like grip of the girl. Orphan Annie, she was not.

"I've got her!" Natalia yelled. At the end of the hall Angel could see Jim and Jay running frantically towards the. Why was her son only in his pajamas? Jim looked like he was one broken shoelace away from losing what was left of his limited cool.

"Jim, what's happening?!"

"They found us!" he declared, trading spots with Natalia. "Stairs, now!"

Angel found herself being dragged along between her son and her ex-lover, with a spry child only feet behind her, toting a gun that she looked altogether too comfortable with. They tumbled through an emergency exit into a dimly lit stairwell. Pounding from two directions, like a marching band closing in around them.

"One floor up!" Natalia hollered. "Go!"

Angel allowed herself to be pushed along, recognizing that whatever was taking place was above her pay grade. These decisions were best left to the professionals.

They burst onto the next floor and sped down the sterile hallway. Jim called out orders to Natalia and she complied, throwing gurneys and fire extinguishers behind her. A means to distract and befuddle those who followed them. Sirens in the distance, and the fire alarm blaring. Nurses were wheeling patients towards emergency exits. Standard protocol. They reached the end of the hallway and Jim turned sharply to the left.

There was a man, no, a biker, toting a large shotgun. Jim dragged Angel and Jayson back as a blast of pellets peppered the floor where they had been standing. Natalia was feet behind now. She yelled for them to duck and fired once, shattering the window at the end of the hall. Jim hauled Angel and Jay by the wrists and jumped. It was a short drop, one storey into a snow bank where they scrambled to move out of the way.

Jim looked up, silent, towards the broken window where golden light streamed through. A shadow of a biker, and Natalia's thin figure. He was struggling with her, and Jim felt the fear hitch in his throat. He levelled his gun.

"You'll hit her!" Angel cried.

Hopefully not.

A single bullet. The biker went rigid and toppled backwards, dragging Natalia with him, out of the window. Angel shrieked and Jay, perhaps shocked to see his father shoot a man, yelled something incomprehensible. The biker landed with a thump in the snow, and Natalia rolled off his mangled corpse. Jay offered his hand to her, but she pushed it away. No time for pleasantries.

Natalia pointed towards the nearest parking lot where people were scrambling around, inhibited by hospital gowns and layers of ice underfoot. "Go!"

"Keep your heads down," Jim ordered. "Low, below the windows. Move, let's go!"

The chaos was spilling into the parking lot that surrounded the hospital. Patients, disengaged from reality, wandered aimlessly through the snow as nurses and doctors tried to corral them into a central location. The police were arriving as the bikers kicked through the front doors of the emergency room and out into the parking lot. Among the calls on the bullhorn for the bikers to put the guns down, Natalia found a rock and smashed a window of a car. A biker's head twitched towards the parking lot.

Her hands were shaking too much to hotwire the damn car; Jim ordered her into the back seat and began to work away at the wires. He would berate her for her failure under pressure later.

The chaos of the moment was blinding. How long ago since she had slept? Was anyone else injured? Natalia couldn't make sense of what was happening. She felt the car rev and glanced over to Jay, who had lowered himself to the floor, hands over his head. The air was rank from the smell of urine.

Angel was crying silently in the front seat and Jim looked as if he was trying to ignore it. Natalia couldn't blame him.

The hospital was growing smaller in the distance. Red and white flashing lights strobed by them, unaware that half their prey was already escaping the scene. The darkness buzzed around them, electrified as the hum of engines began to expand through the darkness, closer and closer.

The hospital was never the target. It was the bait. The Reapers had placed a couple of prospects on the hook to take the fall and draw them in.

"They're coming," Natalia said hoarsely. "Jim-"

"I know. I know. Hold on. Angel, stay down. Kid, you still got your gun?"

Do I?

Jim passed his SIG to her and Natalia mechanically checked the clip. Three shots left. She would have to make them count. Not exactly a comforting thought when she knew her aim left something to be desired.

The streets were slick, black ice, coruscating under the bowed streetlamps.

"Heads down!" Jim roared.

A bike pulled up behind them and the back window blew inwards. Angel screamed, Jay whimpered, and Natalia lifted herself up, shaking pebbles of glass from her hair, and fired a bullet into the darkness. The shot went wide, striking the biker in the arm, but it was enough to shock him into losing his balance. The bike went down and slid back across the highway, struck by a truck traveling too closely behind. A tumultuous crash, screaming.

"Jesus Christ!" Angel cried from the front seat.

"Two more right on our tail, Jim!"

"Keep them busy! I'll try to lose them!"

Natalia's hands were shaking and her vision was blurred from sweat falling into her eyes. She dropped her right hand and shook it violently, as if to loosen the tendrils of uncertainty that had wound around her fingers, and aimed the gun again. Two shots, one wide, one hitting the biker squarely in the chest. She would add him to her list of the dead. Only people she killed herself. Not people that got caught in the crossfire. The car skidded over a patch of ice and there were screams. Her own? No. Angel, Jay.

Upside down and weightless. Gravity ceased to be. Natalia saw stars littering the ground, and above her a sky of black ink.

The car hit the water, and immediately Natalia's head was plunged below the surface of the frigid river. Water flowed through the shattered back window. Jay, without a seatbelt on, was frozen in the thralls of shock. Natalia clawed at her seatbelt, found the release and toppled downwards.

Every second counts. Don't hesitate. She reached out towards Jay, hauling him up by the collar of his shirt so his head was above water. Jim had Angel free and was holding her by the waist. Overhead Natalia could hear gunfire popping along the surface of the water like skipping stones.

"Out!" Jim looked back towards them, pointed to the opposite bank of the river that was dipping out of sight. "To the other side!"

The look in his eyes that said he was terrified; his family caught between his world and the fire that engulfed him. Natalia understood that feeling. She knew what to do, knew someone had to take control, if only to get them out of the water and somewhere safe.

"Take her! I've got Jay!"

Jim began to kick the front windscreen. The current had caught the car and was dragging it deeper into the center of the river where the undertow would grab them and haul them away from the surface world. Natalia rammed Jay through the back window and looked back. The front windscreen crumpled away and Jim pushed Angel through.

"Go, kid!"

The car shifted as Jim moved through the windshield and Natalia turned toward her own escape route. The water was flooding through now, above her chin, her nose. She tipped her head up, inhaled sharply, and ducked below the surface. Water filled her nose, eyes, ears, and blocked her senses. It was like being dunked in a pail of plaster. Murky. Spears of ice raced in through the window as the car began to shift. She pushed against the current as the river made its own path through the car, heedless of whatever might get in its way.

The river took what the river wanted.

The car jolted backwards a few feet and Natalia grabbed the side of the broken frame to prevent herself from being sucked along with it. Hot blood spilled from her fingers as she tightened her grip and pulled herself forward.

With his son in one arm, and his ex-lover in the other, Jim dragged his family up the snowy bank, where Angel and Jay collapsed in a fit of hysteria. Jim turned, saw the last of the car's rear bumper disappear beneath the frothing surf of the river. Headlights from the other side. Bikers watching, waiting to see if they could see anyone break the surface.

Come on, kid. Where are you?

The car slipped out of sight, taken by the river. Was Natalia a strong swimmer? Had it ever come up in her training? It must have, but try as he did Jim couldn't remember what she had told him, if anything at all.

"Jim." Angel's voice was ragged behind him. She crawled over the snow and rocks, reached for his hand, and pulled herself upright. "Jim, where is she?"

"I'm going back in," he declared. "Take Jay, hide and-"

Then he saw it. A movement below the surface, a distorted figured rising from the weeds and current. Natalia broke the surface, four or five meters from the bank. The lights from the motorcycle swivelled as Jim trudged back into the water and grabbed Natalia by the arm. A barrage of bullets scattered the surface and Jim pulled her down into the dreck.

Fronds of aquatic plants snagged at their fingers as they propelled themselves towards the western bank where Jay and Angel still hid in the shadows. Jim pushed forward, his eyes on Natalia's silhouette as she clawed her way through the water like a wounded kitten. Bullets cut through the water around them, and, all at once, he saw her stiffen, a swell of bubbles bursting from her mouth as she instinctively screamed from the unexpected pain.

Catching her by the back of her jacket, Jim dragged her through the muddied water until they could break the surface and crawl, gasping, through the sludge and silt to the bank. Jim could feel the blood swelling through the back of the leather jacket. Beautiful, warm blood that cut through the frigid air. Jim pulled Natalia up to her feet. Angel was at his side, gripping Jay's arm like he might disappear the instant she let go.

Natalia tipped over onto her knees and began to retch and cough in a desperate attempt to expel the river from her lungs.

"Natalia, kid, come on," Jim croaked. "We gotta go."

"I know." She gasped and stumbled upright. "I know."

"Can you-"

"I'm fine!" She swatted away his hand and caught sight of Angel and Jay, tangled together in their fear and confusion. She tried to roll her shoulder back, but the sensation of bone grinding against metal made her stomach lurch. "Come on," she said. "Let's go."

Chapter 16

There was a fine balance between risking hypothermia and wanting to get as far away from the riverbank as possible. Sirens were swirling around, descending upon the neighbourhood, accompanied by a cacophony of locals leaning out of their second story windows, screaming at each other to shut up. It was the sort of neighbourhood that was just seedy enough for a person to disappear in with ease, if they had the wherewithal to know what they were doing, but staying too close to the scene of the crime wasn't possible either, so as they climbed the bank and made their way onto the road, Jim began to scour the area for somewhere safe to store his family while he tried to plot out his next move.

Natalia was bleeding, he knew that for certain. How many of those bullets had hit her? More than one, and they'd be in trouble. Still, at least she was upright, walking, perhaps a bit more hunched over than normal. It was a good sign. She caught his glance and nodded to an alley across the street. Only a few feet in, it was devoured by darkness. It would provide them some semblance of protection as they forged their way deeper into the neighbourhood.

Jim took the lead. Soft whimpering cut through the silence, becoming more pronounced the further they explored the encompassing darkness. Silence was key, but Jim didn't have the nerve to berate Angel or Jay for their fear. Natalia was mercifully silent, but he could hear her awkward gait along the crushed snow. She was limping, caught in the thrall of the new pain. Stabbing was one thing; getting shot was an entirely new experience.

Thank Christ for the cold, I guess.

When at last he was satisfied that they had doubled back and crossed enough roads to dissuade anyone who might have picked up their trail, Jim picked out a quiet set of row houses on a road that breached the middle class. They took the long way around to the back alley until the found the right door.

"Keep an eye out," he said hoarsely, kneeling in front of the door and pulling out a waterlogged leather case. His hands shook as he adjusted the tension wrench and began to pick away at the pins. Every minute they remained outside, not moving, was a risk to their health, and if Angel or Jay got sick, he would never forgive himself.

And Natalia. Natalia's been shot.

The pins clicked into place, and Jim pushed the door open with his shoulder. He held his breath and listened. He could hear the frantic, rapid gasps of his family as they shivered in the darkness. No footsteps, no alarms, no animals. He turned, one finger to his lips, and ushered them inside. The was an old brownstone, like the one Natalia had lived in before everything had changed. Before she learned of the wickedness of men and the cruelty of the night. The house was undecorated for the holidays. Whoever lived there was probably gone for a few days.

"Keep the lights off. Natalia, go find a bedroom. We need dry clothes." Jim turned to look at Angel, whose lips were pursed and blue. "Find a bathroom, hot showers for both of you."

"Jim-"

He stepped forward, took her by the hands. "Please, Angel. Trust me."

She held his gaze for a moment then shook her hands out of his grip. It was a half-hearted effort at showing her frustration. Whatever anger had been brewing was tepid now, made so by their dip into the river. Angel turned towards their son, who looked petrified from his position by the kitchen door. "Jayson, upstairs, now."

Natalia passed Angel and Jayson on the stairs. She had located a heap of clean dry clothes in the laundry room by the backdoor and divided them into piles. Angel accepted hers without a word, and no eye contact. Jay hung back, stretched out the sweater on the pile, and tried to grin.

"Oilers? Come on, Nat. You're killing me."

"Ouch." Natalia forced a laugh. "Come on, timing, man."

Jay nodded shakily and drew the sweater close to his chest. "Thanks," he said quietly, "for the truck."

Natalia felt a smile crack her cold lips and nodded. "Anytime."

Back downstairs, Jim was searching blindly through the cupboards. A kettle was hissing on the stove, and he had lit a candle, offering a weak dance of light across the white kitchen cupboards. They wouldn't be able to risk turning on any lights. Natalia placed the clothes she found for Jim on the counter and slipped into the powder room off the kitchen where she peeled off her soaking clothes.

This must be what getting skinned alive feels like. She bit back a yelp as her shirt pulled away from her bloodied back. She could look at the wound, she reckoned, but that might make the pain somehow more real. At least if she didn't look at it she could feign ignorance for a while longer. Steam was pouring from the sink; she leaned in, running her hands and arms through the water. While soft clouds of steam filled the small space, Natalia sat on the edge of the toilet and began to furiously rub her feet with a dry towel. Somewhere within the house a furnace clattered on, and puffs of warm air began to emanate from a grate on the floor. Natalia placed her feet over it and began to wiggle her toes back and forth until the colour had returned and her skin no longer tingled. Satisfied her core body temperature had returned to something close to normal, she stood up and began to dress.

After donning a long sweater, clearly meant for someone twice her size, Natalia returned to the kitchen where she found Jim with his back to her. A cupboard beside him was open and an empty whiskey bottle sat at his elbow.

"I'll be back in a few minutes," she said, reaching for a dry jacket that hung by the back door.

He turned abruptly. "You've been shot."

Natalia chose to ignore that point. *Out of sight, out of mind,* "I don't know about you, but my phone is ruined, and we need a way to contact *someone.* I'll go to the corner store we passed and get us a couple burners."

Jim leaned back against the counter, sipped his instant pick-me-up, and placed the mug to one side. The cup rattled as it touched down against the granite. "I'll do it."

"No." Natalia shook her head. "You need to stay here with Angel and Jay. You can keep them safer than I can."

"Jesus, Natalia." Two long strides brought him to her side. He reached out, his hand vibrating with the motion. "You can't go-"

"Don't touch me!" she shrieked, pulling abruptly back from him. Her hands flew to her mouth, as if she might be able to silence the cries that were already long gone. Jim jolted backwards. When Natalia acted out, and there had been times enough for him to recognize it, she chose words as her weapon.

Natalia shook her head and frantically rummaged through the pockets of her ruined leather jacket, a desperate measure to avoid his questioning gaze. She found her emergency credit card, tucked into an inner pocket. "I'll max it out," she said, defeated.

For a moment, Jim simply stared at her, his face expressionless other than the exhaustion that had carved itself deeply onto his skin. Natalia expected him to argue the point, to refuse her passage back into the night. Instead, Jim grimaced, nodded his head in acceptance, and stepped aside.

"Buy two burners," he said quietly. "Save the rest. You're going to need to get a gun."

Natalia gave an involuntary shiver and rubbed her arms vigorously. Dry as her clothes were, she could feel the chill from her own body overtaking any warmth she had managed to draw in. The sweater scratched along her open wound. It was nauseating.

"I'll be back soon."

Jim was looking down at his hands, brow creased, as if he couldn't quite understand why a palsy had overtaken him. He gave them a violent shake and looked up, but Natalia was gone.

Changing her clothes had been a mistake. Hypothermia be damned, at least the frozen cloth of her shirt had numbed the spot on her back where the bullet had nestled beneath her skin. Now, warm, tucked into layers of clean, dry clothing, she could feel the blood dripping down her back and staining the shirt of a stranger. She would have to leave them some money as an apology for the petty thievery. Leaving anything behind that might be traced back to them was out of the question.

Natalia shivered, reached back with one arm, and prodded the skin on her back. Her fingers came away bloody, but she could feel the butt of the metal poking out. No risk to her spine. It was the little things that really counted. She unconsciously raised her hand to the nape of her neck. The brand felt tight, like someone had layered clay over her skin and left it to dry and crack.

I might as well be made from porcelain with the way things are going, she thought grimly.

Snow drifts swept up from the street and buried Natalia up to her ankles, forcing her to move in concise, measured steps. Every time a car raced by her, her eyes would be blurred by the falling snow, ignited by headlights. She tried to remind herself that she was supposed to be a normal young woman, out for a walk during a snowfall, perhaps out to get cigarettes for a no-good boyfriend or a carton of milk for cereal the next morning. If she believed the story herself, she could convince whomever she wanted about the accuracy of the narrative. With the corner store in sight, Natalia picked up the pace.

Inside the store, it was warm. No, hot. Natalia's ears felt like they were on fire, and her chest tightened by the sudden inhalation of warm, dusty air. She blinked away the tears and looked around. A single clerk leaned behind the counter, protected by a layer of thick Plexiglas that looked as if it had been beaten on by irate customers many times before. The clerk glanced up from his newspaper, gave her a once over and nodded. Satisfied that she didn't seem like a threat, he returned to reading

Natalia snagged two prepackaged Nokia phones and moved stiffly towards the counter. One of Jim's various lessons had been about the impact of extreme weather changes on the body. She knew she had to keep moving, despite every instinct wanting her to sit down on the floor and cry. The clerk looked up again as she approached the counter.

"Cold out," he said lamely.

Natalia couldn't decide if it was a question or a comment, so she ducked her head shyly and asked, "Any chance of getting a pack of smokes too?"

"You're not old enough."

"No, but my dad is."

"And I suppose they're for him?"

Natalia tried to muster her most angelic expression but found it futile given the way her damp hair was frizzing out from her skull. *Nothing angelic about a stray with matted hair.*

The clerk hesitated a moment longer before shrugging his shoulders and turning to the locked cage behind the counter. "Camels?"

"Perfect," Natalia said with a smile. "Thanks so much. That'll get him off my case."

"Is this it?" the clerk asked, adding the pack to the two phones.

"You bet." If her credit card had been damaged in the water, she would be up a whole different level of shit creek, but a moment later the reader beeped *Approved* and Natalia picked up the phones and pocketed the smokes.

That should keep Jim in an amiable mood until he can shoot something. Moving to the back of the store where a generic bank machine sat, she tried to look casual and peruse the odds and ends that the corner store stocked. Cup noodles and Starbursts. Band-Aids and energy drinks. She just wanted to warm up a bit, maybe give her hair a chance to dry out. The clerk watched her the whole time.

Natalia turned her head as the front bell of the convenience store rang. Three bikers entered. She dropped to the floor, glanced up towards the ceiling where a circular mirror gave the clerk a full view of the back of the store.

Shit.

She scrambled silently around the corner of a shelf, putting her out of sight of the mirror. She could hear the boots of the bikers stomping across the floor, and the scrape of something metal along glass. The barrel of a shotgun? Maybe something less dangerous; a crowbar? Something to frighten the clerk who had no loyalty to a girl who looked liked she was dragged in by wolves.

Quiet talking, more boots and scraping. Natalia inhaled sharply and watched the mirror. One biker was threatening the clerk, brandishing his crowbar like a bat. The other bikers moved around to flank both sides of the store, knocking products aside like they were trying their hand at a child's carnival game. She kept low, quickly moving around the corner of the first row and into the second before one of the bikers entered her line of sight.

And there, on the floor, a dribble of blood, radiating off the white laminate like rubies in snow.

Shit, shit!

Voices were raised, and the biker at the front of the store was arguing with the clerk now. The crowbar was on the counter top, his hand gripped menacingly around it.

"I've been alone *all night, Jesus.*"

"You sure-"

Natalia inhaled and moved between the rows, narrowly putting herself out of view of the man at the counter. If he turned around she would be dead.

"Anything?" he barked over his shoulder.

"Place is empty, Rog."

"Let's keep going then."

Natalia shut her eyes tried to make herself as small as possible. Just a few more seconds and she would be safe. Boots, snow and slush crushed underfoot and the slamming of the door. It felt like the whole store shook with the force. She gripped the edge of the rack and used it to pull herself upright, leaving a smear of fresh blood on the shelving

The clerk was looking at her, wide-eyed, mouth agape.

"If," Natalia said, slowly walking back to the front counter, "a person needed some way to defend themselves around here, where would they look?"

"If," the clerk said, voice shaking slightly, "they were just protecting themselves?"

Natalia nodded.

The clerk pointed over her shoulder to the ATM at the back of the store, then took the keys from his pocket, locked the register and walked out the door behind the counter.

Natalia maxed out her limit on the card and stepped back into the snow. Following the edge of the building, she found an alley where the clerk was frantically going through a pack of cigarettes, chain smoking to calm his nerves, or perhaps to give them a lift.

"It's just over four hundred," she said slowly, holding the handful of bills up like a torch. A small lie. Haggling; another one of Jim's many lessons.

"Enough," the clerk said. He reached into his waistband, pulled out a small snub-nosed pistol, and passed it to her, along with a handful of bullets. She gave him the money and they stared at each other for a moment.

"Thanks," she said finally.

"Fucking bikers," he said, with a shake of his head. "We pay protection to the locals and still get pressured by other assholes." He lifted another cigarette, lighting it on the tail end of the one still clasped between his lips. "This city is goddamned drag."

Chapter 17

"Are you *insane?!*"

Natalia was about to push through the backdoor of the house when she heard Angel lay into Jim with a barrage of words that even Natalia wasn't sure she was comfortable hearing. She paused to listen.

"Angel, please, we need to be qui-"

"Oh *fuck you*, Jim. We were just being *shot* at! The time for being quiet is over. And-and then you let a *child* go back out there? What the hell were you thinking?"

"She's a hell of a lot more capable than you're giving her credit for." Jim was doing his best to stay calm, but Natalia could hear the stress in his voice. A certain intonation that only developed when he was being backed into a corner like an animal. "She knows what she's doing."

"Well good, I'm glad she does! That's still no excuse!"

"Angel-"

"She is a *child.*"

Natalia knocked gently on the door and pushed into the kitchen, stomping her feet dramatically in the hope it would alert them to her presence and stall whatever fight was brewing between them.

"Neighbours can probably hear you, just so you know." A small lie. Worth it if it got them to shut up. Natalia dropped the two phones on the kitchen counter, and looked over. "Am I interrupting something?"

Angel looked at her and for the first time Natalia felt the heat of shame fill her face. She imagined her bruises, all yellow and purple like summer squash, discoloured and emphasized along her cheeks and arms. She imagined Angel, a mother, viewing her as an anomaly, a creature made putrid and corrupt by the world.

"It's nothing," Jim said.

"No," Angel said coldly. "It's not." She turned and marched towards the stairs.

Jim exhaled sharply through clenched teeth and shook his head. "She doesn't like any of this."

"Can't say I blame her," Natalia said, "but it is what it is, right? Nothing we can do about it."

"Did you get a gun?"

That was Jim's way. Avoid uncomfortable conversations. Focus on the important things. One step at a time.

"Nothing special." Natalia placed the pistol on the kitchen table next to the phones and then lobbed the carton of Camels towards him. Jim caught them and Natalia thought the expression on his face might be as close to appreciation as she would ever witness. Popping a cigarette between his teeth, Jim reached for a hand towel on the table and tossed it towards Natalia, touching his head as he went. She caught the towel, but the movement tweaked the open wound on her back and she winced.

"Shit, kid." He dropped the cigarette back onto the counter and pointed to a chair pulled away from the table. "Sit down, let's take a look at it." He began to root around through the cupboards in search of what Natalia hoped were genuine medical supplies but what she suspected would be field medicine instruments.

"Move your shirt up, we need to clean away the blood."

Natalia did as she was told. Had it been three months earlier, she would have clung to her clothes like an extra layer of skin she had been given *just in case*. Her time in Alcatraz had made her uncomfortably familiar with her own body and its unique set of scars. Gangly but female, covered in paint palette of knife strokes that left her discoloured and awkward. Even her bones felt like they belonged to someone else. Jim had no time for her youthful insecurities and told her as much. If one of them was bleeding out from a stab to an artery, he expected her to understand that things *needed* to be done.

The bullet had struck near the bottom of her right scapula, a few inches above where her bra band sat. She leaned over the table to give Jim a flat surface to look at, closed her eyes, and the exhaustion finally closing in around her. A second chair creaked as Jim pulled it close.

"You ok?" Even though Natalia knew he was trying to ask about the pain, she understood the subtext. Are you ok being exposed? Are you ok being touched? Are you ok at all? It was as if what had happened in the kitchen earlier that night was a malfunction, a glitch in their reality that neither wanted to address. When it came right down to it, they didn't talk about Alcatraz or what happened in segregation. It was the one thing Natalia carried with her, beyond the death of Steven and the lives she had snuffed out to protect herself. Beyond it all, when the nightmares came, Natalia still remembered foreign fingers, the scent of sweat, of vile creatures who stalked the night and preyed on her. She thought killing Duncan would end it, but somehow his ghost lingered, along with the others she kept desperately wishing away.

"I'm ok," she confirmed quietly. A cloth, warmed by water, touched her skin, and Natalia winced.

"Tell me what happened out there."

Natalia recounted how she had gone back to the corner store, bought the phones, and nearly run directly into the bikers. Jim listened intently, dabbing away at the blood until the cloth gently worried at the bullet. There was a clinking of metal behind Natalia and she turned her head.

"What was that?"

"I had to improvise."

"Are you using *metal chopsticks* to get a *bullet* out of me?"

"I almost went with a shrimp fork, but that seemed classless." He paused, then added, "It's a kabob stick."

"Holy shit." Natalia exhaled sharply and tried not to squirm as the end of the metal point dug into her skin and Jim began to prod around in a rather fruitless effort to spring the bullet free.

After a few moments of silence, Natalia asked, "You and Angel going to be ok?"

"Not sure. She knew what I did was...unsavory, but not like this. I never told either of them. I certainly never wanted it to impact their lives like this."

"It's not your fault," Natalia said shortly. "No one ever wants the people they love to get hurt. It just happens sometimes."

"Yeah, well, it'll be a while before she'll forgive me for endangering Jay like that. Can't say I blame her. The sooner we're gone the better off they'll be."

Natalia twitched at his words, head snapping to the side so she could look at him over her shoulder. "What do you mean?"

"As soon as we know that the area is clear, you and I will head out. Angel and Jay will stay here and we'll start a fire elsewhere, make sure the Reapers follow us out of the city." Jim paused for half a second. "Not a *real* fire, though."

"You're just going to *abandon* them?" Natalia asked, ignoring the jab at her own distraction techniques.

"Natalia." There is was. That voice that Jim used whenever he didn't want a fight. Whenever he was tired of trying to argue with her. "They don't belong in this world-"

Natalia launched herself up from the chair, knocking Jim's homemade implements aside, angrily scrambling to adjust her shirt and face him head on like an agent. Like her *mother* would.

"You don't get to just *leave* them!"

"For goodness sake, keep your voice down."

"No! They are your goddamned *family*. Family *always* comes first."

"In the Agency-"

"Fuck the Agency!" Natalia snarled back. "The Agency took my mom, and made my dad leave me in goddamned *Chinatown*. Fuck you and fuck the Agency!" She whipped her hand across the counter of the kitchen, sending a glass that had been filled with water to the floor where it shattered on impact. It felt tremendously satisfying to watch something crumble apart just like her.

Jim was unmoved by her outburst. "You don't understand how it works. You don't know what people like Cain will do to get what they want."

"I know leaving your kid and his mom behind isn't going to protect them," Natalia snapped back, "and I know if I had anyone left to give a shit about, I sure as hell wouldn't leave them to their own devices."

"Natalia."

They turned at the sound of Angel entering their battleground. She was standing in the doorway of the kitchen, Jay at her shoulder, arms crossed, pulling a cardigan around her body, warding off the cold? No, warding off the anger.

"He's right," Angel said softly, as she knelt by the counter to pick up the broken glass. The pieces clinked against each other, ringing hollow through the sudden silence in the kitchen. "We don't belong in this world."

Natalia stifled back a frustrated cry and wrapped her arms around her midsection. She hated crying in front of Jim; he saw it as a sign of weakness, of manipulation. But the pain in her chest sat like a burning rock that embodied all her agony at her own abandonment, sending waves of sorrow spilling through her body with every breath she took. It burned so deep that at times she felt sure that she would be split in two by it.

"Natalia-" She knew she was in trouble when Jim called her by her name. Even in Alcatraz she had been *kid*. He only used proper names when he was pissed off or disappointed with her.

"I just-" she inhaled sharply, ran the back of her hand over her nose, and sniffed loudly. "I know what it's like. That's all."

"Yeah," Jim said, sounding defeated. "Yeah, I guess you do."

Angel scooped up the last of the glass, placed it on the counter, and pointed towards the scattered pseudo-medical equipment. "Who's hurt?"

Jim stared at Natalia, and she grudgingly raised her hand.

"Let's take a look at you then." With a tender, guiding hand, Angel directed Natalia back towards the kitchen table. Natalia leaned forward again, this time with her arms as a pillow under her head. Jim pulled up a chair next to her, so they could look at each other as Angel began to gently examine the wound.

"I miss them so much," Natalia whispered.

Jim placed his hand on her head, a foreign action, and oddly disconcerting. She did not try to push him away this time. "I know," he said. "I know you do."

Chapter 18

When Natalia woke the next morning, her body free of bullets and a
handful of makeshift sutures in her skin, she felt embarrassed and foolish.
Sometime after Angel had retrieved the bullet and sewn her up, all without
saying another word, Natalia went to sleep on the living room sofa. She knew
Jim was still awake, out of necessity as much as mental incapacity. He would
wear himself out, Natalia decided, unless she started doing her part. A united
front, that's what he would call it. She already knew she would keep her
opinions to herself from now on, if only to prevent further conflict.

There was whistling in the kitchen, someone's off-tune attempt at a
Weekly Top Fifty pop ballad. With all the shades drawn, only a glimmer of early
morning light freckled the walls. Natalia pulled the duvet over her shoulders
like a robe and sauntered into the kitchen, where she found Jay at the stove.

"Uh," was all she could muster before her voice cracked.

"Morning," he said, without turning around. "Making pancakes. It's
the peace offering food."

"Uh," Natalia said again.

Jay turned around. He was smiling, batter on his forehead. "When I was little, whenever they fought, we always made pancakes together. It was like...Germany and England playing soccer on Christmas Eve. And well," he gestured around with a batter-smeared spatula, "it *is* Christmas Eve."

"You might need a bit more than batter and maple syrup to fix this one." Natalia tossed a hand towel to him and motioned to her forehead.

"It's Aunt Jemima." Jay rubbed away the batter. "It's the best I can do. Not like we live here or anything."

"Yeah, this is my first break and enter, too." Natalia settled at the kitchen table, moving stiffly, and hauled the blanket around herself so she was cocooned in its warmth. The fragrance of the home and its owners had leeched into the folds. Sage and pine and citrus. Warm, comforting. The smell of *normal*, of perfectly *ordinary*.

"Here," Jay said, setting a plate before her. "Eat. You're probably starving."

"Thanks." Natalia didn't have much of an appetite, but Jay had gone to more work than she would have expected from him, and she didn't want to seem ungrateful. He settled on the other side of the table and began to dig in.

"How'd you know," he said, with his mouth full, "about my truck, I mean?"

"Oh," Natalia picked at her food and frowned. "I recognized a guy outside. I saw him at the docks where I was being held. It wasn't much, really, but usually in those scenarios I guess it is better safe than...whatever."

"Well, thanks again. And for the river, and shit." Jay's face reddened slightly and he continued to inhale his pancakes.

"My pleasure." Natalia moved her breakfast around her plate with a fork, hoping it might somehow lessen the quantity of food that she was expected to consume. No such luck.

"I smell pancakes!" Angel's head appeared around the corner of the kitchen. She was smiling, which was a marked improvement from the night before. She looked at her son. "Was it really that bad?"

"Thought you two were going to decimate each other," Jay said without looking up, clearly still a bit sore from watching his parents fight the night before.

"Well, breakfast was a nice thought, even if it wasn't needed. We just needed to talk it out. Evidently we weren't the only ones." She pulled up a chair next to Natalia and settled in to the food.

"Where is he?"

"Showering. He'll be down soon, then we can talk about what happens next." Angel looked at Natalia and frowned. Natalia shifted so Angel was out of her peripheral vision. She couldn't get a read on the woman anymore. "Thank you for going to bat for us like that. I appreciate it."

"Yeah, well." And that was all Natalia said. She didn't want thanks or praise or to be told it was unnecessary, because unless they were in her position, they would never understand the desperation, the desire. Maybe it was selfish, but Natalia enjoyed being around someone else's family, and she didn't want to leave that behind simply because Jim thought it was a safer option. Then again, it was clear she was outnumbered on the issue. She wouldn't push her luck.

When Jim joined them at last, they finished the meal in silence. Angel and Jay began to clear away the dishes.   Jim rubbed his chin. Somehow in his shaving and showering he had still managed to leave a layer of scruff behind. Perpetually dishevelled. "I talked to Tess this morning. She can get supplies to us, but if Caulder starts to suspect anything he might pull her off the street, and Meghan won't be able to overrule him without knowing why."

"But he doesn't have any allies left, does he? At least no one to do his dirty work."

"It will only be a matter of time. You don't spend this long in the profession without being owed some favors. Our best bet is to keep moving around the city, stay ahead of the Reapers, and anyone who might side with Caulder."

"We've already done this, Jim," Natalia protested. "We did the whole *run away until the bad guys give up,* thing. This is exactly why we came home in the first place."

"I am open to suggestions," he said, throwing his hands out.

"Can't we parlay with the Agency? Talk to Caulder face to face?"

Jim snorted and Natalia scowled fiercely. "I know he's not on our side," she said quickly, "but we can't keep running around, hoping to outpace him. If we can get him to lay off, it'll be one less thing to worry about, right?" Natalia lowered her voice and leaned in. "We can get Jay and Angel somewhere safe then, where the Reapers can't find them. Then we can focus on, I don't know, putting sugar in their gas tanks or whatever."

"So, what I'm hearing is that you want to load them off on someone else?" Jim sounded stern, but Natalia could see the smirk rising on his face.

"See the difference between your dumb plan and my brilliant plan is that I wanted to leave them with someone whereas you just wanted to *leave.*" Natalia paused, then said, "That is why I am the brains of the operation, and you are just the muscle."

"Jesus Christ, kid." Jim laughed spitefully and shook his head before looking over at Angel and Jay. "Well?"

"Well *what?*" Angel demanded, looking unimpressed again. "Jim, the last twenty-four hours have been hell for us. We've been shot at, and..." she gestured helplessly around the kitchen. "We need some answers."

Jim sighed, glanced at Natalia who shrugged, as if to say *I don't know where to begin any more than you do.* But that wasn't true. Jim could edit his tale, pick whatever pieces he wanted to form a coherent story. He could tell them Natalia had gotten in someone's way and was subsequently the reason for their suffering. It wouldn't be that far from the truth.

"I'm going to get some fresh air." Natalia pushed back her chair, felt the makeshift sutures in her back tighten with the movement. She didn't want to be there; she didn't want to hear what narrative Jim would weave to protect his family. It would place her in the unwitting role of the villain, and she would accept that if it helped Jim salvage the relationships he had with those he cared most about.

The back alley was quiet. Soft drifts of snow lay undisturbed, and the footprints of the group had long been buried. Settling on the stoop, Natalia placed her palm flat against the snow and shivered. Droplets of ice crystals began to melt away beneath her body heat, leaving tiny diamonds behind to delicately grace her skin.

She had lost track of time when the back door finally cracked open and a blanket flopped over her shoulders. Natalia tucked it under her chin without looking up. She could smell Jim's lingering cologne on the fabric. Another silent act made in trepidation. Did he care at all about what she thought? Jim didn't strike her as the sort of person who put much stock in someone else's opinions.

"All right?" He settled next to her on the step, cigarette already between his teeth. He certainly didn't care what Angel thought about his smoking at this point.

Natalia inhaled sharply, hoping to quell the shake in the back of her throat. If she was going to talk to Jim, she wanted to show strength. She wanted him to admire that, to not see the girl who was stabbed or shot. If they were going to get out of this, and get Angel and Jay out of it, then they needed to work as a team. She rested her hand on the back of her neck where the brand was hard and lumpy against her fingertips.

"What did you tell them?" Natalia asked finally.

"The truth. Most of it, at least."

"Do they hate me?"

Jim looked at her sideways, clearly confused. "No, kid, why would they-" and then it seemed to hit him just why Natalia's thoughts had gone in such a direction. "Shit, you're just a kid. Angel knows you didn't ask for this. She doesn't blame you, and Jay isn't much older than you. Naw." He turned to face the back alley, spat off to the side then returned to his cigarette. "They feel sorry for you if anything at all."

"That's almost worst."

"Isn't it just? But we talked it over and they agreed. We'll call it in. Get them to a safe house. Call in a parlay with Caulder."

"Like a pirate," Natalia said lamely. "*Yarr.*"

Jim smirked in her peripheral vision. "Yeah, kid. Just like a damn pirate."

xXx

Natalia trusted Caulder about as far as she could throw him, and given his girth that wouldn't be particularly far if at all. Judging by the way he was looking at her now from across the conference table suggested that while he could throw her much farther, he was well aware that laying even a finger on her would result in having that same appendage ripped from its socket and shoved down his throat by Jim. Angel, as well, was delivering a look of hatred that Natalia feared might translate into physical action if they weren't careful.

No one in the conference room spoke, each waiting to see who would break the silence first.

"Hey," Natalia said, pointing a finger at Caulder, "What happened to your face?"

In her peripheral vision, Natalia saw Jim grin wickedly. Caulder's cheeks reddened; a stark contrast to the white splint that had been applied over his nose. During the taxi ride to the Agency, Jim had mentioned that he *might* have broken the director's nose in an ill-advised moment of anger. Natalia thought it was hilarious; Angel and Jay both blanched.

Now, Caulder cleared his throat awkwardly and looked over to Meghan, who stood next to the door. She gave him a look, as if to say *you brought this on yourself*, before turning to Angel and Jay. "These are Agents Callum and Brecker," she said, motioning towards the two stoic members of the security force that were standing beside her. "They're going to be on your protective detail until we get this mess dealt with. We've prepared a safe house for you and-"

"Right now?" Jay looked panicked, as if he hadn't expected things to change so quickly. Of course he hadn't. He had no concept of how time worked within the Agency. Choices were made in seconds, not minutes or hours. Jim had made it clear to Meghan when he called that morning that his family needed to be secured and removed from this situation right away.

"I'm afraid we can't waste any time," Meghan replied, "and what we're discussing here is highly sensitive."

"Jim already told us about the gang," Angel said coolly, unaware that there was so much more to the story, then directed her gaze towards Caulder. "*You*," said Angel. "If I hear that you've been trying to do *anything* that might cause this girl harm, I will personally come back here and strangle you with your stupid-looking tie."

A wave of snickers, dissent in the troops, and Caulder said nothing, remaining perfectly motionless, out of fear, Natalia reckoned.

Angel turned and embraced Jim, whispering something in his ear before breaking away and turning to Natalia. They stood in silence for a moment. Natalia could feel Angel's eyes on her, from the top of her head to the tip of her toes, as if searching for something that was not there. She reached out, but instead of embracing Natalia, Angel rested a hand on Natalia's shoulder and offered a weak smile. "You be safe, sweetheart. We'll celebrate Christmas and your birthday when this is all over, ok?"

The sting of loss was like a barb to her chest; a stark reminder that this was not her family. Natalia had been an interloper for the briefest moment, and now Angel and Jay would have to consolidate what they thought they understood about her with what they knew was true. She was a cancer, just as her parents had been, a sickness in the lives of those she interacted with. Natalia nodded stiffly and turned around so Angel wouldn't see her cry.

Jim watched Callum and Brecker accompany his family from the conference room, and took his place at the table next to Natalia, all without emotion, without any indication that saying goodbye caused him any sort of grief. That was his way.

"Let's get down to business." Meghan placed her hands on the back of an empty chair. You didn't have to be a senior agent with a well-developed sense of survival to recognize that she was asserting her dominance over the situation and, perhaps more importantly, Caulder himself. "Director, I believe you have something to say?"

Caulder cleared his throat and adjusted his aggressively patriotic tie. Angel was right; it was stupid looking. "Yes, I... Well, I'll just say it. I didn't explicitly order the Third after you, Agent Artison," Jim opened his mouth and Caulder quickly jumped back in, "but I didn't attempt to stop them either. Obviously, there are certain things that need discussing. Supervisor Sirano and I have agreed we can't waste resources on in-fighting when Cain is a very real threat."

"He means the bigwigs up in Washington dropped the ban hammer," Tess announced bluntly, garnering a wave tittering from the Twelfth. Meghan cleared her throat and the laughter died.

"Sir." Meghan's voice was low, a warning for her people to show a modicum of respect, even when it wasn't deserved. "They need to know."

Caulder sighed and swallowed loudly, his Adam's apple bobbing like an lemon stuck in a turkey neck. "Cain has my nephew." The room rippled again, and Caulder held up his hand to silence them. "He made contact several weeks after the siege on the prison, and offered to trade Kyle for you, Agent Artison. I wasn't particularly *keen* on that option given what it would mean for the Agency, so we began to explore *other* options."

"You thought *killing* her would even the playing field." Bedlam plucked his glasses from his nose and began to clean the lenses on the hem of his shirt. "You thought you could *outsmart* him."

"It was a calculated risk, I'll admit," Caulder said. "Understand, every choice I've made has been to protect the Agency first and foremost. Cain would accept no other payment in exchange for my nephew; and he would never believe you were dead unless he saw a body. There was no other way."

It was oddly satisfying to hear the words come out of Caulder's mouth. To understand now that he felt backed into a corner and brought his violence down on Natalia to protect what he cared about almost made him seem human.

Almost.

"So, as far as you trying to kill me," Natalia said slowly, "Is that still a thing, or what?"

"Consider it cancelled."

Natalia narrowed her gaze at Caulder, pushed back her chair, and walked towards the head of the table. She could feel the eyes of the team following her, analyzing her gait, her facial expressions, searching to find a sign of weakness, of vulnerability to be exploited. She reached Caulder, paused, and stuck out her hand. He stared at it, as if snakes had sprouted in place of her fingers, then reluctantly took her hand. "I'll hold you to that," she said evenly.

From across the table Jim grunted something vaguely crass. Whatever doubts he had, Natalia was sure she shared them. If Caulder was acting agreeable, there was a strong likelihood it was only because he had run out of options and the threat to his nephew's life was imminent.

"Good, we can go back to being one big, happy, dysfunctional family." Meghan pointed to Natalia's empty seat. Natalia complied as Meghan continued speaking. "We pulled this from Federal archives." A grainy black and white photo flashed on the monitors set around the table. Pete's hulking frame looked like it was acting as a centre of gravity for the rest of the bikers. "It was taken two years ago at Sturgis. We need to know if you recognize anyone."

Natalia scrutinized the photo carefully, urging her grey matter to fill in the spaces between the grains that distorted the image. Nestled among the patches and leather vests Natalia saw a family-friendly logo: Mickey Mouse's big ears. "Second row, third from the left. I called him ZZ Top. He didn't think it was funny."

"I'm amazed they didn't shoot you then and there," Jim drawled.

"Lonny Stieber," Meghan said, flipping through a series of folders that were spread in front of her. "Runs a mechanics shop out in the Bronx. Old school Reaper."

"Third row, fifth in on the right. The guy with the scars. He's looking a little worse for wear now, but he was definitely there." She couldn't have forgotten him, or the way the skin had curled back from his face in white and pink scars. He hadn't said anything to her. In fact, the only time Natalia had noticed him was when Pete had been showing her the trailer full of crates and explosives.

And then again, outside of Jim's home, only two nights prior.

Meghan flipped through a file, then used her pen to swipe her screen to the left. "Hayden Meloy." She typed the name into a search bar, and it brought up a prison intake photo of the man in question. "Ex-demolitions expert, used to do contract work. Legit stuff for construction companies, until he joined the Reapers and got involved in their lifestyle. You're sure he was there?"

"I'm hardly likely to forget that face. Duncan said something about the Reapers not knowing that Pete was using the compound. He wanted everyone out as soon as possible, before they found out." Natalia paused, looked over to Jim for guidance. "But Meloy was there when the Reapers found us at Angel's house." She looked over to Jim. His eyes were closed, and his jaw was grinding.

"Meloy and Stieber could be playing both sides of the field," Tess said from across the table. "If Pete didn't want the Reapers to know he was borrowing their space-"

"It's a risky move." Meghan ran a thumb over her chin, and for the first time Natalia saw thin, milky white scars crisscrossing the knuckles of both her hands. Artistic strokes, forgotten slashes of paint. It humanized her beneath the sharply cut dress suit and razor-straight hair. Meghan's gaze caught Natalia's, and she smiled slightly. "Cain would never go to bat for any of his lowly minions. If the Reapers want to bring in members that have gone off the reservation, and they get in the way of whatever Cain's planning..."

"It could be a bloodbath," Jim finished quietly.

"So maybe we encourage it?" Tess suggested. "Point the Reapers in the right direction, make sure they know Cain is poaching their people, stalking in their territory?"

Natalia gave an involuntary shudder at the suggestion. The last thing she wanted to witness was a Westside Story street rumble between a biker gang and a terrorist.

"How do you go talk to a biker gang?" Anna looked over at Natalia and mimed knocking on a door. "*Avon calling?*"

"Sometimes the direct approach is a lot more successful than tradecraft," Meghan replied. "Tess, you take Anna and someone else along to make contact. See if you can't give the Reapers something else to focus on for a day or two while we regroup and try to get eyes on Cain. As for you two," she looked over at Natalia and Jim "no field work. No lighting things on fire. No pissing off any more gangs, ok?"

"I'm *sorry*." Natalia threw up her hands dramatically. "What else was I supposed to do?" But it was clear from Meghan's expression that she was simply teasing the girl, perhaps to lighten the mood, or perhaps to divert attention away from the fact that she had just sidelined both Jim and Natalia.

"Get out there, hit the streets. Let's end this before they decide to camp outside our door."

With Meghan's permission freeing them from the monotony of bureaucracy, the members of the Twelfth began to shuffle and rise from their seats. Natalia could see the exhaustion written in their faces, born from too many truths colliding at once and incinerating their beliefs in the ensuing explosion. She tried to recall if she had ever seen her parents look so disheartened after missions, but in each instance she found their faces were hidden behind a cloudy veil. Each step further into the belly of the Agency somehow seemed to draw her away from her family, and the sensation left her feeling ill.

Jim nudged her in the side and pointed towards the door. "Wait outside," he said shortly. "Don't go far."

Right, Natalia thought, following the last stragglers from the room. She hung back, leaned against the wall of the hallway outside the conference room, and unconsciously let her fingertips wander over the stab wound that punctuated her body with another scar.

"Hey."

Natalia jumped slightly, having lost herself in the silence of the hallway and thoughts of her battle scars. She turned, and found Anna standing there, a clay pot holding a miniature pine tree thrust forward.

"Merry Christmas," Anna said, then ducked her head and added sheepishly, "I'm really glad you're okay, Natalia."

Natalia reached out and took the tree. It listed slightly to one side. She looked up at Anna and smiled, "That's awesome, thanks so much."

"It's from me and Ben and... Well, Martyn too, really. We put his name on the card at least. We figured maybe Jim wasn't big into the holidays and a tree of your own would be nice. Martyn was supposed to water it but-" She pointed towards the limp tree and shrugged her shoulders. "I'm sure it'll perk up."

Natalia wrapped her arms around the pot and nodded sagely. "A little TLC goes a long way."

"I'm really sorry about what happened. I shouldn't have left you there."

At this Natalia laughed. Seeing the dread on Anna's face, she stopped and tried to find her sense of decorum. "I'm not your responsibility, Anna. Honestly, it's fine. It all worked out in the end."

And that was true, even if she was sporting an impressive stab wound and multiple contusions to her face.

Pain can be psychological. Think above it. Be more *than it.*

Anna looked relieved, as a child at confession who was told her mortal sins would not condemn her for all time. Natalia didn't have the heart to tell her that her lack of friends made her keen to forgive even the more grievous errors, if only to have some companionship.

"Anna, let's go!" Tess was at the end of the hall, waving for her ward.

"Merry Christmas, Natalia." She leaned in, embraced Natalia quickly, crushing the already sad looking tree between them, before turning away and running back down the hall.

How about that? She turned the clay pot between her palms and smiled to herself.

Natalia wasn't certain how long she had been standing there when the door to the conference room opened and Caulder stepped out. Having been so caught up in the rush of the agents leaving the conference room, Natalia hadn't noticed that he wasn't among them.

They stared at each other for a moment, like two hungry wolves sizing each other up for a meal or two. He would surely be more satisfying, what with his girth. Natalia imagined how Caulder might choose to pick his teeth with her bones or floss with her sinewy muscles.

"I won't apologize again," Caulder said. "I did what I had to."

Natalia was surprised to find herself agreeing with the sentiment. "I know."

"You'll understand one day, when it's your family at risk."

"Mine are all dead," Natalia said.

"Yes, well, my nephew is still out there." Caulder let the thought hang in the air, as if it somehow explained away his actions. It did to Natalia. If anyone she loved were still alive, she might have done the same thing. She couldn't very well condone Caulder's actions while simultaneously planning her own revenge.

A hand was on her shoulder. She twitched, glanced back, saw Jim standing beside her, ever protective.

"There a problem here?"

"No," Caulder said, taking a single step backwards. He made no effort to hide his grim expression.

"Ok?" Jim asked, as Caulder disappeared around the corner of the hallway.

"Ok," Natalia agreed. "Just tired. Can we go home?"

xXx

Tess blew a grey curl of smoke from her mouth and tapped the head of ash into the cup holder. Next to her, Max shifted in his seat and flexed his bad knee. The cold snap was a stark reminder of the arthritis that was to come. His days as a field agent were numbered. In the back seat, Anna was sitting in silence, watching the snow bluster outside the car and making furious notes about the experience. They had been watching the Road Reapers clubhouse for a solid two hours, their coffees having long gone cold and their mittens no longer keeping the chill at bay, but they had to stay put, because the clubhouse was empty, save for a few prospects, and they needed to talk to the head of the chapter.

Patrick McKim was a beast of a man, nearly blind in one eye, thanks to a close call with a chain during a fight in his youth. He had risen through the ranks of the local chapter of the Reapers until setting up the last president for embezzling funds. Rumor was that McKim was the one who put the bullet in his brain. That had been well over ten years ago. McKim was relentless in his grip on power. He had eyes for the National Presidency and wasn't above throwing troublemakers under the bus if it meant achieving his goal.

McKim valued loyalty above all else, and it was that same loyalty that Tess, Max, and Anna suspected McKim was wrestling with now, as he and his convoy reached the clubhouse and moved their bikes into the garage.

If what Natalia had said was true, then Pete had acted outside of the club and it was fair to assume that McKim was biding his time, waiting for the chance to strike and show Pete that betrayals were not taken lightly.

"Do we wait?" Anna asked from the back seat. "Or do we just go up there and-"

"Knock on the door?" Max suggested, glancing back in the rear-view mirror. "Essentially, yes."

"Seems like a quick way to visit the morgue if you ask me," Anna muttered.

"Only if we're stupid. These assholes are trigger-happy, but they aren't fools. Don't provoke them." Tess tapped the last of the ash into the cup holder and stepped out into the wind. She hated winter, always had. After the massacre of Cain Ferigon's family, she had been sent to the Middle East, where she'd run informants for the SOI who had an in with a local ISIS leader. Her bones had gotten used to the heat of the desert and the grit of the sand. Coming back to New York hadn't been her choice, not by a long shot. Now she was Anna's guardian; another thing that was forced on her, although Anna was a good enough kid. Same old sappy story, lost parents, taken in by the Agency. It didn't matter which walk of life a person came from; everyone had lost something.

Then Cain had come a-calling for her, as he had done for all of them, trying to herd his enemies into one place. It had worked, and every day since the Siege on Alcatraz Tess had kept one eye on the road ahead of her, and one keenly on her own back. The only reason she hadn't retreated overseas was because Jim had adamantly refused to go into hiding with Natalia. He knew as well as Tess did that Cain would be drawn to Natalia; a moth to a candle. Hiding would bring no satisfaction after the years of torment.

Time to focus.

The clubhouse had no qualms in trying to hide its true nature. Large, obtrusive cameras covered all angles and pointedly followed the agents as they trooped through the deep snow and up the sidewalk. Tess felt sorry for whatever city ordinance officer tried to fine the clubhouse for not keeping their sidewalks clear.

There was no doorbell. The walls of the home thumped with the beat of overblown bass and some poor soul screamed his lungs out about the state of his broken heart. Tess curled her fingers and pounded her fist against the door.

No response. She repeated the process, harder this time, and raised her voice to say, "Special agents. Open up." Good and generic.

The music faltered and they heard the sound of heavy books scrambling around inside. Tess glanced back at Max who smirked and said, "Cocaine can be real tough to clean up at a moment's notice."

Finally, the door opened, and Patrick McKim, in all his muscled glory, stepped into the frame.

"What?"

"Special agents." Tess held up her badge, just long enough to McKim to get a glance at the ID, not quite long enough for him to question where their credentials might have come from. "We were hoping we could ask you some questions about a couple of old associates of yours."

McKim glanced over his shoulder, and Tess added, "We're not here to bust you on anything. Just questions. Scout's honor."

If he doubted Tess, McKim made no indication of it. He leaned his bulk against the doorframe and Tess thought maybe she saw the house shift a few inches to the right.

"We're wondering if you've heard anything from a member of your chapter recently. Peter Cobbs?"

"Pete?" McKim feigned confusion poorly, tapped one sausage like finger on his chin, and grinned. "Naw, last I heard he disappeared after the Siege on the Rock. Another body tossed into an unmarked grave outside of the prison walls, probably. *If* he were alive," McKim narrowed his eyes "we'd sure like to see him again. He's a brother of ours, after all."

"Oh, yeah," Max said, narrowly treading the line of sarcasm. "What about Lonny Stieber or Hayden Meloy? Seen them recently?"

At the mention of Stieber and Meloy, McKim's grin twitched and receded back, curling over his teeth like a wild animal that had caught the scent of flesh on the air. "They aren't here right now. Why?"

"No reason." But Tess had already decided how she would play this. Enemy against enemy; send the two groups on a crash course and see which flinched first. "Just a rumor that the three of them were hanging out together recently near a compound of yours. The one that went up in smoke on Staten Island. We were wondering if there was any truth to it."

"That would be," McKim looked as if he was picking his words carefully "*unfortunate*. I'd hate to think Pete was shirking his duties to the club. Or that he'd got anyone else involved in his little scheme."

"No, we can't have that, can we?" Tess narrowed her gaze at McKim, leaned into the doorframe, and moved her hand slowly towards the gun that was holstered clearly at her hip. "In that same vein, we'd hate to hear that any of our own friends are suddenly running into your buddies. People make mistakes, isn't that right? No need to condemn an innocent party for someone else's choices." Her lips twisted into a smile. "It would be, as you said, *unfortunate*."

McKim nodded. "It would be, wouldn't it?"

Satisfied that the message was as clear as she could make it without blatantly telling McKim to stop fucking around with the Agency, Tess turned, showed McKim her back, waved one hand over her shoulder as casually as possible. "Ta."

The agents didn't speak until they were back in the car, McKim's gaze following them all the way across the snowy street. Tess lit up another smoke and watched the clubhouse in her peripheral vision, knowing that it was a matter of principle that they not show any fear in the Reapers' territory. McKim had to understand that the agents were *bored* by this familial infighting, and that they would manipulate the situation to their advantage. McKim knew they wanted him to pursue Pete; it was mutually beneficial.

From the dimness of the clubhouse, Tess saw McKim's head dip in a single nod, as if acknowledging her position, before disappearing back inside and slamming the door behind him.

"Could be a mistake," Max said from the passenger seat. "We don't know how far they'll go to get to Pete."

"They'll irk him." Tess inhaled sharply on the cigarette and cast a glance towards the rear-view mirror, where Anna shifted in her seat and played with a lock of hair. "He'll come out of hiding," Tess said, as if to convince herself. "Then we'll track him to Cain."

"If you say so." Max leaned down and rubbed his hands across his bad knee. "Let's get moving. The cold is bullshit on my gammy leg."

Tess started the car and turned the heat on full blast.

Chapter 19

Christmas at Jim's house passed without any revel. Neither he nor Natalia wanted to acknowledge the holiday out of concern that they might be forced to celebrate when they were hard-pressed to find things to be grateful for. The house remained undecorated, unless they were willing to consider the plastic sheeting and crime scene tape strewn along the upstairs corridor some sort of festive ornamentation. Natalia had to give it to the Agency, they knew how to take care of their own. It hadn't taken long for repairs to be arranged and get underway. Jim figured the upstairs would be back to its naturally dreary self by New Years Day.

Cooper had been taken in by a dog catcher who apparently wasn't doing anything else during the holidays. After a bit of arguing, Rebecca had been able to retrieve him and brought the anxious mutt back to Jim's house not long after he and Natalia had returned. He whined and nuzzled them, searching for signs of potentially fatal wounds. Satisfied both his people would live, he chose to follow Natalia to her room, pointedly ignoring Jim's grumbles about a traitorous animal.

Natalia put the sad Charlie Brown tree on her desk and made a and made a small paper chain out of candy wrappers to give it a little pep. She could hardly claim to be surprised that Martyn's participation in the ritual had been half-assed at best. She certainly didn't blame him for his reticence. In the end, the tree looked quite festive, and found a more permanent home in the sunroom on the east side of the house.

She spent the whole of Christmas with her nose in a SAS survival handbook that she had taken from the small library upstairs. It was worn through, spine broken and the few pages that hadn't been ripped loose were mud-splattered. Jim only came to check on her once, offering her something to eat, which she politely declined.

Neither acknowledged the day, and it seemed better that way.

Jim was pacing, unable to sit still. Natalia listened to him stomp around upstairs, opening and closing cupboards doors, checking for monsters, or perhaps ensuring his own private monsters were still locked away where they belonged. Then downstairs, where he began to furiously rearrange the kitchen. Knowing what she did now about him, Natalia imagined that the Alcatraz assignment must have been hell for him. It had been about patience, taking the time, making the right friends, and acting only when the iron was hot enough to set the ocean to boil. Now here he was, trying to pull some semblance of sanity out of this bric-a-brac life that had been forced on him. Jim was anchorless because there was nothing to do except wait.

By the third day of their internment, Natalia had caught him in the middle of dialing the safe house twice. He always looked guilt-ridden as she pulled the phone away and reminded him that the point of the safe house was to keep those he loved *safe*, and the less contact any of them had, the better.

"Besides," she said, "Angel's probably mad at you."

"Don't beat around the bush, do you?"

Natalia shrugged and retreated to her bedroom. There didn't seem to be any benefit in tailoring her language to protect the feelings of those around her. If anything, she imagined someone like Jim might respect her less if she didn't tell it like it was, and mutual respect was the only thing keeping them afloat at the moment.

Jim knew Natalia was right, that a call to the safe house could raise any number of flags and draw a target on Angel and Jay. He didn't appreciate knowing she was right, because she was a teenager and was supposed to be wrong ninety percent of the time. Still, he had snapped at her with perhaps a tad more vim than was required, and decided to make sure she was ok.

He found her in the sunroom off the east side of the house, where Jim had earnestly stored various plants over the years, all with the best intentions of keeping them alive. It was a fool's mission in the end, given that he could be home one day and jetting off to the other side of the world the next. Natalia was far more patient, and had tended to them unwearyingly, trimming dead branches and watering them daily until small spouts had begun to wriggle free of the old dirt. In the center of it all sat the sad-looking Christmas tree that Anna had given her.

She was sitting in a wicker chair, head tilted back as she watched the light from the street lamps stream through the snow-covered panes of glass overhead. The light created intricate shadows along the snow, like tumors on an x-ray.

"Want me to turn on a light?" Jim asked.

"No," she tipped her head forward, let her chin hit her chest, and rubbed her eyes with the palm of her hand. "I was just spacing out."

"You high? Your folks would kill me if they knew you were getting high."

Natalia smirked, leaning her head back again. "Nothing to worry about. The dead can't hurt you."

Jim sighed quietly to himself, or so he thought. Natalia jolted in his peripheral vision, alert now, and glared at him. "What? It's true, isn't it? They're dead. They don't get a say in what I do anymore."

Jim settled on the edge of the second wicker chair and pulled a crumpled package of cigarettes from his pocket. Natalia stared at him incredulously and he sighed. "Jesus, not you too." But he crushed the packet in his hand and tossed it towards a small garbage can in the corner of the sunroom. "You've been keeping to yourself."

Natalia shrugged her shoulders half-heartedly and leaned down to pull up a knitted throw that had been discarded on the floor. Her hair fell away from the back of her neck, and Jim could see the brand just below her hairline. It was fading now, still pink and shiny but no longer inflamed. That was progress, though Jim figured she would probably wear her hair long for the rest of her life to cover the damage that had been done.

"I want to know about Cain." She said it so simply, like she was asking him about the weather forecast in Mississippi. Like she wanted to know if that was two cups of flour or three. As if nothing in the world could be more ordinary than hearing how a man became the monster that branded her for life. It was, as Tess has said, time to cut through the swathes of lies and half truths Jim had laid over those memories and reveal to Natalia some of the history that she was tangled in.

"It's not pretty," Jim said. A last-ditch effort to avoid confessing his sins.

"With Cain involved? Colour me surprised."

Jim sighed and reached across the table to adjust the paper chain that was balanced delicately on the needles of the miniature tree. "Ten years ago, we were tasked to infiltrate the ring of an arms dealer. Some asshole who was getting his jollies putting guns in the hands of people who didn't care for their government." Jim was surprised by how easily the story filtered through him. He had gone over it so many times in his head, as if memorizing the details somehow made it less real, more fantastical. "We figured he was mid-level at best, but had aspirations to move up in the world of illegal trade. He'd already supplied a few factions that we had been keeping our eyes on and we weren't interested in letting him get any more power."

"Cain." Natalia exhaled slowly.

Jim nodded. "A team of recruits were assembled, including myself, Steven, Tess, Kira Carter, Erin Banks, and Daisy O'Byrne. My role was to infiltrate directly, get hired on, and work my way up the ranks as someone Cain could trust. Steven was my second in command, and I would bring him in once Cain trusted me. Tess and Erin were our outside contacts, acting in whatever capacity we needed them to. Kira ran point and Daisy was meant to go in undercover close to Cain's family, who were living on a family acreage outside of Lancaster.

"Once we were on the inside with Cain, it was easy to get established and build a reputation. He was doing exactly what we thought, traversing the world, greasing palms, making trades, and building connections. Steven and I were in deep cover for six months before we felt like Cain trusted us. Daisy injected herself into the life of Cain's wife, Myra. They were neighbours, lonely women whose husbands were never around. They became close - good friends even. We thought that was it. Daisy was doing her job, always the professional. Problem was she was alone for a long time up there. She missed a couple of rendezvous, but always had a story or a reason for it. A barbeque, a tea date. I should have realized, paid a bit more attention. It was unusual."

"They...*fell* for each other?"

Jim held up a hand. "Just wait, I'm getting there. Nearly a year in, we were scheduled to make a delivery. The idea was we would accompany a van carrying small arms to a ship, pass it off, take the money, and return. Nothing new. We placed a tracer on a crate of ammo heading out east; minor tradecraft. Easy. We'd done it before with no problems. Except this time, we're moving at night and we hit a curve in the road and lose sight of the truck for a minute. We turn the corner and the truck is sideways across the road, cutting us off, and the driver is pointing a MIG right at us. I don't know how we got out of the car. There was fire everywhere. Steven nearly got blinded from the damn explosion. We knew we were made. Kira, Erin, and Tess secured themselves. Steven should have gone to the hospital, but refused when I couldn't get a hold of Daisy. We drove up the valley that night, reached Cain's compound and found them. The whole family. Myra Ferigon; her sister, Lyza and Lyza's twin boys, just *goddamned toddlers*. Daisy. The housekeeper. All of them. Cain... He fucking hung them from the trees in the orchard, every one of them, and set the whole damn thing on fire. The only ones spared from the whole shit show were his kids, off at boarding school. Thank Christ they didn't have to see it."

Jim's voice was shaking with rage, maybe, or sadness. All those emotions started to feel the same after so long. "I couldn't figure out *why*. We betrayed him, us. Not his family, not his wife. Fucking...loneliness and human connection, some bullshit like that. Myra and Daisy, Daisy and Myra. Later we found Daisy's safe in her house. All her notes on his family, diligently taken. I don't know what it was. She never really explained, probably to protect both of them. Before they could get away something went wrong, and it all went to shit."

Silence hung in the air around them like a thick, poisonous fog, and Jim found himself unable to make eye contact with Natalia. He knew when he did they would have to address the heart of the matter.

"How were you made?" she finally asked.

"We never found out," Jim admitted. "The five of us that got away were sent into deep cover. By the time we were allowed to come back, Cain's legacy was a distant memory. If they ever learned the truth, we were never told."

"So, Cain wants the Code because-"

Jim lifted his eyes, just for a moment, and found himself staring not back at Natalia, but the ghost of her mother. Judgement free, mercifully. "He wants to dismantle the Agency, to destroy the people who ruined his life."

"But *he* ruined his life," Natalia protested. "He was the one who killed his family. It doesn't make any sense."

"No," Jim said. "It doesn't, but it was made clear we weren't to pursue it any further. We never did. We were young. We wanted to be free of the whole damn thing. Never even thought about it, not really, until you showed up in Alcatraz."

Natalia heaved a great sigh, one that seemed to indicate all the pain and disharmony of the world had fallen directly on her small shoulders. But Jim saw the spark, that sense of obligation that blossomed from knowledge. A responsibility renewed, as if the exhaustion of the last few months, of being on the run and changing names and hair color and contacts all made sense. All seemed *worth it*, somehow. Jim saw this and recognized it as Amy's genetic contribution forcing its way through in the mannerisms of her daughter.

The mirrored image of Amy faded from view, leaving in its place Natalia in all her feistiness. "That was what those pictures were in Alcatraz, huh? The ones Cain showed me. The trees."

Jim nodded.

"And Steven's wife saw them, too?" Natalia chewed her lower lip for a moment. "He doesn't just want to kill you, does he? He wants to make you watch everything you care about crumble away, just like Steven did."

"Yeah, that about sums it up. Should have probably told you sooner," Jim admitted ruefully, "but those sorts of things. Well, you know. They feel like nightmares, misplaced in the waking world. You try to block them out, pretend they haven't happened. Anything to free yourself from it."

"It's not that easy, is it?"

"No. It isn't."

Natalia leaned forward, touched Jim's arm with one hand. The blanket slipped from around her and Jim saw the shiny pink scar that ran along her left arm. A coarse reminder of the violence that Cain encouraged within his organization.

"This won't be the hill we die on though, will it?"

Jim leaned back, shocked to hear his own words, ancient as they seemed, spoken back to him. He had told her that in Alcatraz. When everything had seemed hopeless.

"No, it won't be. Plenty more hills to climb before then."

Natalia nodded her head, lifted the throw up to her chin. She was curled under it, like a caterpillar nearly completely consumed by its cocoon. "But," Natalia said, "What then? What happens when it's all over?" She had pulled the throw closer, so it muffled some of her words. "I don't know who I am without it. The anger, the sadness."

"Well, figure it out." Jim didn't mean to sound so cold, but by the time he realized how his tone must have come off, he was walking back towards the doorway. "You figure it out or you die. Those are your two options. Reinvent yourself if you have to. Be whatever you need to get through the day."

So you become something better than the rest of us.

So you become better than me.

xXx

The next day they were paid a house call by the Agency doctor who wanted to examine Natalia's wounds to ensure she wasn't at risk of turning into a bulbous ball of pus and grime. She was given a thorough physical and declared healed and, with perhaps a bit of moderation, she could resume some practical training.

When Meghan had cobbled together the plan to make her an official trainee, no one had expected Natalia to take it seriously. It was meant to be on paper only, a bureaucratic roadblock to protect her from those who equated the value of a human being with their ability to turn a profit. As it turned out, Natalia very much took it seriously, and Jim knew he shouldn't have been surprised. She knew how to load a gun, aim down the sights, measure her breath to steady her hands. She could assess a scene for weak points, as she had done at the warehouse. Now she needed to know how to work with her hands and her hands alone.

They covered basic defensive measures. A repertoire of actions that she could turn to if someone decided to stab her again. Up to that point, any conflict she had been part of lacked the proper ballet-like movement. Every action was driven by sheer will to survive. That had to change.

By the end of the afternoon, she was blocking six out of ten carefully plotted attacks. Jim wasted no time in reminding her that any real-world combat scenario would be faster, scarier, and without any proper defense; her best chance was to disarm her opponent if possible, and make a run for it. Always, always run.

"What if they have a gun?" she asked.

"Then take the gun."

"What if they have a second gun?" she asked coyly.

"Then take the first gun and shoot the second gun out of their hands."

"Aren't you supposed to aim for the biggest target, like their torso?"

"I assume by this time in the conflict you've probably just sarcasmed your opponent to death."

That brought a small smile to her face, and Jim was glad to see it. By the evening, Natalia was wan from exhaustion and, despite her own demands for *one more round,* Jim ordered her to bed. As she turned to leave the garage, Jim spoke.

"You did good today, kid."

Coming from Jim, that was likely the highest compliment she would ever receive, and she treasured it.

Natalia woke unexpectedly, still in her workout clothes. Her muscles had turned to jelly the moment she hit the bed, and she had curled up with Cooper without even bothering to take off her sneakers. It took her a moment to recognize the sound of the house phone trilling from the living room. It never rang. It was there for decoration, for telemarketers for Jim to troll when he was bored, and for the government to contact him just in case he missed an obscure line on his taxes. It was coated in a thick layer of dust and its analog buttons still clacked like a hinged trap when you pressed them. Natalia reckoned if she listened closely, she might be able to hear someone manually connecting the call on the other end.

She felt compelled to answer it, if only because the intense ringing cut through the night like a harpy's screech. She would never get back to sleep until it was silenced. With a dramatic groan, Natalia hauled herself out of bed and stumbled down the hallway. She heard Jim's footsteps hurry across the hardwood ahead of her.

"Yeah?"

Natalia reached the edge of the living room and glanced in. Jim's back was to her, his shoulders hunched.

"Jim?"

He waved his hand at her, a motion for her to be quiet.

"Angel, what-" He yanked the phone back from his ear as a horrific shriek echoed through the receiver. Natalia tripped forward, leaned in to listen. When the next voice came onto the line, her breath hitched in her chest.

"You should have just died, Jim."

"*Pete.*"

"Now they gotta clean up your mess."

"Don't you fucking touch them-"

Dial tone. The receiver fell from Jim's hand. He swung around, but Natalia was ready. She had moved back towards the foyer, snatched the keys from the shell dish that sat by the front door, and tossed them towards her guardian.

"Get your coat!" Jim ordered, grabbing the keys out of the air.

"What happened? What did you hear?"

"No time!"

They raced towards the garage, movements blurred by sleep and confusion. Jim was already on his cell, calling someone, trying to warn them about something, or trying to learn something more? Natalia had hardly closed the passenger side door before the car was speeding out into the snowy night. The safe house was out in the Bronx. Jim knew the address, though he wasn't meant to. He managed to wheedle it out of one of the security sector agents the day before last.

"Just in case," he had told her.

Natalia hated that phrase.

Jim was shouting on the phone now, levelling swears at Meghan, promising a violent act unlike anything anyone had seen.

If Jay or Angel were hurt in any way, someone would pay with their life. Natalia didn't want to be around when it happened.

They entered the community of Hunts Point, ten minutes from the safe house, according to the GPS, when Jim finally tossed his phone aside and flexed his knuckles over the steering wheel. "Brecker and Callum aren't answering at the house," he growled.

Natalia swallowed the rocky lump in her throat. The last time security had been compromised, Martyn's mother had been ruthlessly slaughtered, hung from a second story balcony and left to swing like a metronome. That was the moment Natalia had been thrown out of one world and embraced by the next. She couldn't comprehend Angel and Jay joining her alongside Jim in an existence driven by bloodlust and riddles. It wasn't the place for a healer, or her child. Let the world of shadows be occupied by just that, and leave the people who still had a chance at a normal life to their quiet existence.

Too little, too late.

"What do we do?"

They pulled onto a quiet street; Natalia could see the safe house in the distance. Lights brimmed from the windows. It looked homey, occupied. Like an average dwelling, occupied by milquetoast people, recovering from their blasé holidays. Whatever was inside, Natalia was not confident it would be as hopelessly nonchalant as the outside might suggest.

Jim pulled the car to a stop and stepped out into the street. "Stay here."

"Fuck, no!" Natalia stepped out into the snow and caught Jim's dower look. "You're not going in there alone."

"I don't have time to argue-"

"Then fucking *don't*." Natalia didn't wait for a reply. She wasn't going to let Jim sideline her because of some half-assed need to make sure she didn't get her head shot off. He was swearing at her now, using words she felt were better left for individuals that pissed on his shoes.

Natalia picked up her pace towards the front of the house.

Do I just knock on the front door or what? What's the standard protocol for a compromised safe house?

What would Steven have done?

Her foot hit the first step of the porch and the silence around them rippled, and the windows along the front of the house shattered outwards. Fire licked out, snatching into the darkness before curling back towards the house and swallowing the structure. The force of the blast threw them from the porch, tossing their bodies across the sleeted ground as flaming shingles rained down over their heads, sizzling as they struck the newly fallen snow.

Her skull reverberated with echoes of the explosion, as if she had been clapped on the temple by a gong. She turned to look at Jim and found her body moved faster than her mind. He was bleeding from his forehead, scrambling forward in the snow, screaming, screaming, screaming. The blood dripped down his face, splitting into a dozen different paths, as if his face was being rent apart from within by the agony of what had taken place.

Natalia pushed herself forward and grabbed Jim by the collar of his jacket as he lunged towards the inferno where he would surely die. He tried to push away from her, screaming Angel's name, and then Jay's, as if they would be able to hear him above the din. Natalia could feel the rage vibrating through his body, and as her hearing began to return, she realized she was screaming too, not for Jay and Angel, but for Jim to control himself.

"They weren't in there! He wouldn't have left them in there, Jim!"

He tried to drag his arm away, knocked Natalia to the side, but she reached out frantically and pulled him back to the snow.

"They're *fine!* They have to be fine!"

Jim fell to his knees and sobbed at the loss that struck him deeply, gouging at his core. Natalia watched in bewilderment as the safe house collapsed into burning rubble, crushing anyone that might have possibly survived the initial explosion. Jim screamed again, an animalistic cry that drowned out the rising sirens spilling out of the night.

Natalia wasn't certain how she managed to get them home. Jim had been virtually catatonic, and they had to get out of the neighbourhood before emergency services arrived. There would be too many questions that they weren't qualified to answer. She had considered calling someone, Troy maybe, but there wasn't enough time.

Somehow, she convinced Jim to climb into the passenger's seat of the car, and with a modicum of hesitation, Natalia managed to navigate them to the main road. They drove the whole way in silence. Both their phones were constantly buzzing, until Natalia finally had to toss hers into the back seat so it wouldn't distract her while she was trying to drive.

By the time they returned to Prospect Park, Natalia figured she probably had a handle on switching gears without stalling out, but there was hardly time to celebrate that achievement, or any other she might have reached while not getting them killed.

Natalia parked the car crookedly in the lot beside the garage, scraping against garbage cans as she went, and watched in silence as Jim mechanically moved from car to attached garage and disappeared into the house. He had left his cell phone behind, so she scooped it up along with her own and followed him. There were copious texts from Meghan, Rebecca, and Troy, all of which became increasingly less coherent as the minutes had worn on.

Meghan first. Prioritize this. We have to move fast.

At the back door, Natalia began to kick off her wet jacket and boots, and dialled Meghan's number. When she picked up they didn't bother greeting each other.

"The whole safe house is up in flames," Meghan said, grimly.

"I know, we were there."

"Goddammit."

"He insisted."

"How is he?"

Natalia followed the sounds of clattering towards the kitchen and found Jim leaning over the island, a full bottle of something atrocious-smelling sitting before him. She paused, waited, watching as the muscles in his neck bulged and shuddered.

"Not good," Natalia said Meghan, as she turned away from Jim and walked back into the hallway. "Meghan, I don't think they were in there. It wouldn't make any sense for Cain to just..." She let the thought die on her tongue. No need to verbalize what everyone was thinking.

"I agree. He prefers an audience for his bloodshed. And I doubt Pete was in it for the killing. We'll know more once the fire is out and crews can go through the scene."

"And what about the Reapers? Have we been watching them?"

"Natalia, put Jim on."

"He really isn't up to talking. Just tell me. Tess was taking a team to the clubhouse the other day. What happened?"

"I need to talk to Jim."

"For fu-" Natalia heaved an aggravated sigh, pulled the phone back from her ear, and returned to the kitchen. Jim was leaning over the island again, this time with his head in his hands. He wasn't making any noise, no sobbing, no helpless weeping – not that Natalia expected that of him. She placed the phone on the table in front of him and stepped back.

For a moment, nothing happened. Then Jim lowered his hands and Natalia saw what he was trying to hide.

Fury. The anger had pierced something he had long contained within himself. There was a poison in his blood now, reacting with his agony. The chemical equation of wrath. He exhaled sharply through clenched teeth, a fierce hissing, like a snake, and then snatched up the phone so quickly that Natalia jolted backwards at the motion. He looked at her with a fleeting expression of anger.

Don't touch me. She shook her head, and sidled backwards out of the kitchen.

Her body was seizing up from the short flight she had taken off the porch. If she didn't stretch now her body would never forgive her, so she turned away from Jim and returned to the living room. They would be moving out again soon. Jim would take a minute or two more, to calm down, to wrap his head around the way the latest piece had been moved across the board. Then they would go back into the night and begin the arduous process of finding Pete and snipping this single thread of violence before it could choke anyone else.

Natalia shuffled across the living room floor, closer to the door to the kitchen, so she could hear Jim speaking to Meghan.

"I don't fucking know, Meghan, I'm not-"

Oh, I would not try to interrupt her, Jim.

"Listen to me." Natalia could envision him clenching his jaw, gritting his teeth, maybe baring them like a wolf to its prey. "He wants the kid, he's come after *my family* to get to her. How long do you think this can go on?"

Oh.

Natalia slouched back from the door, returned to her stretches, and tried to shake the sense of doom from her mind. *Of course, it's your fault. Stupid for thinking anything else. Cain will do whatever it takes to get to you, and hurt whoever gets in his way.* But it was the anonymity of the conversation that bothered Natalia the most. In an instant, she had been wiped from the secluded position she had earned in Jim's life and returned to her place as *the kid*. The kid who was always in earshot at the most inopportune times. The kid, who was the catalyst to the agony of others.

The kid who got Steven killed.

She shut out the last of the conversation, finished stretching on autopilot, and retreated to her room. One of the first things Jim made her buy was a gun safe. It was a tiny one, tucked into the corner of her closet. It housed everything from knives to guns to ammo which, Jim explained was explicitly against the law, but they couldn't exactly afford to have them stored separately. She had just finished taking the contents out of the safe and begun to check them for any irregularities when Jim appeared at the doorway.

"What are you doing?" he asked lamely.

"I'm getting ready," Natalia replied.

"For what?"

"For what? For going after them. For going after Pete."

"That's exactly what he wants."

"I'm sure it is," Natalia said as she stood up, swinging a shoulder holster over her arm. "But I couldn't possibly give a single shit. He has your family, and we're getting them back."

"Right, my family. Not yours. Not your responsibility."

Don't engage him. He doesn't understand. He doesn't get it. "They're in this position because of *me*. I'll be damned if you're going to leave me behind. They're *your* family, so what? Family comes first."

Jim struck the door jam with a clenched fist; white paint flecked to the floor. "You can't put yourself in harm's way just because you want to hold yourself to some arbitrary standard!"

"I do not want to be fucking *babied* while Angel and Jay are suffering god-only-knows what because of *me*."

"It isn't just because of you-"

"Oh no, it is. That's been made perfectly clear time and time again. Either I stand up and start *doing* something about this, or I keep *running away* and I am *sick of it.*" Natalia was in Jim's face in a wild attempt to assert herself in the face of madness. For a moment, it looked like she had pushed him too far, like Jim might crack and revert back to the single-minded persona of the convict she had first met on Alcatraz. She had never feared for her safety in his presence, always mindful of his black moods and his penchant for sadness.

Is this the breaking point? she thought, holding his gaze.

"I'm coming with you," she said at last. "Don't try to stop me."

Jim broke the stare down first, perhaps out of exhaustion from trying to battle someone as equally strong-willed as himself. "You better fucking be here when I wake up in the morning," he warned, waving a finger in her face. "No midnight jaunts, got it?"

"Whatever." Natalia flopped face first onto the bed, pointedly ignoring Jim's aggravated sigh as he stormed away.

You don't have to be so animal stompy about it.

Natalia searched her memory for that familiar voice, and was sad to discover it was her sister.

Have I really forgotten Beth's voice already?

Natalia heaved deeply, swallowed the sob in her throat, and tried to push against the memories of her sister, long gone; of Angel and Jay, now victims in their own right; of Steven and the Hollow Man. All of it. She wanted all of it out of her, to be purged of the poisonous hate and sadness that seemed to accompany her wherever she went.

Chapter 20

Jim didn't sleep. Fuck sleep. Sleep was for people who didn't lose their families to a biker, to a terrorist. Jim didn't deserve sleep. He hadn't earned it. By 0800 that morning, the call came through. No Angel or Jay found in the carnage of the safe house. No one, in fact. No Callum, no Brecker. Just burnt box springs and minimalist IKEA furniture.

That frustrated Jim even more. If his son and ex had died in the fire, he could have let loose his anger and gone on a destructive rampage. He could have killed everyone standing in his way to exact some semblance of revenge. But no, with them out there somewhere, taken, held hostage, he had to move carefully or risk their lives.

And then there was Natalia. Something had happened. She was annoyed with him, and acting more petulant than she usually did. He couldn't fault her for that. She was young, it was normal. But there was no time for dissent in the ranks. He couldn't afford to have her act out, and, for one of the few times since he had begun to act as guardian to the daughter of Amy Artison, Jim felt a deep, indisputable resentment towards her presence in his life. She was an interruption, temporary at best, but she had appeared at the worst time, and it seemed as if her continued presence was only serving to complicate things.

When he emerged from his bedroom after taking Meghan's phone call and being told what was expected of him, he found Natalia was already awake, dressed, and ready to go. She was sitting on the couch in the living room, petting Cooper and watching the clock on the wall.

"Let's go," he said.

Natalia stood abruptly; Cooper whined and stepped haltingly backwards.

Leave it to a pet to know when shit is going down.

When they were in the car, Jim began to adjust the seat and fiddle with the settings, which Natalia had changed the night before. He didn't recall much from the drive back from the safe house, save that Natalia had somehow managed to get him into the passenger's seat and gotten them home safely.

You ought to say thank you, a voice in the back of his head reminded Jim. *She might be a pain in the ass, but she's damn competent when she needs to be.*

That didn't mean he was going to thank her, though.

"Sweepers didn't find any bodies from the inferno last night." His seat finally clicked into the right position. "Means we're looking for Callum and Brecker too."

"Where are we starting?"

They pulled onto the open road, and Jim said, "Bree Cobbs' house. Pete's ex-wife."

"Why?" Natalia drew out the vowel, and Jim could see her working the idea over. Oh yeah, she figured they were going in guns blazing.

"Despite it all, Pete cares a lot for her, and they have three kids together. If he's in contact with anyone it'll be her."

Natalia tapped the passenger window with a finger. "Those clouds look pretty menacing."

"You trying to change the subject?"

"Nope." Natalia leaned back in her seat and folded her arms. "Just trying not to think about what'll happen to Bree Cobs if she decides to be uncooperative."

"I'm not a monster-"

"No one said you were."

"Listen, if you're going to act like this-"

"Like what?"

"Like some fucking teenager!"

"I *am* some fucking teenager! This is how we *fucking teenagers* act!"

Jim resisted the urge to slam on the brakes, knowing it wouldn't solve anything and a collision would only cause them to lose precious time. Whatever. Whatever. Whatever.

Don't engage her.

The prolonged silence was as awkward as Jim knew it would be, and finally, after several agonizing moments of driving, Natalia finally spoke.

"Sorry."

"Yeah," Jim said. *I bet you are.*

They arrived back out in the Bronx over an hour later. Troy was already parked down the block, away from Bree Cobbs' house, as agreed. He was there at Meghan's insistence. *Someone to keep you grounded and rational* was how she had explained it, but Jim wasn't a fool, and he knew her hidden meaning. *Someone for Natalia to lean on when your attitude gets out of hand.*

As they stepped out of the vehicle, Troy walked up to greet them. Natalia smiled, and Jim thought it looked genuine enough. Whatever had happened between them in the car was irrelevant now.

"Aurora forwarded what she pulled from our files." He handed over a small tablet and Jim flicked through the itemized list as Troy began to recite it from memory. "Born and raised in Raleigh, married to Peter Cobbs, but separated since last spring. They have three kids together, the oldest two of which still live back in Raleigh with her parents. She moved to New York just over two months ago after securing a job as a paralegal. Rumor is she may have made a run for it after hearing that Pete escaped Alcatraz."

"Pete was based out of New York," Jim said. "It doesn't make sense for her to move closer to his home base if she were trying to avoid him."

"That's something you can ask her about yourself," Troy replied coolly, snatching back the tablet, and motioning towards the house. "Movement inside. She's got an infant with her. I'd guess it isn't Pete Cobbs' given how long he was in Alcatraz for." Troy thumbed towards the house and Natalia peered over his shoulder. It was a nice enough looking home; she had imagined some rusted-out trailer park where dreams went to die. Instead, it was a small A-frame house, painted a sunny yellow with pristine white trim. It looked cozy, and reminded Natalia of Angel's house. If Jim made the connection, he didn't say anything.

"How do you want to play this?" Troy asked, realizing that he wasn't going to get any definite response from Jim.

"We don't leave without answers," Jim said, jamming his hands in the pockets of his coat as he trudged up the sidewalk towards the house.

Natalia moved to follow him when she felt Troy's hand on her shoulder. She glanced back to see her godfather staring at Jim.

"Is he going to be a problem?" he asked quietly.

Natalia could only shrug. "I don't know. He doesn't have much to lose at this point."

Troy looked back at her and frowned. "That's not true."

"Try telling him that." She didn't want to have this conversation with Troy any more than she did with Jim. Tensions were running high, vibrating through the group like a current, and Natalia wasn't prepared to step out of line and risk getting electrocuted. "Let's go."

Jim didn't bother to acknowledge their absence; he had already rung the doorbell. The sound of a baby wailing and a toddler crying grew louder, and when the door opened Natalia was surprised to see a perfectly normal looking woman, baby balanced on her hip, staring back at them. Given all she had come to imagine about the wives of bikers, it seemed to Natalia that Bree Cobbs was lacking a few tattoos and piercings. No, she was delightfully average, if a bit frazzled looking.

"Yes?"

"Bree Cobbs? Special Agent Jim Wilkinson." He produced his badge and flashed it at her.

"Oh lordy." She blew a strand of hair away from her face and grimaced. "What did he do?"

"Ma'am?"

"My ex-husband, Pete. Soon-to-be ex, I guess. I assume he's done something. That's the only reason you lot ever stop by. Never mind, it's freezing out. Come inside." She stepped aside, continually bouncing the baby on one hip while motioning towards a living room with her free hand. Bree Cobbs followed them and, upon realizing Natalia was present, tipped her head to one side. "You can't be one of them too, can you?"

"It's, uh, bring your kid to work day."

Jim fired her a dour look and Natalia just shrugged helplessly.

Bree laughed a bit too enthusiastically at the thought and settled the toddler in a small Fisher-Price crib. "Annie! – She's mine, well, mine and Pete's. She's annoyed that I told her Santa wouldn't be taking away her baby brother. Annie! Come here!"

A small child peered around the corner of the foyer, large brown eyes blinking and taking in the sight of the strangers.

"Sweetie, I've got to talk to these folks for a couple minutes. Can you go to your room? Maybe make another picture for Santa, ok?"

The eyes lowered as the head dipped, and the sound of two small feet scuttling down the hallway faded away. Bree watched the empty space for a split second longer than necessary, and then turned her attention back to the agents.

"She's running me off my feet. At least back home she had her brothers to keep her entertained."

"Where are your sons?" Jim asked.

"Back in Raleigh with my parents. I moved to New York after my sister found me a job at a law firm. Once things get settled around here, I'll bring out the boys, but, you know, school was just starting and it didn't seem right to take them away from their friends so quickly. They'll come out in the summer, give them a couple of months to adjust before they start somewhere new."

"New York is a bit of a risk, isn't it?"

"Why, because of Pete you mean?" She chewed the corner of her lower lip. "No. Maybe. I don't know. We were already separated by the time he went to prison, but it wasn't *bad.* The kids and I always came out to New York in the summer to spend time with him. When he was around, that is. He was on the road a lot. And no, I didn't know what he did. Told me he was in construction; only 'fessed up about the gang after Annie was born. Things haven't been right since."

"Then," Jim waved a hand towards the crib "not Pete's?"

"No," Bree said, icily. "Not Pete's. But he knows, if that's what you're wondering. It was a short-lived fling, *after* we were separated. He wanted to go knock the father senseless, but I convinced him otherwise."

"You've seen him recently then?"

Bree nodded, stood up, and walked over to the crib, where she tickled the infant under the chin and smiled. He burbled in response and held up his chubby hands towards her. "The Feds were already out here asking about it, maybe two weeks after the Siege on Alcatraz, but I hadn't heard a thing from him at that point. He got in contact, oh, maybe three weeks ago? Stopped by for coffee, to drop off Christmas presents. Asked me not to call the police," she narrowed her gaze at Jim, whom she rightly seemed to suspect was the greatest threat, "which I did, after he left. He wanted to see Annie, ask how the boys were, and if I was still sure about the divorce." She waved her hand to a coffee table next to the couch. Natalia peered over and saw official court documents. "I sent them to him in prison, told him to send them back on the government's dime. He decided to do it in person."

Bree slumped back on the couch with a *woomp* and sighed. "He told me he had gotten a job and wanted to see it through before he had to go back to prison. I knew what had happened by then. Everyone did. But I figured, shit, can't fault a man for wanting to see his kid. I'm not protecting him, but I'm not persecuting him either." She leaned back, tipped her face towards the ceiling, and closed her eyes for a moment. When she turned back to them, she said, "So, what did he do?"

"We think he's involved in a kidnapping," Troy said.

"Jesus Christ, I told him..." Bree shook her head, disgusted. "He was pretty nonchalant when he showed up here. Said he got a job, doing some construction work. I thought it was funny. Ironic, he'd get a job doing exactly what he pretended to do for years. I don't know. Maybe I didn't want to see it for what it was. We've been on a shoestring budget since he went to prison. I sort of hoped he was...I don't know. You don't *leave* the gang. There's never been any question about that."

"We don't think this is related to the Reapers," Troy said.

"Well, then he's really up shit creek. They won't take nicely to him working for someone else."

"Is there any chance they know?" Jim asked.

Bree shrugged. "I doubt it. They might be one-percenters, but they never tried to be the biggest, meanest group out there. They always stuck to drugs, the odd weapons deal. Never people. Pete always told me he couldn't abide that sort of thing. 'People are people,' he'd say. 'Let them be.'"

Troy was making frantic notes on a tablet. Whatever shorthand he was using might as well have been ancient Sumerian to Natalia. "Any idea where we can find him?" Troy asked. "An apartment maybe? Some place the gang might not know about?"

"He had an old place north end of the borough, but I think it was foreclosed on before he went to prison. When he came back, he didn't say where he was staying. I'd guess, well, no..." She hemmed and hawed for a moment before snapping her fingers. "Lonny Stieber. One of Pete's buddies from the Reapers. Joined up for the camaraderie more than the drug running, and he never liked the way the whole enterprise was moving. He wanted out. If anyone's going to know where to find Pete, it'd be Lonny."

Troy glanced over at Jim, who had a grim look on his face. "We good?"

"For now." As Jim stood up from the couch he said, "If you hear anything from him, give us a call." He produced a single white business card stamped with the Agency's tip hotline. Bree took it without looking at the number. They all knew she wouldn't be calling.

The suggestion to follow up on Lonny Stieber was hardly a revelation. He was next on the list as it was. Unlike Hayden Meloy, Stieber had an address. He owned an automotive shop up north that specialized in bikes and, Natalia suspected, illegal trade.

Next to the cars, Jim didn't waste any time. "Aurora's got us the address on Stieber." He glanced up, eyes darkening in the dying light. It wasn't particularly late, but heavy clouds had settled around them, and the air smelled thick with approaching snow. The forecast called for a blizzard. "I'll forward it to you and meet you there."

Natalia felt the cool tone in his voice, and noticed the lack of inclusion. *I'll do this. I'll do that.*

"As much as I'd just *love* to be left on the side of the road again," she said icily, "am I going with you?"

"No." Jim had already turned away from them, and was moving back towards the car. "Go with Troy."

"Oh, ok!" she called after him. "I'll just go with Troy, shall I?" She turned, huffed angrily, and glanced at her godfather. "How am I supposed to work with that?"

Troy clapped her on the shoulder and offered a weak smile. "You're not. Give him a chance to work it out of his system. We'll grab coffee on the way."

xXx

On a good day, it would have taken them less than a half hour to reach Lonny Stieber's shop. But the snow was falling fast and thick, flexing sideways across the road thanks to a nasty wind that had swept up off the East River. It was a cruel reminder that winter in New York was forever unpredictable. It took them nearly an hour to reach the shop, and the only reason they had been able to distinguish where to park was thanks to the tire treads left by Jim's Agency rental. He was waiting, staring at the dashboard, looking...sad. Natalia's own annoyance at him waned, just a bit.

As Natalia stepped out of the car into a solid foot of snow the wind caught her in the face like a wild haymaker, and she felt the ice drill into her cheek. They crowded together to keep the wind from carrying their voices. The other side of the street had been absorbed into the snow, and Natalia could only make out the vague outline of the shop, low-slung and shack-like.

Natalia wanted to ask Jim where he had gone before arriving in Port Morris, but she got the distinct impression Jim would rather go back to Alcatraz than answer any questions that didn't revolve around *How many bullets can I plant in Lonny Stieber before he dies?* Anyways, he was in a foul mood and wasn't likely to share anything with her unless he had to.

Men.

"We know if Stieber is inside yet?" Troy asked, raising his voice to be heard above the squeal of the wind.

"Open sign isn't on," Jim said, turning his attention towards the front of the shop. Natalia couldn't see much through the blowing snow, but what she did see didn't speak highly of what lay within.

"Let's get this over with," Jim grunted.

Natalia braced herself against a gust of wind that caught the hem of her jacket and sent a whirl of snow up her shirt. Troy and Jim were talking, walking ahead of her and disappearing through a veil of white. She was disconnected from their reality, where investigations grew and bullets flew wide. Behind this partition, she saw a world she was unable to touch, a veil she could press herself against without tasting the air on the other side. She imagined it coated the lips and tongues of those who inhaled it with a bitter film. A palette that could never be cleansed. Despite this, Natalia wanted to step beyond, to experience the world of poison and burnt gunpowder herself. It would connect her to what she had lost; family and friends who had vacated their given place in her life.

Natalia *wanted* it, if only to have somewhere she belonged.

She skipped up the front walk to catch up with the two men.

Jim was already kneeling in front of the door, a set of lock picks in his hand. She could see his hands shaking as he manoeuvred the tension wrench and the pick. Piles of what she assumed were useless car parts settled on either side of the door like some sort of art deco statuary.

It gives the place a lovely sewer-chic look.

The lock clicked and Jim let out a low hiss through his clenched teeth. Natalia and Troy exchanged nervous glances.

The door was heavy metal, studded along the edges and, Natalia guessed, probably a good three or four layers thick in case someone, either a lawman or an enemy, decided to try to bash their way in. Jim had to put his shoulder into it to open it completely.

Natalia wished he hadn't.

The stench of death, of burnt fat and leather, twisted around them before being pulled out the door by the wind. Chains hanging from the ceiling rattled above, caught in the breeze. The lights had been left on, and the white glare reflecting off shined chrome handlebars and disassembled bike parts illuminated the room with medical-like precision.

Natalia followed Jim and Troy from the alcove and let her eyes trail up towards the ceiling, across the mechanical lifts, towards the lengths of titanium bars and metallic cables that were splattered brown and black, to the ground below them, and the skeletal remains of a bike. It was charred, nothing more than a husk. Leather seat and saddlebags eaten away by flames. Natalia stepped forward behind Jim and Troy, both of whom were staring at the chains dangling overhead.

She saw the black bones clutching at the tangle of chains. Femurs and skull twisted together, caught in a spider web of looped metal that swung softly in the air. Particles of ash drifted sullenly from the human remains, sifting over the burnt-out bike. Natalia leaned down, grabbed a nearby wrench, and began to prod the mess.

She nearly missed the charred Mickey Mouse pin that Lonny Stieber's grandkids had bought for him at Disneyland.

He had wanted out, and it looked as if he got his wish.

"This was Stieber's," Natalia said, lifting the pin and rubbing some of the black smudge from its surface. She didn't have to say any more.

"Damn." Troy stepped away, turned his back to the man who had been roasted alive beneath his own flaming bike. "This the sort of shit the Reapers get up to?"

"They don't go around planting flowers, Troy," Jim replied sharply.

Natalia averted her gaze from the skeleton that was caught in the jumble of chains. The Reapers were relentless, but it was equally possible that Cain had decided to string up Lonny Stieber, and Natalia wasn't sure why Jim hadn't suggested it yet.

He's blinded by rage, Natalia decided. *We're a sightless sort of species.*

She left Jim and Troy there to talk, not wanting to be with the dead any longer than she had to. She circumvented the makeshift funeral pyre and moved behind the counter of the shop. The till had been opened and emptied, probably in an attempt to make it look like a burglary gone very wrong. Strapped beneath the counter was a sawed-off shotgun. It was firmly in place. Whoever had interrupted Lonny Stieber had been a friend, or at least someone he trusted for long enough to be attacked from behind.

Behind the counter was another door that led deeper into the shop and a fully-equipped garage. Numerous bikes, all in various states of disrepair, stood at attention. What was outside, beyond the door, was for show only. This room, with all its tools and machinery, was where the magic happened.

"An impressive setup," Troy said from behind Natalia. "Almost makes you think he was trying to run a legitimate business."

"Oh yes," Natalia said. "Very legitimate. Definitely not evading taxes or running drugs."

"I don't remember either of your parents being this snarky." Troy smiled, offering a light pat on the shoulder.

Natalia could hear Jim's teeth grinding audibly behind her. Classy.

"Troy, check the back, see what the living situation is like."

Natalia moved to follow her godfather, hoping to put some space between her and Jim so he could cool down, as Troy suggested. As she turned, Jim's hand was on her shoulder, holding her back.

"There's a gun under the counter," she interjected before Jim could berate her for *whatever* it was she had done wrong. "But it doesn't look like it's been moved at all. Maybe he knew the people who attacked him? He wasn't scared of them?"

Jim nodded sharply, looking where Natalia was pointing. "That would make sense, especially if the Reapers lit the match."

Troy called out, and Natalia followed her sullen guardian through the door into the garage proper. There were chrome pieces littered everywhere; half-disassembled bikes that looked like they were being scrapped for parts. Across the garage, Troy was emerging from a greasy door marked *bathroom*, waving a cell phone between two fingers.

"Someone was living in that rat's nest," he said as he approached. "We've got a sleeping bag, some old beer cans that the Sweepers might be able to pull DNA from."

Natalia grinned at her godfather as Jim grabbed the phone and began to scroll through the contacts. The scientific process was too time-consuming for someone like Jim. Better to put evidence he could see with his own two eyes in his hands and let the man go to work on that.

Like a dog with a bone.

"It's not Lonny's, he's listed in here. Same as-" His voice stalled and he glanced up to Natalia and said, "Pete."

"Do it," Natalia said, skipping forward. "Jim, we have a *line* to him now."

Jim hesitated, and in that moment Natalia saw his uncertainties for the future filling every line of his face. Would he find his son dead, dismembered, as Natalia's family had been? Would Angel be hung from a tree and set to burn until she was nothing more than papery ash, dissolved by the next snowfall?

They will be if we don't act. Natalia snatched the phone from Jim's hands and hit the call button.

Silence. Then, from the storefront of the garage where Lonny Stieber had been burned along with his bike, a ringing, cheerful melody. Ninety-Nine cents in the App Store. Some 8-Bit rendition of *Chim Chim Che-ree.*

Jim put a finger to his lips, narrowed his eyes, and motioned for Natalia and Troy to follow him. They reached the doorway behind the counter and ducked low. The chaotic trill was louder now, and Natalia could hear something brushing past the chains that strung up what was left of Lonny Stieber.

The ringing stopped, she lifted the cell to her ear, and heard Pete's voice coming from the phone and from beyond the counter, in surround sound. "I'm not talking to Meloy, am I?"

Jim jumped the counter before Natalia could tell Pete where to ram his cell phone. She and Troy leapt up to see the back end of Pete throwing himself through a door, out into the blistering snow, with Jim in pursuit.

Natalia, without a thought to what might be waiting on the other side of the door, did the same.

The frozen squall swept snow and ice into her face, dragging her forcefully into an unpainted canvas, without detail beyond the footprints that were already being filled in by rolling sheets of white. Natalia took one step forward, and then a second, only to turn and realize the entire world around her had been erased. Troy was gone, as was Jim. Where was the back door of the shop? She scrambled to orient herself, throwing one hand out in the direction she thought she had come from, but there was nothing behind her, nothing ahead; only wind that buffeted her from all directions.

There was a gunshot to her left. Or was it right? She couldn't tell. The blizzard was oppressing, all-encompassing. She felt it, like hand gripping her heart and squeezing as the beating increased. The snow filtered around her, and the fear of it all created a whiteout in her brain. There was nothing to focus on, no where to escape, to calm herself. Her lungs were burning now, but everything was cold. Cold and white, in all the nothingness that surrounded her. She felt her knees buckle, but didn't feel her body collide with the ground.

Snow soaked through her jeans, and the wind whipped her hair and screamed in her ear like a harpy released from Hell. No other voices, no other comforts. Nothing but silence beyond the wind.

Another shot, closer this time, like a starting gun. Natalia scrambled back to her feet, across the wasteland towards the echoing pop.

It was easy enough to imagine a splash of violent colour across the canvas, a shocking slash of blood bursting from the whiteout, drawing her towards death, but no matter how far she seemed to stumble, there was nothing ahead or behind her save for snow.

"Jim!"

No response. Natalia plunged forward further. Another round of bullets flying around her, like a swarm of gnats hovering over a lake. A hand reached from the nothingness that surrounded her, caught her by the throat as the barrel of a gun pressed into the tangle of her hair.

"Stay still."

That voice. She knew it. Knew the voice, knew that smell that was in her nose and then torn back into the storm by the wind. She knew the one who had carted her away in Alcatraz, who had whispered *hush* in her ear, and who had tried to take her when Steven died. A Hollow Man.

A break in the snow and ice, a figure emerging from the depths, like he had been summoned out of hell, and for a wondrous moment Natalia thought it was Jim and that he had turned back for her, because that was his job as a guardian. Protection, safety.

Don't go chasing mad men into the middle of blizzards. Don't abandon your protégé.

But it was Troy who had come back for her. Troy who had found her in the storm, and it was Troy who stood a mere ten yards away from them, gun directed towards her but aimed at the person who held her in a precarious position. Even as the wind churned up snow and ice, as if trying to erase Troy's visage from her gaze, Natalia saw the shock written in his face.

"Put the gun down!" Troy ordered. His voice trembled.

Tell me, Natalia thought wildly. *Tell me who you see.*

The gun nestled deeper, as if her captor were trying to bury it right into her skull and then bypass it to her brain. It might be worth it, she decided, if Troy could just see the face, know who it was, and answer the questions that had been lingering in the wake of all the destruction Cain had levied against her.

Then out of the snow, she saw a glint of silver reflect the underside of Troy's chin. She saw it plunge in to the side of his neck. She saw the splash of blood, staining the snow at his feet.

Natalia screamed, horrified, as Troy fell to his knees, hands rising to his neck. Behind him Pete looked on with anguish, the small, bloodied knife hanging limply from his hand. Natalia wrenched herself free from the one who held her, the instincts that Jim had spoken of kicking into high gear. She spun and used the back of her hand to push the gun away from her skull. There was no time to search the blizzard for her attacker's face, to try to find something familiar there. He was already disappearing back into the storm. Natalia stumbled towards Troy. She fumbled at his body, forcing her hand down against the blood that was pumping from his neck.

"Troy, oh no, no, please not you, too-" Natalia's head snapped up to look at Pete, whose eyes were now locked on something straight ahead. The silence and stoicism broke; he turned and launched himself back into the storm. Natalia heard snow crunch behind her, felt Jim's fleeting presence as he bypassed her in pursuit of Pete.

"Jim! *Jim!* Troy's hurt!"

He wouldn't. He wouldn't abandon us for his vengeance. I know it. I know.

"Jim, *please!* He's going to die!"

Jim halted, back still to Natalia and his fallen comrade, watching the whitewashed world ahead as if he were silently calculating the odds of destroying Pete versus the odds of Troy's survival. Natalia knew he felt that pull towards anger and revenge and whatever else lay behind his own veil. If she weren't there, if she weren't a figure in his life or a problem to be solved, if all things were equal, Natalia knew Jim would pursue Pete until the end of time.

He turned back towards her and she saw the reluctance. He struggled through the snow and knelt next to Natalia, ordering her to call it in, replacing Natalia's shaking hands on Troy's neck with his own firm grip. She already knew he wouldn't forgive her for asking him to choose between the two worlds.

Chapter 21

He would live, miraculously. If the knife had sliced a few millimeters in either direction, if it had plunged any deeper and completely severed the external jugular vein, he wouldn't have survived. If Natalia had been alone, trying to call for help while keeping pressure on the wound, lost in the blizzard... Yes, Troy would be dead. But he wasn't. The blood loss was substantial, and when he was taken to the nearest hospital the doctors had advised that his survival was unlikely.

Natalia knew she wouldn't be able to stand another death. She would wither away, blow out to the East River, caught in a current, before descending to the stony bed where she would become hollow and broken and her body would become home to fish.

But Troy survived, and, after two days by his side, Natalia was taken back to the Agency where she could change her clothes and report to Aurora. She hadn't seen Jim since they had followed the ambulance to the hospital. He left her there. She wasn't even mad. The idea that he might choose following Pete over saving Troy was horrifying; she had seen his true colours shine through in that moment of hesitation. She didn't hate him for his desire to pursue the biker; she just couldn't speak to him.

It was Rebecca and Bedlam who came to retrieve her from the hospital, with the promise that Troy would be transferred to the Agency as soon as he was stable enough to move. She had saved his life, they told her.

No mention of Jim.

Whatever.

She still had the phone in her pocket. Jim hadn't asked for it, nor taken it. What had Pete said? *This isn't Meloy.*

Hayden Meloy, the man with the half-face, who knew how to wire bombs and destroy things with white-hot flames. Rebecca was chatting away in the front seat. Natalia turned the phone on and quickly copied down Pete's number.

At the Agency, she passed through security and immediately handed off the cell phone to their crime scene analysts. From there Rebecca took Natalia up to the locker room where she could have a shower, clean up, and put on fresh clothes. Aurora was waiting for her, and took her to a small lunchroom, where she proceeded to putter around, making Natalia a snack, stopping occasionally to make notes on what had happened at Lonny Stieber's shop.

"Has Jim contacted you since the hospital?"

Natalia stopped mid-bite into a sandwich and eyed Aurora suspiciously. "No. He hasn't called in?"

"He contacted Meghan to say he was fine, following some leads. Senior agents like him get a bit more leash when it comes to pursuing investigations, so she isn't worried. I think her biggest concern is that he might go on a bender."

Natalia shook her head, finished her mouth of food, and said, "Not while Angel and Jay are still out there."

"We figured as much," Aurora said as she sat on the other side of the table. "We just want to make sure he doesn't try to go after Pete and the Reapers by himself." Her tablet chimed and she glanced down at it. "The body you found at the shop has been confirmed as Lonny Stieber."

Natalia already knew it would be. She wondered how old Stieber's grandkids were, and what they'd be told when Grandpa couldn't go with them to Disneyland again.

"And," Aurora said as she kept reading, "it looks like the hair samples they pulled from the sleeping bag and pillow that Troy found belong to Hayden Meloy. Sweepers found a blood sample near the burn site, a seventy percent match to Patrick McKim."

Natalia hummed at that and finished the last of her sandwich. Either way, Pete was on the Reapers' radar now, and if they got to him before the Agency there was a solid chance Angel and Jay would be lost forever.

"Now what?" Natalia asked finally.

"Troy's being transferred here in the next couple of hours. You can go see him then. Bedlam will take you home tonight, stay over if you need the company."

"I'll be fine."

"Until then, you can come and get the run down on some of the comm work we do and try your hand at running plates and credit cards."

"Big Brother is alive and well, huh?"

"Such a cynic for a young thing," Aurora said with a wink. "People forget there is a price for the life we lead. You tell them they can't have that life, they kick up a fuss. You tell them they can have it but we need to be a bit more secure, watch personal things, and they lose their shit then, too. There's no winning. To be fair, there isn't a good answer either. No one *wants* to live in a surveillance state. Our society is in a transitionary phase. Eventually something will break, whether it's our technological advancements or what the people want. Something's gotta give. Until then, we do it under the radar, try to be good, stay in the realm of law and order, and don't step outside the bounds."

"Unless you're Caulder."

"Yeah, well, I think that's going to come back to bite him in the ass. Meghan's been sending detailed reports to Washington, and they aren't happy that he abused his power in going after you. I'd reckon that once his nephew is home safe and sound they'll probably call him to a tribunal."

"Nothing says *hey, you, don't do that* like a light slap on the wrist."

Aurora shook her head. "The public wants to know that people are being held accountable. Even if we work outside their scope of vision, we need to show that everyone is held to a certain standard. There's no room for power-tripping in the SOI."

"That's reassuring, I think."

Aurora chuckled, shook her head, and held out her hand to take Natalia's plate. "Let's go teach you some invasive technical shit."

Troy had arrived at the medical ward just after dinner. At the announcement of his arrival, Natalia wasted no time in beelining it from the Hive so she could check on him. The on-call doctor gave her a basic update on his status. Another blood transfusion. A badly scarred neck. Alive. Beyond that, he couldn't say. She was family, but not *family*. Natalia crept into the private room and stood at the door, watching as the EKG gently spiked and dipped with each heartbeat. Alive. His chest rose and fell in a peaceful rhythm. Alive. A breathing tube down his throat and IVs on his arms. Alive.

"You acted fast."

Natalia jolted at the unexpected voice behind her and turned to find Meghan standing at her shoulder. The supervisor pressed past her and settled in the chair next to Troy's bed. "He'd have been a goner if you hadn't been there."

"That always seems like such a weird saying."

"Hmm?"

"*If you hadn't been there.* Like, if I hadn't been there, Troy would have died. But if I hadn't been taken in by Jim then Angel and Jay never would have been targets. If I didn't make it home that day, I never would have found the Code, Steven would be alive. If I hadn't been born..." Natalia trailed off, then flipped her hand through the air. "If, if, if. It's like, how far back do we take it?"

Meghan smiled slightly, a wisp of her black hair catching the corner of her mouth. She blew it free and shrugged. "Deep thoughts."

"If I'd done the same for Steven, if I hadn't panicked there in Alcatraz, he'd be alive too."

"Maybe," Meghan nodded. "Maybe not. We can never be sure where the path goes. We make the best decisions we can with what information we have. We live our lives, try to be good people, that's it. That's all we can do."

"What if I'm not a good person?"

Meghan smirked and raised one eyebrow. "Do you think you are?"

Natalia shrugged one shoulder lamely and broke eye contact. The scars along Meghan's fingers caught the light. A sort of waffle pattern. Natalia couldn't figure what might make such precise, thin scars. "I don't know."

"I don't think people would care so much about you if you were a little shit," Meghan said wryly.

"Except maybe Jim," Natalia added with a grin. *I could be more like him. That'd probably suit him just fine.*

"He called me a couple hours ago to say he was back at the house. Whatever he was doing, it didn't pan out." Meghan paused. "This isn't on you, Natalia. With Angel and Jay, and even Jim's bad attitude. None of it is on you."

"But, if I-"

"Yeah, if. There are a lot of *ifs*. You need to understand, though, what happened to Jim with Cain, all that bullshit, it was before your time, and it's what damned Jim to this. He's built a lot of misery around himself, a lot of guilt that he never should have taken on. Cain's been waiting for a chance to exploit that for ten years, and he's only doing it now because *he's* done waiting. It's not on you. And Jim's family – Angel and Jay? They would have always been the target. For all his faults, Jim has always protected them. They keep him grounded, and he knows it. He knows damn well that if he fails them, he's failed himself, and all the other people he's worked to protect over the years. Don't take that guilt on yourself, Natalia. It's easy enough to take someone else's medicine, but that doesn't mean it's good for you."

Is that what she had been doing? Natalia wasn't sure. She had let Jim be himself, for all intents and purposes. In many ways, he was just as she remembered him from Alcatraz; withdrawn from the world, protective of both his secrets and his truths. Was he taking that pressure out on her, or was she just incapable of separating herself from the misery of others?

Meghan stood up and faced Natalia. "I know he can be ornery, but he's one of the best we have for getting things done. The thing is, there might come a time when you don't need things to *get done*. You might need to learn skills, trades, the parts of the job that aren't learned sneaking out of a motel room at two in the morning. Jim's not the person for teaching the...human aspect of the job. The rest of us are here for you when that time comes, because it will, Natalia. Keep your mind open enough to recognize that."

"Sounds like some hippy mumbo jumbo to me," Natalia said.

"Spoken like the ward of Jim Wilkinson," Meghan replied with a sigh and a roll of her eyes. "Go home and get some sleep, Natalia. None of us are broken yet."

xXx

Natalia waved to Bedlam from the porch of the house in Prospect Park. He flashed the headlights, yelled at her to "stop faffing about," and pulled away from the curb. Natalia watched until his car rounded the corner and disappeared into the darkness. The blizzard had only lasted the day, and left the world blanketed in thick puffs of snow that looked like marshmallow whip. The thought made Natalia smile, because it reminded her of a Christmas song she couldn't stand that Beth would insist on singing every year.

Fuck you, Marshmallow World.

Inside was warmly lit, and Natalia knew Jim was home. His cologne lingered in the air, as did the scent of bourbon.

Classy as hell.

She dropped her shoulder bag on the floor of the hall with a *thump*, just in case Jim hadn't heard her arrive in his drunken stupor. Make noise, alert him to your presence, prepare for a fight in three, two, one...

She poked her head around the open archway that led into the living room and stared in confusion. Jim sat on the couch, bent over the coffee table, head in his hands. Crying?

No, probably just leaking liquor out of his eyes. Natalia shuffled her feet loudly, giving Jim a moment to recover. He inhaled sharply, ran his hands down his face, and turned to her. A man reluctant to reveal the weakness that he knew was written all over him.

"You're back," he said.

"I wanted to wait until they transferred Troy back to the Agency." She stepped forward and settled on the piano bench. Even with the space between them Natalia could smell the booze seeping from his pores. How long had he been drinking alone? How many hours? Days? Weeks?

An entire lifetime.

"He's going to be fine," she added simply.

"Good."

After an extended silence, Natalia said, "I learned how to trace a license plate today, and how to find someone's credit card records. I got my own cubicle in the Hive."

"Glad to hear it."

Natalia knew that was as far as the conversation would go. She had seen Jim in moods like this before, though none had ever quite matched this particular brand of bitterness. There was no use in trying to talk to him. He would have to work out his agony in his own time, his own way.

"Ok." Natalia turned around and was a step from the living room when she heard Jim speak again and turned back to face him. "What?"

"How many people have you killed?"

"Five," she said, without missing a beat, because she knew each one of them. Their astral presence nipped at her heels and followed her like a black, oily sickness that was smeared on her skin. Something she could never completely rid herself of.

"I make it six."

"Preacher was an accident," Natalia replied coolly, taking another step back into the living room. She wasn't sure what Jim was getting at, but the fact that he was talking seemed like a move in the right direction.

"Ain't no accidents in murder, kid."

"Six, then," Natalia conceded.

"You remember all of them?"

Carmen, stabbed; Fish, neck sliced open; Preacher, shot; unnamed guard, head smashed in; another guard, skewered; Duncan, gutted. Direct contact; that was how she quantified it. She had to have personally taken their lives.

"Yes."

Jim leaned back from the coffee table and ran his hands over his face with such force that Natalia wondered if he weren't trying to pull his skin free from his body. "I've lost count of my kills," he admitted dully, "but I see them all, like some goddamned horde of the undead, lurking around every corner. Even the people I didn't kill, the victims, the *accidents.*"

"Like Cain's wife?"

"Like my son and his mother. Like Steven. Every mistake. Every person caught in the crossfire. I see all of them, I know their names. I know them."

Natalia eased herself onto the end of the couch, perched in such a way that she might be able to bolt if necessary, though wholly uncertain why the sensation was present. She didn't reach out to him, because Jim was not a man who found comfort in a human touch, and even if he were, she knew that a wall remained between them. It was built from the bones of the dead.

"Jay and Angel aren't dead," Natalia said, because it was the only thing she was certain of, even though she had no reason to be.

"They are. They will be. You don't come back whole from this sort of thing."

"I did," Natalia reminded him quietly.

Jim laughed. "No, you didn't, kid. You came back in fragments. Knuckles and joints and screws that you'll never be able to reassemble properly. We leave pieces of ourselves behind with the ones we kill. You're just too goddamned innocent to see it."

Natalia had opened her mouth to protest when Jim gripped his glass and flung it hard across the room so it smashed against the stonework of the fireplace. Natalia leapt from her spot on the couch and stumbled back a step.

Jim held his head in his hands, gave a hoarse sob. "I'd have left him in a heartbeat," he said at last. "I'd have left Troy there to die if it had been anyone else with him. Just for the chance to get to Pete, to finish it."

"I won't tell him if you don't."

Jim forced a sad laugh. "Jesus, kid."

"What? What do you want me to say? Am I supposed to be pissed that you nearly left us there, or-or that you *did* leave me at the hospital? Or that no one knew where you were? Like, really, Jim. Tell me what part of this I'm supposed to be angry about and I'll summon all the wrath I've got in me."

Jim was unfazed by the sharpness of her words. "I imagine it's a lot."

"Yeah, it's a whole goddamn lifetime of pissed off," she said, and frowned. "But I'm not an angry person, Jim. Not really. I don't *want* to be angry. I want to stop feeling bad, like I brought all this shit on you."

Jim looked surprised. "You didn't. This has nothing to do with you."

"Yeah, well, sure feels like it does." Natalia slumped over on the piano bench. "I'm sorry you couldn't go after Pete, and about Angel and Jay. I want to make it better. I want to be able to fix it."

"Shit, kid. This isn't... There isn't some magical cure here. It's just a bad hand, all right? Things go wrong and we deal with it as it comes. I'm just... Fuck." He shook his head and laughed. "Cards on the table? I'm a major fuck up. Steven, he had some problems, but they stemmed from something, from tragedy. Me? I've been the screw-up my whole life. Even with Angel, but I always wanted to do right by them, *always*. There's never been any doubt about it in my mind. Keep work and home separate and everything will be fine. It just didn't last nearly as long as I hoped it would."

"I bet it never does," Natalia replied. "Or else neither of us would be in these shitty positions."

"Yeah, you got that right."

"I'm sorry I asked you to choose one over the other. It wasn't fair of me."

"Yes, it was. You had every right to do what you did. I couldn't just let Troy die."

"But you couldn't let Pete go, either," Natalia said slowly.

"No, I couldn't."

"Did you find him out there, Jim?"

"No, I didn't, kid. Didn't find much of anything besides regret."

"Ok." Natalia exhaled slowly and lifted her eyes to her guardian. His attention was diverted now by a framed photograph that Natalia didn't remember seeing before. It was a family portrait; a younger, happier looking Jim with Angel and, she guessed, a young Jay.

"Get some sleep, Jim. Things will look better in the morning. I'm sure of it."

Natalia left the living room without another word to her guardian. She went to her room, copied the number on her hand, nearly faded away now, onto a legal pad, and then pulled out her cell phone.

Pete picked up on the first ring, and Natalia laid out the rules.

xXx

Natalia caught a cab to the Pitkin rail yard. It was where she had agreed to meet Pete. He hadn't been surprised to hear from her.

"You been planning this?"

"Call it *Plan C*," she said, doling out a hefty tip to the cabbie. He glanced at her, tried to tell her it was too much, but she shook her head and smiled. If she was paying someone to take her to the mouth of Hell, she ought to give a decent tip.

Besides, if he remembers the kid who tipped him well, it'll leave another thread behind. Something for them to follow back to me.

She stepped out of the cab and gave the driver a friendly wave. Another ounce of humanity. Another thread. *Remember that girl you dropped off at the rail yard a few days after Christmas? Remember the generous tip and the big smile? People are going to be asking about me; I need to you tell them what you saw.*

"Come inside."

The line went dead and Natalia sighed. Her phone battery was on full. They would make her get rid of it, probably toss it in the snow. The cabby had instructions to circle the block a few times, but give the rail yard a wide berth. Using her limited tradecraft, Natalia figured one of two things would happen; Jim would realize she was gone and try to catch up, or Angel and Jay would be able to catch the cab on his circle around the block and get to safety.

The only thing she had to contend with now was allowing herself back into Cain's hands.

Allowing. The terminology made her shiver, as if she had no agency. The world expected her to be tossed by waves and worn like pieces of glass on a beach. A shard of something long gone. Natalia had to prove them wrong; her very survival depended on it.

The gates to the yard were open, and Natalia could see deep ruts in the snow. The yard had been closed for renovations; it was a cemetery of abandoned trains in desperate need of repair. Vandals had clambered over the fence, tagged the cars, left their vibrant neon marks on the isolated world. They wouldn't dare interrupt this, of that Natalia was certain. Even with her minimal training, she could smell the blood in the air. This place would be more than a graveyard for trains soon enough.

Was this what it was like for Steven? Did he know he was going to his death as he climbed up those rickety stairs on Alcatraz?

"Were you scared?" she asked the wind, half-heartedly hoping an answer would reach her on the tail end of the wind, directed down from above, or wherever it was the dead *really* ended up. All that followed her question was silence and the sound of a cab pulling away from the curb.

xXx

While Natalia was halfway towards her destination with the unsuspecting cab driver, Jim was just waking up from a nightmare. In it he could smell roasting apples and flesh on the wind, but the trees were lost beneath sheets of snow that whirled about in all directions. As he staggered towards a tree, he saw a half-naked figure huddled beneath its charred branches. It was as he had found her in Alcatraz, after Cain had sent her to the wolves in Segregation. In his dream, Jim knelt before this quivering child and saw she was without a mouth to scream; her eyes showed intense terror. He took her face in his hands and told her to be strong, that this was not the hill she would die on.

If she understood him, she could say nothing in response.

As he tried to soothe the girl who both was and was not Natalia, Jim saw the blood flowing from the side of her neck. The blood began to arc in bright, red twists like spun sugar, splashing against the charred wood of the apple tree. He grasped at her throat, hoping to stem the tide of blood, fingers curling around her fragile neck until the tendons were fully enveloped. She clawed at his hand and Jim gripped harder, squeezing off the last narrow passage that might have given her a breath of air. Of life.

He woke up as her body fell backwards into the tree and was enveloped in ash.

The cold air on his face was the first indication that something was wrong. He never left the windows open; never invited the unexpected to find an easy route into his domain.

Cooper was by his feet, whining. Another bad sign. Since she had entered his life, Cooper had clung to Natalia's side like a shadow, as if he understood her need for something soothing and reliable. A protector.

Jim launched himself out of bed and down the stairs, across the hallway, cutting a corner sharply, slamming his shoulder into the wall as he bolted into Natalia's bedroom. The light was still on; the window, wide open. A single sheet of paper fluttered on her desk, caught by the wind but held down by a water glass. The snow has caused the ink to bleed, but Jim could still make out the important details.

Tell them I'm sorry.

Always family first, and despite Jim's misgivings he was forced to accept that Natalia had accepted Angel and Jay as pseudo-family; replacements for the irreplaceable. They, in turn, had done the same.

Jim had been too stubborn to see it happening, or maybe just desperate to keep the two diametrically opposing worlds separate. He didn't want to share Natalia, nor did he want to share Angel or Jay. He wanted them safely tucked away from each other, surrounded by velvet and cotton. Pristine condition, collector's editions.

But there was no time for those sorts of regrets now, because Natalia had done something very stupid, and was about to pay a heavy price for it.

xXx

It occurred to Natalia, as she followed the ruts in the snow around a disassembled train car, that at some point in the past she had promised Meghan, Steven, and even Beth, that she wouldn't pull what they called a *disappearing act.* Running away in a wild attempt to exert some control over her life, or at least limit the strategic advances of her enemies.

Now she had done it again, and she was certain Meghan Sirano would not hold back on the reprimanding if she somehow managed to get out of this alive.

Looking ahead, she saw the back end of a single trailer, open and exposed. It was deep and black, like a cavern carved into rock, and Pete emerged from it like an animal that had caught the scent of his prey on the wind, readying himself for the attack.

Behind him limped Jay, and then Angel, supported by equally dishevelled-looking Brecker and Callum. Everyone looked like they still had their limbs attached, which was more than Natalia could have hoped for given the nature of who she was dealing with.

"You have a weapon?" Pete called, halting at the lip of the truck.

Natalia held one hand up while carefully easing back her jacket to pull out her pistol. She tossed it sideways into the snow, where it was instantly buried. Brecker looked like the less injured of the two security agents; he hollered at her as she tossed her gun aside, telling her to run.

"And your phone!" Pete shouted.

Natalia rolled her eyes and pulled it from her pocket, running her finger over the power button to ensure it was on. The snow would damage it soon enough, but if she was lucky Aurora would be able to trace it prior to its inevitable malfunction. She dropped it.

"Walk slowly towards me!" Pete levelled a shotgun at Natalia. It was a sign of authority, nothing more. At that range, he was hardly likely to kill her if he suddenly became trigger-happy.

"Jayson first," Natalia called back. She was new to the hostage exchange process, but figured she shouldn't give away her only card, herself, right away. Pete looked unimpressed. With one gentle push, he sent Jayson over the edge of the trailer and into the snow. Angel squeaked and reached out for her son, who quickly scrambled to his feet and looked hastily between Natalia and his mother.

"Go," Angel croaked. "Go baby."

Jay stumbled through the snow, digging a trench with his legs as he went. He reached Natalia and she grabbed him by the arm.

"Are you hurt?"

"No," he said shakily.

A lie. She could see the lingering shadows of bruises along his neck, and hear the crackle in his throat. Still, if he was willing to pretend, she could do the same. "Good," she said. "Get back, behind that train."

"But Nat-"

"Do what I say. *Trust me.*"

He complied, and Natalia watched Pete with a steady gaze, unsure if she ought to wait for him to take control of the situation. She knew what Jim would say in these scenarios; he would tell her that she needed to be in the driver's seat, but Natalia knew better than to feign that sort of power. Pete would see right through it, and more importantly, he would punish her for her arrogance.

"Now you!" Pete demanded over the din of the wind and snow.

Angel was her priority, but she couldn't leave Callum and Brecker. Pete's truck was the trolley taking her to Hell, and Cain wouldn't hesitate to axe any extra hostages who were unnecessary to his end game.

"Angel first!"

Pete wasn't having any of it. He collared Callum, tossing the limp security agent off the edge of the truck. Callum looked as if he couldn't believe his luck as he struggled to his feet and took a step forward towards Natalia. Then realization of what was happening dawned on him and he stumbled, grabbing her by the arms.

"What are you doing here?" he demanded, shaking her by the shoulders. "*You can't be here!*" He was babbling now as the full consequences of Natalia's actions dawned on him. He began to pull at her, trying to drag her back towards the entrance of the rail yard, but Natalia was stubborn; she dug her heels into the snow and earth and refused to give an inch to Callum.

Pete had watched the scene with interest until he saw the strength Callum was trying to exert over Natalia. Grabbing Brecker by the collar, he flung the security agent to the floor of the truck next to Angel, aimed his gun, and pulled the trigger.

The horrific blast of the single bullet ricocheted out of the truck. Angel screamed, her face splattered with blood and brain matter. Callum loosened his grip on Natalia, groaned in agony, and fell to his knees.

Natalia was shaking as she turned her head to look at Callum. "Please, just... Just go. Make sure they get back safe." Pete was calling her name again.

No time to waste, then.

"I'm not fucking around!" Pete declared. "You start walking, I'll let her go!"

That was more along the lines of what Natalia had been expecting. She watched uneasily as Angel was pushed unceremoniously off the back of the truck, landing in a heap of snow that smeared Brecker's blood around her clothes. She had to lean into the truck in order to stand, and as she began to walk her legs wobbled like a newborn lamb's. Angel made the first hesitant step forward and Pete hissed through his teeth.

That's my cue.

Natalia stepped forward. The snow was up to her thighs at some points and made moving sluggish and slow. It also bought her time. Desperate seconds that the Agency, Jim, anyone might be able to stumble upon them in. She could still hear Callum behind her, screaming at her to run away.

No. I won't.

At the halfway point, she and Angel would be close enough to brush shoulders. And that would be all. That would have to be enough. One last taste of mothering, of love, before Natalia accepted her place beyond the veil, where spiders clung to flesh and bullets punctuated each sentence. She understood now why Jim had gone to such lengths to protect his family. She understood and she could never begrudge him that.

As they brushed by each other, Angel rested her hand on Natalia's wrist and whispered, "He'll *kill you*."

Natalia couldn't help but smile. "Tell Jim I'm sorry."

That was more than Steven had given her.

"Keep moving!" Pete hoisted his shotgun and Natalia scowled in his general direction.

"Ass," she muttered.

"Natalia-"

"I'm really sorry you got involved in this."

Natalia reached the truck without looking back, trusting that Angel would be wise enough to continue moving towards freedom. She couldn't worry about anyone else now. Pete was offering her a hand to hoist her up; a strange action for a man who had rammed his fist into her side only weeks earlier.

"You're taking me straight to the devil. You know that, don't you?"

Pete grimaced. "Y'know, I'm pretty sure the devil don't know what he's getting himself into." He rested a hand on her shoulder, pushing her down to her knees.

Jim ignored the speed limits, the icy road, the warning signs. Looking back, he had ignored so much, it was a wonder he had managed to function at all. It was all laid out so clearly. Cain knew him, knew his quirks and his habits and his desperations. Cain knew damn well that drawing a sword against Jim's own family would blind him to the actions of anyone else.

And Cain knew that Natalia would never let another person take the hit for her if she could help it.

Aurora narrowed Natalia's cell phone signal to a two-block radius surrounding Pitkin rail yard, where the CCTV feed had picked up a cab circling the area for the last fifteen minutes. When pulled over by the irate guardian, the driver explained that a young woman had been his last passenger, let off at the rail yard gates, and had paid him extra to stay in the area for a half hour.

Jim followed the heavy ruts of a single vehicle through the front gate, and tracked them beyond an area where disused cars had been abandoned to the elements. Just beyond that was a clearing, open like an arena.

He saw Agent Callum first, frazzled, a man who had somehow managed to pull himself off the battlefield. He was facing away from Jim, screaming. Behind him sat Jay, unkempt and hunched over in the snow, half-embracing his mother. Angel had collapsed and was gripping her son frantically. Relief hit Jim like a torrent, propelling in towards his family. But the moment he was within arm's length, Angel pushed him, screaming, incomprehensible. Anger? No. Fear. Jim looked up, saw where she was pointing. The other end of the yard where Callum was staring; a single truck with its container open to the world.

Natalia stood in the truck, head bowed like a misbehaving child who had been reprimanded for sneaking a cookie before dinner. Pete stood over her like the unrepentant executioner he was. With a kick, he sent a bloody sack of flesh and bones over the edge of the truck. Brecker. Callum snarled something, stepped towards the van as Pete levelled his gun. Natalia snatched at his arm, pulled it down and shook her head vigorously before looking over her shoulder towards Jim.

Jim saw fear rise over her face as the reality of the trade she had consented to began to dawn on her, but it was too late to turn back. She jolted forward, one hand outstretched, summoning Jim to her side. Ever the fighter; an abused dog with one last kill left in it, if only it were given a chance. Pete brought the butt of his gun down against her back, sending her sprawling across the bed of the truck.

Pete looked up with a dark smile, as if to say, '*Look at what you did to her. Fucking despicable*,' before pulling down the rolling door and disappearing from sight. God help him, Jim wanted to go after them, but wanted to hold his family more. And he understood the futility of it. There was nothing he could do without risking Jay and Angel, himself, and even Natalia. Because Cain had seen his weakness long before Jim had recognized it in himself, and Cain had been wily enough to exploit it.

The truck pulled from the yard, lumbering towards a back exit, and Jim watched, dazed, as his ward was carted away into the night. He could have gone after her, but as he turned with the intention of tossing Angel and Jay into the cab with Callum before attempting a pursuit of the truck, he saw his son's face contorted with pain, and the monstrous black bruise that had spread across his neck and collarbone. Jim knew then that he couldn't leave them.

Chapter 22

Angel wouldn't talk to Jim, and the doctors refused to tell him what tests they were running. The only thing they could confirm was that there was no need to run a rape kit. A small mercy. But Angel was angry, so goddamned angry, that the moment Jim had appeared at the doorway of the medical ward she had screamed at him to leave. The force of her hand against his face was unexpected. She was not the violent sort; quite the opposite, but she screamed and hit him repeatedly as he cowered under her anger, until a nurse forcefully pushed him towards the door of the room.

Jay was moderately more forgiving, although Jim suspected that was more due to exhaustion than a willingness to fight.

"I'm not supposed to talk to you about what happened," Jay said, voice breaking. He was sporting a brace on his neck; a sign of a strangulation. Jim knew better than to question him about it. "They said you're *too* involved."

Jim conceded that point without hesitation. "I'm sorry, I never-"

"He's going to kill her, Dad. He said...terrible things. What he's going to do to. It was..." Jay couldn't finish the sentence and shook his head.

"Cain is going to pay," Jim said. "He's going to *pay* for what he did to you."

Jay tried to shake his head, but it was just a strained tip from side to side. "It wasn't Cain."

"How do you-"

"Because he introduced himself, *Dad*. Because that fucking monster smiled and wanted to shake my hand and told us we only had you to blame." Jay shifted his jaw, ground his teeth, and said, "We were blindfolded after that. They talked around us sometimes, Cain and someone else. The things he said-"

A throat cleared behind them, and Jim turned to see Meghan standing in the doorway.

"You aren't supposed to be here, Jim."

"I'm talking to my son."

"Be that as it may." She stepped aside, spread out one arm wide to indicate she was holding the door for him. "We have things to discuss."

Jim turned back to Jay, hoping that his son might protest his absence. Instead, and perhaps unsurprisingly, Jay looked back at his father with an air of disgust. "Go, Dad," he croaked. "I want to rest anyways."

"I'll...come back to see you later."

"Just-" Jay shook his head again. "Just go."

Meghan led Jim towards the elevator. When they were well out of earshot, she turned to speak to him. "This is a major clusterfuck."

"You don't say."

"No, no, you don't get to be smarmy with me, *Agent Wilkinson*. You don't get to be a douchebag in this situation. Your family is safe, all right? And they're going off the grid the minute the doctors clear them. I'm talking complete name change, made up history, and *you* are to have no contact with them until we end this."

Jim had known this was coming. Even under the protection of the Agency, Cain had tracked them down and utilized Pete's anger and resentment to snatch them. As much as he disliked the thought, Jim couldn't help but concede that the best way to protect his family was to ensure they simply no longer existed. They entered the Agency as Angela and Jayson Holloway. They would leave under assumed names that Jim would probably never learn.

That was just the way it had to be.

Meghan punched the button for the elevator. "The doctor told me Angela won't see you."

"And refuses to let them give me an update on her," Jim added.

"That's her prerogative." Given Meghan's tone of voice, Jim figured Meghan was probably not the person to go to for sympathy. "She's pissed at you for getting her involved in this."

"She isn't the only one."

"Or," Meghan continued as if Jim hadn't spoken. "She's pissed that Natalia traded herself like that. And that makes *all of us*. It was a fucking *idiotic* move. I'm sorry, I get they are your family, but Natalia is more important than them, and there's no point mincing words. She's fucking irreplaceable, and now she's back in Cain's hands."

"I know."

"Do you? Do you even understand how royally screwed we are? If she breaks, we'll have hundreds of other Angelas and Jays, families ruined in an instant. I thought we made it clear to Natalia how vital she was. She really seemed to *get* it, so why, Jim? Why the fuck would she think trading herself for two civilians was somehow a good idea?"

"I don't know, Meghan. I'm not a fucking *mind reader*."

"No, but you *are* her guardian. You really expect me to believe she didn't say or do anything at all that suggested she was thinking of doing this?"

Did she? Jim went back over his last conversation with her, but it had been so one-sided. He ranted, he bemoaned his failures, and she gave him a hard time for his stupidity. It really seemed like a normal conversation to Jim.

"Nothing that stands out, Meghan. If I had realized, I would have put a goddamned lock on her window."

Meghan shook her head and laughed in spite of herself. "What's done is done. We can't afford to dither around. Take Tess and Bedlam and go back to Bree Cobbs, see if she's got any idea who else we might be able to turn to in the Reapers. We need to find Pete; he'll be the key to getting to Natalia." Jim opened his mouth to reply, but Meghan held up a hand. "I don't want you fucking around on this. You aren't some vigilante out to burn the world. Do this the right way so we can get her back safely."

xXx

She wasn't scared in the chapel. She could have been, easily. Infection ran deep in her blood. The island itself, the prison, a pulsating wound that had been poisoned by too many deaths. Infection. Her own body, rebelling against her. Infection. Steven's own drive, his desire for revenge, an infection.

She sat beside him in the chapel and, for the first time since arriving on the island, felt safe. Because he was beside her again. An infection of the mind, but not one she wanted to cure just yet.

The space between her and Steven felt like an ocean, though if she leaned over she was sure she might be able to touch him, yet Natalia knew better. He was of another world, a something else, and to touch him was to breach the barrier between worlds, and that was forbidden.

"I miss you," she said. It seemed like the most logical way to begin any conversation with the ghost of a guardian past.

"Your father didn't."

"You said that." Natalia shifted on the old wood and looked over at him.

"Your father didn't."

"Didn't what?"

"Your father didn't."

Natalia shook her head, not angered by the incessant repetition of her ghosts. It was in her subconscious, wasn't it? A piece of her, caught in the background of a mirror. Something she needed to glimpse. Something she needed to reach towards and pluck out of nothingness to make sense of her waking world. Her father didn't, her father didn't, her father didn't.

"What didn't he do, Steven?"

"He didn't."

"Steven."

Steven turned his head, slowly, joltingly, as if it were on a rusted cog. He looked at her, but his eyes were empty. His jaw fell open and a dozen spiders clawed their way from between his lips. He spoke without breaking eye contact.

"He didn't."

In her dream, Natalia had pressed her back into the wood of the pew, and an electric shock of pain had coursed through her body, waking her. She might have tried to work through the strange repetitive phrasing if the pain emanating from her bruised back was not stifling her mind. She groaned, rolled slightly, and inhaled deeply. Perfume. Jasmine and vanilla; fancy, Chanel No. 5. She could feel the particles clinging to her skin, leaving a chalky residue. But there was more; outside her person, her sense of self, she felt the world bulge and expand in response to all that was happening around her. Tendrils of the real world, in scents and sensations and memories, beckoning her out of the gloom. Natalia opened her eyes.

She was lying on her back. The first indication that something was wrong was the coolness at her fingertips, not frigid but...deformed, as if she were reaching for something through the cold air and couldn't quite grasp it. She could curl them and clench to make a fist, but her body responded slowly. She would have to hope that whatever had gone awry would straighten itself out in time.

Overhead were lengths of stark, grey fabric, draped in long, languid pools to form a sort of canopy. Even from where she lay, Natalia could see that the cloth was old, worn and moth-eaten. The bedding beneath her felt the same; crusty, flecked with dust and the ancient particles of things long since past. Natalia clenched at the bedding, felt her fingertips prod the intricate quilt-work, and exhaled to match the rhythm of the rest of her body. Jim's training, kicking in again.

Pace yourself, don't force your body to respond if all it wants to do is curl up. You need to ensure that every choice you make is calculated. Christ knows your enemies will do the same.

Inhaling sharply, Natalia pushed off with her right arm, forcing herself to roll to the left. She cried out, the bruise on her back making its presence known. She rolled, gasped for air and stared, shocked, at what looked back at her.

Two large brown eyes set with a spray of freckles across cheeks and nose. Raggedy, earth-coloured hair that hadn't been cut recently and stood in wild waves across his head. Only half the face was visible, but the smooth curves and lack of crow's feet told Natalia all she needed to know.

"Kyle?" Her voice came out in ragged rasps, and, for a moment, Natalia wondered if this were what she would sound like in ten years if she adopted Jim's smoking habits.

The big eyes blinked in response and slowly ducked down until only a scruff of hair was visible next to the bed. Natalia could hardly blame the boy for being timid. She wasn't exactly the picture of mental health after her own kidnapping either.

She pushed herself up with her left arm, felt a new cut crinkle and weep gently under the motion. "Kyle, is that your name? Kyle Powell?"

The tuff of hair had disappeared, and a muffled scrambling came from around the bed, as if the boy were moving on hands and feet around the room. A moment later, he was at the foot of the bed, wide eyes staring back over the sheets at Natalia.

"I'm..." she paused. How best to introduce herself. She was a stranger, and he was a child hostage. His mind could be warped, splintered by what he had seen and endured from Cain. Natalia looked beyond the boy and saw nothing but an empty bedroom, covered in lengths of disturbed dust. She looked back at Kyle, leaned forward, and felt her back protest the motion. She forced a smile and offered her hand. "I'm Natalia."

The boy stared at her fingers warily, as if he had never seen such an alien action before. She half expected him to spit in his palm and offer her the head of a rat in greeting. The child looked feral.

I probably did too.

Tentatively Kyle reached out with a pale hand and touched his fingers to Natalia's palm, as if confirming for himself that she was indeed real. At first touch, he retracted quickly, a hissing sound escaping from between his crooked, youthful teeth, but it seemed like he had confirmed her existence. He disappeared beneath her line of sight and scuttled around the last quarter of the bed so he appeared on her right-hand side, this time completely upright. In the pale light of the room, Natalia could see he was gangly but not underfed. He was just a boy in the grips of growing up.

"You are Kyle Powell, right?" Natalia turned, twisting the sheets around her. Suddenly, she felt very grown up. It was silly, given she was only six years older than the boy, but he seemed completely bewildered, caught up in the experience, unable to process. Natalia wasn't sure if Kyle Powell would ever have the capacity to ram a knife into a man's neck.

At last, the boy nodded his head and took a step back. He turned, facing the boarded-up window, and stepped forward until his nose was pressed against the wood and he could peer through the slat.

Natalia followed his movement, groaning as she pushed the sheet from across her body and shifted her feet to dangle over the bed. She ran one last diagnostic on her body and found that apart from her right hand being inordinately cold, everything seemed to be functioning properly. Natalia eased herself off the bed and walked around to the other side where she leaned down next to Kyle and looked through the boards.

It was a cloudy night and she couldn't make much out of what lay beyond their room. The roof sloped downwards before flattening off to the eavestrough. Beyond that, the world looked like nothing more than a black canvas, but the light radiating from the other windows along the house was enough for Natalia to see what had captured the boy's attention. Half buried beneath the snow on the slope of the roof was the skeleton of a bird. Its carcass had been picked nearly clean, leaving a flap of red feathers across its chest, as if it had been hollowed out for taxidermy. Kyle seemed fascinated with it, though Natalia could hardly guess why. Its head was bent at an obtuse angle and its tiny feet were discoloured and rigid from the snow and ice.

"Kyle." Natalia pulled herself away from the boards and looked down at the boy. "I need you to talk to me, ok? I know I'm a stranger, and you probably don't trust me, but-"

Natalia yelped as the boy swung about and threw his arms around her waist, pulling himself close. Instant waterworks; the tears soaked through the front of her shirt and she held her hands up, as if unsure what to do with them. Then she remembered Jim and his reticence; his refusal of even the most basic human connection. She remembered how badly she had wanted a goddamned *hug* in Alcatraz; it would have made everything seem better.

Natalia wrapped her arms around Kyle and pulled him close. "It's ok. It's all going to be ok."

She wasn't sure how long they stood there. As Kyle continued to cry his words became clear, and his fears focused. Natalia felt the chill of familiarity as he mimicked a common refrain. *I want my mom. I want my family. I want to go home.*

Me too.

"Look, look at me." Natalia knelt on the floor before him and wiped a snail line of tears from his cheek. "Kyle, this isn't the hill you die on, do you know what that means?"

The boy snuffled loudly and shook his head. Natalia couldn't help but smile. "It means this won't break you. You'll survive this. I'm going to take you home, ok? I know your uncle. He's working *really* hard to find you."

He sniffed again, tipping his head back dramatically, as if that would somehow help clear his nasal passages. It didn't. Natalia smiled sadly, placed her hands on his shoulders and was about to offer another gram of comfort when the lock on the bedroom door turned. Natalia threw herself up to her feet, ignoring the sting from her shoulder blades as her body adjusted to the sudden movement. But pain was a state of mind as much as a state of one's body, and Natalia couldn't afford to let it get in the way when Kyle could be at risk.

Cain Ferigon looked as if he hadn't changed. The same eyes, same hair, same smile, but Natalia saw him in a different light now; he was no longer just *her* monster, as Jim had so aptly put it, but the monster that spawned a hundred different tragedies. He was the monster that consumed those who stood in his way. He was the monster that was relentless in his pursuit of righting supposed injustices.

Natalia Artison stood to face her monster.

Cain seemed impressed, or at the very least amused by her; Natalia wasn't sure if there was a difference. His eyes flitted to one side, connecting with Kyle, who stood behind her, peering out towards the man. Cain had one hand behind his back, and as he brought it out, Natalia flinched and pushed Kyle back behind her. An instinctive, gut reaction.

Cain grinned wolfishly. "Jumpy, aren't you?" His voice was weary, beaten, and as he stepped forward, Natalia could see that the creases on his face were deeper than when they had last met, and shadows circled his eyes. He looked exhausted. In his hand was a white case, the size of half a book. Kyle's eyes went wide, and before Natalia could tug him back, he had stepped around her and moved towards Cain to accept the box.

The boy grabbed a small blue handheld console from the dresser, flipped it open, and replaced a cartridge with the one in the case. A moment later his face was illuminated by the duel screens of the console; soft beeps indicated that whatever it was he was playing, he was relatively proficient at it.

Neither Natalia nor Cain shifted, caught on a bridge between two worlds, waiting for one of them to break the silence.

"You're looking well," Cain said at last, and Natalia immediately begrudged him the first words.

"You still look like an asshole," she replied.

Cain smiled, glancing over at Kyle, who had pulled himself up onto the bed and didn't seem to notice the swearing.

"Where are we?"

"My home." He paused, considered the answer, then added, "Once."

That made sense. The lingering scent of smoke, the strange inhuman silhouettes that waited beyond the darkness of the house and the roof with the dead bird. A burnt orchard, where people had been strung up like meat. Natalia couldn't imagine why anyone, let alone Cain, would want to return here, but maybe he drew power from a place where he had once summoned death with such success.

"I heard what Pete did," Cain said. "He should have known better. I hope you're feeling all right."

Natalia imagined burning apple trees and the scent of flesh on the wind. She imagined the fear of Daisy O'Byrne, who had been discovered. Of Myra Ferigon, as a man she must have trusted implicitly strung her up like a pig in a slaughterhouse before setting her alight. Of the children, who had no concept of the monster they had blood ties to.

Cain Ferigon was a dangerous man, and no ounce of normality projected through clothing and good grooming would convince Natalia otherwise.

"Where is Pete?"

Cain shrugged one shoulder and looked casually back towards Kyle, now thoroughly engrossed in the game. "He paid his dues and was released from service." Cain said it with such flourish; Natalia despised that dramatic air.

If she was hoping to utilize Pete's vague connection to her, she was out of luck.

Plan D.

Cain took a step forward and Natalia shifted back. Out of the corner of her eye she saw Kyle twitch, glancing up from his game. When he spoke next, Cain's voice was soft, genteel even. He was trying to be civil in front of the boy, and on some level Natalia admired his dedication to the ploy.

"I need the Code, Natalia."

Natalia smiled sweetly. "No."

She had imagined that might frustrate Cain, but he only shook his head, bemused, and said, "I don't know why, but I think I'm a little surprised by that. Can't blame a man for trying."

He leaned forward, ruffled Kyle's hair, as if the child were his own, and Natalia had to resist the urge to leap forward and snap his fingers backwards one by one. Without another word, Cain turned and left the bedroom, locking the door behind him.

Natalia let her shoulders slump and roll forward with the exhaustion; the very sight of Cain was mentally draining, to say nothing about the bruise to her back, which was aching fiercely now. Kyle had crept across the blanket and rested a tiny hand on the back of her head, and Natalia lifted her face from the covers, giving him a weary smile that felt fake plastered over her anguish.

"Show me what you're playing," Natalia said, hoping to buy herself a few hours of rest, so she might refocus before assessing her surroundings. It was time she couldn't take, but dammit, she needed it. Kyle pushed the handheld console towards Natalia and began to show her how to level her enemy with the push of a button.

Chapter 23

Jim was becoming a staple in the medical ward until one nurse pointed out that he was taking up valuable room usually reserved for people who were bleeding to death. He appreciated the snark. No doubt it was at Angel's urging that the order was given; someone in a shared profession made an excellent ally. He regretted leaving, but as Meghan had told him, he had wasted half a day in the med ward. The trail for Natalia had grown frigid the moment the truck had pulled from the rail yard and avoided the local CCTV. The only choice was to take two steps backwards and hope that Bree Cobbs might be able to lead them to Pete.

Jim told the afternoon nurse to tell his family that he was sorry they had gotten involved, that he would make it right. That he would bring Natalia home. If the nurse was unconvinced of this, he didn't say anything, instead patting Jim courteously on the shoulder and telling him to take care of himself.

In the locker room, he ignored the whispers and stares of his fellow agents, certain that if he stopped for even half a moment to listen in on their conversations he would find they were trying to offer help and sympathy, not berate him for his failures. He was more comfortable assuming the worst.

He always had been.

Jim rarely used his locker, if only because it brought him too close to the rest of the Agency, and he preferred keeping friends and enemies at arm's length.

As such, the last time he had bothered to open it was, well, before Alcatraz, at the very least. A last-minute transfer to the West Coast that he had thought would be semi-permanent. Meghan had let him leave his possession behind with the promise that she would send them along if he decided he liked the hippies and the weed too much to come home. He had left a jacket behind, and a pair of runners that looked like they had seen better days. Tacked on the inside of the door was an old picture of Jim, Angel, and five-year-old Jayson. It was crinkled at the corners from the times Jim had thoughtfully rubbed the photo between his fingers before going on a mission. Ritualistic. For luck. Maybe if he had followed through before being sent to the island things would have turned out differently.

There was no point in prayer now. Even if they did end this with Cain, even if Natalia was brought back from the land of the Devil, his family would want nothing to do with him.

Or he would want nothing to do with them. Jim could already hear Angel's voice berating him, accusing him of some self-serving sacrifice that wasn't really for them but for his own benefit. She would be right. He couldn't focus on the job and keep them safe at the same time, that much was very clear. He wasn't a fool; Jim understood that family came before his job, but when his job ran the risk of infecting the rest of his life, well, something had to break eventually.

He lifted the edge of the photo, revealing a second image hidden below. This one wasn't quite as old, and not nearly as worn. He kept it more out of necessity than anything else, because memories were strongest when they had reminders, and he didn't want to ever forget. These memories fueled a lifetime of hurt and rage and anger. These were the memories that stood as a fork in the road during his last days in Alcatraz. These were the memories that forced a promise from his lips when Meghan asked him to protect Natalia.

The image showed a young Amy Artison, smiling, holding an infant. A baby girl with blue eyes and a wide, gummy smile. Amy, holding up the chubby hand, forcing the child to wave for the camera. The picture had been ripped along the side, severing some poor bastard from the construct.

Yes, there were things to be dealt with before he could remove himself from the world of the Agency.

By late afternoon, Tess had prepped whatever it was that had been holding her up. Along with Anna and Bedlam she located Jim, told him to stop being "a big dumb baby", and handed him a gun.

"You can't solve anything sitting on your ass," she declared. "Get up. Let's go talk to Bree Cobbs."

The ride to the small A-frame out in Hunts Point was made in silence. There wasn't much to say. Words never had a place in the moments after one of their own was lost. Callum had wanted to come along, said he owed it to his partner, but he was sequestered to the med ward, where he would be under constant supervision. He was lucky to be alive, and it would haunt him for years to come.

Jim was hard-pressed to feel any empathy for the security agent. They all had their demons, and Jim had been living with his long enough to know that it only defeated you if you gave it an inch to fester in your soul.

The streets had been cleared after the blizzard. Now Bree Cobbs' quaint home looked all the tinier, huddled beneath sheets of snow. The sidewalk had been scrapped and sanded, and children's boot prints could be seen across the yard, stopping near a half-formed snowman that slumped awkwardly to one side thanks to a severe case of scoliosis.

Up the sidewalk, onto the concrete front porch. Tess raised her hand to knock on the door and then paused.

It was open a crack. Enough to let in a deathly breeze; something a reasonable woman like Bree Cobbs would never let happen, not with a toddler and an infant in the house.

Guns out. Tess eased the door open with her shoulder, stepped beyond the snowdrift that had formed along the hardwood. The floor creaked under their weight, reminding Jim of dry bones grinding together.

The living room was torn apart. Couches had been overturned; lamps on the floor, their bulbs now powdery dust that graced the floor like newly fallen snow. The house was silent, as if the cold that had permeated its walls had siphoned what sound might have emanated from anyone still within.

They found Bree Cobbs in the hallway, struck down by a barrage of bullets that had opened her back to the air, leaving her flesh bubbled like discoloured popcorn kernels. The blood around her was brown, tacky to the touch. She had been dead a while. Bloody boot prints trailed down the hallway, away from her body.

"Two kids," Jim said in a whisper. "One toddler, one infant."

Bedlam stiffened behind him. Jim understood that instant visceral reaction. Bedlam's son was only a few months old.

The footprints careened down the hallway and made an abrupt turn to the right, towards a door painted princess pink and covered with glittery butterflies. It had been pushed open by the toe of a bloodied shoe. Jim's stomach clenched. They followed the trail in silence, aware only of the creaking floor and the wind buffeting through the door at the front of the house.

The bedroom had been spared the violence that had scarred the rest of the home. It was chaotic, but only as a child's room might be in the post-Christmas haze. Wrapping paper and presents scattered across an unmade bed. A crib in one corner, with a single quilt covered in tractors and airplanes. The footprints disappeared on a bright purple and green shag rug. The agents peered under the bed first, then behind the crib. The closet was cold and empty.

As they moved back towards the hallway, Jim paused, turned back to the closet, and narrowed his gaze.

"What?" Bedlam asked.

Jim didn't reply. Two short steps brought him back to the closet doors. Kneeling, he pushed back the rows of carefully hung toddler onesies and ballerina skirts and reached into the darkness. A cold bluster of air touched his fingertips, and he reached further until he felt what he was searching for. A small sliding lock, open. Jim pulled on the door and clicked on his flashlight.

Annie Cobbs sat in the crawlspace, legs curled up towards her body with a small blanket wrapped around her shoulders. Her skin was ghastly pale and her brown hair flew in all directions. She blinked once at Jim, then raised a hand to protect herself from the light. Nestled in her tiny arms was her baby brother.

She retracted from Jim, arms tightening around her brother. "He's sleeping," she squeaked, retracting from Jim's shadow. "Don't wake him up. Mommy will be mad."

Jim fell backwards, his gun and flashlight clattering to the floor bedside him as he watched Pete's daughter clinging to her half-brother. And there in the musty space of the closet, Jim heard Natalia's own voice echo the same sentiment among thunder and pouring rain.

We have to stay until he wakes up.

Bedlam was in front of him, in full father mode. He called out for Tess, and gently reached towards Annie Cobbs, beckoning her to release her grip on her brother. She eyed him suspiciously, a stranger, probably one of many she had seen in the last few days, and reluctantly held out the bundle. Jim saw the pale blue skin of the infant's hand and felt a surge of anguish.

Tess settled next to Jim, and offered Annie a smile that Jim knew had been gathered from the pit of her stomach and forced onto her face. Tess was feeling the guilt as sure as any of them. Annie, seemingly understanding that Tess might be able to provide more comfort than someone like Jim, scrambled out from the crawlspace and latched herself onto Tess' legs.

Jim stood, shaking, and left the bedroom to make the call. Anna was still standing in the hallway, staring down at the back of Bree Cobbs. As Jim stepped past her, he heard her muffle a cry in her palm.

xXx

Natalia watched Kyle play his game for a few hours. It was an excuse to adjust to her surroundings and try to recover some stamina lost when Pete had struck her. Kyle gabbled on about characters, weapons, skills, and magical lore, all things that seemed mightily complex and highly unimportant given their current predicament. That being said, at least he was distracted. He had stopped crying. He wasn't talking about home. It was a relief to Natalia. She had unwittingly taken on Jim's mentality of wanting to push emotions to one side in favour of action, and as such, she had no idea how to deal with Kyle, aside from patting him awkwardly on the shoulder and telling him that things would be ok.

She had drifted off for a few hours of uninterrupted sleep and woke to find cold, winter sunlight streaming through the boards that had been haphazardly nailed over the windows. The air rushing between them was frigid, the sort of that stalled out your lungs if you inhaled it too quickly. Fat flakes of snow were drifting in from the outside, reminding Natalia that heat conservation was of the utmost importance. Any escape attempt would involve traversing foreign territory in the dead of winter, and neither of them were equipped to survive out there for very long.

Kyle was sleeping on the bed beside her, tiny hands clutching at his game mid-battle. Natalia leaned over and gently closed the console before rolling from the covers. She didn't want to disturb him. He would need his rest if they were going to find a way out of this predicament. It would mean moving at a moment's notice, and she had to trust that he would be up to the challenge.

As if I'm somehow more up to it than he is.

With daylight streaming in, Natalia took the opportunity to peek through the boards and see what she could make of their surroundings. The first thing she noticed was the bird. Its red breast was more vibrant in the daylight, speckled with deep brown crystals where blood had dripped over its plumage and been left to freeze. It had been dead a while, the skin and feathers receding along its thin bones. Were it summer its whole body would have long since decayed. As it was, the poor creature looked horrific. Natalia gave an involuntary shudder and trained her eyes beyond the bird.

Just as she had thought, the malicious shadows from the night before were nothing more than the burnt husks of apple trees, left to wither in the vibrant Massachusetts seasons. They must have been large trees in their prime, left to go wild. Natalia was having a hard time picturing Cain as the sort of man who was content to watch nature take back the world of man, but the gangly skeletons of the trees suggested that was exactly what he had let happen.

Or maybe he was too busy sending weapons to warlords to care for his garden.

The forest surrounding the acreage seemed to stretch on forever. Natalia had been secretly hoping she might look out the window and see evidence of civilization peeking out in the distance. It would have given them something to aim for in their escape. Instead she was faced with rolling hills of white; trees covered in heavy gobs of snow.

Aw, hell, she thought. Weather and distance aside, Natalia had no idea how far Cain's land stretched. If they somehow managed to escape the house, they would leave a trail. They had to know where they were going before they could think of crafting an escape plan.

Lancaster. But where the fuck is Lancaster? Geography hadn't exactly been her forte.

Something was rumbling in the distance and Natalia narrowed her eyes on the horizon. A convoy was rolling up the road and stopped behind the hill, out of sight. Below, the front door open and Cain emerged, winter jacket tucked around him, his hands shoved into his pockets. At the other end of the orchard a small group appeared, trooping up the hill to the burnt trees. Natalia saw one shadow, tall and gangly young man, turn his attention to the window. She ducked instinctively.

Dummy, he can't see you all the way up here.

Still, she held her breath as she returned to her post, watching as Cain strode across the snowy orchard and embraced the young man.

Watch and memorize, Jim's voice echoed in her mind. *Every little piece of information helps.*

Cain and the young man were too far away for her to clearly make out a face, but she saw the intimacy, the longing in their embrace. She knew she was watching a reunion.

The lock of the bedroom creaked and Natalia spun, instantly repressing the desire to hush whoever was on the other side of the door lest they wake the sleeping boy. The door swung open; Nicholas Thellion stood there, far too proud for his own good. Natalia knew him only as Cain's right hand man, the death dealer, who took on the more vicious tasks when Cain didn't want to get his hands dirty. Thellion's actions had nearly cost Natalia her life, and left her with a scarred left arm that still ached every time the humidity changed.

"Thought I'd come say hello." He was a man of relatively few words. Still, Natalia was surprised how he kept his voice quiet, hardly above a whisper.

"Oh, lovely," Natalia drawled. "I'm so happy to see you. It's like I couldn't sleep knowing you hadn't graced me with your presence up to this point."

Thellion smirked and winked. "How's your arm?"

"Still attached, despite your best efforts." Natalia unconsciously rubbed the thick, pink scar, sending ripples of pain down her arm and into her fingertips. The doctors who had tended her during one of their many stops while on the run had reckoned there might be a small amount of nerve damage, but Natalia decided she was better off telling herself that such a thing wasn't possible. She would take that denial all the way to the bank.

"In my defense, I never wanted it to go that far," Thellion said shortly. "Things just escalated."

"Yeah, imagine that," Natalia replied lamely. "Things escalating with you. Wow."

Thellion grinned wolfishly, and Natalia could see one of his front teeth had been cracked half off, leaving him with a jagged, jack-o'-lantern-like smile. The moment passed and his brow furrowed in concern. "You've got someone else to look after now," he observed. "Best if you gave up the Code. Save both your skins."

"That song's getting really old." Natalia moved in front of the bed. It was fruitless to try to engage Thellion in combat, but if he planned on launching himself at Kyle, the least she could do was plant herself like a rock in the ocean and take the brunt of the attack. "If I kick you like a jukebox, will you sing something else?"

Thellion arched an eyebrow and took one step towards Natalia. She flinched, and he smiled. "That's what I thought. Good luck to ya, kid. You're going to need it."

Natalia watched, keenly aware of the embarrassed heat that rose in her cheeks. She wanted to be brave, especially now, as Thellion pointed out, she had someone depending on her. She found, in his presence, that it hadn't just been her arm that was scarred, but her nerve.

You're going to have to get it back if you want to get Kyle out of here in one piece.

With the room silent once more, Natalia turned back to the covered window and peered through the crack in the boards. A breeze had picked up and caught the flap of skin and red breast on the bird carcass, flipping it back to reveal the rotted meat beneath the surface.

xXx

No children. That was the rule. No children should be harmed, nor be dragged into the world of the Agency. No children should have to wash their parent's blood from their hands or experience nightmares of death arriving in the middle of the night. No children.

Never children.

Annie Cobbs was still asking for her baby brother; the doctor was gently deferring the question, telling her that she needed to rest, that she was safe now. But Annie Cobbs knew she would never be safe again, and so she asked for her brother, to hold him, because he was so hungry and needed to be fed.

The early reports from the Agency coroner indicated that Bree Cobbs had been dead for just over three days. Neighbours had reported hearing some commotion the night of the attack, but had equated it with Bree's no-good ex-husband being back in the picture. In that part of town, people tended to turn a blind eye to the anger of strangers. But it wasn't Pete; Jim knew that without question. Pete was not a good man, but he had loved Bree, and his child, and probably even had a soft spot in his heart for the baby that was not his.

Neighbours also reported the sound of motorcycles tearing up the street. A risky maneuver given the new snowfall, but that was the Reapers for you. When they had things needing to be done, they acted without hesitation. Bree Cobbs' life had been forfeit the moment Pete aligned himself with someone else; the Agency knocking at her door had only sealed the deal that much sooner. Chances are they learned where to find her right before they put the match to Lonny Stieber's ride.

At least Annie would be safe. She would be given a new name and a new life and sent far away from the house where her mother had been gunned down and her baby brother had died from exposure. She would be given countless people to talk to, to help her through the coming years. She would not be forgotten, and, in time, perhaps memories would soften to a dull ache and her days in the crawlspace would seem like a nightmare and nothing more. The ghost of her brother, who she had tried her best to save, would lift from her arms and, God willing, she would become someone else, someone better.

Less than twenty-four hours after they returned from the Cobbs home, Jim, Bedlam, and Tess were sitting in a conference room with the other members of the team, being debriefed by Aurora on what they had learned through Annie's eyes.

"According to Annie, and corroborated by neighbour's reports, four men entered the house just before 2200 hours on the night in question." Aurora ran a finger along a tablet in front of her, and the projection on the screen changed to show the crime scene. "Annie Cobbs was able to retrieve her half-brother, father unknown, and hide in a crawlspace within the closet, where she stayed for three days. Her brother, Tyler, passed away due to exposure within the first twenty-four hours."

Coroner's images. Those sitting around the table suddenly found themselves interested in the pens they held and the pieces of lint clinging to their clothes.

Meghan stood up, offering Aurora a reprieve. "It is unclear at this time if Pete Cobbs knows that his ex-wife is dead and his daughter has been taken into Agency custody. We are running on the assumption that if he did, he would have made contact by now."

"What are the chances it was Cain?" Caulder had been sitting in on every meeting related to the case thus far, and stubbornly interjected his opinion even when it wasn't asked for. A man who had been off the streets for too long, forgetting that there were rules and methods that the agents adhered to. He was desperate, looking for connections where there were none.

"Nothing the Sweepers pulled from the house suggests it was Cain," Meghan replied patiently. "Skin cells found under Bree Cobbs' fingers were matched in the system." A new picture flashed on the screen. Tess recognized the face.

"Patrick McKim," she said shortly. "Chapter president of the Reapers."

"They came looking for Pete?" Rebecca suggested.

"And Hayden Meloy." Jim replied. "It's likely. Were we able to make contact with the chapter before…" His voice dropped off, not wanting to verbalize Natalia's abduction out of fear that it might become that much more real to him.

"We did. He was…*amicable* to our suggestions," Tess replied, glancing towards Meghan, who had narrowed her eyes at the image of Patrick McKim.

"Time to go pay him a proper visit," Meghan said coolly. "Aurora, get your people on recon. I want eyes on everyone from McKim to the sergeant-at-arms. We need to cripple these bastards before they have a chance to spread the bloodshed any further."

Before they find Pete or Hayden Meloy, Jim thought sourly. *If the club gets to them first then the next time we see Pete we'll be hauling him out of a river piece by piece.*

"Jim, Tess, I want you two as team leads. If we're lucky, we can get them all together in one place, but if we need to hit multiple locations then we need to do it simultaneously. Sit down and figure out a game plan once Aurora comes back to you with some locations."

Jim gave Tess a wary glance that she returned grimly. Neither of them wanted to be running lead, even with circumstances as they were. Being the first through any door was always a risk, a fifty percent chance of taking a fistful of buck straight to the chest, followed by a mid-week funeral with poor attendance. But the boss had spoken and that was that. Jim had no intention of getting killed before he had the opportunity to crush Pete's windpipe, and he reckoned Tess was as just determined to prove to Cain that he couldn't take her down.

They would do what they could; lay Bree Cobbs' body to rest and ensure her surviving children weren't lost in the shuffle. They would take down the Road Reapers, and find Pete. They would do all of that and more because it was the only way any of them would get a good night's sleep ever again.

xXx

Food had been delivered by an unnamed trained monkey working for Cain. Natalia didn't recognize the woman from any of their other encounters and wondered how Cain had managed to grow his organization in three months while still staying under the radar. Sandwiches, fruit, vegetables. Natalia picked through them carefully before she passed a plate to Kyle and let him indulge. She watched him devour the food, then, realizing she had her own strength to maintain, she began to nibble away at the meal. From the corner of her eye, she observed Kyle in the dying light of day. He looked remarkably unharmed given how long he had been in Cain's care. A bruise on an elbow, which Natalia figured was the result from colliding with one of the many pieces of furniture in the room. No scrapes, no cuts, nothing to indicate anyone had dealt the boy any harm.

Natalia was annoyed by this in spite of herself. Why had she been branded, cut, and bashed around so much when Kyle was given a warm bed and two meals a day? But that wasn't fair, and she chided herself for being envious of the treatment a kidnapped child had received.

After they had finished eating, Kyle washed his face in the ensuite and crawled into the bed. Natalia tucked the edges of the quilt around him. It seemed like the right thing to do under the circumstances. He was exhausted, and asleep before she had a chance to wish him goodnight.

She spent the next few hours entertaining herself by looking through the drawers and cupboards. The bathroom had been stripped of all but the necessities. A packaged toothbrush, an opened tube of toothpaste, and obligatory feminine hygiene supplies. The last items amused her the most, and seemed the most telling. They obviously expected to keep her here a while, and, on some level, she resented the fact that she wouldn't be able to make her captors decidedly uncomfortable by telling them she needed tampons and Midol.

The dresser was dotted with personal mementos; smudged picture frames that had been forgotten by time and now hid their secrets beneath thick layers of grime. Natalia went through them, one by one, and began to rub the mess clean, revealing images of complacent happiness beneath. Cain's family, on a picnic, beneath the apple trees; vacations in Paris, Rome, sunny beaches; wedding portraits and school photos. It all seemed so horrendously normal. Natalia felt sick. She plucked a picture frame from the corner of the dresser and stepped towards the window, running the back of her hand along the murky glass to reveal a family photo beneath.

She knew Cain instantly. He was older now than in the photo, but still had his hair trimmed the same. Smiling beneath an apple tree, his arm around a woman with a bright smile, he seemed almost...sane. They sat on a checkered sheet, the remains of a picnic scattered around. Beside them sat two children, a boy and girl, who seemed to be in the midst of harassing each other in a way only siblings could when the photo was taken.

Is this the family he burned to death? Natalia searched her memory for what Jim had told her. His wife, sister-in-law, and nephews. But his own children were spared. They were at boarding school at the time of their mother's murder.

What do you live with? Natalia thought, running her fingers over the faces of the two children. *Do you have any idea about the burden you carry with you?*

She was just putting a frame down when Cain entered the bedroom.

He stepped up behind her, reached to pluck the image off the dresser, effectively drawing her towards his body. It was frighteningly intimate and Natalia froze, lest her body touch his own. "My children...they never knew. I was always their hero." He put the frame down. "I don't know how I was able to fool them all for so long."

Natalia briefly considered snapping back something snarky, but the moment was lost and, she thought, perhaps inappropriate. Cain's fingers glanced across the back of her neck, drawing her hair clear so her nape was free and cold against the winter air. She knew he was looking at her brand.

"It's healed well," he said simply.

"I've got a good doctor," Natalia said, forcefully turning around and pushing Cain away from her. Her hand grasped the picture frame and she shoved the image towards his chest. "Jim told me what you did," she said through clenched teeth. "You're a fucking *freak*."

Cain stepped back, as if the accusation was more than some schoolyard taunt. He glanced at the photograph, pressed his thumb along the glass almost lovingly, and looked up. "A man can make terrible choices when he's pushed to the edge, Natalia. We've all been there."

"Yeah, but we haven't all murdered our families," Natalia shot back. In her peripheral vision, she saw Cain clench his fist.

Is that your weakness? Your guilt?

"You're just a coward who lost his temper, aren't you?" she continued to sneer. "Couldn't handle the responsibility; couldn't accept that you had been caught. You had to take everyone who loved you down, and then you were too cowardly to finish yourself off. That's what happened, isn't it?"

She knew the hit was coming. In many ways, Cain's hand colliding with her cheek was what she needed to ignite the spark that had been flickering near extinction since Angel and Jay had been taken. She had let Jim's negativity sink into her, draw her back to the sorrow that compounded with the loss of family, of friends. The strike to her cheek was no more consequential than flipping a switch, but it *energized* her. Natalia's hand drifted back towards her face, probed the already throbbing flesh. A smile touched her lips.

"That's the limit, huh?"

"Like I said." Cain placed the photo back on the dresser and turned away from Natalia. "Terrible mistakes. Some are easier to live with than others."

Part III

Chapter 24

Patrick McKim had bundled down for the storm. He'd missed Christmas with his girlfriend, and lord knew she was making a goddamned deal about it. His side piece wasn't much happier given the only present he had time to get her was a fucking KitchenAid blender she saw in a Target flyer. With the way things had played out, it was looking like he'd miss their New Year's ride out west for the rally in Nevada. The whole thing was a fucking disaster and McKim knew it. Bree Cobbs had always been a loose end, McKim thought, but Pete had insisted that she be left alone even after their separation, but when a couple of suits who looked about as inconspicuous as a man on fire had gone to visit Bree, McKim got worried.

He hadn't wanted to kill her. She had four kids, she was a single mom. *Life was hard for her.* But things got out of hand. She had called Pete, she explained, to tell him that a friend had come looking for him. McKim had gotten on the line and while stupidly distracted by Pete, Bree had tried to shoot him with an old pistol. She knew that Patrick McKim was a killer, and not a pleasant one at that. She knew he was a risk to the safety of her children.

McKim had figured someone was bound to call the cops and the two
kids hiding in the closet would probably be found in a matter of minutes.
After all, now that Pete knew his old friends were visiting his ex, he'd surely
want to stop by. If they were lucky, he would bring Hayden Meloy with him,
and McKim could finish off the last of the members who had gone AWOL.
The president had made it perfectly clear; leaving the club was fine if you
were old, wanting to retire to some sunny beach off the coast of San Marc-
Who-Gives-a-Shit. But leaving to serve another? That was unacceptable.
McKim and his chapter had been given clear orders to deal with Cobbs,
Meloy, and Stieber, no matter what, and that was exactly what McKim aimed
to do. Stieber was easy. Old bastard loved his shop, and didn't seem to think
he'd done anything wrong. They showed him the error of his ways. Rumor
had it Meloy had been staying there, but he wasn't around when they strung
up Lonny Stieber and set the match to him. As for Pete, well, if anything
would draw him out of hiding, it would be the death of his ex-wife. Certainly,
McKim could have gone to him, but he wanted Pete to understand that *he
didn't care.* Pete's betrayal was a nuisance, a fly in his beer. He was more than
willing to wait until Pete felt the pressure, and came back to his old hunting
grounds to bend the knee.

Patrick McKim would find locate Meloy, put a bullet between Pete
Cobbs' eyes, and that would be the end of it.

It was three days after the killing of Bree Cobbs that news of her
death hit the airwaves. McKim admittedly felt a little sick when he learned
that one of the kids had died. He hadn't counted on the silence of the
neighbours. Still, Pete's biological daughter survived; if anything was going to
draw him out, it would be the fact that his kid had been left with a couple of
rotting corpses for nearly three days.

Given it was the holidays, the clubhouse wasn't busy that evening. Most of the prospects were home with their families, indulging in leftover turkey sandwiches and cans of cranberry sauce that had been squished down with the back of a spoon. Those that were left had conglomerated at the club, most unaware that there was fresh blood on the hands of the senior members

McKim had put his sergeant-at-arms on duty outside. The guy had wanted to kill the little girl and McKim figured standing in the cold for a few hours would do him some good.

Sometime after sunset, the lights for the whole clubhouse went out. It wasn't much of a surprise. They had jerry-rigged it to 'borrow' electricity from a neurotic right-winger down the block who they figured was one racist remark short of becoming the cast of *Guess Who's Coming to Dinner*. McKim reckoned it was only a matter of time until the moron moved and cut his electricity. Even then, the recent blizzard had put a lot of strain on the grid. Members groaned in annoyance and McKim ordered the nearest prospect to go get some candles and a few flashlights from the closet. While that went on, he fumbled his way to the window, shoved the sash open with his shoulder, and leaned out.

"Eh! Tucker! You see anything?"

Tucker, the goddamned sergeant-at-arms, didn't reply, probably still pissed off at being stuck on guard duty. McKim laughed at the idea. He wasn't ever worried about dissent in the ranks. Standing at over six feet tall and made primarily of muscle and tattoos, McKim figured he had the ability to crush a man's skull in his hands if he tried. Tucker could be a little bitch about his assignment if he wanted. He'd be cooking for the rest of the house for the next two weeks, frilly apron included.

There was shuffling behind him, the sound of the door opening and closing, and then a cry in the darkness from the living room. The sound of a punch against an immovable target. McKim whirled around on his heel and felt a rifle butt crash into the side of his jaw, dislocating it and knocking a few lackluster teeth astray. He fell to the ground and plunged a hand into his vest, hoping to grip the switchblade he kept tucked near his heart, when the end of the rifle came down sharply into his gut once, then twice, forcing the air from his chest and leaving him doubled over. He struggled to move, keenly aware of his own girth. He clawed across the carpet, a figure following, walking alongside like a vulture waiting for his prey to perish. McKim's fingers were back under his vest now, searching for his blade. If he could grab it... Outside was screaming, gunfire. The cries of his brothers. Weak, all of them.

There, his fingers were on the hilt of the blade. Now if he could just-

A booted foot slammed down on his wrist and McKim cried out in agony as the bones snapped effortlessly. The figure was closer now, leaning over him, breathing heavily. In the darkness McKim saw frightful black eyes, narrowed in anger.

"No," the voice said coldly. "Not yet."

With the electricity back on in the clubhouse, the members subdued and two on their way to the nearest medical center for some much-needed attention, Jim stepped back to observe the scene. It was much as Pete had described it in Alcatraz; a place where hedonism went to die. Empty cheap-ass beer bottles and stray lines of cocaine were strewn about, along with some escorts who, more than anything, looked annoyed at having been caught in whatever the Road Reapers had gotten themselves involved in.

Patrick McKim had made a half-assed effort to escape, but the shock of the invasion had sent him reeling, and now he sat hogtied on the stained, mustard yellow couch. Jim figured it probably wasn't the sort of treatment the president of the chapter was used to.

"Wake up." He leaned over McKim and gave him a gentle slap on his bruised face. McKim groaned, squirmed a bit, and rolled back so his face wasn't pressing against the couch. One eye was bloody from a hit he had taken from the rifle.

"We're looking for Pete Cobbs. You murdered his ex-wife recently, remember?"

McKim shook his head, opening his mouth to show teeth covered in blood. He smiled wolfishly, like it was all a joke. Jim glanced over his shoulder to where Bedlam, Max, and Rebecca were all standing around, their prey corralled into a corner. For the most part, they looked like they were rolling their eyes.

"You really want to play that game?" Jim asked, leaning in so his face was inches from McKim's. "Look around, you've got a hell of a lot to lose."

"Sure, sure." McKim coughed, horked up a wad of bloody saliva, and tried to spit it towards Jim, only for gravity to send it into his own face.

"Let's try this again..." Jim brought the switchblade into McKim's line of sight and flicked it open. He slowly drew it back and forth, as if attempting to hypnotize his kill. "I don't have time for this. You tell me where to find Pete, or I start doing what I do best."

"Yeah?" McKim choked out a laugh. "What's that?"

Jim smirked and pressed the tip of the blade into McKim's inner thigh; delicate skin, sensitive to changes in weather and garments. McKim grunted, them cried out as blood spurted from the wound, covering Jim's hand. But he didn't dig it in fast, nor far. The idea was to hurt, maim, but not kill. A man like Patrick McKim had a pre-determined place in prison, isolated from the rest of the criminals in a segregated cell where he would only have his ribbed scars for company.

Jim certainly didn't want him to be lonely.

Jim was washing his hands in the kitchen sink when his phone rang. McKim hadn't held his tongue for long after blood had begun to stream. It was the cut to his Achilles heel that did it. He would walk with a limp for the rest of his life. If he ever made it out of prison, he'd never be able to ride the same way. Chances were the club president would have him silenced in prison before he had a chance to spill any gang secrets. That wasn't much of a concern to Jim. Let the evil die. Let them rot until their bodies slipped in between the cracks in the pavement and join with the foundation of the house. Let them be forgotten among all the other dead, all the other hopeless ones. McKim had given up Pete. That was all that mattered.

Jim quickly dried his hands on a sheet of paper towel and snatched his phone from the counter.

Unknown number. Fantastic.

He answered, "Yeah?" There was a pause, a click. When the voice spoke, Jim went on high alert.

"Did I catch you in the middle of something, Jim?"

Cain.

"Nothing that I can't put on hold." He stamped his foot on the ground and Bedlam's head appeared around the corner. Jim pointed to the phone and mouthed Cain's name.

"Even when your ward is MIA?" Cain clucked his tongue. "That sort of laziness is what gets people killed."

Jim's mind cleared. Experience had taught him to focus on Cain's words; he was a precise man who rarely wasted his breath.

"What do you mean?"

A lengthy pause, then a haggard sigh. Jim felt his chest tighten.

When Cain spoke next, Jim struggled to stay upright.

"Our children are such fragile things, Jim."

In the silence that followed, Jim's mind spun to Natalia, to the girl who flew at him, draped in a sheet, and drove her small blade into his shoulder. He carried the shame of that moment, for the snap of anger that overtook him, blinding him to all rational thought as he threw her to the wall and tried to squeeze the life from her body. All small bones and veins and stature, emboldened by something larger than herself. "What have you done, Cain?"

"Oh," Cain said, and Jim could hear the smile in his voice. "I lost my temper. You know what that's like, don't you?"

Jim felt the world tilt at an angle and grasped the edge of the kitchen counter, hoping he might steady himself for what he knew what was coming, but was so ill-prepared to accept.

"If it's any consolation, she didn't suffer. If anything, I think knowing death was coming must have been a relief to her."

"I'll kill you," Jim declared, voice wavering against the shock. "I'll fucking *kill you!*"

Cain had hung up. The phone slipped from Jim's fingers and clattered on the floor. From the doorway to the kitchen, Bedlam, Max, and Rebecca stared, wise enough to understand that whatever had been relayed over the phone had been a cruel truth that they had all been battling to prevent. Jim felt a burning pain, like fingers pulling his heart from his chest. He doubled over and gasped for breath, one arm around his stomach as he tried to focus.

Breathe.

I can't.

You can breathe. Move through it.

But the failure was embedded in him, part of him. Cain wrenched all the miserable memories from the past decade back up, letting them roam freely. And now Cain let them burn, just as he had burned the apple trees. Just as he had burned his family. He cast a killing blow with Natalia's death.

Whatever part of Jim had been able to keep the darkness at bay flickered and was consumed by shadows, and in that instant he felt every terror, every fear, clamor out of the night and descend upon him with claws extended and mouths dripping with saliva. In his sadness and fury, Jim allowed himself to be consumed by the souls of the dead.

Natalia wrenched against the hands that covered her mouth, that pinned her against the wall like a butterfly on display, as she was forced listen to Jim's anger rise in a way that she had only ever heard once before, when Duncan was upon her in Alcatraz. And she knew, in that instant, what Cain meant to do.

A man can make terrible choices when pushed to the edge.

She could see it play out. Jim, seeking revenge, heedless of danger, allowing himself to be drawn directly into Cain's web.

When the call ended and the hands flew away from Natalia, she fell to her knees.

Cain's eyes burned with an anger that Natalia had never witnessed in him before. Was this the same vitriolic hate that forced his hand into killing his own family?

If it is, we're all fucked.

"You'll see," he said, kneeling and tipping her chin up so their eyes could connect. "You'll understand. We all do what we have to do to survive." He stood up, leaving Natalia crumpled on the floor. Kyle was beside her a second later, having landed a keen kick on Thellion's shin, freeing himself from the grip the killer had on his arms. Cain watched, bemused, as Kyle placed his arms protectively around Natalia, as if he was capable of somehow saving her.

"Let's go," Cain said to Thellion. "We have work to do still."

Natalia watched, horror-struck as she desperately tried to process what had just happened, and to include this new variable into her calculation of possibilities, of what might happen next. As he passed by the dresser, Cain paused. For an instant she wondered if he had been horrified by what he saw reflected through the smeared glass, as if the decade of planning and months of torture had somehow given way to a different sort of creature that he was entirely unfamiliar with.

"I'm sorry," he said, without turning around.

Natalia waited. She waited because even then, in her horror, Jim's mind echoed in the back of her head.

Show them fear, show them terror, but never show them your true hand. Never show them you have a plan. Never show them that you plan on acting out.

Don't ever let them see you cry.

When the door was closed and the lock set in place, Natalia lifted her head, stood on shaking legs, and fumbled her way towards the window so she could take in a cold gasp of winter air and use it to settle her brain. The bird still lay there, dead as before, but as Natalia watched, focused, playing through half a dozen scenarios in her mind, she saw the belly of the dead bird bulge and shake. Feathers and flesh split, and one long, shiny brown leg, graced with delicate hairs, emerged from the bird, then another, and another, until the spider that had made its home in the carcass of the bird rested upon its breast.

Natalia gasped, blinked, and narrowed her gaze. The spider was gone. She turned abruptly to Kyle. "We're getting out of here."

Chapter 25

Even with Bedlam and Max racing to catch up with him, with Rebecca calling his name, frantically trying to direct the additional security forces that had arrived to keep the bikers in line, Jim felt compelled to leave the compound and throw himself out into the snow and wind. The cold did nothing to soothe him, nothing to extinguish the heat that had surged up his throat and singed his brain. He lost what was little food had been in his stomach and groped at the frozen ground, hoping to dig himself a shallow grave.

I'm sorry, I'm sorry.

In the wintery darkness, the ghosts of the dead descended around him, claws raking his flesh, burying themselves into his chest as deep as they might go.

God, Amy. I'm so sorry.

He saw her, staring at her from across the street, lost between worlds. He saw her mouth open to reveal pearly teeth that gnashed in agony as she tore at her golden hair and screamed at him for his failure. But the shrieks held no sound, for the dead did not speak to Jim, they simply held him in their claws, dragging him about by the back of his neck.

A hand rested on his shoulder and Jim felt himself wrenched from the moment of hysteria. Bedlam stood over him, face downcast, not requiring an explanation for the agony.

"How?" he whispered.

"Cain." Jim rose on shaky legs, gripping Bedlam's arm for support. Looking across the street, he saw the visage of Amy turn her back on him, one final shunning for his failures. "He...*fuck!*" Jim punched the ground, the pavement splitting his knuckles, sending a shot of pain through his arm and setting his brain alight once more.

"It's not on you," Bedlam said shakily, gripping Jim's arm fiercely. "Cain, he would have...no matter what. We couldn't have stopped him."

Jim yanked his arm away, stepped back from Bedlam. "Wait for backup to take in the rest of the Reapers."

"Where are you going?" Bedlam shouted after him. "Jim! Where the hell is Pete?"

Jim didn't reply. He knew. McKim had told him, and in due time the Agency would surely be able to acquire that information again. But Jim wasn't interested in sharing. He wanted to feel the life leave Pete's body as his fingers curled around his neck and crushed his windpipe. He wanted to feel the blood bulge in Pete's jugular, struggling to bypass the fingers that gripped the tube closed. He wanted to look Pete in the face as he died and tell him that it was for Natalia.

Then Jim would find Cain, and destroy him.

xXx

Natalia twisted so she could catch a glimpse of herself in the frosted-over mirror. With a bit of scrubbing she had been able to make a clean patch of glass sparkle. For some time she observed her brand on the back of her neck, gently pressing her fingers against the raised skin. She had memorized the image long ago. In her dreams, the burnt flesh on her neck was overlaid by the tattoos of Jim and Steven, mutilated over the years in desperate attempts to hide their youthful shame. In the waking world, her wound was hers and hers alone. Every curve, every indentation was unique to her body. A marking to remind her of man's vulnerability.

After Cain and Thellion had left them, Natalia was quick to explain to Kyle why now was the time to escape. There was no question in her mind that Cain's untimely phone call had been made with the intention of manipulating the Agency, *no*, Jim. He was playing on the rage, the need for revenge, drawing those he hated close to his breast. It was as Jim had said; Cain's loathing for the Agency was powerful, and Natalia couldn't afford to forget that.

Kyle had looked increasingly pensive as Natalia explained her theory about Cain. And, he said, there was a way out.

"They used to let me walk around until I went into the basement an' saw what they were doin'," Kyle explained quietly. "I followed them. They had lots of tools, like Minecraft. We went into a big hole, and it went all the way, out to the other side." Kyle walked up to the window and pointed through the slats towards the western side of the property, out beyond the orchard. "That way, I think."

A tunnel, Natalia thought quickly. *Cain is building a tunnel right under his killing grounds.*

A few more minutes of questioning and Natalia learned that the house was generally quiet during the evening and all the doors and windows had been boarded up long ago. From the outside, it appeared as if the whole homestead had been abandoned.

Just as Cain wanted it to appear.

"We'll wait until night," Natalia said. "Then we'll head for the basement as see if we can't find a way out of this place."

"But the door is locked." Kyle pointed a small finger towards the entrance to the bedroom, lower lip trembling, clearly concerned that this single obstacle would be the end of all their hopes.

"Leave that to me," Natalia replied with a shaky smile. She wanted to be strong, to reassure him that she was not afraid of what was coming.

Truth be told, she was terrified. She was certain she understood Cain's methodology. He was trying to overwhelm her, to break her spirit with new information that would play on her emotions and make her sloppy in the heat of battle or shut her down mentally.

The day stretched on, and Cain had decided to torture them by denying food. Kyle complained about an empty stomach, and Natalia commiserated. She promised him they would eat the moment they were safe, and he just had to be brave for a little while longer.

"Hamburgers," she said with a smile.

"Nu-uh," Kyle kicked his feet out and flopped backwards. "*Pizza.*"

"Pepperoni?"

"Hawaiian!"

Night descended over the orchard. Natalia kept one eye glued to the outside world and tried to keep track of the workers that seemingly appeared out of nowhere from the side of the hill, carting away covered loads of what she now knew was dirt. There was no reason to make a secondary escape route when Cain had a perfectly reasonable front door he could use, and for the life of her Natalia could not fathom why he might dig a tunnel beneath the orchard.

The last of the plodding feet patrolling the hallway died away not long after sunset, and Jim's training had been echoing in her head since then.

You need to look at every angle, every possibility. You need to be prepared for any outcome.

She had run the possible scenarios backwards and forwards, until she was certain her best bet was to find a weapon first, and formulate an escape plan second.

Natalia took a pillowcase, wrapped it around the length of her arm, and, with her head turned to the side to avoid any flying shards, slammed her elbow into the mirror. It shattered after the third hit; Natalia's elbow stung and her fingers prickled with sudden numbness. The tinkling shards of glass were muffled by the duvet she had spread over the dresser. Glancing towards the doorway, she held her breath, waiting for the sound of feet thundering towards the room.

Silence. She looked to Kyle, who had clamped his hands over his mouth. He relaxed at her smile. Natalia lowered her arm and shook the pain away, flexing her fingers until feeling returned. Only a handful of mirror shards had broken into something of useful size and shape. Natalia picked a dagger-like piece and wrapped a length of ripped sheet along the bottom. It was a feeble weapon at best, but she figured that if worst came to worst she could drive it into someone's neck.

"We still have to get out," Kyle said, as if Natalia had forgotten. She rolled her eyes, flipped the duvet over, and began to search the top of the dresser.

It didn't take long to find a handful of bobby pins tucked into a small green enamel box. Lengths of faded golden hair still clung to them. Natalia wondered if Cain ever looked at them in a fruitless search for memories of his wife.

"Can you really..." Kyle gawped as Natalia knelt in front of the door and pressed a finger to her lips. She wasn't confident in her ability to open it. Jim had made her study the mechanics of locks. She understood pins and tumblers, but the age of the lock and the fact that she didn't have the proper equipment meant even a slight miscalculation could reset her hard work. One pin, two pins, three... Her fingers twitched and the pins reset. She rubbed her damp hands on her pants and exhaled slowly. It was an agonizing process. She felt a pin shift and stay in position, and made a mental note of where it sat in the whole mechanism.

There was a clock in the room somewhere. The ticking was annoying. Behind her, she could hear Kyle breathing through his nose. He might as well have been screaming in her ear.

Natalia stood up, frustrated, shook out her hands and paced once across the length of the room.

Focus. Focus. Focus. You've got this. What's your other option if you don't? Pull the boards off the window and climb over the roof? That's a quick way to a three-storey death.

Natalia turned, marched back towards the door, and knelt in front of the lock. Her hands weren't shaking now. She wasn't a fan of heights.

The minutes wore on as she worked at the lock. She could hear Kyle beginning to shift behind her. One pin, then a second and a third.

The thin, ornate clip she had been using as a tension wrench turned unexpectedly, and the lock clicked.

Jingo-jango. Natalia made a mental note to tell Jim about her success. Knowing him, he would probably grunt something vaguely passive-aggressive. She would take it as a compliment though, because passive aggressiveness was as good as it got with Jim.

Assuming she saw him again.

Natalia glanced back at Kyle. He was staring at her, wide-eyed.

"Stay here," she whispered. "I'm going to make sure it's clear."

With the makeshift dagger in hand, Natalia eased the door open. It squeaked as she went, and for a horrifying moment Natalia wondered if this would be when Thellion, in his skeletal-like glory, decided to swoop down and pluck her out of this reality.

Now able to take in the full majesty of the house, Natalia realized how successful Cain must have been in his previous profession. It was three stories, with rounded balconies that stretched along each floor, looking down upon a massive open foyer, supported by elegantly carved pillars reaching from floor to ceiling. Overhead, stars peeped through the snow that had fallen over the rounded glass domed ceiling. It was elegant, but cold. No electricity, and layers of dust that had been disturbed by the repeated marching of Cain's mercenaries.

It was the sort of house Natalia expected to be occupied by unhinged poltergeists who wailed and tipped over candelabras.

Creeping forward across the empty third floor landing, Natalia hunkered down and glanced between the rails of the balcony. Below she could see a single mercenary pacing around the front door, moving between pillars in a dedicated pattern.

Jim would be horrified, Natalia thought with smile. *It's too easy.*

She gulped for air; the lack of food was making her lightheaded. Or perhaps it was the fear. Up until now, every death, every kill, was the by-product of the moment. She had killed to survive. This death would only be for convenience, because they couldn't risk alerting anyone. This death would be different because there would be eyes on her back, watching her make the move.

Back in the bedroom, Natalia found Kyle picking through the bits of glass, trying to make his own dagger. She smiled. The effort was appreciated, but something she wanted to avoid. Killing her first man back in Alcatraz had been horrifying experience, and something she had to actively push from her mind on a daily basis.

Hot, hot blood pouring down your arm. Splashing your face, like a fountain at a water park.

She wouldn't subject Kyle to the same nightmares if she could avoid it.

"Here." She knelt in front of him and ripped a length of sheet free, wrapping it around the bottom of the glass. "You hold on to it for me, ok? Be careful, it's sharp."

Kyle pressed the shard flat against his chest, like a favourite toy, and nodded earnestly. Natalia saw that he had found more bobby pins and tucked them so they stuck out of his jean pockets.

He's trying to be prepared, Natalia thought grimly. *Good for him.*

"We're going now. I want you to stay up here until I tell you it's safe. There's a man down there, and I need to deal with him, ok?"

"Ok."

"Keep your eyes closed, Kyle. Don't look until I tell you."

"Ok."

Natalia leaned back, looking at Kyle as the moonlight illuminated his pale face and thin, prepubescent body. He was a fragile thing, and Natalia wondered what it had been like for him, these last few weeks. How frightened had he been? How much confusion had driven his thoughts towards the darkness where he imagined a horrible fate for himself? She had done it herself enough times.

"We're getting out of here, ok? But if something happens to me, if we get separated, you keep running, all right? Don't stop for anything."

"But-"

"Trust me, Kyle. He doesn't want you. Now." She stood up, offered a hand to the boy. He accepted it shakily. "Let's get out of here."

Natalia discarded her shoes, not wanting to draw any more attention to herself with the squeaking of her sneakers. The rainbow laces still radiated brightly, and Natalia smiled as she remembered how proud Jay had been when he presented them to her.

Kyle, for his part, watched Natalia curiously as she untied her laces and set her shoes aside.

"I don't want them to hear me," she explained, and then as Kyle began to pull on his own sneakers, she placed a hand on his shoulder. "Keep yours on. It's ok."

Timing is everything. She waited until the merc had his back turned to the bottom of the stairs, facing the door that led to the cellar. She took the stairs two at a time in her sock feet and pounced from the last step, driving the length of sharp mirror into the merc's neck. He gasped, flailed, his gloved hands reaching towards Natalia's as she drove the shard in further and then yanked it free, sending an arc of red across the foyer, staining the moonlit floor scarlet. Leaning down, she clamped a hand over his mouth to prevent his wet gurgles from raising the attention of anyone who might be nearby. She caught a glance at herself in the shard of mirror, bloodstained and solemn, and ran the sleeve of her jacket over her face. The man at her feet was long dead. There was no point in trying to hide the body; the blood had spread like syrup and they couldn't afford to waste time trying to cover their tracks. Natalia whispered up the top of the stairs and Kyle came trotting down. No time to retrieve her shoes. She reached out, and Kyle took her hand.

"Don't look," she said.

Kyle squeezed her bloody fingers and said nothing.

xXx

Jim knew he would have to move fast if he wanted to take Pete down. It would be a matter of hours before word spread that the Reapers' clubhouse had been invaded and Pete would know who was behind it. He would go into hiding, and that would be the end of that. Jim drive drove quickly, breaking the speed limit the whole way home, and didn't waste any time once he was inside. He fed Cooper and let him into the yard to romp, but instead of frolicking in the snow the shepherd sat at the back door, whining. The damn dog knew something was wrong.

Jim let him back in and watched as Cooper trotted down the hallway, turning towards Natalia's room, where he settled at her door and peered in, as if to see where the female of the house had gone.

"She's not here."

Cooper didn't move.

"Dammit, Coop! She isn't coming back!"

At Jim's raised voice, Cooper whined gently and turned away from Natalia's room, slinking towards his master. Jim knelt before the dog and rubbed his ears, content in the sensation of the moment that this was life, and life was good. What lay beyond the door, out in the winter and lost among the snow, was different. Where the ghosts made no prints, no marks to show they passed among the living, Jim felt them around him, crowding, wailing, and full of anger. But for now, in that moment, he focused on the dog. Cooper leaned in, sniffed loudly, and pressed his nose into Jim's hand.

"It'll be ok. Things will work out."

In the pseudo-gym that had once been a workshop connected to the back of the house, Jim began to pull loaded mags from the safe and check his favored weapons for cleanliness. He would go from Pete directly to Cain, and from there he would end it. The result didn't matter much to Jim, as long as he dragged Cain straight to hell with him.

In hindsight, he shouldn't have answered his cell, but instinct trumped even the most intense emotions at that moment.

"The fuck are you doing, Agent Wilkinson?"

It was never a good sign when Meghan used someone's title.

"I'm dealing with this."

"You're dealing? Jesus." She laughed mockingly. "Don't start with me. You don't get word that your ward is dead and then just go on a one-man killing spree. This is not a game."

"I agree. It's fucking deadly, and I'm ending it. We've lost too many to Cain; he needs to be finished off."

"By the Agency. By the team. You can't just march into wherever the hell he's holed up and blast away until there is nothing left! We have rules, we have-"

"We have nothing!" Jim declared. "We placed all our eggs in one goddamned basket, and lucky for us she set down somewhere safe before he killed her. Everyone got their wish, Meghan. She's not a threat: she took her secret to the grave."

"Say her name," Meghan replied coolly.

"What? What the fuck..."

"Say her goddamned name, Jim. She was a person, she was important to you. She was Amy's daughter and- Christ, you can't be blinded by this. Natalia's dead, yes, and we'll mourn her in time, but this disaster that Cain's crafted isn't anywhere close to being finished yet. I need you to pull yourself together. I need you to say her name."

Natalia. Natalia. Natalia.

Jim slammed his fist into the metal cabinet with an angry yell.

When Meghan spoke next, she was controlled, calm. "Get it out of your system and come in. We've got bigger problems than the fact She's is dead."

"What the hell-"

"Just come in. Troy's awake. He saw something."

xXx

As they descended the staircase towards the cellar, the smell of wet earth was overpowering. It reminded Natalia of sunshowers and mud puddles, of times spent with Beth before they became too old to appreciate each other's company. At the bottom of the stairs, they found themselves in a cellar that extended into a long hallway, just as Kyle had described it. Then, at the far end of the corridor, another door. Makeshift at best. It was a piece of plywood on springs and had been propped open by an artistic cobblestone pulled from the ground under their feet.

Natalia was uneasy with the sensation of being followed, as if something had risen out of the shadows of the house after her killing of the mercenary and followed them deep into the earth, spreading inky shadows in its wake. But there was no time to stop, no time to turn and confront whatever it was that had caught their scent and decided to pursue them with saintly patience.

She knew, without putting much thought into it, what it was.

The Hollow Man.

She gave Kyle's hand a reassuring squeeze, pointed towards the door. "That's it, right?"

Into the bowels of hell and beyond.

Kyle nodded earnestly, having apparently decided it was in his best interest to simply say nothing.

"Let's go then."

The stone was cold under her feet, bleeding into her socks and freezing her toes. It would make traversing the snow a problem, but they couldn't turn back now. If they couldn't find some place to hole up overnight, then Natalia would have to try to make a fire for them, which seemed like a dreadful idea given she had never taken to Girl Scouts the way her parents had hoped. Another childhood experience that was beginning to make a bit more sense. Her parents had kept encouraging her to give it another shot despite her showing no inclination towards navigating the outdoors. Unless it was by tree.

Still, one step at a time.

They moved down the corridor, careful to ensure that every door they were about to pass was solidly shut, until they reached the hole in the earth.

Someone had jerry-rigged a string of bare wire from what barely constituted a ceiling in the tunnel. It was just under six feet in height, with bare light bulbs strung every five feet or so, forcing Natalia to ease carefully to the side so as to not knock one out of place. The sides of the tunnel were bare dirt and had been supported with wooden pillars that were set in place by cement blocks. Rebar criss-crossed overhead, supporting the frozen, cold earth from collapsing on those building the tunnel. Reaching out from above the rebar were fresh, spongy roots that curled out from the earth in all directions.

The orchard, Natalia thought. *We must be beneath the orchard.*

The tunnel curved down and flimsy plywood stairs had been added. Far ahead Natalia could hear the faint whistle of wind.

There's an exit.

With one eye on the ground, watching for stray nails, Natalia stepped down the stairs and deeper into the earth.

Dear God, if this is where I die then at least make it fast.

Being crushed by thousands of metric shit tonnes of earth wasn't top of her *Ways to Die* list, but Natalia figured it was better than whatever Cain planned on doling out.

The tunnel spiraled down into the earth. The air around them was cold, nipping at their cheeks. Natalia glanced back once to see Kyle's pale face, now patchy and red. She took off her jacket, already too big for her, and handed it to the boy. It was like watching a child play dress-up. Here he was, pretending to be an adult, on his way to the office to do all sorts of business.

Maybe if he was three five-year-olds stacked on top of each other. The visual made Natalia smile, but when Kyle asked her what was so funny, she just shook her head.

After nearly a half-hour of walking, the ground began to arc upwards. The whistle of the wind was nearly screeching, and Natalia could feel the cold breath of winter on her bare arms. Then she saw it, there, at the end of the tunnel. Another plywood door set in place by springs. The force of the wind was catching it and swinging it open so it banged roughly against the support beams.

"When we get to the end we run, understand? Don't stop, no matter what."

"Natalia, what if- what if they catch us?" Kyle's eyes were wide with panic, as if he only now realized what they were doing.

"Then we try again. And if you can, if you get the chance, you leave, ok? Don't wait for me. They'll let you go before they let me go."

"But *why*?"

"Because." Natalia straightened, felt the top of her head scrape the rebar supporting the earth. "Because I know something I shouldn't, and Cain wants it. That's why you're here."

"But...I didn't even know you. Why would he take me if I didn't know you?"

Because you're one more way to manipulate me. Natalia kept the thought to herself. "We're not sticking around to find out."

Natalia's left ear twitched at a new sound. Feet, shouting, coming from behind them.

"We have to go! Come on!"

Taking Kyle's wrist, Natalia raced down the length of the tunnel and threw her shoulder into the plywood door. The wind nearly blew them both sideways, but Natalia had her feet planted firmly in the snow and held fast to Kyle. One step out and the snow plunged halfway up her thigh, and past Kyle's knee.

"Move!" she screamed over the wail of the wind. The rush of snow and ice was suffocating, but Natalia pulled Kyle cruelly over the knoll, out into the raging storm. Whichever way they went, whatever they ran into, it would surely be better than whatever Cain had planned. They scrabbled sluggishly through the snow until a blackened treeline rose out in front of them. Shadowy ancient pines that stretched upwards, threatening to pierce the sky.

The treeline cut the wind, giving Natalia a moment of respite to see what lay ahead of them. Endless forest silhouetted against the moon. Breaks in the vegetation came only with stumps or small snow-covered glades.

Ducking below the wide branches, Natalia knew she was all but dragging Kyle with her, completely disregarding the earth beneath their feet and his panicked gasps for breath. A spiny branch sliced across her cheek, but the pain and heat were instantly swept away by the wind. Up ahead she could see a break in the trees, and then another thicker bramble of dark branches.

We can lose them there.

The tree line was only a few yards away now, and Natalia felt the leap in her chest as fear was unexpectedly overtaken by determination and, perhaps, just an ounce of pride. They would make it, they would make it, they would-

The ground below their feet slipped, and for a desperate moment Natalia and Kyle froze. The wind continued its helpless weeping, but was joined by the unexpected harmonization of cracking, like the shards of the mirror descending onto the duvet over the dresser, the crackle of fragile things everywhere. Natalia glanced down to her bare feet, carefully pushed the reams of snow aside, and saw the ice below their feet.

A river, raging beneath a skimpy layer of ice.

Kyle squeezed her hand and gave her a terrified look.

"I can't swim," he said, desperately.

"I'll hold on to you, ok? I won't let you go, I promise."

"No, please-"

The shouting behind them was becoming louder, and Natalia could see beams of light split the trees and scatter at their feet. "We have to Kyle, come on!"

It would break beneath their weight. She knew that. But if she could get Kyle to the other side, or close enough that she could push him to the bank, then maybe Cain would let the boy go. One step forward, then another. The ice crackled under her heel. Turning around she reached towards Kyle. He shook his head fearfully, glanced over his shoulder, and took a step backwards, unable to comprehend that any watery grave would be a hundred times better than whatever remained for them back at that house where the dead still clung to fabric and nails.

The time for gentleness was long gone. Natalia reached forward, grabbed the boy by the wrist, and pulled him forward as he flailed in her grip and tried to pry himself free.

"Stop!" Natalia screamed above the din. The shock must have been enough, for Kyle allowed Natalia to lead him forward, step by step, across the ice. They were halfway when Natalia risked looking down and saw that there was nothing below them. No river bottom, no aquatic life. Just black, emptiness. The water was deep. If they fell in, she might be able to keep Kyle's head above the surface, but-

Her heel dropped, just enough for Natalia to feel it register in her bones, like a Rube Goldberg machine, setting off a series of events, of warning signs. Natalia dragged Kyle forward and gave him a wild push towards the opposite bank as her foot split the ice and the whole of her body dropped suddenly into the water. Into the darkness. Into the nothingness.

Just breathe it in.

She struck a rock, and felt her ribs groan from the injury as she tried to bypass the current and break through the surface of the water.

Breathe in the darkness and let it take you away.

The water was cloudy; billows of silt puffing out from the river bottom as her body was dragged along. Then a flare of colour, of tiny fingertips scrambling along the ice as beams of yellow and white light began to blaze through, distorted. People were screaming, but she wasn't sure if it was in her head or above it.

Dead is dead.

She saw a thousand small black bodies scramble for traction; individual eight legs tip-toeing, as if that might make the movement easier. Her body crashed against a boulder, her ribs flexing to take the blow, and Natalia saw the glassy surface above her shatter, sending a hundred spiders drifting helplessly through the water just as a hand reached down towards her.

Dead is dead.

She was tossed into snow, face striking a rock hidden beneath the cottony tufts. She tried to blink the water from her eyes, cough up river from her lungs, and look around, praying she might see a familiar face from the Agency. But no. Thellion was taking Kyle up the snowy bank, cradling the child in his arms. Beyond him, already absorbed into the forest, she saw the familiar glow of the Hollow Man's eyes.

Natalia could hear voices warbling at her feet. Her toes twitched, and she was overcome with a strange sensation of something being both inside her foot and outside of it. She felt the flesh of her heel part, as if someone were drawing a string out of her. She jerked her leg back and felt a warm hand rest on her calf.

Turning her head to one side, Natalia saw Thellion sitting next to Kyle on the edge of a bed, speaking to him; almost familial, kind. Kyle was tying a pair of shoes. He looked up at Thellion and wiggled his foot, which was propped on the bed. "It doesn't fit."

"We didn't take your measurements," Thellion replied dryly.

Kyle looked heartbroken.

She wanted to scream a warning, to vocalize her intense rage for anyone who dared come close to Kyle. Her voice erupted from her chest in a broken wave, hollow from her distorted hearing.

Then came the sensation of spiders nipping at her foot.

"Just a nail." Then came a voice from the end of the bed, warbled, like she was hearing it through gushing water. "She probably picked it up in the tunnel."

"Christ." The hand on her leg vibrated as the voice spoke.

From his place on the bed, Thellion looked back at her and gave a broken-toothed grin. "She'll be lucky if she doesn't lose any fingers or toes."

"If she does," the voice attached to the hand said, deathly quiet, "I'll break the rest of your goddamned smile for putting her through more bullshit-"

"She's not going to lose any appendages." Cain. His voice was clear. Always calm, warm, as if amused by some small detail.

The voice that was attached to the hand spoke, close to her ear, and Natalia felt her heart pound. "Hush, sweetheart. You're safe now."

Your father didn't.

Hush.

Your father didn't

Hush.

"D-dad?"

Chapter 26

Jim listened to what Troy had to say without expression, because what he was hearing might have been outrageous, but he didn't think the newly-conscious agent needed to see his look of disbelief. The wound pulsating at Troy's throat broke his voice into a weak whisper, and when he finished talking, he slid backwards into the hospital bed and sighed in relief, as if he had been clinging to an anchor in a storm and just been told he was now safe.

Meghan looked over at Jim with one eyebrow arched. "What do you think?"

"It's not fucking possible," Jim said with a casual shrug. "Just not."

"I know what I saw." Troy glowered at Jim. One hand at his throat, another unconsciously pressing the button that would deliver morphine directly into his veins. They had cut him off hours ago, but hadn't told him. That was the Agency way. Grit your teeth. Fight it. "Marcus-"

"Was killed by Cain," Jim interjected. "Shotgun to the face. Leon, Rebecca, they both saw it. Even if they didn't, why would Marcus hold a gun to his own daughter?"

"Jim." Meghan tipped her head towards the doorway, then looked back at Troy. "I'm glad you're still with us, Troy. Just take it easy, all right? We'll look into this."

"I know what I saw, Meghan." Troy had pushed himself up on his wrists. "I *saw* him."

Meghan smiled, and Jim recognized the look. Pity; the worst thing for an agent to endure. He could read her thoughts at a hundred yards. *Such a shame, such a good agent, cracking under the pressure.* Because it simply wasn't possible.

Up to that point, Caulder had been listening diligently without question to Troy's story. Now, as he took the lead from the medical ward, Jim saw how his meaty fist was clenched, fingers white from the strain. A thick bobble of blood welled in his palm and was shaken away. When he turned to face them, Jim averted his eyes.

"Well?" Caulder asked.

"It can't be right," Jim said. "Cain had no reason to keep him alive. Besides, it was a goddamned blizzard out there. Troy probably imagined it."

"There was obviously *someone* else out there," Caulder said, leaning past Jim and calling for the elevator.

"Probably just another poor schmuck that Cain's hired. It couldn't have been Marcus Artison because he's *dead.*"

The silence stretched between them until the elevator doors slid open and they stepped inside. Meghan was the first to break. "We worked on a theory early on, after Amy's death," she said, "that Cain had taken Marcus in order to manipulate Natalia and Beth. Threaten their father, their last relative. The last of their family. The girls would break."

"But they didn't. *Natalia* didn't. She told us that herself. He was executed in front of her."

"When we finally got the whole story from her it was nearly a month after Alcatraz," Caulder reminded Jim slowly.

Jim remembered. He and Natalia had been on the run, and she had abjectly refused to speak about what had happened to her father until a brief phone call with Meghan had convinced Natalia to tell them what she could. He had been executed. Cain had threatened to kill Marcus and Natalia had let him. That was the guilt she lived with every day. Neither Meghan nor Jim had asked for details, because they knew pushing her any further was a risk they couldn't afford. Besides, *execution* had a very clear meaning in their line of work.

But perhaps Natalia had used it more loosely. A different definition entirely.

"That still doesn't explain why we found a goddamned *body*. Who was that poor bastard with his head half blown off if it wasn't Marcus Artison?"

"The eternal question," Meghan replied slyly. "We buried him, whoever he was."

That tweaked something in Jim's mind. A memory. What was it? It felt like a lifetime ago, but it hadn't been. Just a few weeks, really. She had been annoying him, being less than forthcoming, trying to *force* conversation because it amused her, and they both knew it.

Weird.

A waste of space to get buried.

The elevator rolled to a gently stop and the doors opened. Meghan held back half a second as the two men walked in front. "I just don't think Troy would say anything unless he was absolutely sure," she said. "He doesn't have a history of exaggerating things."

"Would Marcus have really allowed his surviving child to suffer in such a way if he was in a position to stop it?" Caulder asked, turning and beckoning Meghan forward. "If it is true, it raises more questions than it answers."

Jim agreed, even if he didn't want to. What Natalia experienced in Alcatraz, hell, even before that... No, Marcus Artison was a lot of things, but he wasn't the sort of man who would let his child suffer if it could be avoided. Even so, Jim couldn't fathom him being alive. It seemed preposterous, and he would defend that position to the death. "Marcus would have tried to contact us if he were still alive," Jim said finally.

And yet...

Mom said it was a waste of space to get buried.

"He may have not had any chance," Meghan suggested. "If he was somehow under Cain's thumb, unable to escape, it would make sense to keep his head down to protect Natalia. We don't know what he might have done to try to save her in Alcatraz. We don't know what he's been through."

"What about Beth? Marcus is good, but I doubt even he'd have the skills to feign cooperation with a man who killed one of his kids." He halted, swallowed the lump in his throat. "*Both* of his kids."

"Unless he thought it was the only way to protect the only one who was left." Meghan stopped halfway down the hallway and mindlessly adjusted a picture that was off-centre. "Marcus was always a pragmatic person, never run by emotions alone. He always looked at the bigger picture, and he might have realized that to keep Natalia alive he would have to sit quietly for a while."

"Lot of good it did him."

Meghan nodded sagely. "Troy doesn't know yet. The doctor thinks we should wait until he's more stable"

"Smart move."

Caulder had moved on without them. It was hard to ignore the fact that Natalia's death had impacted him in *some* regard, but he was reluctant to give in to his emotions, and neither Jim nor Meghan were particularly interested in psychoanalyzing him. It was, Jim suspected, at least partially a sense of loss, and of the last of his hope going up in smoke. Caulder understood as well as any of them that Natalia might have very well died protecting Kyle Powell. That was an ineffable guilt to carry.

"There's something else you need to know," Meghan said quietly, watching Caulder turn the corner, out of earshot. "After Troy told us what he saw, I had Aurora pull the Artisons' files."

"And?"

Meghan pulled her cell phone from her pocket and began to flip through a series of pictures, not looking up. "Days before they left for Russia, Marcus and Amy both changed their funeral instructions from cremation to burial. Closed-casket." She held up the first image, and Jim immediately recognized the formatted will that he, like so many others, had been forced to create when he joined the Agency. Near the bottom of the page rested Marcus Artison's signature.

"Could be coincidence," Jim said, without believing a word of it.

"Sure," Meghan said, then thumbed to the next photo and held it up again.

This peculiarity Jim could see more clearly. It was a copy of Amy's will, same format, same request for a burial in a closed casket.

But the signature at the bottom was not Amy's. If anything, it was remarkably close to Marcus'. The same loops, the same slants. As if someone had been trying to hide their forgery, but not particularly well.

"When I took Natalia to their graves she made an offhand comment about Amy wanting to be cremated."

Meghan nodded, returning the phone to her blazer pocket. "It was forwarded to us from the London Branch. Amy and Marcus geared up there before heading to Russia. London is being remarkably...*difficult* about the circumstances surrounding their visit to the branch."

"So, what are they hiding? We know that's Marcus' signature. At the most we know he forged Amy's."

"Someone had to witness it," Meghan replied, slowly, "and right now we don't know who. The copy we were sent might as well have had the secret blend of twelve herbs and spices written on it for all the redactions it contained. We didn't think anything about it at the time; Marcus and Amy changed their plans, it happens. But now with Troy... well, it raises a lot of questions. I'm waiting for London to get back to me on it."

"What are you thinking?"

"It's a problem," Meghan said, "either way it's spun, it's a problem. The trouble I'm having is whether it's a *today* problem, or a *next week* problem."

Jim understood that, but found himself struggling to care any more than he already did. Marcus couldn't be alive, because it was preposterous. A change in funeral arrangements was hardly something to call out the cavalry for. Or perhaps it was, and he was simply too focused on the immediate future and his inevitable struggle with Pete. A *next week problem* indeed.

"I know you can't focus on it right now," Meghan said, finally, "and you shouldn't."

"Why's that?"

"You're going after Pete." She levelled her stony gaze at Jim and frowned. "Let's not dick around. You think it's your battle and yours alone, but there are other people who are part of this fight, Jim."

Jim shook his head. "This isn't just about Natalia. On the Rock... There are rules. I broke 'em. That's why he did what he did, to punish me. I know it's everyone's fight, and I'm fine with you all being there when it comes to gunning down Cain, but this one is mine, Meghan. You've got to give it to me. I'm not going be able to survive this if I'm not the one to end it."

Meghan tipped her head at him, mouth pursed in a thin line. Even then, Jim could see, he had won her over. She understood the pull of it, the desire to destroy that which had been snarling and snapping at his heels for so long. At last, she nodded, just once, and said, "You call when it's done. I'll have the team ready to go."

xXx

No. it isn't possible. Not this. Anything but this.

Natalia wanted to crawl away from the voice, the touch, the face of the dead. She wanted to turn from the ghosts that had descended over her. She wanted to be anywhere, with anyone else, experiencing any tragedy other than this.

I saw him die. I saw him.

No. She thought, over and over, until the words were spilling from her lips in dry, hoarse sobs and she felt her ability to function or form a coherent thought shut down in a desperate attempt at self-preservation.

"No, no," she cried, shaking her head and clawing across the bed, pushing herself away from Marcus Artison. A dead man risen. She had buried him under earth and snow and tried to give herself leave to mourn and move on with her life. It was a struggle she never mastered, and now it was all in vain. He had never died. Never sacrificed himself so his children might live.

Your father didn't.

It began to make sense, like gears of a clock that had been grinding against each other, wearing down until they crumbled apart, taking her closely held beliefs with them. The last pieces of conversation in the chapel that had been so rudely interrupted by gunfire. Steven and Natalia, talking about bravery and cowardice and the sort of man who might...how had she put it? Kneel, take a bullet to the back. That was what had tipped Steven off, because whatever they had found, *who*ever they had found, had not died from a bullet to the back. That was what Steven had wanted to tell her.

Give me back those seconds, Natalia begged of time. *Give them back so I can tell him that I know. I understand.*

Marcus was reaching to touch her face. She wanted to flee because the sensation of his ghostly fingertips freezing her skin was sickening. But his hand met her cheek in a gentle caress, and Natalia inhaled sharply, shocked by the familiar cologne. Earthy, like pine needles gracing a forest floor after a storm. Comforting. It warmed her skin. She closed her eyes, mentally willing away the tears that were fighting for release.

Don't let them see you cry.

"It's me, sweetheart. It's Dad."

Natalia found her voice, buried under too many long nights of endless crying and mourning for the family she was so certain she had lost. "You're *dead*. I saw him kill you. I saw *Cain* plant a bullet in your back. H-he made me *choose!*"

"I know, I know, sweetie. I'm sorry, I'm so sorry. The only way I could protect you-"

"Beth." Her sister's name was a poison capsule waiting to dissolve on her tongue. As she spoke, Natalia saw the devastation on her father's face, as if she had spat acid on him, and understood that of all the questions she had, Beth was one better left alone, for both their sakes.

He clutched her hand with such ferocity that Natalia thought her fingers might disintegrate under the pressure, but she couldn't remove herself from him, fearful that a broken connection might sever his hold on her reality and send him spinning backwards to wherever it was the dead ended up.

Then, at the foot of the bed, Natalia saw Cain come into her peripheral vision, and she felt Marcus' grip tighten.

"We have to go, Marcus."

The casual familiarity was sickening. Who was Cain to speak to her father as if he was a friend? The pressure on her hand increased, and Natalia felt a sense of relief. It was her father playing a part, embracing the darkness of Cain's world to accomplish something. He would never align himself with a man like Cain; he would never support the one who killed his wife, his eldest child; who left the youngest to be absorbed by the ancient evils of man.

Then Cain stepped forward and clapped Marcus sympathetically on the shoulder, and Natalia's illusion shattered. Marcus' hand retracted from her, and he turned to face Cain.

"Just another minute, please."

Not begging. Not desperately trying to buy time with his last surviving child. No. It was a simple ask, one friend to another. *Pass the sugar, pour me a beer, just one more minute, please.* Natalia felt her skin crawl and pulled her legs back, scrambling against the comforter to push herself away from her father. Marcus looked on in confusion.

No, not confusion. Understanding. Sad, regrettable understanding.

"Natalia, sweetie, please-"

"You know him," she said, bewildered. "You...*know* him."

Marcus leaned forward, tried to caress her hair, but Natalia slapped his hand back forcefully, gaze snapping between her father and the one who had severed their connection and then drawn them back together. For what purpose? It didn't matter now. No, all the lies, piled on each other, weighing her down like the brickwork of a fallen building, were crushing her under the enormity of what it all had to mean.

"Do you have any idea what he's done to me? What almost happened to me in Alcatraz?"

Yet she held out hope. Hope that it might be a long con, some elaborate ruse that her father had crafted in the minutes after he abandoned her and Beth on the side of the street in Chinatown. But no, the familiarity between the two men was too personal, too affirming. Their connection stretched backwards, long before Steven, before Alcatraz, before Beth, before her mother. Natalia could see the ghostly threads between them, woven together, linking them in their cruelty.

"He killed Mom," she whispered. She felt the edge of the bed with her toes and swung her legs over, using the bedpost to support herself as she found the floor beneath her. "He-he killed my mom and you're...you're working for him?"

"Baby, it's not that simple. I..." Marcus cast a desperate glance in Cain's direction, but the terrorist, in all his anger and temper and manipulation, could only shrug his shoulders sadly. Marcus was chewing the inside of his cheek now, creating a ghastly grey hollow in his skin. Natalia saw how the months had worn on him. His strong, well-defined cheeks were now sharp and jutting at all angles. His skin was no longer perpetually tanned from some long-forgotten ancestral DNA sequence. No, he was a man broken by the world, scrambling to stay above the water. "I've known Cain for a long time. I've made mistakes."

Cain cast her a withering look, as if to say *See? I told you so*. And, for the briefest moment, Natalia was willing to let her mind create whatever excuses she needed in order to survive this mystifying world. She would willingly make excuses if it meant finding some semblance of normality. Then, out of the corner of her eye, she saw Kyle Powell. Thellion had one hand on the shoulder of the boy; not a threatening gesture by any means, but a controlling one. Natalia remembered the heat of the blade as it entered her arm and the agony of loss at Beth's death. Natalia felt shame as Duncan tried to violate her. And, in all of that, Natalia remembered Jim's own suffering, withheld, contained, personalized, as a decade later he continued to pay for mistakes he had never really made. Yet he had been there in the dank prison, and saved her life. Looking back now, she understood.

Natalia knew who had betrayed Jim and Steven and all the others a decade ago. She knew who had told Cain that there were rats in his enterprise, and sent the whole event spiraling out of control.

She knew, because for sixteen years she had called him *Dad*.

"You," she said, because now she was looking at a stranger. "It's all you. It always has been. You've been working for him all along, haven't you?"

"Natalia, *please*. Just let me explain-"

"No." Two hobbling limps took her backwards until she could feel the door behind her. "No, I'm tired of excuses. He destroyed our lives, he killed my mom, and my sister! And you think you can stand there beside him and, what? Call him a *friend*?"

"Oh," Cain said brightly. "Are we? That's nice to know."

"Shut the fuck up," Marcus growled over his shoulder, before his head snapped back towards Natalia and he reached out with a pleading hand. "Please, if you'll just let me explain. I wanted to save you-"

"*You don't get to decide!*" Natalia shrieked, taking a frantic step backwards, hoping to put a world between her and her father. "Kyle! Come here!"

The boy jolted at the command, skittered over the hardwood and allowed Natalia to push him protectively behind her.

"This is, this is just...fucking bizarre." Natalia's gaze snapped from the face of her father to Thellion, to Cain. "For you to be alive, to come back, to think you can just throw a Band-Aid on this, kiss it better. You're a monster!"

"Sweetheart, *please-*" But something caught Marcus' eyes as Natalia heard the door behind her creak open. A hand over her mouth, shoving the screams back down her throat. Kyle, crushed between her and the newest person in the room, scrambled free and began to scream, pounding at the arm with tiny, determined fists.

"No!" Marcus' hand shot out towards Natalia, but his cries faded away as she inhaled sharply and felt a punch of ether hit her brain, a sickly-sweet scent that spread through her gray matter with lacy tentacles that snatched at her senses and dulled them. Her legs buckled, but she didn't feel her body hit the ground. Instead she stared up, bewildered as Marcus' face appeared in her blurring vision, shouting something horrific to the figure that had clamped a cloth over her face. She twisted her head, hoping to see Kyle, who was being pulled back from the scene by Thellion.

Then, somewhere amid the tears and confusion and sadness, Natalia decided it was simply time to close her eyes and let go.

Chapter 27

Jim checked the address he had pulled up on Google Maps for a final time, compared it to the Street View image, and felt a stir of unease in his chest. He had done his best to focus on the crisis at hand. Destroy Pete, find Cain, kill Cain. Top three goals in life. Anything that came after, including Marcus Artison's brazen impersonation of Lazarus, was secondary. Even then, he wasn't entirely convinced that Troy hadn't been hallucinating, perhaps seeing what he wanted to see in the gale that had nearly claimed his life.

Yes, Jim had questions, all of which he desperately wanted answered. But they could wait if need be; they could even be pushed out of his mind, lost in the dust of the years, if it came to that.

Jim could forget a hundred years' worth of questions in exchange for the life of Cain Ferigon.

Now, sitting in the car parked outside of a dingy apartment in the North West of the Bronx, braced against Van Cortlandt Park, Jim figured it might be time to start planning for life after Natalia. She hadn't been present in his world for very long, not long enough to create some incorporeal manifestation of herself that would linger after death. Eventually this chapter in his life would close, and Natalia's place within it would be relegated to the odd distorted memory. What would happen next? Jim imagined finding Angel, maybe trying to be a proper family again, living under the same roof. That was silly though, because Jay would be off to university or college or Reno, wherever, soon enough, and then there would be nothing to keep them bound together. They might survive a bit longer as a couple than they had on the first round, but ultimately their connection would be tenuous at best, and Jim didn't want to risk it.

What about Marcus?

No, Jim shook his head. Marcus was a conversation for later. Much later.

The apartment before him was scheduled for demolition, and Jim could hardly blame the owner. The revitalization of the Bronx was sweeping through streets like the spirit of God come to collect the souls of the first-born children. One inanimate object after another collapsed into rubble, only to rise from the ashes with a chic, post-modern look, as if it had been assembled by a toddler who couldn't fit the circle into the square, but still tried their damnedest.

Before he had gone to prison, Pete Cobbs had lived in a small apartment across the street. It was long gone but, Jim figured, with the death of Bree, Pete had probably sought out something familiar that he could lean on while he made his next plan. Either he had come back hoping he could slip right into his own bed, dusty as it may be, or he had arrived, discovered it was gone, and figured if the view was the same, what did it matter?

He would be shocked to see Jim. It would immensely pleasing to see the look of dismay on Pete's face when he realized how badly he had fucked up.

Jim waited until darkness fell. Pete was a bigger man by no small margin, and in a straight one-on-one fight he would easily best Jim. No, the only way Jim was going to win was through stealth and, as Natalia wasn't around to jab a broken bottle into Pete's shoulder, Jim knew he had to move somewhat cautiously.

And there it was. His mind had rolled back to Natalia once again, and Jim felt a twinge of shame for his failure to protect her. If any piece of Amy Artison were left out there in the world, in some haunting, incorporeal form, she would surely be prepared to drag her claws through his flesh and devour what was left of his ill-fitting soul.

Darkness fluttered over the neighbourhood, like a feral animal darting over streets, around cars, and down back alleys, leaving a trail of shadows behind. All at once it was night, and the dilapidated apartment building was a black monolith looming over the neighbourhood.

Jim saw a flicker of a weak light in a tenth-floor window, glowing between boards that had been hammered over it. A fence surrounded the building, but the lock on the gate had been jimmied long ago and was set in place with a loose chain, giving the illusion of security where none existed. One look at the graffitied sides of the building told Jim all he needed to know. The neighbours probably couldn't wait for the monstrosity to be gone. Any illicit activities taking place would probably help the local community leader get it torn down that much sooner.

The front door squeaked as it swung inwards, like a screeching violin in a horror film. Jim winced internally and braced himself for Pete's tank-like stature barrelling into him. Nothing but silence in all directions.

Jim began his ascent of the stairs, manoeuvring around gaping holes in the stairwell that had been casually fixed by imperfect placement of plywood and picture frame nails. The closer he came to the tenth floor, the more aware Jim was of a familiar sound above his head. The rattling of empty bottles and cans, clacking against each other as they rolled across the floor or were crunched underfoot. A bender that had gone on too long and left its participant in dangerous shape. Jim had only lost himself to drink that spectacularly once in his life, and he had vowed never again. No, now, his liquor came in small, constant doses like an IV of watered-down adrenaline, just enough to keep him moving. If Pete was on a bender, then that was a problem. Alcohol and grief were unhealthy bedfellows.

Glass shattering, muttering, maybe even...crying?

He knows about Bree then.

As much torment as Pete had caused her, as toxic as their relationship had been, Jim knew the thought of trying to repair things with his ex-wife had been a driving factor behind Pete's survival in Alcatraz. He loved Bree, and loved his children, and would have, Jim reckoned, died for them if it had been asked of him. The problem was Patrick McKim decided not to ask.

On the tenth-floor landing, Jim began to move more carefully. The hardwood was old, and he was certain that a single wrong move would result in him plunging through the boards to be impaled on a forgotten lamp several floors below. He moved across the hallway, hugging the walls, edging towards the apartment Pete had made his home.

Pete hadn't even bothered to close the door, perhaps too lost in his regret to realize he was letting in the monsters that stalked in the night.

And Jim.

At the open doorway, Jim peered in and saw an overturned couch and broken kitchen table. A fridge door had been half ripped from its hinges, rotting food dripping from it, landing in wet, sucking splatters on the ground. In the middle of the apartment sat a small coffee table covered with boxes of crackers, open tins of meat, and a single hand-crank lamp. Bottles and cans littered the ground.

Jim adjusted his grip on the gun. "Pete? You in here?"

There was a long grunt from the other side of the tipped-over couch. Jim saw a meaty hand fly up from the floor, and narrowly dodged a half-empty bottle of Georgia Moon that flew towards his head and smashed against the doorjamb.

Pathetic.

"Get the fuck up, Pete. We're finishing this."

Laughter now from beyond the couch. Pete grasped at the furniture, pulling himself upright. In the glow of the lamp, Jim could see that Pete wasn't nearly as drunk as he had hoped. Maybe just recovering from a bender, or had planned on getting blackout drunk. Either way, Pete was coherent enough to be a viable threat, and that was a problem.

"You fucking found me, so what?" Pete was gripping the side of the couch, another bottle of something in his free hand. "Doesn't fucking matter in the long run, does it?"

Jim shrugged, kicked a shard of glass from the broken bottle with one foot. "You took something from me."

Pete lifted another bottle, as if to toast the action, then took a swig. "And then I gave it back."

Jim shook his head and inhaled sharply, not wanting to let his anger at Pete's casual demeanor cause him to make a mistake. "The kid did, not you, and she's paid the price for it."

The look of anguish on Pete's face was fleeting, the grimace submerged as he convinced himself that he had done nothing wrong and was not to blame for Natalia Artison's demise.

"Sorry to hear that."

"Fuck you, no you're not. You're the one that took her to him."

"A man's got a job to do," Pete replied, closing the gap between them. He was close enough now that Jim could smell the booze oozing from his pores.

"Your job got some people killed, didn't it?"

"Lonny knew the risks. I told him to get out of town after the kid decided to play pyromaniac. Idiot didn't listen."

"What about Meloy?"

"Meloy?" Pete slung himself up so his girth rested on the back of the couch. "Fuck Meloy. He wants it all. Cain made him an offer." Pete looked ill. "Can't say you didn't warn me."

"I gotta know, before we do this..." Jim stepped forward, making note of the crumbling walls in his peripheral vision. The whole apartment was disintegrating around them. Any fight inside its walls could prove deadly for both of them. "Did you really think the Reapers wouldn't go after you, after Stieber? Hell, even Bree? You fucked up, you betrayed them. What did you expect?"

"I thought-" Pete shook his head, groaning as he pushed himself from the couch. "I owed her money, support for the kids. She wouldn't stop me from seeing them, but I just..." He grimaced, eyes flaring towards Jim, "I just *hate* owing people. Cain's job had a good price tag attached to it."

"Was it worth it? Was getting your ex gunned down in front of your kid worth it?"

Jim knew Pete was capable of summoning intense rage when reason left him. He had witnessed it in Alcatraz and, at the time, had promised himself he would never again do anything to position himself on the other side of that anger. The dig at Pete's failure to protect his ex and their child was more than enough to cause him to snap, though, and in an instant he was barreling forward, launching himself at Jim.

The impact sent them both sprawling towards the open doorway, catching the edge of the wall and cracking through the plaster like it was a nothing more than a sheet of ice. They rolled across the hallway, punching ribs, noses, temporal lobes, anywhere that might cause enough damage to silence the other. The old banister of the stairwell cracked beneath their combined weight, and Jim felt the floor disappear beneath him. He rolled and plummeted two feet onto the stairwell and down to the ninth floor landing. Pete was on top of him, fist raised and prepared to punch through Jim's orbital lobe, and, he figured, right down to the next floor. Jim twisted to one side and felt the reverberation as Pete's fist struck the hardwood, sending a smattering of splinters towards both their faces. Jim dragged a bottle across the floor, then smashed it into the side of Pete's head. With a wild roar he stumbled backwards off Jim, shaking the shards of glass from his face.

The recovery didn't take much. Pete was already snatching up a broken length of banister and brandishing it like a club, swinging wildly at Jim's head. He was in it for the kill, but Jim wasn't. He needed information. Without it, their investigation would be at a veritable standstill. Jim ducked the wild swing and landed a punch in Pete's stomach, winding him. They ducked and dodged and grappled at each other. Cuts, bruises, and wounds appeared on them seemingly without any cause. Jim saw a flash of silver in his peripheral vision and threw himself under Pete's arm, forcing the hand that brandished the knife up at an awkward angle, and used the momentum to push Pete's bulk backwards into the wall.

There was a cracking below their feet, and Jim felt the floorboards flex and tremble. He dashed sideways as the years of wear and tear and intrusive termites finally forced the floor to succumb to Pete's weight. The ground disappeared beneath his body, and Jim snatched out, grasping Pete's wrist.

For a single moment, they froze in that position, Jim clinging to Pete's wrist, keeping him suspended above the rickety floor below as his own shoulder bulged and dislocated from the sudden jarring. Pete looked down, then back to Jim, eyes wide as if he could not comprehend how he had gotten himself into this compromising position.

Jim pulled Pete up, just a few inches, ignoring the throbbing in his arm. "Where the hell is Cain?"

"Fuck," Pete grunted, clawing at the edge of the hole for support. "Fuck you, Jim."

"You said you would help her!" Jim yanked on Pete's wrist again, forcing him to dangle freely. "Then you *sold her out*. And for *what*? What did you get out of it, Pete?"

"He said-"

"He fucking always says shit! He *lies*, you asshole. He *always lies*."

Pete looked pained, like he was struggling with hysterical crying building up within himself. When he spoke, it was in a broken, defeated voice. "Annie."

"She's fine," Jim spat. "*She* gets to live."

Pete hung his head, and, for a moment, Jim thought Pete might cry, out of grief for what he had lost or out of bewilderment, that despite it all, he was being offered some guarantee that his child would be safe, protected. When he looked up again, his face was creased with exhaustion.

"He said, if you came asking, to tell you to go where it all started. That's all I know."

"Fine."

Jim let go, turning away at the sound of Pete's body crashing through the floor below and continuing down, one dilapidated floor after another. Jim stood, placed his weight on his right leg, and let his arm hang as he rolled his shoulder backwards until the joint reset itself with a sickening pop. No sound from the floors below. Wherever Pete had landed, Jim didn't much care to see what was left of him. Pete Cobbs was a closed chapter.

xXx

Natalia couldn't rightly call herself conscious. She was aware; of air, cold on bare flesh, and of pain coursing through her head as the back of her skull was dragged along the ground. Stairs. Hollow thunks that indicated they were moving her. Up or down? She wasn't sure. The bumping was brutal, sending her mind into a tailspin as she tried to focus on anything other than the pain that was like a fuse in her brain.

She didn't black out, but at some point Natalia simply gave up trying to fight the pain and let it carry her away to another place.

When she could focus again, Natalia found herself in a brightly lit bricked room. Tables with outlandish, obscure equipment filled most of the space. Brightly coloured wires, snipped to a variety of lengths, had been scattered across the floor like a discarded preschool art project.

Natalia lifted her gaze to the door on the other side of the room, and watched, confused, as Hayden Meloy, whose face she had gotten to know perhaps a little too intimately, pressed a brown paper package into the hands of the young man Natalia had seen Cain embrace in the middle of the orchard days earlier. There was no reason for her to believe that he was the same person; she hadn't seen his face then, and couldn't see it now, but something in the way the shadows clung to his cheeks, and the way the darkness clawed around him, was familiar.

Hayden Meloy laughed and shook the hands with the man. Natalia strained to move, but her body ached and the pain was ringing through her head like brass bells. The shadowed figure left the room, floating spectrally, and when she blinked again, he was gone.

Meloy was inches from her nose now, peering at her with his scarred face, blinking heavily in the bright light. He gave Natalia a little push on the forehead with his index finger and sent her collapsing back onto the floor.

When her mind settled between her ears again, Natalia decided to move more carefully, with more intent. *You are conscious, but don't open your eyes. You need to pace yourself. Focus on what happened first.*

Dad. Dad is alive. That's what Steven was trying to tell me.

Her head was throbbing. A terrible pounding, like a speaker. She could see waves of colour explode with each hard note, an acoustic art piece. It felt blinding and muffling at the same time.

Natalia cringed at a familiar touch; a hand brushing back lengths of hair that had fallen astray. That familiar cologne, the scarred fingertips that had so often flicked peas at her from the other side of the dinner table, or dug splinters out from her feet that she had gotten from climbing where she wasn't meant to. Her mother had always scolded her for her climbing, but Marcus, Dad, he had encouraged it.

How high you can go? Maybe one day you'll see the whole world.

Now those fingers touched her forehead and held her hand, and Natalia felt her abused emotions compress the thunderous pounding in her head until there was only darkness and she could think clearly.

Jim is still in danger.

There. That was the goal. She had to warn him, warn the whole Agency. Cain was drawing them in. Marcus being alive was...glorious and horrifying and painfully sad, but she could deal with all those sentiments once she was certain her guardian would not be caught in the undertow.

Natalia opened her eyes and let her vision settle on her father, alive and well, sitting on the edge of the couch that she was lying on. His face brightened momentarily at the sight, then he leaned back, as if wanting to put space between them. As if that would somehow protect him from her anger.

It wouldn't.

"Thought it was all a bad dream," she croaked, shifting her body away from him. Marcus looked saddened that Natalia might react in such a way, but she wouldn't give him the benefit of the doubt. "You're a traitor," she whispered, pushing herself up on her elbows so she could wiggle herself into the corner of the couch. "You betrayed the Agency, didn't you?"

"I-" Marcus paused, shook his head, dismayed, then frowned at his daughter. "The Code, Natalia. I need it. Do you remember it, sweetheart?"

"Six," she replied lamely, and a giggle bubbled up her throat, as if the simplicity of the whole thing was absolutely hysterical. She knew it was a side effect of coming off the drugs that had infiltrated her system, and yet she didn't mind. "Six sixes all in a row. Add them together, divide by my age when you fucking *betrayed* all of us."

"Natalia, *please*."

"It's so goddamned *bizarre*. Is-is *Mom* alive? What about Beth? Is this some immortal curse we've got to contend with here? What if I shoot myself in the head? Will *I* die?" As if to make a point, she lunged for the gun that Marcus had holstered at his hip. He pushed her back. They both knew it was a half-assed effort at best.

"I can *end* this," he said gently.

Natalia shook her head. She understood what he meant, and admired his naivety in the face of the situation. How could he possibly understand that there was no *ending* anything now? That even if she gave up the Code, even if Cain relinquished his claim on her life, Natalia would still be intricately tied to this world forever? It would never end for her. And for others...it was already done.

"It's already ended for Beth," Natalia replied quietly, "and Mom, and Steven. Too many people, Dad. For me, though? It's forever. Cain branded me, but you *marked* me, and it'll never end."

"This is about more than you and me. This has been a lot time coming. I can stop it. You don't have to give Cain the Code, you don't have to betray anyone. Give it to *me*. Trust *me*."

Natalia blinked hazy, tired eyes. "Me?"

In that moment, Marcus must have realized he had made a terrible mistake. Me. Not as a father and daughter, but as a singular entity who no longer had any attachment to the world. *Me.* An inmate running the asylum. *Me.* A one-man army. Because *me* was a separate entity from *us*, from the father and daughter that ought to work in tandem. *Me* separated Natalia from her father, her family, forever.

"Fuck you," she whispered hoarsely, "and fuck whatever *side* it is you're on. You want to talk about *me*? Steven gave his life for *me*. Your friends, coworkers, have given their lives for *me* when you ran away. I'm not concerned about *me* anymore. I'm part of something much bigger than you or *me*."

"This is so more complicated than you think. Please, don't risk your life-"

She barked a cold laugh. "I didn't risk my own life!" She jolted forward, pushed him back with her palms on his chest, and glowered. "Don't you get it? I'm here because of you! I've been stabbed and threatened and assaulted because of *you*. This isn't some moral code I'm trying to adhere to. I'm trying to stay alive. You sure as shit haven't done anything to help."

However deeply the words cut, Marcus made no suggestion that he was wounded by them. Something during the months of separation from his family had hardened him, and Natalia suspected he wouldn't emote even if he were still capable of feeling anything. "I'm sorry, sweetheart." He stood up, took a step back, and averted his gaze. "I'm going to make it right. I promise."

Natalia tracked her father as he moved across the room to a door that had been propped open haphazardly with a brick. Just beyond she could see him converse with someone, hands flashing back and forth for a moment, before he was gone.

How strange, she thought as she watched the empty doorway. *He can walk in and walk out so easily. Out of a room, out of a life. It doesn't matter. It's all easy to him.*

Even if she had the capacity to make a dash for the open door, Natalia knew it would do her no good. She couldn't leave without first finding Kyle, and there was little doubt in her mind that the moment she stepped outside she would be tackled by any number of mercenaries who were looking for an excuse to fulfill their bloodlust.

Might as well look around and see where you've ended up.

Her legs wobbled beneath her as she stood up. Fragile, like a newborn animal. She reached for the couch to balance herself and gave both leg a furious shake until she could feel the blood flowing freely once again. Then, and only then, did she begin to look around.

The room was nothing more than four red-bricked walls, with large burlap sacks lining filled to the brim with something malleable, stacked four feet high. Along with the couch she had woken on, Natalia saw there was a collection of small tables scattered with lengths of colourful wires and odd items that she couldn't place. There were bits of what looked like old putty formed into various shapes and pressed into the bottom of small containers. Leaning closer, Natalia caught a whiff of something familiar, like Lonny Stieber's garage. There were small boxes filled with black gunpowder. She recognized the scent. A sundry of other items she couldn't identify, handfuls of ball bearings and pieces of metal that looked like they had been culled from someone's home repair project.

It didn't look particularly friendly.

Another table was against the far wall, but before Natalia could examine it further, the door was pushed open and Cain strode through. He didn't falter as he reached forward and threw her forcefully against the wall, pinning her by her shoulders.

"Tell me, you *must* tell me!"

His expression was indecipherable. Equal measures of fury and desperation.

For the first time, Natalia wondered if she had been wrong about her father, was it possible for her to be wrong about Cain, about what had driven him to this dark place and given rise to the monster standing before her? If all she had believed had been built from falsehoods, then what else in her world was a lie?

"For Christ's sake, Natalia!" He shoved her shoulders into the brickwork and Natalia felt her spine grate against the wall. "This isn't a game."

"I won't," she said through gritted teeth. "I won't ever give you the satisfaction of taking someone important away from me ever again."

"Innocent lives are at risk."

"*I* was innocent!" she declared, knocking his hands away from her arms as Jim had taught her during one of their many late-night training sessions.

"And now you aren't! Now you are part of this world just as much as I am. But you can *save* other people. Tell me the Code!"

Natalia was about to open her mouth, prepared to fly off another sharp reply, when the table on the far side of the room caught her attention. She had almost missed it, her mind consumed with the strange objects littering the other tables, but the old leather jacket was difficult to ignore, as was the pair of boy's sneakers that had been irreparably damaged after their escape into the wild.

Natalia moved past Cain mechanically, eyes latched on the items, afraid that she if she blinked they would disappear. But no, they sat there, as real as anything she had ever seen before in her life.

Kyle's shoes. Her jacket.

Next to them, an outline of a foot, a cross-section of a runner. Someone had opened up the heel of one shoe and packed it tight with a greyish putty that stank of grease monkeys and garages.

That was when she recognized the smell. It was as familiar to her as the smiling face of the mechanic who, thinking she was a gearhead in the making, had showed her how they disposed of old motor oil. It was familiar, because less than a month prior she had stood in a storage container and watched as Hayden Meloy went through his supplies and told Pete about a spill. It was familiar, because someone had bathed Lonny Stieber in it before lighting him up.

Natalia turned slowly to face Cain, certain that the look on her face reflected absolute horror. "His shoes didn't fit," she whispered. "Why didn't his shoe fit, Cain?"

Cain seemed to snap out of his trance, stepped towards her, and took her hand in his own.

"Please," he said, voice cracking from the strain.

She yanked her hand back, shaking her head in confusion. "You really are everything they say," she said. "He's just a kid, and you'd kill him. For what? What do you get out of it?"

"You really have to ask?" Cain tipped his head to one side, his brow furrowed by confusion. "Why would I have Pete interject to save you when the Third tried to execute you? Caulder wanted you dead, still does, I'm sure. And he'll try again. I can't have that, do you understand?"

"You're a monster," she whispered, bewildered.

"I am," he conceded sadly, "and just like you, I'm too far down this path to turn around. Too many people are relying on me." Cain stepped back from her, so thoroughly shamed it was as if she were talking to a different person.

Not my monster.

"I'm sorry, about your father, I mean. The dead should be able to stay dead. When they don't...people like you and me both suffer."

From the third-floor balcony, Marcus Artison watched Cain's men spool a length of wire through the darkness. It wound around the entire compound and out through the tunnel that had been carefully dug into the hillside, down away from the orchard and on the opposite side of the acreage from the only paved road in the area. Those who were considered essential elsewhere had already left the compound earlier in the day, taking a back road that wove east towards Boston, where they would separate until Cain called for them again. The only exception was Hayden Meloy, whose face still made Marcus cringe every time the bastard made eye contact with him. Meloy would head west, following the courier, ensuring the young man got on his flight, and then disappear with a sizeable cash reward tucked into his wallet. If he could stay ahead of the Road Reapers it would be a miracle.

Marcus gave him a couple of months at best; Meloy would blow his money on cheap cocaine and cheaper women before a local chapter of the gang would get word that he was nearby. They would deal with him. Another loose end, snipped off and detached from Cain.

"She's stubborn."

Marcus didn't turn at the sound of Cain's voice. "She takes after Amy."

"She won't talk." Cain stepped forward, leaned against the balcony, and began to unconsciously run his fingers along the marks that had been dug into the old wood years ago.

"Did you really think she would?" Marcus smiled sadly. "I didn't."

"I like to imagine she might have."

"Jesus, Cain." Marcus turned abruptly. "What sort of monster have we aligned ourselves with?"

"The only one that can give us both what we want," Cain reminded him carefully. "No matter what the cost."

"The cost is our goddamned souls. Are you really all right with that?" Marcus gestured towards the orchard. Wires were being wound along the blackened trunks of the dead apple trees. "I know you don't care about seeing this place burned to the ground, but the rest of it-"

"We agreed," Cain said, somewhat more reservedly this time. "Whatever it takes to make this right. No matter who gets in the way, no matter who suffers. We make this right."

"Kyle Powell is just a boy," Marcus said quietly. "He shouldn't have to pay for anyone else's crimes."

"Your daughter is paying for yours."

"That's *my* weight to carry. That's *my* burden. With Kyle we can make a difference, we can be better than what they think we are."

"Letting the boy live would create more problems than solutions."

"Letting him live would give us a chance at redemption; maybe our only chance in all of this." Marcus glanced towards the door of the balcony. Thellion had been there, longer than either of them were probably comfortable with, but he deserved to have a say. He was in it as deep as the rest of them. "What do you think?"

Thellion looked contemplative as he ran a tongue over his jagged tooth. "We're all monsters in our own right," he said finally, "but we've never gone this far."

"And if we don't?" Cain shot back. "We lose everything; every extra inch we've gained. He'll take it all back." He turned to Marcus, gaze steady. "And then in the end he'll still take Natalia, too."

The three of them stood in silence for a moment, watching the sun sinking in the sky and the shadowland beginning to rustle to life around them. It would only be a few more hours now.

"There has to be another way," Marcus said at last. "A way to end this without killing the boy."

"Think of it as a test," Cain said, without missing a beat, "to see how much she's learned. To see if she's learned enough to save him."

The thought made Marcus ill, and rightly so. He saw the fight in his daughter's eyes, and knew it was as much a by-product of her hatred for him as it was the result of her experiences. She had no choice but to fight, and he held much of the blame for that. But to kill a boy, or at the very least allow him to be killed, to prove a point if nothing else... No. Marcus wouldn't stand for it. He would find his own way to end this, as soon as he saw Natalia safely out of this carnage. There were other options, other threads he had left hanging because part of him had always known that it would never be easy. Natalia was her mother's daughter.

"Whatever it is you're thinking," Cain said from beside him, "I'd remind you of what we're up against. We're the only allies you have left, Marcus."

"Not entirely true," he said, turning his back to Cain, the orchard, and a world laced in copper. "But I'll keep your suggestion in mind."

Chapter 28

Where it all started. Jim didn't need to search his memory for a clue; he knew exactly where it had all started for Cain. He knew the place where the orchard burned and the scent of roasted apples and meat filled the air. Jim knew the place that haunted his dreams so vividly for the last ten years.

He was not prepared to return to that place, because he understood the way memories could poison one's mind even after being separated from them for so long. The truth was, Jim was scared to go back there. It represented everything he was frightened of: of failure, betrayal, weakness. Of losing everyone he cared about.

But Cain had taken that from him long ago, or at least had set the loss in motion. Angel and Jay could never have been safe forever. It was fortunate for Jim that any past lovers he still cared about were long gone, married with children, happy in their suburban illusions. As for Natalia, Jim figured what had happened with her was only a matter of time. He couldn't have saved her, and repeating that mantra was what would get him through the coming days and weeks.

The team was waiting for the news, which Jim delivered the moment he was free of the creaking apartment and able to breathe the clear, crisp winter air. It filled his lungs and soothed the lumps he had taken from Pete during their brief fight. It shocked his mind back to life and gave him the edge he needed, along with adrenaline, to push forward, back to his car, to make the call.

Northwest of Lancaster, Massachusetts, sat an isolated acreage where, a decade earlier, a family had been burned to death in an orchard. It seemed poetic that Cain would return home, perhaps because he sensed that his own time was drawing to a close. But Jim wouldn't act foolishly here; he would bring the cavalry with him. Inside the car, Jim called Meghan.

"I know where Cain is."

"Where?"

"His old home, outside of Lancaster. Get the team on the road. I'm heading up there."

"Any chance of you waiting for us to catch up?"

Jim decided to not grace Meghan with an answer, and she knew exactly how to interpret that. "If you can, try not to kill him. If we can bring him in to question him-"

"You'll have to pry my hands off from around his neck."

"Just...try to leave something intact, all right? And if you see Marcus-"

"I won't."

"If you do, do whatever you have to, all right? I'll get the team on the road right now; we'll be an hour behind you, tops. If you get a bad feeling, if it seems like a trap, then get the hell out or wait for us." Meghan paused for a moment, then said, "What about Pete?"

"Dead."

"How much did you contribute to his death?"

"I let gravity do most of the work, really."

Meghan sighed. "Be careful, Jim. Remember, there's still life on the other side."

"You think I'm going to make some stupid mistake, like I've got some death wish?"

"I think you're running on emotions just like the rest of us. I don't blame you for that, but I just want you to keep it all in perspective. Now get going. We'll see you there."

Meghan ended the call, and Jim adjusted his grip on the steering wheel. His knuckles had split where he had laid into Pete's head, and blood was draining from a cut along his hairline, threatening his sight. He swiped wildly at the blood, smearing it across his face, away from his eyes, and focused on the road. The trip would take three hours; Jim figured he could make it in two, maybe less if he pushed it. He wouldn't wait for the rest of the team. He had gotten the taste for blood while fighting Pete; a kick of adrenaline that was now pushing him towards a confrontation that had been a decade in the making. For everyone they had lost to Cain. Daisy and Kira, Amy and Steven.

Natalia.

He owed her nothing, had kept her at more than an arm's length out of fear of dragging her into a past that had had constantly been threatening his carefully balanced existence. He had been a fool to think the two could ever remain separate, and in many ways, Natalia had paid the price for that naivety. Now, Jim thought, there would be justice for all of them.

xXx

At first, Kyle thought it had been a mistake. Cain had taken him from the bedroom after Natalia had freaked out at the new person. Kyle was accompanied to another bedroom down on the second floor and told in no uncertain terms that he ought to put the new clothes on because he was going to catch his death sitting in his wet shirt and pants.

Kyle did was he was told because he thought that would make it easier. If he was good and didn't argue and didn't try to escape then they might bring Natalia back.

But Natalia never came back. Cain returned with food, hot soup and crackers, and told Kyle that he just needed to hang tight, that his uncle would come for him very soon.

When Cain left, Kyle didn't hear the door lock. He didn't move, afraid that perhaps it was a trap and shifting a single inch in either direction might spring it and bring the anger of the strange man down on him. Minutes ticked by, silence marked by more silence. Finally, Kyle stood up and approached the door.

The handle turned without any resistance.

Kyle paused. Whatever it meant, he had to think about it *carefully*. *What would Natalia do?*

She would find me, so I should find her. Kyle took a step back from the door. *Except she told me to run if I had the chance.*

Run and get help for her. That's the right idea.

Kyle pushed on the door gently, held his breath as it swung open soundlessly. He stepped out cautiously, poking his head around the corner of the room, just as he had seen Natalia do, albeit with slightly less grace. With no one in sight, Kyle inhaled sharply, thrust out his chest in a vague act of defiance, and left his small prison.

xXx

Two things were very clear to Natalia once Cain had left her alone in the strange, brick room. The first was that she had to get to Kyle, to snatch the shoes from his feet like a rich socialite determined to ruin the life of a lowly street urchin. The second was a longer, outstanding fear.

Jim.

He believed she was dead and, she imagined, that might upset him a little bit. Ideally, it wouldn't. Ideally, he would have shrugged his shoulders at the news and gone on with his day, but Natalia knew him better than that. Even if he didn't feel responsible for her, he wouldn't be able to stand by while Cain openly mocked him. So yes, Jim, assuming he could locate Cain, was probably on his way to wreak havoc and was walking right into a trap.

Save Kyle, warn Jim. There, only two tasks. Break it down into its simplest components and Natalia was certain she could handle it.

Simple like quantum mechanics.

Cain took her out of the room with the wires and lumps of C4, out into the hallway Natalia recognized as the basement. For a moment she thought he was going to take her upstairs, which would have been a wonderful move and convenient for what she needed to do. Instead, Cain took her across the hall, unlocked a door, and motioned for her to go in like some dramatic doorman. Inside it was nearly pitch black, save for the light coming in from the hallway. Cain gave her a forceful push and Natalia collided with the back wall. The room was far smaller than the one she had been in previously. Before she could react, he gripped her wrist and pressed it against a cold, metal cuff that was attached to the wall.

"I warned you," Cain said as he stepped back, a thin beam of light stretching past him and blinding her in the right eye. "Just...remember that. I gave you a chance."

"Cain, *please.*"

He stopped halfway towards the door, glancing over his shoulder at her.

"You don't have to do this," she whispered, a final act of desperation. No longer defiant or sarcastic or determined to push the dozen buttons that she thought might drive her opponent insane. Just...desperate.

"I wish," he began to speak, but his voice faded and for a moment he stood there with his back to Natalia and didn't move. When the moment had passed, Cain didn't turn to face her again; he simply walked away and shut her in the darkness.

That was when the spiders descended upon her. She felt their legs on her bare flesh first, like the tiniest pinpricks. Not painful, only to make her aware that in the cold of the basement something unnatural was walking with her. Then she felt their pincers; microscopic teeth burying into her flesh, delivering lethal doses of poison that would surely end her life. She would die there, on the cold stone floor of a makeshift room, built illegally into the basement of this once-magnificent home. She would froth at the mouth and begin to spasm and die from the swelling of her tongue or the explosion of her heart, and that would be the end of Natalia Artison.

Unless, she thought, her father decided to intervene. But it would be foolish to count on his help. He was on his own side at this point.

Whatever side that is.

For the first time, Natalia felt a toxic combination of sadness and exhaustion well up inside her. It was like a punch to the centre of her chest. It felt insurmountable and left her winded and on her knees, gasping for a simple breath of air that wasn't poisoned by everything around her. She wanted her family back, her life. She wanted that familiar sense of knowing her place in the world, even with all the confusion that accompanied her in adolescence. She wanted to feel something beyond the intensity of this exhaustive anguish that was spreading through her whole body.

Natalia buried her head on her knees, shielding her face from the darkness, and began to gulp in lungfuls of air that it might purify her of all this poison.

Your father didn't.

There was nothing to see in the darkness, but, as Natalia raised her head, she thought she saw him. Just for a split moment, kneeling in front of her, ghostly hands outstretched to tip her chin upwards. She felt his familiar warmth and wondered, if ghosts were truly real, how could their touch be warm when they existed in such a cold place. Never mind that Steven was dead and gone; in that moment she saw him there, smiling at her, and she felt...

Something.

And perhaps, if only for this moment, that something was all she needed to escape the darkness.

Chapter 29

Jim passed through Lancaster just after midnight. He didn't stop for gas or coffee, his mind and body running entirely on adrenaline and the enthralling idea of finally killing Cain. The blood on his face had long since dried, leaving a crusty mask that he attempted to wash off with a handful of snow when he stopped to take a piss. It didn't do much good, but what did that matter? He'd be layered in the stuff in no time at all. Meghan had called him, telling him that the team was on the way, maybe a half-hour behind him at the most.

Driving through the woods that led to Cain's old home, Jim was overcome by déjà vu. The last time he had made this journey was after he and Steven had nearly been gunned down in the road. They had known then that they were walking into the lion's den, and might not be leaving it, but Daisy had to be warned and she wasn't picking up her phone. They knew then that Cain would be long gone, his car taking the back road south, towards New York.

The same road Jim was travelling now.

Would they greet each other in the darkness, both knowing that the other could not survive any longer?

Jim tightened his grip on the steering wheel and tried to push Cain Ferigon's face from his mind, but each time he did, Natalia was there waiting in his place.

xXx

The cuff fell from Natalia's wrist, a glorious release for her pinched skin. It had taken longer than she liked to navigate the lock in the darkness. She had been down to her last hairpin and couldn't risk breaking it. She would tell Jim of her success, and the next time they did any sort of practice he would probably make her wear a blindfold just so she could get used to navigating locks without the power of sight on her side.

With one hand outstretched to prevent her from smashing into a wall, Natalia walked forward and tried to place the door in her memory. Her fingertips touched brick, so she moved to the left, figuring she probably overshot the door on her dominant side. Less than half a foot to the left, her fingers brushed the metal of the door.

With some blind manoeuvring, she began to make a mental list of the properties of the door. Three old hinges kept the door in place, and a doorknob with no keyhole. She began to feel the top of the hinges, hoping the pin keeping them in place might simply pop loose with a little bit of encouragement. She had bitten most of her nails down to stubs, making them useless for prying. Her right index finger was the only exception, and even as she tried to get her nail beneath the pin to clean out the years of grime and dirt, she could feel it tearing free from her nail bed. She bit the inside of her cheek, hoping to prevent herself from screaming.

The pin rotated free, taking her fingernail with it.

One down. The pain was awful, and her mouth was filled with blood, but hell, she was a third of the way there.

Bracing the first pin against the head of the second one she began to carefully turn them, using the force of one to pop the second free. Now with two rusted pieces of metal to her name, Natalia moved to her tiptoes, put the pins on either side of the third one, and began to turn them like a tap. Physics had never been her strong suit, but it made enough sense to try it. Slowly, but surely, the last pin eased free and clattered to the floor.

With a bit of gentle pressure from her shoulder, she felt the door shift, fall free from its hinges, and crash to the floor. Any hope she had of being even remotely sneaky evaporated. She ducked back into the room, held her breath, and waited for the commotion of feet stomping across the floor above her head.

Nothing. Silence. Natalia couldn't remember the last time she had heard so *little*.

The temptation to turn and flee through the tunnel was troubling. She wanted out of this strange upsidedown world that Cain had thrown her into; back to reality where she could count on the brash, unrelenting rational mind of Jim to help keep her grounded.

Kyle.

Natalia inhaled sharply and moved towards the stairs that led back to the open foyer.

The monstrous pillars that reached towards the domed ceiling stood as silent sentries. Beside one of them, a bloodstain had been smeared around in a fruitless effort to clean it. Natalia crossed the black and white parquet flooring, heedless of who might be watching and waiting for her. She took the stairs three at a time in long, wild strides, until she had reached the first balcony. Hearing soft footsteps, she paused and looked over the railing.

Emerging through the darkness from behind a pillar, Natalia saw the familiar gait of her father. He stood in the center of the foyer and stared up to the balcony.

"He's not there," Marcus said.

Natalia's voice emerged as a whisper, hardly audible even to her own ears. "Dad."

"Come here, Natalia."

She wanted to keep climbing, to reach the third floor, if only to separate herself from the lingering pain of Marcus' betrayal, but her feet disobeyed and carried her haltingly back down the stairs. Every instinct, every part of her that despised him for what he had done to her was screaming for her to run. But it was the child who won, the obedient girl who still understood when she was about to be reprimanded for her actions by a *disappointed* parent. Natalia knew she would have to take her medicine eventually, so why not get it over with?

She could see the handgun hanging listlessly in his grasp and wondered how many bullets were in the mag, and if any of them were meant for her.

She paused at the foot of the stairs. The nail bed of her right index finger was bleeding, and hot, wet, droplets splattered along the floor next to her feet.

"Closer," Marcus ordered, but Natalia shook her head, and leaned on the railing for support.

"Natalia-"

"I can't," she said hoarsely. "You know I can't."

"I never wanted it to go this far," he said. Natalia saw the tremor running through his body as he raised the pistol towards her.

"How far is that?" Natalia asked, genuinely curious. "Where's the line? It wasn't in Alcatraz, it wasn't when they killed mom or murdered Beth. How much more can you really sacrifice after me or Kyle? Where does it stop?"

Marcus hesitated, hand dropping to his side. Natalia imagined what must have been running through his mind, a dozen scenarios, all the outcomes the same. Death, alone and forgotten. If he had raised the pistol to his own skull in that moment she wouldn't have been surprised. Misery was the only thing waiting on the other side for a person like Marcus Artison, and he probably figured he deserved it.

He tossed the gun aside, the skittering of metal against the floor echoing up to the domed ceiling.

Without another word, Marcus walked past his daughter, and disappeared into the bowels of the house.

It was only then that Natalia realized she had been holding her breath. Try as she might, she couldn't release the air from her lungs. It burned her, enveloped entire body, and threatened to consume her. A pain, so violent that it felt like two hands had been driven into her chest and were now pulling her apart.

When she could hold her breath no more, she expelled a haggard sob. The betrayal and the confusion that accompanied it filled her up like a burst cyst, poisoning every part of her. She gasped, hoarse, violent sobs and doubled over from pain. Then, in her line of vision, the pistol. Natalia scrambled across the floor, snapped it in her fingers and pulled it towards her chest. Jim would have a conniption if he could see her handling it so carelessly, but Natalia couldn't be bothered to care anymore.

She curled on the parquet flooring and clutched a hand to her face. She would tear it off, everything that connected her to Marcus Artison. Strip herself of her identity, or what was left of it, and let something else grow organically in its place.

Your father didn't.

Didn't care. Didn't love. Didn't die. What did it matter? She would shed her skin, her name, her DNA, the very atoms that connected her to the lies and deceit of Marcus Artison. Then she could be free.

This is not the hill you die on.

And there, Jim's first lesson, drilled into her mind during every late-night car ride, every last-minute escape out a motel window. Every close call. She was not defeated yet, not broken despite it all. A low thrum in the base of her skull sent ripples through her mind, igniting images of Kyle, still in need of help.

Feet, crossing the floor from the other side of the foyer. Natalia pushed herself upright, unsteady on her legs, and aimed the gun.

From the shadows came hope, a reminder that not all was lost. Though Natalia would have never expected hope to be in the form of a blood-stained Jim Wilkinson, with a face that looked like tenderized meat. He was pointing his own gun towards her, alert to the noise she had made. They stood, stared at each other, bewildered.

Jim dropped his gun and ran to her. There was no hesitation as he pulled her into his arms, clutching her so tight Natalia thought she might very well snap in half. They stood there, neither speaking, until Jim pushed her back and ran a hand over her head, her hair, the scar on her chin.

"I thought-" He shook his head in disbelief. "I thought you were gone."

"My dad, Jim! He-" Natalia's voice cracked. The exhaustion and sorrow that had been welling up inside of her finally burst through the dam. Her head snapped in the direction of the foyer, to where she had last seen her father disappear into shadow and obscurity. Jim's hand rested on her head, pulling her close again, drawing her against his chest.

"It's ok, I know, I know. The whole team is right behind me, they'll get him." He pushed her back gently so her back rested against the wall. "We need to get out of here."

Suddenly, memories rolled over her in one, all-powerful wave. She reached out, gripped Jim's sleeve, eyes wide, and said, "Cain - he's put a bomb on Kyle!"

"What?"

"I was going to find him! Cain separated us, and..." Natalia shook her head, trying to clear the images that were compounding. A dozen questions, points, ideas that she needed to work through her mind to make sense of them when, ultimately, sense wouldn't help her catch up to Kyle. "My dad said he was gone."

"I didn't see him out there." Jim looked around frantically, as if Kyle might magically knit together in the air.

Natalia, however, knew differently. "He'd never go out the front door," she whispered. Then realizing what it meant, she snatched at Jim's hand. "Come on!"

Had the circumstances been different, Natalia might have moved with more caution to the stairs, down into the cellar, and towards the tunnel. But with Jim at her side she felt reassured that harm *had* to stay at arm's length, lest it raise his ire and succumb to the violence that Natalia knew Jim was capable of. Her thoughts split between her father, resurrected from the earth where she had thought him placed, and Kyle, dissolved in flame and ash. Natalia dragged Jim along the length of the corridor, beyond the door she had knocked from its hinges. If she thought they had even a moment to spare, she might have proudly pointed it out, telling the valiant tale of her escape.

Kyle, focus on Kyle.

As they neared the end of the corridor, Natalia began to hastily explain to Jim that they had tried to make an escape through the tunnel, foiled by Mother Nature and her own hesitation. She was babbling so quickly that it took an extra second to recognize the pungent, sweet smell emanating from past the plywood door, cutting through the scent of freshly dug earth.

Motor oil. Natalia raised her eyes towards the low-slung ceiling of the tunnel and saw the rebar was now covered in lengths of wires and small bundles of the gray, clay-like substance. Even the support pillars were dotted with the stuff.

All the way down the line of the tunnel.

"Jim," Natalia said quietly, "you said the whole team was coming, right?"

"Run!"

He snatched her wrist and dragged her forward, down the makeshift stairs, along the dirt hallway, ducking below low-hanging bulbs on wires and lengths of rebar that jutted out from the earth above their heads. As they raced along the air became clearer, as if the monster that pursued them was being held within the confines of the home itself.

They tripped along the dirt, shoulders scraping the stony walls, frozen earth biting into their bare flesh. The lengths of bare wire and bulbs hung like dotted lines on a map, guiding them towards freedom. The tunnel somehow seemed longer than when Natalia had raced through it with Kyle. Perhaps it was knowing that all around them the walls were plastered with handfuls of grey dough that waited for a single shock to ignite them.

Then, behind them, a bullet tinged off the rebar close to Natalia's head.

"Jim! Behind us!"

"Keep moving!"

She could hear the wind now, the howl of the gale cutting across the entrance of the tunnel up ahead, threatening to rip the plywood door off the frail hinges that held it in place. Natalia could feel winter biting her skin, and braced herself for the cold to suck the air from her lungs. Another gunshot and the familiar metallic ting of metal upon metal.

"Up ahead!" She could see it now, the break in the light and the endless, absorbing darkness that existed outside of the tunnel. Another world consumed by the unknown, poisoned by the hands and actions of another. She didn't want to enter it. She wanted to turn heel, run back into the strange stasis that Jim had pulled her from.

Their pursuer was gaining speed, and Natalia's feet were bare and frozen, her toes white and seemingly unresponsive. Jim was pulling her along now, faster, dragging her up every time she fell behind. They crashed through the plywood door and Jim threw her forward into the snow, braced his shoulder against the door, and shoved a long knife in through the small slit where the door didn't quite meet the jamb. There was a wet, sticky sucking noise as Jim wrenched the knife violently up and pulled it back.

It came back red and sticky.

In the distance, they could see a convoy of headlights arriving down the main road, some already stopped near the side of the hill where the burnt orchard sat with curls of copper wire decorating the trees.

"Go find Kyle!" Jim ordered, already throwing himself towards the convoy, hoping he might warn those who had converged on the home, to force them away lest they get caught in what was about to devour the whole compound.

Natalia's eyes tracked the smell set of prints, nearly indistinguishable in the heaping snow that Kyle had forged his way through. Up the hill, towards the orchard. Natalia's head snapped up and saw his figure, bounding towards his uncle. A living, breathing bomb, sent by Cain to destroy their shared enemy. Natalia screamed Kyle's name, certain her voice was lost in the din of approaching sirens and the wailing wind.

The snow around the orchard was packed down, and Natalia bolted her way up the hillside, grief-stricken as Caulder swept his nephew into his arms, the boy so light that he dangled freely above the ground in his uncle's loving embrace.

Shoeless.

Images of Kyle mimicking her actions, of observing guards with a keen interest born of his desire to follow the lead of the older girl. He would have made a knife and plunged it deep; would have kept a handful of hairpins and learned how to pick a lock, as if he knew or had the capacity to use them if push came to shove.

Like Natalia, Kyle had gone shoeless in his grand escape, so as to not make a sound.

Natalia plowed her way through the snow, up the hillside, and screamed Kyle's name again.

The explosion from their cell on the third floor billowed out into the night sky, devouring the top of the house. Natalia felt it as a chain-reaction beneath her feet, the rumbling of kinetic energy preparing to burst. In her mind, she could see the spark of electricity, from one wire to the next, setting off the reaction that caused the ground below them to shudder. She threw out a hand and saw Caulder's eyes widen, as if he too understood that all actions had consequences; every choice created a thousand new possibilities. And his decisions, his choices, had all led him here.

Caulder flung his nephew backwards as the ground beneath his feet disappeared. The trees around him exploded into ash and flame, and Caulder disappeared over the lip of the pit. Natalia dove forwards, catching Kyle by the waist as the earth below his feet crumbled and dropped. But Kyle's weight plummeted in her arms, and he hung over the edge of the pit. The ground crumbled and Natalia felt the earth sink under her belly, causing her to slip forward so she was hanging over the edge.

She saw Caulder, half a dozen meters below, body pierced by the rebar that had been supporting the tunnel. He was gazing up resignedly as the flames curled and dashed up his body. He opened his mouth to scream, but no words could escape his lips. They were already crawling back over his jaw, bubbling and receding.

Kyle shifted his weight and Natalia hauled him closer towards her. "Don't look! Don't look down, Kyle!"

She wasn't sure how he managed it, but Caulder raised a hand, frail, skeletal, as the fat sizzled away from his knuckles and tendons. Natalia thought she saw him mouth words with what was left of his face. *Run.*

She dragged Kyle backwards, throwing him over and curling her body around his own as a second explosion from the crater threw them back, devouring the last of the trees with a wild snap and decimating what remained of the small hillside. Natalia could feel the heat nip at the back of her neck, igniting the brand that bound her to Cain. They were airborne, sailing through the night, cleaving through the ghosts that lingered so close to Cain's ruined home, before crashing violently into a snow bank.

Chapter 30

Ambulances. Lights. Sirens. Smoke, so much smoke. Natalia blinked her eyes, closed her ears to the sounds, and imagined letting go. Shadows from another time, another place, as if the veil between this world and the next was pierced by the explosion, letting through all she had lost and left behind. Mother, sister, guardian, and innocence, all pouring back in from the past for this single opportunity to touch the living once again. She watched them sweep over head, interact with the living, drag the spirits of the dead back with them, direct them towards the other place.

Someone was shouting her name. So many people, in fact. She could hear Beth, and her mother, and then a shadow fell over her and she saw Steven, gazing emphatically down at her, but when he opened his mouth to speak, it wasn't his voice but Jim's. Natalia knew that once again it was her mind, seeking to find what wasn't truly there.

"Natalia, hey, kid, can you move your feet?"

She responded, involuntary, because on some level she understood that this was vital to the whole process. Wiggles your toes. Move your fingers. Mental checklist.

"Does it hurt anywhere?"

Back, ribs, cracked and bruised, and her lungs, full of smoke. But nothing felt broken. How far had they been flung? Fingers worked around her neck, her ribs, arms, and legs, checking for damage, then retracted.

"Can you get up?"

She lifted one hand, a silent demand for assistance. She felt familiar fingers clasp her hand, pulling her gently upwards so she was on her feet.

In front of her was a giant chasm, a hole blown into the core of the world where there had once sat an orchard, a house, and a lifetime of horrifying memories.

"Kyle?" she managed to choke out his name, a weak question.

"Already heading to Lancaster."

Natalia tipped sideways against Jim.

"My feet are cold," she said dully.

"Come on," Jim whispered, taking her by the shoulder. "There's an ambulance waiting."

How long had she been lying in the snow? Her ears were ringing from the explosion, but there had been so much happening around her. People were screaming, why wouldn't they stop screaming? And then she was sitting on a stretcher, unsure how she had moved from point A to point B. No recollection of climbing into the back of the ambulance, or of the hands that put the heated blanket over her shoulders. Someone had placed warm, damp cloths over her feet. Hot and cold all at once. Bandages and gauze, alcohol rubbing around her face, along wounds that she didn't even realize she had incurred until the sting on her face shocked her brain back to life and she felt like she could breathe.

She could breathe, even if she didn't want to.

Ambulances were parked down the drive, far away from the smouldering remains of the orchard and the house. A few fires were being attended to by the local emergency response department, police and investigators standing around the crater, mulling over what had taken place. Emergency officials were dragging things from the pit; bodies on short plastic boards, strapped down and covered with white sheets.

Natalia turned her head from the sight, trying to identify members of the crowd that were walking around in a daze. Meghan, George Bedlam, Rebecca, people she knew and trusted.

A bright light entered her eyes, thin as the head of a pin, and Natalia winced. A voice commanded her to follow the light and she did as she was told. When the light retreated there was a paramedic crouched next to her.

"We should take her in for an MRI to be on the safe side."

"No." She turned and saw Jim sitting on the bench of the ambulance, hunched over, hands clasped in what she imagined equated to silent prayer. "No, we need to get her back. We've got people that can look her over."

The paramedic looked unconvinced, but Natalia imagined that whatever face Jim was making was more than enough to convince the woman otherwise.

"Good to go?"

Natalia looked up and saw Meghan standing at the door of the ambulance. Her hair was a mess and she looked exhausted, but there were no streaks on her cheeks, nothing to indicate she shed a tear for the death of Harrison Caulder.

"As long as she's looked at by a doctor the *moment* you're back in New York," the paramedic said.

"She will be." Meghan offered a hand to Natalia. "Come on. I need to get back to the office."

"My dad," Natalia said hoarsely, "and Cain."

"They're gone," Meghan said shortly. "Probably not long before we got here. We've got agents in pursuit but the back road is a mess, so..." She waved her hand impatiently, and Natalia leaned forward. Her entire body protested the simple action. It would be a fun few days of recovery.

But at least I will, right? I'll recover.

Natalia took Meghan by the hand, felt Jim's hand on her back, gently guiding her, and stepped out of the ambulance, back into the snow.

She had imagined that the ride back to New York would be made in isolating silence, as the passengers, herself, Jim, Meghan driving, and Bedlam, tried to come to terms with what had happened. But Meghan was on the phone before the car was even in drive, and Bedlam was on his own phone. Only Jim, sitting in the back seat, next to Natalia, didn't say a word. Stunned, perhaps, by the turn of events and the violence that had nearly consumed them. Or perhaps just grateful that his body was not being hauled from a pit on a board.

Natalia couldn't stop trembling, despite the blasting heat. She felt a curious mix of caffeine and adrenaline forcing her stomach to squirm as she tried to find a comfortable position. As she tried to sort through the mess in her mind.

Jim's hand was on her shoulder now, drawing her sideways, across the back seat so her head could rest against his shoulder.

For the first time in many days, Natalia let herself cry without shame, without holding back in some makeshift show of strength.

She curled next to her guardian, oblivious to any discomfort the close contact might have been causing him. Jim drew her close and said nothing as her tears soaked his shirt.

Somewhere among the crying and the exhaustion and the strange sensation of being disembodied from everything around her, Natalia closed her eyes and resolutely refused to open them. It wasn't just that the chaos of what had been taking place around her had become too overwhelming; Natalia felt cracked. When she had been taken from Alcatraz, she had knowingly and, perhaps willingly, left a piece of herself behind among the carnage. She had cried her tears and shed her blood, and then deposited a piece of her innocence, carefully carved from herself, into the earth where it now lay in a state of decay.

She had thought that this was all there was to it. Innocence lost. Crushed. There was nothing more to be destroyed among her flesh and bones, surely. She could rebuild herself after Alcatraz, pick up the remnants of herself and construct a new Natalia.

Now she understood so much better. She wasn't shattered, but built of fractals that continued to break down, leaving behind smaller halves of the same person. She had left the greatest piece of herself in Alcatraz. And half of that was now buried in the frozen ground of Massachusetts. Cain could continue to chip away at her, but there would always be some piece of her left. It was both a blessing and a curse. Natalia closed her eyes and imagined fractals of herself, the size of an endless field, and utterly unconquerable to someone like Cain or her father, whose mortal eyes could never see how much more of her lay beyond the horizon.

When she woke next, Natalia found herself under familiar white lights, with a sickly-clean smell infiltrating her senses. She hated hospitals; bad memories and worse pain always seemed to accompany her. Now, at least, she felt warm and secure. Someone had tucked flannel blankets around her, pinning her arms to her sides with aggressive care. It might have been unnerving had she not recognized the pointed face staring at her from over a clipboard. The Agency doctor raised one eyebrow in her direction.

"Welcome back, Agent Artison."

"How long-" she stopped midsentence, realizing her voice crackled and her throat ached. Too much crying and smoke. She swallowed, her throat dry, and looked as the doctor pointed with his pen to a purple plastic cup that sat beside her bed. She fished an ice chip from the cup and placed it on her tongue. It melted, washing through her mouth, and Natalia felt oddly serene. One quick glance to her right showed why; an IV was hooked up to her wrist. She could only guess whatever they were giving her had to be potent.

"A light sedation," he explained. "We thought it might be...useful, given your experience in Lancaster."

"How long have I been asleep?" Natalia fished another block of ice from the cup and dropped it on her tongue.

"In and out for two days now. You've been conscious, but I expect you don't remember much."

"I remember...the car."

The doctor removed his glasses and gave them a casual and unnecessary cleaning on the corner of his white coat. He pushed them back on his face with his index finger and frowned. "I'm sure you have questions. I believe Aurora is waiting outside to talk to you. She's been there for a few hours now, since we adjusted your sedation."

Natalia opened her mouth, intending to inquire about Jim's status, when the doctor held up his hand to silence her. "And he's fine. He'll be around to see you soon enough."

There was a gentle knock on the door of the private ward, and the doctor glanced to his left. Natalia tried to follow his line of sight, but found that her body moved far more sluggishly than she anticipated. Aurora was standing there, a mountain of files and loose papers stacked in her hands, topped with a single tablet and a bright pink coffee mug. She looked tired, overworked no doubt.

"Sorry, is it ok if I-" Her stack of papers tilted precariously to one side, and Aurora shifted on her feet to regain her balance, all without spilling a drop of whatever it was she was toting in her mug.

"By all means." He motioned towards the empty chair beside Natalia's bed and stepped aside. "Agent Artison, if you need anything just call for the nurse. I'll see if I can track down Agent Wilkinson for you."

"Thank you."

As the doctor left the private room, Aurora, in total silence, began to sort out her papers and files on a small table in front of her.

"Ok." Aurora cleared her throat, propped the tablet up on the side table, and set it to record. "I know you're probably exhausted, but we have to go through what happened to you, from the moment you were taken at the rail yard. If you can just tell the story, I'll ask questions to fill in the blanks as we go, ok?"

Natalia nodded. This wasn't the first time someone had asked her to repeat the story of what had happened to her from beginning to end. She had learned long ago that there was significant value in being able to remember tiny details. Faces, words, voices, eyes, and noses. They all helped build partial pictures that could then be coloured in by the bits and pieces that came later on, when the fires were out and the bullets had been pushed into Ziploc bags.

Natalia recounted her decision to make the trade with Pete, the ride to the orchard outside of Lancaster, and waking up in the strange, old bed. Kyle Powell, their escape, Cain's odd behaviour, seemingly desperate in his actions, not for the code but for something else. Eventually the memories came out in a jumble, timing and order irrelevant because there was no timing or order to all the horrors. The young man, the paper packages. Hayden Meloy. The scraps of C4, the wires, the tunnel.

Her father. At this point, Natalia had to pause. She would have preferred talking to Jim about it first, to make a plan, because she was certain a plan was in their future. If Jim's anger at Marcus being alive were at all tempered by the fact that she was alive, it wouldn't last for long. Jim's anger, she understood, had a place in all of this. Because she was angry too, and wanted to do something about it. At the mention of her father, Aurora only nodded sharply, jotted on a notepad, and told Natalia to continue.

Kyle and Caulder. The frantic motion on Caulder's part to save his nephew. Not just save him, but throw him towards the one person he had expended so many hours trying to bury. And his body, burning, less than half the man he had been. Ruined. The crater, the emptiness, both inside and out. Natalia came to the end of her story and knew that the only thing she had to add were expletives and anger, nothing that would help the Agency track down Hayden Meloy, or Cain Ferigon, or Marcus Artison.

Jim watched through the small window in the door. It wasn't double-paned glass, but he still struggled to hear Natalia as she relayed to Aurora everything she had seen and experienced since trading herself for Angel and Jay. Aurora didn't balk at the mention of Marcus, and Jim could hardly blame her. Everyone knew by now. The truth was a cage that walled them in, forcing them to reconcile its reality with the illusion they had built around them. Natalia said it all without emotion or personal interjections – something that Jim knew was generally a challenge for one who had much to say.

Then she spoke about a betrayal, and Jim felt his whole body try to drop out beneath him. He held steady, out of necessity and nothing else. He wished he hadn't, because as Natalia spoke, as the story spilled from her lips, Jim began to piece it together, and he recognized the indisputable truth of it all.

Marcus Artison, a double-agent. Ten years ago he had made the decision to alert Cain to the presence of the SOI Operatives among his team of men, setting the whole damn thing into motion. If he had known that his betrayal of the Agency would ultimately lead to such pain for Natalia, would he have still done it?

Probably, Jim decided. *He wasn't exactly the forward thinking sort.*

Meghan was standing beside Jim, exhausted and wan from the last two days of non-stop action. She had been on the phone with Washington, already finding a successor to Caulder. She gritted her teeth at Natalia's mention of Marcus, and whispered, "Well, that settles it, then."

"You know what this means," Jim said quietly, turning his head towards her. "For her and me both."

"I do," Meghan replied with a grimace. "Her future with the Agency, too. It won't be pleasant. Marcus and Amy were hard enough to get along with. Throw treachery into the mix and it's likely she'll be a pariah, even within the Twelfth."

"She shouldn't have to carry her father's sins."

Meghan's head snapped towards Jim, and in his peripheral vision, he could see her lips twitch and an eyebrow rise. "No," Meghan said. "She shouldn't. But then again, she's not likely to escape them, is she?"

"I can't look after her, Meghan."

"You made a promise."

"We had a discussion like this a few months ago."

"We did." Meghan clapped him on the shoulder and nodded towards the window. "We both know how it'll end." Meghan paused for a moment, then handed Jim a sheet of paper. It was an official document, signed and sealed by some local judge who was probably sitting in his office right now, feeling up a paralegal. He had no concept of what he was unleashing by signing the documents allowing for the exhumation of not one but two graves.

"This'll hurt her," Jim said, handing the papers back. "It might be too much."

"I have a conference call with London tomorrow," Meghan replied. "There are too many questions. We buried someone in Marcus Artison's grave, and we need to find out who."

"And Amy's?"

"Call it a pre-emptive exploration of possibilities." Meghan folded the paper, placed it in her breast pocket, and patted Jim on the shoulder. "Whatever we find, she'll need *you*, now more than ever."

Jim watched the girl through the window, a twinge of pain nestling itself in his heart for all she had endured, and for everything that was to come. It was true, on some intrinsic level, he knew her. More than that, perhaps, he knew what the future would hold for her if she weren't given the right guidance. If she were left to rot in the wake of tragedy, as he had been ten years ago, it would be a very bleak future indeed.

At the end of the story, Aurora finished writing her notes and then looked towards Natalia. "You should know, Director Harrison Caulder was killed in the explosion. Kyle Powell survived, but he's lost part of his right leg." Natalia cringed, and Aurora hurriedly added, "He would have lost his life if you hadn't intervened. You saved him. It'll be a long road to recovery, but he *will* survive. Two separate cars were tracked down the southern back road, which we believe contained Cain Ferigon and Marcus Artison respectively. A third flipped after hitting a patch of ice, and, by the time our respondents arrived, it was abandoned. Fingerprints inside have been linked to Hayden Meloy. We're tracking him now."

"You don't seem shocked to hear about my dad."

"There has been a lot going on around here. Marcus being alive isn't the surprise you might think."

"To you, maybe." Natalia frowned. "What happens next?"

"Next?"

"Caulder is dead. Cain is gone. My dad is alive. What's our next step?"

Aurora pushed back the table and stood up, leaving her piles of papers and tablet where they sat. "That's entirely up to Meghan. I'll go get her. You just hang tight."

Aurora seemed altogether too eager to leave the medical ward, and Natalia could hardly blame her. The stench of cleanliness was overwhelming and the drama of the last few days left Natalia feeling like being trapped inside these four walls was a sort of punishment to keep her out of 'real life'. Inside the medical ward she could hardly get involved with terrorists or people rising from the dead, could she?

Watch me. Natalia threw the covers off her legs and leaned forward to stretch. Every muscle was tense and spasming against the motion. Not surprising, given the way she and Jim had been tossed through the air at the height of the explosion. It was reassuring to see all her toes attached, none of which looked like they were at risk of falling off at a moment's notice, despite the repeated exposure she had suffered. In one faltering movement, she swung her legs over the edge of the bed and wiggled her feet. Everything responded as well as she could expect under the circumstances. She planted her feet on the ground and pushed herself up.

The world immediately tilted out of focus and Natalia's knees banged together as she tipped forward. Hands were on her shoulders, and then she was sitting on the edge of the bed, looking at Jim and Meghan. Neither of them seemed particularly impressed, which, Natalia began to suspect, might actually just be their everyday faces.

"Couldn't even give yourself a couple hours, huh?" Jim stepped back, folding his arms over his chest. His voice suggested a certain level of humor in her actions, but when Natalia looked at his face, it was cold.

"I was bored," Natalia croaked. Her heart wasn't in it.

Meghan seemed less impressed by the response. She rolled her eyes, and settled next to Natalia on the bed. "We need to talk."

"I'm sure we do," Natalia replied, kicking her feet out gently in a wild hope that they might begin to cooperate with the rest of her body.

"Your father." Meghan cleared her throat. "Marcus is alive. You saw him, so did Troy. That brings up a lot of questions."

Natalia wasn't interested in Meghan's rhetoric. She looked towards Jim, and said, "He was the one who told Cain about you and Steven. He-" she lowered her eyes. Was it shame? Sins of her father, somehow falling on the daughter? Natalia wasn't sure. Jim could easily hate her because she was the closest target, right? Marcus had poisoned their lives, and if he weren't there to be held accountable, it would fall onto Natalia's shoulders.

Jim said nothing. The silence was disturbing.

"I'm sorry."

"Why?" asked Jim. "It's not on you." Not a moment of hesitation. It seemed wonderfully rehearsed.

"Be that as it may," Meghan said, "Internal Affairs Division will have to look into his activities. All of them, from the moment he joined the SOI. It's probably fair to say that whatever they find won't be pretty."

"Sounds about right."

Meghan sighed and ran a hand through her hair. "It would be best if you weren't-"

"No." Natalia knew what was coming. She had already made up her mind long before Marcus Artison had pulled off the greatest magic trick since Jesus of Nazareth. Hell, Meghan had said it herself. Having Natalia join the Agency was a Band-Aid, and one Natalia would have been willing to rip off if Cain were lying dead in the crater outside Lancaster.

But no. Cain was still alive, and there were too many questions remaining. She saw the way the world was laid out before her now. It was clear, the veil drawn back, allowing what had been – family, home, a normal life – to dissolve into her future with the Agency. Every decision Marcus had made, every betrayal and lie, had cleared the air around her.

"I'm not leaving. I won't be a coward."

"This isn't about cowardice," Meghan replied sharply.

"Pride, then." Her greatest sin. "I won't let them bully me. I won't let myself get pushed around just because they need someone to blame." She thrust out her jaw and turned to look at Jim. "I'm not leaving."

Natalia hadn't expected Meghan to be particularly thrilled about the verdict, but the eye-roll the supervisor produced was one that rivalled even the most obstinate teenager.

"Fine." Meghan threw her hands up in defeat. "If you insist. But don't go crying to Human Resources when things start to get a little difficult to manage, all right?"

Natalia figured it was best not to respond, lest she antagonize the monster further. Meghan was already storming away from the medical ward. When she was long gone, Natalia turned to look up at Jim. He had stepped away from her, and was looking over his shoulder to the door, as if trying to will it closer so he might make a faster escape.

The silence was sickening, but she knew it shouldn't be. It was Jim's way. He preferred it over talking; action over words. There were some elements of him that had been the true and real Jim in Alcatraz, and it had taken Natalia a long time to know the difference. Now, however, there was much to discuss, and one question particularly had been digging its claws in Natalia from the moment she had been able to piece together her father's story.

"Do you hate me?"

"What?" Jim narrowed his gaze at her.

"With all this." She waved a hand around the room, as if it indicated what she meant. "With my dad – *Marcus* – and looking after me still. I just thought maybe you'd be *upset*."

"It ain't exactly like winning the lottery," Jim admitted, "but no. His sins are his alone."

"That seems a little oversimplified," Natalia said quietly. "We've been through a lot and I know I push your buttons and I've made mistakes. I just don't want things to be weird now."

"If they're going to be weird it's only because you brought it up."

Natalia smirked, holding it until she felt her lip tremble and she let the smile drop away. "Is it really going to be as bad as Meghan says?"

"People are dead; friends and good agents. Put yourself in someone else's shoes. Think about how someone like Martyn Garland must feel."

Martyn had hardly been on her mind, but at the mention of the trainee, she felt a twinge of hot fear in her stomach. Natalia wasn't the sort to actively alienate those around her. She *wanted* to get along with Martyn, and all the other trainees, if only because one day she might need to depend on them. Knowing that Marcus' amazing rise from the dead would anger Martyn and put him off her even more left Natalia feeling sick. She hadn't thought through the price of staying with the Agency. Not enough.

"It can never be simple, can it?"

"Not even slightly."

Chapter 31

Three days later, Natalia stood at the base of a snowy knoll, watching as a small industrial digger carefully split through layers of frozen frost and ice, six feet down. Jim had driven her to the cemetery, citing his own desire for answers as a reason. They didn't speak during the ride. They both understood the gravity of the situation. Cain was a vicious man, for many reasons, but to violate the sanctity of death, to play with the delicate emotions of those who survived, somehow painted over all the images they had devised of Cain previously and recast him in a hellish light.

She glanced at Jim in her peripheral vision. He was pressing his foot into the snow, making some sort of warped smiley face with his boot. Among all his scars and tattoos and personality defects, of which there were many, Natalia saw a man she trusted implicitly because he had been there. He had seen it all for himself and while he would never discuss it with her, because that wasn't his way, Natalia was certain Jim had a certain level of respect for her survival.

"I never said thank you for what you did."

"Huh?" *Think. What did you do? Feed the dog? No. Laundry, you did laundry. You were very helpful when you did laundry.*

"For Angel and Jay." Jim turned to look at her, while machinery rumbled in the background. "It couldn't have been easy."

"They're your family." She didn't elaborate, didn't feel the need to. It was simple. A person fights and dies for the ones they care about.

"You could have died." It wasn't accusatory on Jim's part, just an observation.

"Yeah, well." Natalia turned to look back at the hill. "Pretty sure at least part of my family is immortal, so I wouldn't be too worried."

Jim grinned, and Natalia felt the heaviness that had been sitting between them lift, if only a little bit. "It couldn't have been an easy decision to make on your own."

Natalia didn't reply. She wasn't about to engage Jim in some philosophical banter about ethical choices. She didn't have the energy. "Are they still at the safe house?" she asked.

Jim nodded slowly. "Some mid-western piece-of-shit town where no one will ask any questions. They'll stay there until... Well, until it's safe for them to come back."

Natalia laughed bitterly. "That could be a while."

"It could," Jim agreed.

"And you don't get to see them until-"

"Until Cain's finally out of the picture, yeah. No idea where they are, what they're calling themselves now. Hell, even after Cain is dealt with they might choose to just stay there. It'd probably be safer for them in the long run."

"Safer, not better."

Whatever Jim thought of that, he wasn't about to say. He grunted in response. The silence settled around them again.

"What'll we do next?" Natalia asked finally.

"Hm?"

"Cain, my dad, Hayden Meloy. Three different angles to follow. Three different choices. And those shipping containers. We never found them. Cain can arm a lot of people with that."

"I think Meghan wants the team to pursue Meloy first and foremost."

"Yeah, but what about *us*? Who are *we* going after?"

Jim smirked. "Smart ass."

"They're all threats in their own way, right? How is anyone supposed to prioritize them?"

"Everyone will take a different lead."

"And we'll go after Cain."

"Yes," Jim said. But Natalia narrowed her eyes at him. His face suggested his intentions were slightly different.

She shifted in the snow. Her shoes were tight; her toes were still wrapped, and resting against heated packs. It made her feel sick. Now every aspect of herself felt wrong, and she wondered if this was what Kyle felt when he slipped his one shoe on. Did he know instinctively that something was wrong and simply lack the capacity to verbalize it, or was he oblivious and simply caught in his own sadness and exhaustion, a by-product of his fear?

She wouldn't lose any toes, and given how Kyle ended up, it seemed like the least she could ask for.

There was whistling at the top of the knoll, and Jim and Natalia both turned to see the cemetery caretaker, shovel in hand, motioning for them to come up the hill. The small crane next to Marcus' headstone was whirling, and the top of the coffin, covered in chunks of frozen dirt, was just beginning to breach the grave.

"Come on," Jim said, pushing her backpack lightly with the toe of his boot. "Let's get this over with."

Natalia hauled her backpack over one shoulder and followed Jim up the steep incline towards the grave. The coffin had been swung out of the hole and settled awkwardly on the mound of snow and dirt. The caretaker had a crowbar slung across his shoulder, like exhumation was an everyday occurrence and this was the most casual thing he could possibly engage in a mere week after Christmas.

With a short nod from Jim, indicating it was all right to proceed, the caretaker wedged the crowbar in the slit between the coffin and the lid, which was protecting the man who was not Marcus Artison from the earth and snow and cold. It seemed feeble, given the intensity of the weather, and took Natalia a moment to remember that the dead didn't feel much of anything and she shouldn't be concerned about the state of a drafty coffin. No, it was the contents that were her priority.

The lid gave a satisfying crack, and the caretaker stepped back, allowing Jim room to grab the lip of the coffin and give it a shove with his good arm.

The scent of embalming fluid, formaldehyde, and cologne was dizzying, pouring out of the coffin as if a thousand years of pressure had built up. Natalia felt sick from the wave of familiarity and foreign scents striking her, puncturing her memories, slipping into them, giving them new life.

Together, Natalia and Jim peered over the edge of the coffin. The body had been embalmed, but Natalia thought no amount of embalming could really preserve what had already been ruined.

Your father didn't.

The face was all but gone. Hands and feet cut off. In their place, someone had thoughtfully placed shiny black brogues and leather gloves. It made the body look as if it were in the process of disappearing, limb by limb. Some slow-motion *Invisible Man*. Natalia exhaled through clenched teeth and stood back, making way for the technician who had come to try to salvage samples from the body. They needed to know who they had buried. It was only right.

From behind them, one of the gravediggers cleared his throat and pointed towards the matching headstone that stood as a marker over Amy Artison's final resting place.

"This one next?"

Natalia turned rigid, gaze snapping towards Jim, who nodded grimly. "Yeah."

"Jim?"

"I didn't want to tell you."

"I don't understand. They're digging her up, too?" She shifted back from her not-father's coffin. "What's going on?"

"We have to be sure."

She didn't wait for Jim to respond, too caught up in the sensation of a wave breaking over her body and drowning her. It was as if her father's miracle resurrection had been a rock tossed into a pool, and the impact of it was just now rippling over her entire world. Natalia turned abruptly and stormed down the hill, where she planted herself in the car and didn't move. From there she could see Jim atop the knoll, staring in wonderment in her general direction before turning back to the gravedigger and giving a wave of his hand.

An all-clear to dig up the dead.

Natalia heaved, gulping air to calm the sick that was bubbling up her throat. She watched as they raised the second coffin and pried open the lid. Jim leaned forward, then stepped back. Natalia couldn't make out his expression. Emotionless, probably. He said something to the technician, who was already leaning over the coffin and picking at the corpse inside. Was it black? Husk-like thanks to the fire? How had they laid the head in there with the body? Had the skin on her mother's face crawled away from the bone like burning paper?

Was that even her I saw in there?

As Jim approached, Natalia threw herself out of the car and leaned over the asphalt, throwing up what little she had eaten that day.

Jim rested a hand on her back, an awkward consolation, and then returned to the car.

They didn't speak the whole way home.

Cooper greeted them at the front door. Natalia kicked off her damp shoes and hobbled down the hallway to her bedroom. For having spent only a week and a bit in the confines of the house, Natalia found herself oddly at peace with the foreign territory. Her room was now *hers*, and no longer a space she had invaded, much to Jim's chagrin. It would never be the Brownstone on Boerum Hill, but it was as good a place to start over as any, so why not start thinking of it as her own?

Natalia settled on the edge of the bed, running her fingertips over the quilt that she had bought. All bright colours, bold, vibrant. Amy would have never approved.

No. Mom. Mom would have never approved.

Somewhere in the confines of Cain's home, Natalia had seamlessly transitioned to thinking of her parents from *Mom* and *Dad* to *Amy* and *Marcus*. They lost all perceived honor, all right to the title of parents. Yet the guilt was astonishing all the same, as if they knew she was lowering their parental clearance. Wherever they were, they could feel her lack of faith.

She wasn't certain how long she sat there, looking around at her things, imagining how they might have looked in the old house. Cooper joined her, settling under her feet and heaving a sigh, as if to ask *Why are you sitting there being morose instead of petting me?*

Natalia scooted off the bed and began to scratch the dog behind his ears. Amy never liked dogs; hated them, in fact.

"Lazy bastard."

She looked up. Jim was standing in the doorway of her bedroom. Yes. *Her* bedroom. It was starting to feel normal, now.

"Can I come in?"

"It's a free country." Natalia narrowed her gaze. "Right? Or is there some big government secret that I don't know yet?"

"Ha," Jim said lamely.

"Lizard people in Congress?"

"There's a good chance," Jim said, slumping onto the bed and running a hand through his hair. His knuckles were badly cut up. "You ok?"

"Honestly? No. I'm not." She lowered her head and ran her fingers over the nape of her neck, retracting suddenly as she touched the brand. She had almost forgotten it was there. "I *know* what I saw, Jim. She can't be alive."

"It was a really traumatic moment for you. Your first corpse." He faltered, then offered a wicked smirk. "I'm *guessing* it was your first corpse."

She punched him lightly on the leg, grateful for his carefree attitude regarding the whole situation. It somehow made the possibilities, the uncertainties, more bearable. "I'm the unreliable narrator in my own life," she said at last. "I saw things, and I've experienced things, and at least before I could put it in order. Every action had a reason and a response and it made one timeline that I could follow and understand. Now it's all changed."

"Not yet, it hasn't."

"No," Natalia agreed. "But I can feel it in my bones. It's coming."

"Sagely." Jim groaned as he stood up, cracked his back, and rubbed his right shoulder.

"Jim, if she's still alive... Why hasn't she come for me?" There is was, the indisputable fear that was borne from her mother's grave. "She would be here, if she was still alive."

"Yeah, she would."

"Cain." Natalia curled her fingers until her knuckles were white and she could feel her nails slicing into her palm, drawing up tiny worms of blood. "He has her, doesn't he?"

Jim said nothing.

Natalia ran her palms over her knees, leaving streaks of blood on her jeans. "I have to get her back. I *have to.*"

In the silence that followed Natalia half expected Jim to berate her for her words. She looked up at him, and found that he was watching her, head cocked to one side, as if she was a specimen placed under an ultra-violet light. He saw something different in her now that hadn't been there before. "Hold on," he said finally. "I've got something for you."

Natalia leaned down to kiss Cooper between the ears. The old dog looked up towards her and whined, as if to commiserate with the agony. A moment later Jim was back in the room. In one hand, he held a stack of manila folders bursting with papers. In the other was a long, black box, wrapped with a bow that looked like it had gone through a shredder.

Wrapping was evidently not Jim's forte.

Natalia managed to pry the knotted bow from the box without losing more fingernails, and popped open the lid. Inside was a small leather pouch tied with string. She tugged the string off and lifted the lip of the pouch to reveal a set of brass lock picks. Every conceivable type of wrench, rake, and curved pick that she would need to pry open even the most stubborn pin. It was uncharacteristically thoughtful.

Natalia looked up at Jim. He was scratching Cooper's head with intensity, pointedly avoiding eye contact.

"Jim, thank you."

"Yeah," he grunted. "Happy birthday or Merry Christmas. Whatever. You can stop wasting money on your damn bobby pins."

"And save my fingernails, too." She held up her right index finger and wiggled it. "I really appreciate it, thank you."

Jim nodded towards the files he had left sitting on the side of the bed. "Those too."

Natalia pulled down the first folder, full nearly to bursting with all the paper. She recognized the date and time stamped on the cover, having watched two guardians piece through the papers and pictures in a foolhardy attempt to understand the intricate web Cain had woven around those he sought to destroy. She had wondered endlessly about what was contained within, if her eyes, her own, private knowledge could somehow find a clue. It was her story, and her parent's story. A door that had been closed to her for months.

And now she had the key.

"Seriously?" she asked, looking up.

Jim nodded. "It's time. You need to know what we're up against."

Natalia exhaled sharply through her clenched jaw and ran her fingers along the cover. The fate of her family, of Steven and Beth, of Cain, all of it, contained neatly between manila covers, waiting to be pried open and looked on with fresh eyes.

Her eyes.

"No more secrets?" she asked.

Jim sighed, and, for a moment, Natalia thought he might stand up and simply walk away. Instead, he plucked the next folder from the top of the pile, flipped it open, and began to lay the papers out on the floor. Line by line, piece by piece. Memory by memory.

"No more secrets," he lied.

Acknowledgements

I'm always struck by the oddity of people claiming that writing a novel is no easy task. I love writing. It's easy! (Wait, don't be mad, let me finish!) On the other hand, what comes after that last full-stop is on the page, and you have a completed draft sitting in front of you is a very difficult thing indeed. Draft after draft. Variation after variation. I have countless people to thank for their contributions to the completion of The Skeletal Bird. This is only a handful of them. My apologies to everyone I've missed. Chances are if I've never called you a rude name and meant it, you've probably helped me in some way.

Ashley Whitt, a very dedicated critique partner, has yet to tell me that my ideas are stupid. I've emailed her at two in the morning with flashes of brilliance, and she has helped me massage them until they fit into the final product. The folks at the Unofficial Critique Circle Chat have once again proven to be invaluable in all that they offer. Aries75, Gretchen, Ferris, Linnea, Pat, and Evensong have spent countless hours, not only helping dissect my plans in the search for holes (of which there have been many) but hours upon hours helping write and rewrite the blurb you see on this back cover. It nearly drove me insane, but we managed. These are all incredibly talented people whose real names have been withheld because I am certain they are also quite mad and potential dangers to society.

Once again, David Fross has taken time out of his busy life schedule to create a cover that I have fallen in love with. His talent knows no bounds (at least none that I have found yet). I remain ever indebted to him for his time and patience in helping craft the completed book that you are holding now.

My suffering editor, Michelle Heumann, took on this project in the midst of her own education. Her dedication into double checking facts (like the rights of 'side-pieces' in gangs) as well as her keen eye for flow and my tendency to repeat certain words makes her brilliant. Any mistakes remaining the book are entirely my own, because I am impatient and didn't take the time to read through the final proof. Or I did, and I'm just blind.

I have received remarkable support from not only my family, but from my coworkers and my friends. The enthusiasm all of you exhibit is reason enough to continue Natalia's journey. I am always grateful for each of you, every day of my life. Dr. Greg Sawisky, who is my go to every time I stab someone (metaphorically). Sergeant Nicholas Sawisky, who is my go to every time I want to shoot someone (also metaphorically). Maureen Sawisky, who is my go to every time I need a hug (not metaphorically). Dana Christakos, who has unknowingly taught me about sisterhood and those unbreakable bonds. Kelti Boissonneault of Theoretically Brewing, and my sister from another mister, whose beers have accompanied me during the majority of my writing sessions. Shawna Yanke, who completes me, and isn't animal stompy in the slightest.

As in all things, those professionals who have provided me with insight have done so knowing that I am somewhat wordy and perhaps overly liberal with the realism of things. As such, any and all errors within the novel are mine and mine alone and should not be considered reflections of the skills of those providing advice. In other words, I'm pretty sure my brothers are excellent in their doctoring and militarying. Don't hold this novel against them.

Finally, I can't complete the acknowledgements without mentioning the one who harasses me on a daily basis. His inability to control his sarcasm, or understand why such a deadpan attitude might sometimes annoy others, is truly awe inspiring. He has never questioned my dream of writing, and has only intermittently tried to stand in its way by his frequent shouts from the ground floor of *"Kat, come here!"* every five minutes or so while I am trying to write.

I love you, Goose. Come here.

Kathleen Sawisky is "just a chick with a sore back", according to some dude on reddit. When not crafting the next big explosion or managing her chronic pain, she can be found in her home in Calgary, Alberta with her husband, Alex, and their ridiculous cats. Her favourite fruit is lime and her favourite smell is a pine forest after the rain.

You can stay in the loop on all things *Code* and sarcasm-related at her website www.kathleensawisky.com

77021793R00264

Made in the USA
Columbia, SC
20 September 2017